MORE ADVENTURE STORIES

MORE ADVENTURE STORIES

Edited by
Hayden McAllister

Illustrated by
Sam Thompson

octopus

CONTENTS

First published 1981 by
Octopus Books Limited
59 Grosvenor Street,
London

This collection copyright © 1981 Octopus Books Ltd.

ISBN 0 7064 1550 7

Printed in the United States of America

ESCAPE FROM WAR FORT 9

A. J. Evans

In the early days of the War Fort 9, Ingolstadt, had been a quiet, well-behaved sort of place, according to its oldest inmates. But for the six months previous to my arrival before its forbidding gates at the end of 1916, the Germans had collected into it all the naughty boys who had tried to escape from other camps. There were about 150 officer prisoners of different nationalities in the place, and at least 130 of these had successfully broken out of other camps, and had only been recaught after from three days' to three weeks' temporary freedom. I myself had escaped from Clausthal in the Harz Mountains – but had been recaptured on the Dutch frontier after I'd been at large for a few days.

When I arrived at Fort 9, Ingolstadt, seventy-five per cent of the prisoners were scheming and working continually to escape again. Escaping, and how it should be done, was the most frequent subject of conversation. In fact, the camp was nothing less than an escaping club. We pooled our knowledge and each man was ready to help any one who wished to escape, quite regardless of his own risk or the punishment he might bring upon himself. No one cared twopence for court-martials, and nearly every one in the fort had done considerable spells of solitary confinement.

It is scarcely necessary to say that the Germans, having herded some

150 officers with the blackest characters into one camp, took considerable precautions to keep them there. But there were some of the most ingenious people in Fort 9 that I've ever met – particularly among the French – and attempts to escape took place at least once a week.

Fort 9 had been built in 1866 after the Austrian wars. There was a wide moat, about fifteen yards broad and five feet deep, round the whole fort and inside the moat the ramparts rose to a height of forty feet. Our living rooms were actually in the ramparts and the barred windows looked down upon the moat, across a grass path along which a number of sentries were posted. It looked as though there were only two possible ways of getting out: to go out the way we'd come in, past three sentries, three gates and a guardhouse; or to swim the moat. It was impossible to tunnel under the moat. It had been tried, and the water came into the tunnel as soon as it got below the water level. An aeroplane seemed the only other solution. That was the problem we were up against, and however you look at it, it always boiled down to a nasty cold swim or a colossal piece of bluff. We came to the conclusion that we must have more accurate knowledge of the numbers, positions and movements of the sentries on the ramparts and round the moat at night, so we decided that one of us must spend the night out. It would be a rotten job; fifteen hours' wait on a freezing night, for it was now winter. For the first three and last three hours of this time it would be almost impossible to move a muscle without discovery, and discovery probably meant getting bayoneted. We cast lots for this job – and it fell to a man named Oliphant. I owned I breathed a sigh of relief. There would be two roll-calls to be faked, the roll-call just before sunset and the early morning one. How was this to be done? Our room was separated from the one next door, which was occupied by Frenchmen, by a three foot thick wall, and in the wall was an archway. This archway was boarded up and formed a recess which was used as a hanging cupboard for clothes. Under cover of these clothes we cut a hole in the boarding big enough for a man to slip quickly through from one room to the other. The planks which we took out could be put back easily and we pasted pictures over the cracks to conceal them. It was rather difficult work. We had only a heated table knife to cut the first plank with, but later on we managed to steal a saw from a German carpenter, who was doing some work in one of the rooms, and return it before he missed it. You must remember that there was absolutely no privacy in the fort, and a sentry passed the window and probably stared into the room every minute or two. We then rehearsed the faking of the roll-calls. One of us pretended to be the German NCO taking the roll. First he tapped at the Frenchman's door and counted the men in the room, shut the door and walked about seven paces to our door, tapped and entered. Between the time he shut the first door till he opened ours only six or eight seconds elapsed, but during these seconds one of the Frenchmen had to slip through the hole, put on a British warm, and pretend to be Oliphant; the German NCO's knew every man by sight in every room, but so long as the numbers were correct they often didn't bother to examine our faces. That accounted for the evening roll-call. The early morning one was really easier. For several mornings the fellow in bed nearest the hole in our room made a habit of covering his face with the bedclothes. The German NCO soon got used to seeing him like that, and if he saw him breathing or moving didn't bother to pull the clothes off his face. So the Frenchman next door had simply to jump out of bed as soon as he had been counted, slip through the hole, and into the bed in our room, and cover up his face. We practised this until we got it perfect, and the rehearsals were great fun.

The next thing to do was to hide Oliphant on the ramparts. Two of us dug a grave for him there while the others kept watch. Then just before the roll-call went we buried him and covered him with sods of grass. It was freezing at the time. It was about 4.30 pm when we buried him, and he wouldn't be able to return to our room till 8.15 the next morning, when the doors were open. The faking of the evening roll-call went off splendidly, but the morning one was a little ticklish, as we couldn't be quite sure which room the NCO would enter first. However, we listened carefully, and fixed it all right, and when he poked our substitute, who groaned and moved in the rehearsed manner, we nearly died with suppressed laughter. About an hour later Oliphant walked in very cold and hungry but otherwise cheerful. He had had quite a successful night. A bright moon had prevented him from crawling about much, but he had seen enough to show that it would be a pretty difficult job to get through the sentries and swim the moat on a dark night. However, Providence came to our help.

The winter of 1916 was a hard one, and the moat froze over, and although the Germans went round in a boat every day and tried to keep the ice broken, they eventually had to give it up. It was difficult to know whether the ice would bear or not, but I tested it as well as I could by throwing stones on to it, and decided one morning that I would risk it and make a dash across the moat that evening. A man named Wilkin, and Kicq, a little Belgian officer, who had accompanied me on my previous attempt to escape, agreed to come with me.

Our plan was to start when the 'appell' or roll-call bell went at 5 pm, for it got dark soon afterwards, and I trusted that this would cover our flight. We had to run down a steep bank on to the ice, about forty yards across the ice, and then another two hundred yards or so before we could put a cottage between ourselves and the sentries. There was sure to be some shooting, but we reckoned the men's hands would be very cold, for they would already have been two hours at their posts. Moreover they were only armed with old French rifles, which they handled badly. We arranged with some of the other officers to create a diversion when the roll-call bell went by yelling and throwing stones on to the ice to distract the attention of the two nearest sentries. Our main anxiety was: would the ice bear? I felt confident it would. Wilkin said he was awfully frightened, but would go on with it. Kicq said that if I was confident, so was he. It would be extremely unpleasant if the ice broke, for we would be wearing a lot of very heavy clothes. Still, any one who thinks too much of what may happen will never escape from prison. We filled our rucksacks with rations for a ten days' march and enough solidified alcohol for at least one hot drink a day. We then concealed them and our coats at the jumping-off place.

A few minutes before the bell went we were all three dressed and in our places. It was a bad few minutes. At last it rang and almost immediately I heard laughter and shouting and the sound of stones falling on the ice. We jumped up and bolted over the path and down the slope. I was slightly ahead of the others, and when I got to the moat I gave a little jump on to the ice, think that if it was going to break at all it would break at the edge instead of in the middle. It didn't break, and I shuffled across at good speed. When I was about half-way over I heard furious yells of 'Halt!' behind me, followed by a fair amount of shooting; but I was soon up the bank on the far side and through a few scattered trees. Then I looked back.

The ice had cracked under the weight.

The others were only just clambering up the bank from the moat, and were a good hundred yards behind me. It turned out that instead of taking a little jump on to the ice as I had done they'd stepped carecully on to the edge, which had broken under their weight, and they had fallen flat on their faces. Wilkin had somehow got upside down, his heavy rucksack falling over his head, so that he couldn't move, but Kicq had freed himself and pulled Wilkin out.

The covering parties had done their job well. They'd managed to divert the attention of the most formidable sentry until I was well on the ice. He had then noticed me, yelled 'Halt!' loaded his rifle as fast as possible, dropped on one knee, fired and missed. Cold fingers, abuse and some stones hurled at him by the party on the ramparts above had not helped to steady his aim. After one or two shots his rifle jammed. Yells and cheers from the spectators. He tore at the bolt, cursing and swearing, and then put up his rifle at the crowd of jeering prisoners above him, but they could see that the bolt hadn't gone home, and only yelled louder.

Meanwhile, I'd nearly reached the cottage, when I saw a large, four-horse wagon on the main road on my right with a number of civilians by it. They were only about 150 yards away, and they started after us, led by a strong, healthy-looking fellow with a cart-whip. The going through the snow was heavy, especially with the weight we were carrying; so the carter quickly overtook me and slashed me across the shoulders with his whip. I turned and rushed at him, but he jumped out of my reach. His companions then arrived, and I saw, too, some armed soldiers coming on bicycles along the road from the fort. The game was up, and the next thing to do was to avoid being shot in the excitement of re-capture. So I beckoned the smallest man and said in German: 'Come here, and I'll give myself up to you.' The chap with the whip immediately came forward. 'No, not to you,' I said, 'you hit me with that whip.' The little fellow was very pleased, for there was a hundred marks reward for the capture of an officer, so he hung on to my coat-tails as we started back to the fort. I tore up my map and dropped it into a stream as we went.

The scene in the Commandant's office was quite amusing. We were stripped and searched. I had nothing more to hide, but both Kicq and Wilkin had compasses, which they smuggled through with great skill.

Kicq's was hidden in the lining of his greatcoat, and Wilkin had his in his handkerchief, which he pulled out of his pocket and waved to show that there was nothing in it. All our foodstuffs and clothes were returned to us, except my tin of solidified alcohol. I protested, but in vain. I was given a receipt for it and told I could have it back at the end of the war. As we left the office I saw it standing almost within my reach, and nearly managed to pocket it as I went out. However, I found a friend of mine – a French officer – outside and explained to him the position of the tin and suggested that he should go in with a few pals and steal it back for me under the cover of a row. This was the kind of joke that the Frenchmen loved, and they were past-masters at it. They were always rushing off to the Commandant's office with frivolous complaints about one thing and another, just for a rag, which never failed to reduce the Commandant and his officers to a state of dithering rage. Within ten minutes I had my solid alcohol back all right, and kept my receipt for it as well.

Compasses and maps were, of course, forbidden, but we managed to get them smuggled out in parcels all the same and watching a German open a parcel in which you knew there was a concealed compass was one of the most exciting things I've ever done.

For the next six weeks life was rather hard. It froze continuously, even in the daytime, and at night the thermometer registered more than 27° of frost. Fuel and light shortage became very serious. We stole wood and coal freely from the Germans, and although the sentries had strict orders to shoot at sight anyone seen taking wood, nearly all the wood work in the fort was eventually torn down and burnt.

The Germans didn't allow us much oil for our lamps, so we used to steal the oil out of the lamps in the passage, until the Germans realized that they were being robbed and substituted acetylene for oil. However, this didn't deter us, for now, instead of taking the oil out of the lamps, we took the lamps themselves, and lamp-stealing became one of the recognized sports of the camp. How it was done has nothing to do with escaping, but was amusing. Outside our living rooms there was a passage seventy yards long, in which were two acetylene lamps. The sentry in the passage had special orders, a loaded rifle and fixed bayonet, to see that these lamps weren't stolen, and since the feldwevel, or sergeant-major, had stuffed up the sentries with horrible stories

13

about our murderous characters, it isn't surprising that each sentry was very keen to prevent us stealing the lamps and leaving him – an isolated German – in total darkness and at our mercy. So whenever a prisoner came out of his room and passed one of the lamps, the sentry would eye him anxiously and get ready to charge at him. The lamps were about thirty yards apart, and this is how we got them. One of us would come out, walk to a lamp and stop beneath it. This would unnerve the sentry, who would advance upon him. The prisoner would then take out his watch and look at it by the light of the lamp, as if that were all he had stopped for. Meanwhile a second officer would come quickly out of a room further down the passage and take down the other lamp behind the sentry's back. The sentry would immediately turn and charge with loud yells of: 'Halt! Halt!' whereupon the first lamp would also be grabbed, both would be blown out simultaneously, and the prisoners would disappear into their respective rooms leaving the passage in total darkness. The amusing part was that this used to happen every night, and the sentries *knew* it was going to happen, but they were quite powerless against tactics of this kind.

At about this time an officer named Medlicott and I learnt that some Frenchmen were trying to escape across the frozen moat by cutting a window-bar in the latrines which overlooked it. The Germans, however, smelt a rat, but though they inspected the bars carefully they couldn't find the cuts which had been artfully sealed up with a mixture of flour and ashes. Then the feldwebel went round and shook each bar violently in turn until the fourth one came off in his hands and he fell down flat on his back. They then wired up the hole, but Medlicott and I saw a chance of cutting the wire and making another bolt for it about a week later, and we took it. We were only at large however for about two hours. The snow on the ground gave our tracks away; we were pursued, surrounded, and eventually had to surrender again. This time we had a somewhat hostile reception when we got back to the fort.

They searched us and took away my tin of solidified alcohol again. They recognized it. 'I know how you stole this back,' said the senior clerk as he gave me another receipt for it, 'but you shan't have it any more.' We both laughed over it. I laughed last, however, as I stole it back again in about a week's time, and kept my two receipts for it as well.

It may seem extraordinary that we weren't punished severely for these attempts to escape, but there were no convenient cells in which to punish us. All the cells at Fort 9 were always full and there was a very long waiting list besides.

After this failure I joined some Frenchmen who were making a tunnel. The shaft was sunk in the corner of one of their rooms close to the window, and the idea was to come out in the steep bank of the moat on a level with the ice and crawl over on a dark night. It was all very unpleasant. Most of the time one lay in a pool of water and in an extremely confined space and worked in pitch darkness, as the air was so bad that no candle would keep alight. Moreover, when we got close to the frozen surface of the ground it was always a question whether the sentry outside wouldn't put his foot through the tunnel, and if he did so whether one would be suffocated or stuck with a bayonet. It was most inpleasant lying there and waiting for him to pass within six inches of your head. All the earth had to be carried in bags along the passage and emptied down the latrines.

Unfortunately, just before the work was finished the thaw set in, and it was generally agreed that we couldn't afford to get our clothes wet swimming the moat. However, the Frenchmen were undaunted and determined to wade through the moat naked, carrying two bundles of kit sewn in waterproof cloths. The rest of us disliked the idea of being chased naked in the middle of winter carrying two twenty-pound bundles, so we decided to make ourselves diving suits out of mackintoshes. We waterproofed the worn patches of these with candle grease, and sewed them up in various places. The Frenchmen would have to fake roll-call, so they made most life-like dummies, which breathed when you pulled a string, to put in their beds. Whether this attempt to escape would have been successful I can't say, for, thank Heaven, we never tried it. When we were all ready and the French colonel, who was going first, had stripped naked and greased himself from head to foot, we learnt that the trap-door which we had made at the exit of the tunnel couldn't be opened under two hours owing to unexpected roots and stones. We had to put off the attempt for that night, and we were unable to make another as the end of the tunnel suddenly fell in, and the cavity was noticed by the sentry.

This was practically the end of my residence in Fort 9, for soon after the Germans decided to send the more unruly of us to other camps. We learnt that we were to be transferred to Zorndorf, in East Prussia, an intolerable spot from all accounts, and a man named Buckley and myself decided to get off the train at the first opportunity and make another bid for freedom. The train would be taking us directly away from the Swiss frontier, so it behoved us to leave it as soon as possible. We equipped ourselves as well as we could with condensed foods before starting, and wore Burberrys to cover our uniforms. Although there were only thirty of us going we had a guard of an officer and fifteen men, which *we* thought a little excessive. We had two hours' wait at the station and amused ourselves by taking as little notice as possible of the officer's orders, which annoyed him and made him shout. Six of us and a sentry were then packed rather tightly into a second-class carriage. We gave him the corner seat next to the corridor, and another sentry marched up and down the corridor outside. Buckley and I took the seats by the window, which we were compelled to keep closed, and there was no door in that side of the carriage. The position didn't look very hopeful, for there wasn't much chance of our sentry going to sleep with the other one outside continually looking in. Just before we started the officer came fussing in: he was obviously very anxious and nervous, and said he hoped that we would have a comfortable, quiet journey and no more trouble. The train started, night fell, and the frontier was left further and further behind. We shut our eyes for an hour to try to induce the sentry to go to sleep, but this didn't work.

The carriage was crowded, and both racks were full of small luggage, and, noticing this, I had an idea. I arranged with the others to act in a certain way when the train next went slowly, and I gave the word by saying to the sentry, in German: 'Will you have some food? We are going to eat.' Five or ten minutes of tense excitement followed. Suddenly the train began to slow up. I leant across and said to the sentry, 'Will you have some food? We are going to eat.' Immediately everyone in the carriage stood up with one accord and pulled their stuff off the racks. The sentry also stood up, but was almost completely hidden from the window by a confused mass of men and bags. Under cover of this confusion, Buckley and I stood up on our seats. I slipped the strap of my haversack over my shoulder, pushed down the window, put my leg over and jumped into the night. I fell – not very heavily – on the wires at the side of the track, and lay still in the dark shadow. Three seconds later Buckley came flying out after me, and seemed to take rather a heavy toss. The end of the train wasn't yet past me, and we knew there was a man with a rifle in the last carriage; so when Buckley came running along the track calling out to me, I caught him and pulled him into the ditch at the side. The train went by, and its tail lights vanished round a corner and apparently no one saw or heard us.

I have not space to say much about our walk to the German-Swiss frontier, about 200 miles away. We only walked by night, and lay up in hiding all through the hours of daylight which was, I think, the worst part of the business and wore out our nerves and physical strength far more than the six or seven hours marching at night, for the day seemed intolerably long from 4.30 am to 9.30 pm – seventeen hours – the sun was very hot, and there was little shade, and we were consumed with impatience to get on. Moreover, we could never be free from anxiety at any moment of those seventeen hours. The strain at night of passing through a village when a few lights still burnt and dogs seemed to wake and bark at us in every house, or of crossing a bridge when one expected to be challenged at any moment never worried me so much as a cart passing or men talking near our daytime hiding-places.

We went into hiding at dawn or soon after, and when we'd taken off our boots and put on clean socks we would both drop asleep at once. It was a bit of a risk – perhaps one of us ought to have stayed awake, but we took it deliberately since we got great benefit from a sound sleep while we were still warm from walking. And it was only about an hour before we woke again shivering, for the mornings were very cold and we were usually soaked with dew up to our waists. Then we had breakfast – the great moment of the day – and rations were pretty good at first, as we underestimated the time we would take by about four days. But later on we had to help things out with raw potatoes from the fields, which eventually became our mainstay. All day long we were pestered with stinging insects. Our hands and faces became swollen all over, and the bites on my feet came up in blisters which broke and left raw places when I put on my boots again.

On the fifteenth day our impatience got the better of us, and we started out before it was properly dark, and suddenly came upon a man in soldier's uniform scything grass at the side of the road. We were filthily dirty and unshaven and must have looked the most villainous tramps; it was stupid of us to have risked being seen; but it would have aroused his suspicion if we'd turned back, so we walked on past him. He looked up and said something we didn't catch. We answered: 'Good evening' as usual. But he called after us, and then when we took no notice, shouted: 'Halt! Halt!' and ran after us with his scythe.

We were both too weak to run fast or far, and moreover we saw at that moment a man with a gun about fifty yards to our right. There was only one thing to be done, and we did it.

We turned haughtily and waited for our pursuer, and when he was a few yards away Buckley demanded in a voice quivering with indignant German what the devil he meant by shouting at us. He almost dropped his scythe with astonishment, then turned round and went slowly back to his work. Buckley had saved the day.

The end of our march on the following night brought us within fifteen kilometres of the Swiss frontier, and we decided to eat the rest of our food and cross the next night. However, I kept back a few small meat lozenges. We learnt the map by heart so as to avoid having to strike matches later on, and left all our spare kit behind us in order to travel light for this last lap. But it wasn't to be our last lap.

We were awfully weak by now and made slow progress through the heavy going, and about two hours after we'd started a full bright moon rose which made us feel frightfully conspicuous. Moreover, we began to doubt our actual position, for a road we'd expected to find wasn't there. However, we tramped on by compass and reached a village which we hoped was a place named Riedheim, within half a mile of the frontier. But here we suddenly came on a single line railway which wasn't on our map. We were aghast – we were lost – and moreover Buckley was fearfully exhausted for want of food, so we decided to lie up for another night in a thick wood on a hill. The meat lozenges I'd saved now came in very handy and we also managed to find water and some more raw potatoes. Then we slept, and when daylight came studied our small scale map and tried to make head or tail of our situation.

We had a good view of the countryside from our position but could make nothing of it. Perhaps we were already in Switzerland? It was essential to know and it was no good looking for signposts since they'd all been removed within a radius of ten miles of the frontier. I think we were both slightly insane by now from hunger and fatigue; anyhow I decided to take a great risk. I took off my tunic and walking down into the fields asked a girl who was making hay what the name of the village was. It was Riedheim – as I'd originally thought. The railway of course had been made after the map was printed. I don't know what the girl thought of my question and appearance; she gave me a sly look, but went on with her work. I returned to Buckley, and when it was quite dark we left our hiding-place. We had three-quarters of an hour to cross the frontier before the moon rose – and we had to go with the greatest care. For a time we walked bent double, and then we went down on our hands and knees, pushing our way through the thick long grass of water meadows. The night was so still – surely the swishing of the grass as we moved through it must be audible for hundreds of yards. On and on we went – endlessly it seemed – making for a stream which we had seen from our hill and now knew must be the boundary line. Then the edge of the moon peered at us over the hills. We crawled at top speed now, until Buckley's hand on my heel suddenly brought me to a halt. About fifteen yards ahead was a sentry. He was walking along a footpath on the bank of a stream. *The* stream. He had no rifle, and had probably just been relieved. He passed without seeing us. One last spurt and we were in the stream and up the other bank. 'Crawl,' said Buckley. 'Run,' said I, and we ran. It was just after midnight when we crossed into Switzerland and freedom on our eighteenth night out.

A FIGHT FOR LIFE

Denis Wheatley

British Agent Gregory Sallust has entered wartime Germany in a bid to contact the ring leaders of the anti-Nazi movement.

In a private house in the town of Ems, Gregory meets Pastor Wachmuller who is sympathetic to the anti-Nazi cause. Gregory is about to be given vital information when an SS man breaks in and shoots the Pastor dead. In return, Gregory manages to kill the SS man – but finds the house surrounded by Nazis . . .

Gregory's racing thoughts moved at lightning speed. Only a second or two had elapsed since the SS man had fallen dead in the doorway when sounds of movement below caught his ear. Snatching up his overcoat he slipped it on and strode to the door, his gun still in his right hand. Opening the door quietly but quickly he slipped out on to the landing and stood listening. Excited voices came up from the hall below, followed by the sound of a footfall on the lower stairs.

One cautious glance over the landing-rail showed him the tops of uniform caps worn by men who were already running up towards him with drawn guns in their hands. The Nazi whom he had shot must have secreted himself in the room adjoining the library and left his men below to guard the exits of the house. Gregory was trapped: his only chance of escape lay in getting away over the roof-tops before the Nazis had time to search the building.

With catlike swiftness he tiptoed to the foot of the upper stairs; then, crouched and silent, he began to ascend. He had just reached a bend in the flight when the leading Nazis arrived with a rush on the landing below. By an evil chance one of them happened to glance up, and caught sight of him moving in the semi-darkness.

With a shout of '*Da ist jemand!*' he raised his automatic and fired.

The bullet crashed into the baluster-rail a few inches above the crouching Gregory's shoulder and sent splinters of woodwork flying into his face.

Then his own automatic spat as he pressed the trigger, firing between the balusters. The Nazi clutched at his throat: blood oozed between his fingers and spurted suddenly from his mouth. With a half-choked scream he fell back among his comrades.

The next second a fusillade of shots crashed out as the others blazed away into the gloom, but by that time Gregory was round the bend. As he sprang on to the upper landing he heard the killers come pounding up behind him.

★   ★   ★   ★

In the dim light on the upper landing Gregory could just make out three doors, one of which was lower than the other two. There was no time to examine the rooms to which they led, as the slightest hesitation meant that he would be exposed to the bullets of his pursuers. He had to make an instantaneous choice. If the room he chose had a skylight there would still be the fraction of a chance that he might get away; if not, he would be cornered and captured, or more probably dead, within the next few minutes.

The larger doors looked as though they led to bedrooms, whereas the lower one might well be that of the boxroom of the house – and boxrooms are more usually lit by skylights than are bedrooms.

Grabbing the handle of the lower door Gregory wrenched at it. Fortunately it was unlocked, and as it swung open he flung himself inside. For a second he could see nothing. The place was as black as pitch, but jerking his head upward with frantic anxiety he saw a long rectangle of dimmish light above him. It was a skylight; he had been granted that hundredth chance of getting out alive.

How slender his chances were he knew only too well. If there was a key in the lock of the door it must still be on the far side, as he had had no time to remove it, and as people do not usually have bolts inside their boxroom doors it would be merely a waste of precious moments to fumble about in the hope of finding one.

Pouching his gun he reached down and groped about in the darkness.

His hands came in contact first with a perambulator, then with a heavy wooden box. As he stooped to lift this and fling it against the door another fusillade of shots rang out. The house was old and the door a thick one, but even so several of the bullets penetrated the panels, and the fact that he had stooped just at that instant probably saved his life.

The heavy box now temporarily held the door, but the Nazis were already battering on it and a faint streak of light showed that their first assault had opened it a crack. Lying full length on the floor Gregory set his shoulder against the box and drew his gun again. Raising it and placing it against a panel on a level with his head he pulled the trigger twice to give his pursuers a taste of their own medicine. There was a yelp of pain followed by a blasphemous spate of curses, and the pressure on the door eased a little. As it did so he wriggled back until his feet touched something, and reaching behind him he found that it was a ladder.

The Nazis charged the door again. It creaked under their weight and the sudden broadening of the band of light showed that they had now forced it open a good six inches. Judging from its weight the box was probably full of books; it had taken a big effort for Gregory to heave it against the door. But there was nothing but its weight to hold it in position, so a series of determined assaults would soon force it back. If Gregory had had more time he could have piled other things upon it, for he could now see the faint outlines of a number of cases and trunks in the boxroom; but to stand up and move them would mean exposing himself to any bullets that might come through the door. He knew that he would have to risk such exposure for a moment in any case, but he meant to do so only for the better purpose of attempting to reach the skylight.

One of the Nazis emptied the remaining contents of his pistol through the panels of the door and the bullets streamed over Gregory's head. Immediately the smacking of bullets into the far wall had ceased Gregory swung round, grabbed a rung of the ladder and launched himself up it.

Another crash below told him that his pursuers had made a further assault on the door, but by that time he was crouching at the top of the ladder and fumbling frantically with the perforated iron strip by which the skylight could be adjusted at various angles.

As he thrust up the skylight he glanced down and saw that the door was now open a foot. A black patch, shoulder-high in the band of light down its edge, could only be a man's arm thrust round it. There came a rapid succession of flashes which lit up the whole room as the owner of the arm sprayed it blind with his pistol.

Gregory had always prided himself upon his marksmanship. Raising his automatic he aimed carefully and let the fellow have one in the shoulder. There was a cry and the pistol dropped from a nerveless hand. Gregory heard it crash on the floor-boards as he wriggled out on to the roof.

Drawing the fresh night air gratefully into his lungs he let the skylight fall back with a bang and looked swiftly round him. The houses in the row were of the old German type with sloping roofs and many gables; dangerous, tricky ground for any man to attempt to negotiate in the darkness; but darkness was his friend, and if only he could manage to avoid slipping and falling headlong to the street they would afford excellent cover.

The rain had stopped, and a few stars were showing through a break in the clouds. They gave just a little light, and owing to his brief sojourn in the boxroom Gregory's eyes were by now accustomed to the darkness. He could see that he was standing upon a flat portion of the roof about two feet wide, and that it sloped sharply down on either side.

A tall chimney-stack some fifteen feet away, where the Pastor's house abutted on the next, showed as a patch of deeper blackness to Gregory's left, beyond the skylight. Drawing himself up, he stepped carefully towards it.

As he moved there came a sharp challenge from the roof of the neighbouring house: '*Wie gehts?*'

'Fritz,' he called out quickly; that being the commonest German Christian name that he could think of on the spur of the moment; but the challenge showed him that his position was even more desperate than it had been in the boxroom a few minutes before. The Nazis had posted men on the adjoining roofs, and if they had done that they would certainly have surrounded the whole block also. In a moment the men below would be scrambling up behind him, and he would be caught between two fires. Even if he could break through and reach the street he would find himself faced by the men of the cordon while the others followed in hot pursuit. It seemed that nothing now remained but for him to sell his life dearly.

'Fritz who?' came the swift question.

Instead of answering, Gregory asked another question in reply. 'Where is he? Haven't you seen him?'

'No!' shouted the other man.

'*Himmel*! Are you deaf and blind?' Gregory cried urgently. 'He came up out of the skylight less than a minute ago.'

'He's somewhere on the roof, then. Must be behind you,' said the German, moving forward and disclosing his position near the chimney-stack.

Already the sounds of feet below warned Gregory that the Nazis had forced the door of the boxroom and were streaming into it. Another moment and they would be dashing up the ladder. This was no time for scruples; raising his gun he pointed it at the dark shadow by the chimney-stack and fired.

A gasp was followed by the sound of feet slithering on slates, the fall of a heavy body and then a shriek of fear as the Nazi on the adjoining roof lost his balance and went hurtling over and over down the steep slope until he pitched off over the gutter.

One of the men inside the boxroom sent a pot-shot crashing through the skylight. Lowering his weapon and firing blind, Gregory emptied all the bullets left in his automatic down through it, aiming it at the spot where he knew the ladder to be. A whimpering moan followed by the thud of someone falling to the floor told him that one of his bullets had found flesh and bone. Before another Nazi could get up the ladder he turned and padded as quickly as he dared across the narrow, level stretch of roof to the point where the man on watch had been standing.

Halting there in the shadow of the chimney-stack he slipped a spare clip of cartridges into his own gun and pulled from his coat pocket one of those which he had taken from the Nazis at Coblenz. Crouching down and invisible in the darkness he waited, tense with the thrill of battle, for the enemy's next move.

Since his pursuers did not lack courage, it soon came. One of them scrambled out on to the roof, then another, then a third. Gregory held his fire, waiting to see whether any more would appear. There was just enough light for him to make them out as they crouched by the sky-light, but they could not see him. Once he pressed the triggers of his guns he might never again have the chance of snaring them in so perfect an ambush.

The Naxis were muttering together. 'Where is he? Which way did he go?' 'Where's Förster?' 'He must have killed him. That shot up here, just now.' Cautiously they stood to peer round, and Gregory let them have it.

Aiming both guns at the centre man he blazed off; then slowly turned both barrels outwards while keeping his fingers pressed down on the triggers. The effect was like that of two machine-guns simultaneously spraying bullets outwards from a central point.

Cries, a gurgling moan, a curse cut short, penetrated faintly to him through the banging of his automatics. One Nazi crashed headlong through the skylight; another rolled down the slope of the roof and pitched off; the third slumped in a still, silent heap.

As he ceased fire to ascertain the result of his murderous attack Gregory could not tell whether the third man was dead or shamming. To make certain of him he took careful aim and put another bullet in his body, but he did not even moan. Gregory knew then, with a thrill of satisfaction, that he had scuppered the whole of the party which had broken into the Pastor's house.

But his elation was short-lived. As he drew himself upright a single shot cracked out from the roof beyond the skylight. Another Nazi had either been lurking there or had just come up, and had fired at the flash of Gregory's gun.

He felt a sharp pain, like the searing of a red-hot iron drawn across his left thigh; staggered, lost his balance and slipped off the narrow, flat portion of the roof.

With a gasp he realized that he was about to die in the same way as the sentry whom he had shot on that very spot only two minutes earlier.

His pistols were knocked out of his hands as he fell; one exploded and both clattered loudly as they slithered down the slates beside him. His hands clawed desperately at the empty air. As he rolled towards the gutter he glimpsed the double flash of his enemy's gun as the man put two more shots into the spot by the chimney-stack where he had been kneeling; next instant he felt a terrific jolt which nearly drove the breath out of his body. His whirling descent had been brought up short against a gable which broke the outline of the gutter.

It was a quite small affair, and had he rolled down a single foot further either to the right or to the left he would have slithered round it to crash into the street forty feet below, but as it was it had caught him full in the centre of the spine, so that his head and arms were flung backwards on one side of the ridge and his heavy boots crashed on the slates at its other side.

For a minute he lay there, bent backwards like a bow; then he cautiously eased himself up, scrabbling on the slates with his hands and feet until he was lying flat on the slope of the roof with his head uppermost and his feet wedged firmly against the gable.

The man who had shot him must have thought at first that he had fallen into the street, but a minute later would have heard the noise that he had been compelled to make as he hauled himself up into a safer position. Gregory's fear that this had been so was soon confirmed. He heard the man stealthily approaching along the top of the roof, then saw him vaguely as a moving black blur against the skyline.

Very gently Gregory withdrew one of his hands from the flat surface of the slates and wriggled his third gun out of his overcoat pocket.

The man above had paused and was peering down, uncertain as to whether Gregory was still there or not, for he could not see him in the blackness.

Gregory knew that he was temporarily safe while he remained hidden; to shoot would give away his position and would draw the enemy's fire in reply if his bullet went wide, but as he was a crack shot he decided to risk it. Resting his right hand on his left wrist as it lay on the slates in front of his face he aimed for the black blur above him. Placing his first finger along the side of his pistol, he very slowly squeezed the trigger with his second.

The flash of his gun stabbed the darkness; there was a loud cry, and the man above suddenly sprang into the air. But Gregory had not foreseen a possible result of his shooting. Next moment the man had pitched forward and came sliding down the roof towards him.

He had just time to jam his gun back into his pocket before he faced the peril of being swept from his precarious footing and whirled to the street with the wounded German.

Splaying his legs backwards like a frog round the sides of the gable, he lowered his head and clung to the slates with the flats of his hands. As he did so the German came tumbling, feet first, right on top of him. The Nazi would have gone right over the edge of the roof but for the fact that one of his hands came in contact with Gregory's right shoulder-strap. He grabbed it with all his strength, and though his legs were already well over the gutter on Gregory's right he succeeded in checking his fall.

The strain on Gregory was terrific. He was almost dragged over, but his leg-grip saved him, and the weight of the German was lessened almost at once as he managed to support himself by wedging one of his feet in the gutter.

Gregory turned sideways and lashed out with his fist in the direction in which he believed the man's head to be, but he missed it and barked his knuckles badly on the slates. The Nazi was still half on top of him, and with a swift wriggle he succeeded in throwing his whole weight on Gregory while he bashed at him with both fists, thus showing that he had been wounded only in the leg or body.

The fact that Gregory was lying face-downwards saved him from the worst effects of the blows; but, on the other hand, he was unable to get to grips with his enemy.

The Nazi was a big, heavy fellow who puffed and panted as he strove both to retain his balance and to knock Gregory out. Gregory was more wiry and since his fall had had time to get his breath, so he fought with silent ferocity.

Hugging each other in a bear-like grip, but not daring to move anything but their hands and arms for fear of falling off the roof, they struggled desperately until Gregory, now lying sideways and half twisted over, managed to get his hands upon the throat of the man above him. His was no amateur strangler's grip, for he did not press with the flats of his thumbs, but deliberately forced their points into the man's throat below his chin.

The wretched Nazi gurgled horribly; the pain must have been excruciating, but he could not scream. His hands loosed their hold on Gregory and began to flap wildly. For a full minute Gregory kept up the pressure, while he could feel the warm blood running over the backs of his hands from the places where his nails had gored the man's throat. Suddenly the Nazi slumped forward as though his neck had been broken, and Gregory knew that he was now unconscious. With a cautious heave he pitched the body from on top of him, and it disappeared into the blackness.

For a few seconds he lay there panting. When he could once more take stock of things, he could hear the Nazis in the street below talking round the body of their dead comrade while one of their officers issued fresh orders.

Easing his position carefully, he tried to haul himself up the steep slope of the roof, but there was not a thing to grip, and he had made hardly a couple of feet headway when he slithered back again to the gable that had proved his salvation. A second attempt met with no more success, and he realized with dismay that it was impossible for him to regain the roof-top. With that realization, a wave of black despair engulfed him. Sooner of later the Nazis would smell him out and pick him off at their leisure.

But his despair was only momentary, for it soon occurred to him that although he could not get up, there was a chance that he might be able to get down. Wherever there is a small gable breaking the gutter-line of a roof there is nearly always a dormer window below it. This new thought gave him fresh courage, and with the utmost caution he lowered himself round one side of the gable until his legs were dangling over the gutter. Very gingerly he began to feel about with his feet round the angle of the wall below.

It was difficult to judge what was below him in the darkness and at first he could find nothing with his groping feet. Lowering himself a little he tried again, and this time his foot struck something which gave out a low rumble, like the faint quivering of a drum.

With a sigh of thankfulness he realized that his luck still held. There *was* a window below the gable, and the upper half of it was open; he had kicked the lower part with his foot, and it was the glass which had rumbled; but it was going to be a devilishly tricky business to get inside it.

Just as he was about to make the attempt he caught the sound of fresh footsteps on the roof-top. Another party of Nazis must have come up through the skylight. Fortunately, the only man who had known his exact position was now lying dead in the street below, and providing that he could remain very quiet it might be some time before the new squad would be able to locate him.

Straining his ears until it felt as though their drums would burst he remained rigid, listening, until the Nazis above him spread out and began a systematic search for him along the roof-top. They were not to know that he had been wounded and was precariously perched upon a gutter some twenty feet below them; they naturally supposed that he had stuck to the narrow, flat treads on the roof and was hiding behind one of the chimney-stacks, probably on one of the more distant houses.

From the sounds they made he could tell that they had split up into two parties and were moving in opposite directions with the intention of beating the roofs until they had cornered him at one of the extremities of the block.

Directly the group which had moved in his direction had gone past he lowered himself still further, until his whole body was dangling over the roof-edge and supported only by his elbows in the gutter. The houses were old, and the gutter bent under his weight until he feared that it might give way at any moment, and he dared not rest too long upon it. He had to make his attempt quickly or he might go crashing into the street without having made it at all.

Both his feet were now well inside the open window, but unless he could find some other support for the top half of his body immediately he let go of the gutter he would pitch backwards and descend head-first on to the paving-stones. Reaching down with his right hand, and supporting his weight with his left only, he felt along inside the top of the open window until to his immense relief, the tips of his fingers found a curtain-rail.

The rod was only a thin one, but he thought that it might bear his weight just long enough for him to gain sufficient impetus to fling himself in through the window. Drawing a deep breath he gripped the curtain-rail firmly, let go of the gutter and launched himself downwards, twisting his body as he did so. The thin rod snapped; for a second he hovered in mid-air, his left hand flung out, his feet kicking wildly. Then he landed with a bump on the wooden window-frame, hanging half in and half out of the window. During his drop he had turned in the air so that he was now facing out across the street. With a desperate jerk he pitched himself backwards, banged his head on the upper part of the window-frame and fell in a heap on the floor inside.

Picking himself up he stepped forward into the darkness like a blind man, with his hands outstretched, until he came in contact with a bed. He did not dare to strike a light as the windows were uncurtained and to have done so would have given away his position, but to his relief the bed was unoccupied and he groped his way along until he found a door.

Pressing the handle firmly into its socket so that the catch should make no noise he turned it slowly and opened the door a fraction. A dim light filtering up the stairs showed him a landing. There were splashes of blood upon its floor, and next minute he realized that he was back in Pastor Wachmuller's house.

The door of the boxroom stood open. One dead Nazi was stretched out inside it; another lay on his face beside him, groaning loudly. At first it seemed to Gregory that he had hardly improved his position. Almost certainly there would be Nazis occupying the hall below and on guard outside the door, as this was the house that they had raided and the centre of their operations. But on second thoughts he decided that even if he had been able to plan his movements he could hardly have done better than to return to the Pastor's house.

In all the others there would be civilians who, even if they had gone to bed early that night, would have been roused by all the shooting and excitement in their street. He could hardly have hoped to have got downstairs without one of them seeing him and raising the alarm, whereas here, in the upper part of Wachmuller's house, he was safe for the moment, at least. While the Nazis were probably already searching the other houses, this was the one place in which it would not occur to them to look for him.

For a moment he considered returning to the unoccupied bedroom and hiding in it, but he quickly abandoned that idea. When daylight came his pursuers would be able to get a full view of every roof in the block, and when they found that he was not concealed upon any of them they would resume their search of the houses. Every room, every cupboard and every cellar would be ransacked in case some anti-Nazi family had agreed to hide him. When that had failed the thorough Germans would conclude with their admirable logic that he must have got back into Pastor Wachmuller's house and search that; so that to conceal himself in the bedroom would be simply to postpone his capture and death until the morning. The almost total darkness of the ARP* black-out was his one ally; his sole chance of escape lay in acting while it lasted.

Having peered over the baluster-rail and seen that there was no one on the landing below, he tiptoed downstairs. The Nazi whom he had shot in the throat had been removed by his comrades, but splashes of blood on the wall showed where the wounded man had collapsed against it. The light was still on in the Pastor's sitting-room; the door stood open. No sound disturbed the grim silence. Drawing his spare gun again Gregory edged his way round the corner of the door. The Pastor and the dead SS officer still lay there just as he had left them.

Returning to the landing he crept down the next flight of stairs. The hall was empty; the heavy, wooden street-door shut. Still that uncanny silence. He wondered what had become of the old housekeeper. Either she was in the semi-basement or the Nazis had carried her off before laying their ambush. He paused for a moment in the stone-flagged hall, listening intently; then, as he still heard no sound, he softly turned the handle of a door on his right and opened it a crack.

The room was in darkness, but opening the door a little further he saw by the light in the hall that it was the dining-room. Slipping inside, he held the door wide open for a second to get his bearings. It was a longish room with three tall windows; the curtains of the farthest window billowed slightly from the draught. Having noted the disposition of the furniture he shut the door behind him and walked slowly forward into the darkness until he touched the table. Feeling his way along to its far end he turned half-left and took three good strides, which brought his outstretched hand in contact with the curtains of the farthest window.

Kneeling down on the floor he returned his one remaining gun to his pistol holster; then very gingerly he parted the curtains a fraction. There was another, thinner, calico curtain behind them, evidently put up for black-out purposes, and he lifted it until his fingers touched the edge of the window-sill. Raising it a little more he peered out into the street.

* ARP = Air Raid Precautions.

At first he could see nothing except two spots of light some way to his left, on the roadway in front of the street door, but as his eyes grew accustomed to the darkness he gradually became able to make out the main details of the scene. The spots of light came from two black-out torches specially constructed to shine downwards, which were held by two uniformed men. Two others stood near them, and this group was evidently guarding the entrance to the house.

Farther along the street in both directions he could see other, smaller patches of light on the road, which clearly indicated that similar groups were posted at intervals to watch the exits of the other houses.

As all the houses in the street had semi-basements their first-floor windows were only about eight feet from the ground and Gregory saw that an easy drop from the window behind which he was crouching would bring him unharmed into the street below. But for how long could he hope to survive once he had gained it? The street had apparently been closed both to traffic and pedestrians, and it was very quiet; the stillness broken only by the occasional shouts of the Nazis as they called to one another.

Swiftly Gregory weighed up his chances. As a tall man, his toes would just about touch the pavement if he hung from the window-sill at the full stretch of his arms. He would have at the most only an inch or two to drop, but the rattle of his buttons and equipment against the woodwork as he wriggled himself through backward and the scraping of his toes on the wall as he lowered himself would cause a commotion in the utter stillness of the street quite sufficient to put the nearest groups of watchers instantly on the *qui vive*.★ Even in the shadows he would be shot before he had gone twenty yards.

He had already abandoned any idea of attempting an escape that way as absolutely suicidal when he suddenly heard someone speak in a low voice just below the window. Another voice answered with a monosyllable; then silence fell again, broken only by the faint, distant cries of men calling to each other while they still searched for him among the chimney-pots.

More from curiosity than for any other reason, Gregory raised his head slightly so that he could look down at the men who were standing below him in the street. As he did so another beam of light caught his

★ qui vive = the alert.

eye. It came from the thin, horizontal aperture cut in the black-out shade of a motor-bicycle head lamp. He could make out the silhouette of the machine where it stood propped up in the gutter just in front of the men, who wore the flat caps of Nazis, and evidently it belonged to one of them.

Should he, or should he not! It would be a most desperate gamble, but any other exits from the house were sure to be equally well-guarded, and if only he could seize the bike and get it going its speed would at least give him some chance of breaking through the cordon before he could be shot down.

'Nothing venture, nothing win!' muttered Gregory. 'Here goes!' And coming up under the curtains he placed one foot on the low sill of the window.

For a second he paused there to make certain that the men below had not heard his movements. Apparently they had not, for they were still standing side by side just beneath him with their faces turned away towards the road.

Drawing up his other foot, he balanced himself in a crouching position, then jumped; not outwards towards the motor-cycle, but downwards, straight on top of the two Nazis.

He landed as he had planned, right between them, so that both of them were bowled over as he pitched forward on to his knees. Scrambling to his feet, he grabbed the handlebars of the motor-bike, opened the throttle, jammed the gear-lever into low, and, exerting every ounce of his strength, ran forward with it.

Time seemed to stand still as he forced the heavy, twin-cylinder BMW along and waited for its engines to start firing. Both the men whom he had knocked over had begun to shout from the moment they had hit the pavement. The little blobs of light further down the street instantly began to move. Shouts, challenges and cries broke the stillness of the night as the waiting patrols sprang into action.

At last, after what seemed an eternity, there was a loud explosion as the cycle backfired. Cursing *Ersatz* petrol, Gregory retarded the spark and dropped the decompression control. Another yard, and the powerful machine nearly jerked his arms from their sockets as it leaped forward, roaring suddenly into life.

When he landed in the saddle with a desperate spring he was already

33

The machine hurtled forward at even greater speed.

halfway towards the nearest group of Nazis. The road was narrow, and by seeking to avoid them he would only have presented a better target. Lying flat along the tank he jerked the throttle wide open and charged straight at them, the engine screaming deafeningly in bottom gear. They scattered and had evidently only just drawn their guns without having time to aim as none of them fired until he had flashed by them and was roaring down the street towards the next group, which the light of the headlamp suddenly brought into view.

Still crouching low over the handlebars, he set his teeth and risked a racing change into second gear. By a miracle it came off, and the machine hurtled forward at even greater speed. The pistols of the Nazis ahead flashed almost in his face, but he had swerved a split second before, and their shots went wide. Scraping one man with his elbow he bowled him over, and raced on just as a shot from the first group, now well behind him, whistled past his ear.

An instant later a yell of pain sounded above the roar of his engine. A man in the second group had been hit by another bullet intended for Gregory and fired by one of the men in the first, who were now pounding vainly down the street after him.

Orders, counter-orders; cries of stop him, to shoot him, to cease fire or they would kill one another, rang out in gutteral German.

Behind him the darkness veiled a scene of consternation and confusion: before him at the end of the street, there waited yet another squad of Nazis, and although it was barely half a minute since he had thrown himself on the motor-cycle they had had that much more time in which to prepare for his reception.

They blazed off as he came charging down the street, but, gripping the handle-bars with savage determination he wrenched the machine right up on to the low pavement, skimmed inside an unlighted lamp-standard, roared past the group of men and bumped down off the pavement beyond them. Swerving again he careered first to one side of the street and then to the other until he shot round the bend, miraculously immune from the hail of bullets that were now striking sparks from the roadway and whining loudly as they ricocheted from the walls of the houses.

In his anxiety to get clear of Ems before a police cordon could be drawn across its exits he took a wrong turning, but he soon picked up his route again and striking the main Coblenz road slipped the BMW into top gear. Regardless of all danger of a smash he streaked at over eighty mph past a police patrol which yelled at him to halt and two minutes later was clear of the town. At last he breathed a little more freely and eased up the speed of the machine. By the mercy of Providence and the use of his own quick wits he had escaped when escape had seem next to impossible.

TRAPPED AMONGST ICEBERGS

Jules Verne

At one stage of their amazing and often dangerous underwater journey on board Captain Nemo's submarine 'Nautilus', three friends – Professor Pierre Aronnax, his servant Conseil and the Canadian Ned Land – find themselves near the great icebergs of the Antarctic . . .

The cold was great; the constellations shone with wonderful intensity. In the zenith glittered that wondrous Southern Cross – the polar bear of antarctic regions. The thermometer showed twelve degrees below zero, and when the wind freshened, it was most biting. Flakes of ice increased on the open water. The sea seemed everywhere alike. Numerous blackish patches spread on the surface, showing the formation of fresh ice. Evidently the southern basin, frozen during the six winter months, was absolutely inaccessible. What became of the whales in that time? Doubtless they went beneath the icebergs, seeking more practicable seas. As to the seals and morses, accustomed to live in a hard climate, they remained on these icy shores. These creatures have the instinct to break holes in the ice-fields, and to keep them open. To these holes they come for breath; when the birds, driven away by the cold, have emigrated to the north, these sea mammals remain sole masters of the polar continent. But the reservoirs were filling with water, and the *Nautilus* was slowly descending. At 1,000 feet deep it stopped; its screw beat the waves, and it advanced straight towards the north, at a speed of fifteen miles an hour. Towards night it was already floating under the immense body of the iceberg. At three in the morning I was awakened by a violent shock. I sat up in my bed and listened in the darkness, when I was thrown into the middle of the room. The *Nautilus*, after having struck, had rebounded violently. I groped along the partition, and by the staircase to the saloon, which was lit by the luminous ceiling. The furniture was upset. Fortunately the windows were firmly set, and had held fast. The pictures on the starboard side, from being no longer vertical, were clinging to the paper, whilst those of the port side were hanging at least a foot from the wall. The *Nautilus* was lying on its starboard side perfectly motionless. I heard footsteps, and a confusion of voices; but Captain Nemo did not appear. As I was leaving the saloon, Ned Land and Conseil entered.

'What is the matter?' said I at once.

'I came to ask you, sir,' replied Conseil.

'Confound it!' exclaimed the Canadian. 'I know well enough! The *Nautilus* has struck; and judging by the way she lies, I do not think she will right herself.'

'But,' I asked, 'has she at least come to the surface of the sea?'

'We do not know,' said Conseil.

'It is easy to decide,' I answered. I consulted the manometer. To my great surprise it showed a depth of more than 180 fathoms. 'What does that mean?' I exclaimed.

'We must ask Captain Nemo,' said Conseil.

'But where shall we find him?' said Ned Land.

'Follow me,' said I to my companions.

We left the saloon. There was no one in the library. At the centre staircase, by the berths of the ship's crew, there was no one. I thought that Captain Nemo must be in the pilot's cage. It was best to wait. We all returned to the saloon. For twenty minutes we remained thus, trying to hear the slightest noise which might be made on board the *Nautilus*, when Captain Nemo entered. He seemed not to see us; his face, generally so impassive, showed signs of uneasiness. He watched the compass silently, then the manometer; and going to the planisphere, placed his finger on a spot representing the southern seas. I would not interrupt him; but, some minutes later, when he turned towards me, I said, using one of his own expressions:

'An incident, Captain?'

'No, sir; an accident this time.'

'Serious?'

'Perhaps.'

'Is the danger immediate?'

'No.'

'The *Nautilus* has stranded?'

'Yes.'

'And this has happened – how?'

'From a caprice of nature, not from the ignorance of man. Not a mistake has been made in the working. But we cannot prevent equilibrium from producing its effects. We may brave human laws, but we cannot resist natural ones.'

Captain Nemo had chosen a strange moment for uttering this philosophical reflection. On the whole, his answer helped me little.

'May I ask, sir, the cause of this accident?'

'An enormous block of ice, a whole mountain, has turned over,' he replied. 'When icebergs are undermined at their base by warmer water or reiterated shocks, their centre of gravity rises, and the whole thing turns over. This is what has happened; one of these blocks, as it fell, struck the *Nautilus*, then, gliding under its hull, raised it with irresistible force, bringing it into beds which are not so thick, where it is lying on its side.'

'But can we not get the *Nautilus* off by emptying its reservoirs, that it may regain its equilibrium?'

'That, sir, is being done at this moment. You can hear the pump working. Look at the needle of the manometer; it shows that the *Nautilus* is rising, but the block of ice is rising with it; and until some obstacle stops its ascending motion, our position cannot be altered.'

Indeed, the *Nautilus* still held the same position to starboard; doubtless it would right itself when the block stopped. But at this moment who knows if we may not strike the upper part of the iceberg, and if we may not be frightfully crushed between the two glassy surfaces? I reflected on all the consequences of our position. Captain Nemo never took his eyes off the manometer. Since the fall of the iceberg, the *Nautilus* had risen about a hundred and fifty feet, but it still made the same angle with the perpendicular. Suddenly a light movement was felt in the hold. Evidently it was righting a little. Things hanging in the saloon were sensibly returning to their normal position. The partitions were nearing the upright. No one spoke. With beating

39

hearts we watched and felt the straightening. The boards became horizontal under our feet. Ten minutes passed.

'At last we have righted!' I exclaimed.

'Yes,' said Captain Nemo, going to the door of the saloon.

'But are we floating?' I asked.

'Certainly,' he replied; 'since the reservoirs are now empty; and, when empty, the *Nautilus* must rise to the surface of the sea.'

We were in open sea; but at a distance of about ten yards, on either side of the *Nautilus*, rose a dazzling wall of ice. Above and beneath the same wall. Above, because the lower surface of the iceberg stretched over us like an immense ceiling. Beneath, because the overturned block, having slid by degrees, had found a resting-place on the lateral walls, which kept it in that position. The *Nautilus* was really imprisoned in a perfect tunnel of ice more than twenty yards in breadth, filled with quiet water. It was easy to get out of it by going either forward or backward, and then make a free passage under the iceberg, some hundreds of yards deeper. The luminous ceiling had been extinguished, but the saloon was still resplendent with intense light. It was the powerful reflection from the glass partition sent violently back to the sheets of the lantern. I cannot describe the effect of the voltaic rays upon the great blocks so capriciously cut; upon every angle, every ridge, every facet was thrown a different light, according to the nature of the veins running through the ice; a dazzling mine of gems, particularly of sapphires, their blue rays crossing with the green of the emerald. Here and there were opal shades of wonderful softness, running through bright spots like diamonds of fire, the brilliancy of which the eye could not bear. The power of the lantern seemed increased a hundredfold, like a lamp through the lenticular plates of a first-class lighthouse.

'How beautiful! How beautiful!' cried Conseil.

'Yes,' I said, 'it is a wonderful sight. Is it not, Ned?'

'Yes, confound it! Yes,' answered Ned Land, 'it is superb! I am mad at being obliged to admit it. No one has ever seen anything like it; but the sight may cost us dear. And if I must say all, I think we are seeing here things which God never intended man to see.'

Ned was right, it was too beautiful. Suddenly a cry from Conseil made me turn.

'What is it?' I asked.

'Shut your eyes, sir! Do not look, sir!' Saying which, Conseil clapped his hands over his eyes.

'But what is the matter, my boy?'

'I am dazzled, blinded.'

My eyes turned involuntarily towards the glass, but I could not stand the fire which seemed to devour them. I understood what had happened. The *Nautilus* had put on full speed. All the quiet lustre of the ice-walls was at once changed into flashes of lightning. The fire from these myriads of diamonds was blinding. It required some time to calm our troubled looks. At last the hands were taken down.

'Faith, I should never have believed it,' said Conseil.

It was then five in the morning; and at that moment a shock was felt at the bows of the *Nautilus*. I knew that its spur had struck a block of ice. It must have been a false manoeuvre, for this submarine tunnel, obstructed by blocks, was not very easy navigation. I thought that Captain Nemo, by changing his course, would either turn these obstacles, or else follow the windings of the tunnel. In any case, the road before us could not be entirely blocked. But, contrary to my expectations, the *Nautilus* took a decided retrograde motion.

'We are going backwards?' said Conseil.

'Yes,' I replied. 'This end of the tunnel can have no egress.'

'And then?'

'Then,' said I, 'the working is easy. We must go back again, and go out at the southern opening. That is all.'

In speaking thus, I wished to appear more confident than I really was. But the retrograde motion of the *Nautilus* was increasing; and, reversing the screw, it carried us at great speed.

'It will be a hindrance,' said Ned.

'What does it matter, some hours more or less, provided we get out at last?'

'Yes,' repeated Ned Land, 'provided we do get out at last!'

For a short time I walked from the saloon to the library. My companions were silent. I soon threw myself on an ottoman, and took a book, which my eyes overran mechanically. A quarter of an hour after, Conseil, approaching me, said: 'Is what you are reading very interesting, sir?'

'Very interesting!' I replied.

'I should think so, sir. It is your own book you are reading.'

'My book?'

And indeed I was holding in my hand the work on the *Great Submarine Depths*. I did not even dream of it. I closed the book, and returned to my walk. Ned and Conseil rose to go.

'Stay here, my friends,' said I, detaining them. 'Let us remain together until we are out of this block.'

'As you please, sir,' Conseil replied.

Some hours passed. I often looked at the instruments hanging from the partition. The manometer showed that the *Nautilus* kept at a constant depth of more than three hundred yards; the compass still pointed to the south; the log indicated a speed of twenty miles an hour, which, in such a cramped space, was very great. But Captain Nemo knew that he could not hasten too much, and that minutes were worth ages to us. At twenty-five minutes past eight a second shock took place, this time from behind. I turned pale. My companions were close by my side. I seized Conseil's hand. Our looks expressed our feelings better than words. At this moment the Captain entered the saloon. I went up to him.

'Our course is barred southward?' I asked.

'Yes, sir. The iceberg has shifted, and closed every outlet.'

'We are blocked up, then?'

'Yes.'

★   ★   ★   ★

Thus, around the *Nautilus*, above and below, was an impenetrable wall of ice. We were prisoners to the iceberg. I watched the Captain. His countenance had resumed its habitual imperturbability.

'Gentlemen,' he said calmly, 'there are two ways of dying in the circumstances in which we are placed.' (This inexplicable person had the air of a mathematical professor lecturing to his pupils.) 'The first is to be crushed; the second is to die of suffocation. I do not speak of the possibility of dying of hunger, for the supply of provisions in the *Nautilus* will certainly last longer than we shall. Let us then calculate our chances.'

'As to suffocation, Captain,' I replied, 'that is not to be feared, because our reservoirs are full.'

'Just so; but they will only yield two days' supply of air. Now, for thirty-six hours we have been hidden under the water, and already the heavy atmosphere of the *Nautilus* requires renewal. In forty-eight hours our reserve will be exhausted.'

'Well, Captain, can we be delivered before forty-eight hours?'

'We will attempt it, at least, by piercing the wall that surrounds us.'

'On which side?'

'Sound will tell us. I am going to run the *Nautilus* aground on the lower bank, and my men will attack the iceberg on the side that is least thick.'

Captain Nemo went out. Soon I discovered by a hissing noise that the water was entering the reservoirs. The *Nautilus* sank slowly, and rested on the ice at a depth of 350 yards, the depth at which the lower bank was immersed.

'My friends,' I said, 'our situation is serious, but I rely on your courage and energy.'

'Sir,' replied the Canadian, 'I am ready to do anything for the general safety.'

'Good, Ned!' and I held out my hand to the Canadian.

'I will add,' he continued, 'that being as handy with the pickaxe as with the harpoon, if I can be useful to the Captain, he can command my services.'

'He will not refuse your help. Come, Ned!'

I led him to the room where the crew of the *Nautilus* were putting on their cork jackets. I told the Captain of Ned's proposal, which he accepted. The Canadian put on his sea-costume, and was ready as soon as his companions. When Ned was dressed, I re-entered the drawing-room, where the panes of glass were open, and, posted near Conseil, I examined the ambient beds that supported the *Nautilus*. Some instants after, we saw a dozen of the crew set foot on the bank of ice, and among them Ned Land, easily known by his stature. Captain Nemo was with them. Before proceeding to dig the walls, he took the soundings, to be sure of working in the right direction. Long sounding lines were sunk in the side walls, but after fifteen yards they were again stopped by the thick wall. It was useless to attack it on the ceiling-like surface, since the iceberg itself measured more than 400 yards in height. Captain Nemo then sounded the lower surface. There ten yards of

The men set to work on the ice.

wall separated us from the water, so great was the thickness of the ice-field. It was necessary, therefore, to cut from it a piece equal in extent to the waterline of the *Nautilus*. There were about 6,000 cubic yards to detach, so as to dig a hole by which we could descend to the ice-field. The work was begun immediately, and carried on with indefatigable energy. Instead of digging round the *Nautilus*, which would have involved greater difficulty, Captain Nemo had an immense trench made at eight yards from the port quarter. Then the men set to work simultaneously with their screws, on several points of its circumference. Presently the pickaxe attacked this compact matter vigorously, and large blocks were detached from the mass. By a curious effect of specific gravity, these blocks, lighter than water, fled, so to speak, to the vault of the tunnel, that increased in thickness at the top in proportion as it diminished at the base. But that mattered little, so long as the lower part grew thinner. After two hours' hard work, Ned Land came in exhausted. He and his comrades were replaced by new workers, whom Conseil and I joined. The second lieutenant of the *Nautilus* superintended us. The water seemed singularly cold, but I soon got warm handling the pickaxe. My movements were free enough, although they were made under a pressure of thirty atmospheres. When I re-entered, after working two hours, to take some food and rest, I found a perceptible difference between the pure fluid with which the Rouquayrol engine supplied me, and the atmosphere of the *Nautilus*, already charged with carbonic acid. The air had not been renewed for forty-eight hours, and its vivifying qualities were considerably enfeebled. However, after a lapse of twelve hours, we had only raised a block of ice one yard thick, on the marked surface, which was about 600 cubic yards! Reckoning that it took twelve hours to accomplish this much, it would take five nights and four days to bring this enterprise to a satisfactory conclusion. Five nights and four days! And we have only air enough for two days in the reservoirs! 'Without taking into account,' said Ned, 'that, even if we get out of this infernal prison, we shall also be imprisoned under the iceberg, shut out from all possible communication with the atmosphere.' True enough! Who could then foresee the minimum of time necessary for our deliverance? We might be suffocated before the *Nautilus* could regain the surface of the waves! Was it destined to perish in this ice tomb, with all those it

45

enclosed? The situation was terrible. But everyone had looked the
danger in the face, and each was determined to do his duty to the last.

As I expected, during the night a new block a yard square was carried
away, and still farther sank the immense hollow. But in the morning
when, dressed in my cork jacket, I traversed the slushy mass at a
temperature of six or seven degrees below zero, I remarked that the
side walls were gradually closing in. The beds of water farthest from
the trench, that were not warmed by the men's mere work, showed a
tendency to solidification. In presence of this new and imminent danger,
what would become of our chances of safety, and how hinder the solidification of this liquid medium, that would burst the partitions of the
Nautilus like glass?

I did not tell my companions of this new danger. What was the good
of damping the energy they displayed in the painful work of escape?
But when I went on board again, I told Captain Nemo of this grave
complication.

'I know it,' he said, in that calm tone which could counteract the
most terrible apprehensions. 'It is one danger more; but I see no way
of escaping it; the only chance of safety is to go quicker than solidification. We must be beforehand with it, that is all.'

On this day for several hours I used my pickaxe vigorously. The
work kept me up. Besides, to work was to quit the *Nautilus*, and breathe
directly the pure air drawn from the reservoirs, and supplied by our
apparatus, and to quit the impoverished and vitiated atmosphere.
Towards evening the trench was dug one yard deeper. When I returned
on board, I was nearly suffocated by the carbonic acid with which the
air was filled. Ah! if we had only the chemical means to drive away
this deleterious gas. We had plenty of oxygen; all this water contained
a considerable quantity, and by dissolving it with our powerful piles,
it would restore the vivifying fluid. I had thought well over it; but of
what good was that, since the carbonic acid produced by our respiration
had invaded every part of the vessel? To absorb it, it was necessary to
fill some jars with caustic potash, and to shake them incessantly. Now
this substance was wanting on board, and nothing could replace it. On
that evening, Captain Nemo ought to open the taps of his reservoirs,
and let some pure air into the interior of the *Nautilus*; without this precaution, we could not get rid of the sense of suffocation. The next day,

26th March, I resumed my miner's work in beginning the fifth yard. The side walls and the lower surface of the iceberg thickened visibly. It was evident that they would meet before the *Nautilus* was able to disengage itself. Despair seized me for an instant, my pickaxe nearly fell from my hands' What was the good of digging if I must be suffocated, crushed by the water that was turning into stone? A punishment that the ferocity of the savages even would not have invented! Just then Captain Nemo passed near me. I touched his hand and showed him the walls of our prison. The wall to port had advanced to at least four yards from the hull of the *Nautilus*. The Captain understood me, and signed to me to follow him. We went on board. I took off my cork jacket, and accompanied him into the drawing-room.

'M. Aronnax, we must attempt some desperate means, or we shall be sealed up in this solidified water as in cement.'

'Yes; but what is to be done?'

'Ah, if my *Nautilus* were strong enough to bear this pressure without being crushed!'

'Well?' I asked, not catching the Captain's idea.

'Do you not understand,' he replied, 'that this congelation of water will help us? Do not you see that, by its solidification, it would burst through this field of ice that imprisons us, as, when it freezes, it bursts the hardest stones? Do you not perceive that it would be an agent of safety instead of destruction?'

'Yes, Captain, perhaps. But whatever resistance to crushing the *Nautilus* possesses, it could not support this terrible pressure, and would be flattened like an iron plate.'

'I know it, sir. Therefore we must not reckon on the aid of nature, but on our own exertions. We must stop this solidification. Not only will the side walls be pressed together; but there is not ten feet of water before or behind the *Nautilus*. The congelation gains on us on all sides.'

'How long will the air in the reservoirs last for us to breathe on board?'

The Captain looked in my face. 'After tomorrow they will be empty!'

A cold sweat came over me. However, ought I to have been astonished at the answer? On 22nd March, the *Nautilus* was in the open polar seas. We were at 26°. For five days we had lived on the reserve on board. And what was left of the respirable air must be kept for the workers. Even now, as I write, my recollection is still so vivid that an involuntary terror seizes me, and my lungs seem to be without air. Meanwhile, Captain Nemo reflected silently, and evidently an idea had struck him; but he seemed to reject it. At last, these words escaped his lips:

'Boiling water!' he muttered.

'Boiling water?' I cried.

'Yes, sir. We are enclosed in a space that is relatively confined. Would not jets of boiling water, constantly injected by the pumps, raise the temperature in this part, and stay the congelation?'

The thermometer then stood at seven degrees outside. Captain Nemo took me to the galleys, where the vast distillatory machines stood that furnished the drinkable water by evaporation. They filled these with water, and all the electric heat from the piles was thrown through the worms bathed in the liquid. In a few minutes this water reached a hundred degrees. It was directed towards the pumps, while fresh water replaced it in proportion. The heat developed by the troughs was such that cold water, drawn up from the sea, after only having gone through the machines, came boiling into the body of the pump. The injection was begun, and three hours after the thermometer marked six degrees below zero outside. One degree was gained. Two hours later, the thermometer only marked four degrees.

'We shall succeed,' I said to the Captain, after having anxiously watched the result of the operation.

'I think,' he answered, 'that we shall not be crushed. We have no more suffocation to fear.'

During the night the temperature of the water rose to one degree below zero. The injections could not carry it to a higher point. But as the congelation of the sea-water produces at least two degrees, I was at last reassured against the dangers of solidification.

The next day, 27 March, six yards of ice had been cleared, four yards only remaining to be cleared away. There was yet forty-eight hours' work. The air could not be renewed in the interior of the *Nautilus*. And this day would make it worse. An intolerable weight oppressed me. Towards three o'clock in the evening, this feeling rose to a violent degree. Yawns dislocated my jaws. My lungs panted as they inhaled this burning fluid, which became rarefied more and more. A moral torpor took hold of me. I was powerless, almost unconscious. My brave Conseil, though exhibiting the same symptoms and suffering in the same manner, never left me. He took my hand and encouraged me, and I heard him murmur: 'Oh, if I could only not breathe, so as to leave more air for my master!'

Tears came into my eyes on hearing him speak thus. If our situation to all was intolerable in the interior, with what haste and gladness would we put on our cork jackets to work in our turn! Pickaxes sounded on the frozen ice-beds. Our arms ached, the skin was torn off our hands. But what were these fatigues, what did the wounds matter? Vital air came to the lungs! We breathed! We breathed!

All this time, no one prolonged his voluntary task beyond the prescribed time. His task accomplished, each one handed in turn to his panting companions the apparatus that supplied him with life. Captain Nemo set the example, and submitted first to this severe discipline. When the time came, he gave up his apparatus to another, and returned to the vitiated air on board, calm, unflinching, unmurmuring.

On that day the ordinary work was accomplished with unusual vigour. Only two yards remained to be raised from the surface. Two yards only separated us from the open sea. But the reservoirs were nearly emptied of air. The little that remained ought to be kept for the workers; not a particle for the *Nautilus*. When I went back on board, I was half suffocated. What a night! I know not how to describe it. The next day my breathing was oppressed. Dizziness accompanied the pain in my head, and made me like a drunken man. My companions showed the same symptoms. Some of the crew had rattling in the throat.

On that day, the sixth of our imprisonment, Captain Nemo, finding the pickaxes work too slowly, resolved to crush the ice-bed that still separated us from the liquid sheet. This man's coolness and energy never forsook him. He subdued his physical pains by moral force.

By his orders the vessel was lightened, that is to say, raised from the ice-bed by a change of specific gravity. When it floated they towed it so as to bring it above the immense trench made on the level of the water-line. Then filling his reservoirs of water, he descended and shut himself up in the hole.

Just then all the crew came on board, and the double door of communication was shut. The *Nautilus* then rested on the bed of ice, which was not one yard thick, and which the sounding leads had perforated in a thousand places. The taps of the reservoirs were then opened, and a hundred cubic yards of water was let in, increasing the weight of the *Nautilus* to 1,800 tons. We waited, we listened, forgetting our sufferings in hope. Our safety depended on this last chance. Notwithstanding the buzzing in my head, I soon heard the humming sound under the hull of the *Nautilus*. The ice cracked with a singular noise, like tearing paper, and the *Nautilus* sank.

'We are off!' murmured Conseil in my ear.

I could not answer him. I seized his hand, and pressed it convulsively. All at once, carried away by its frightful overcharge, the *Nautilus* sank like a bullet under the waters, that is to say, it fell as if it was in a vacuum. Then all the electric force was put on the pumps, that soon began to let the water out of the reservoirs. After some minutes, our fall was stopped. Soon, too, the manometer indicated an ascending movement. The screw, going at full speed, made the iron hull tremble to its very bolts, and drew us towards the north. But if this floating under the iceberg is to last another day before we reach the open sea, I shall be dead first.

Half stretched upon a divan in the library, I was suffocating. My face was purple, my lips blue, my faculties suspended. I neither saw nor heard. All notion of time had gone from my mind. My muscles could not contract. I do not know how many hours passed thus, but I was conscious of the agony that was coming over me. I felt as if I was going to die. Suddenly I came to. Some breaths of air penetrated my lungs. Had we risen to the surface of the waves? Were we free of the iceberg? No; Ned and Conseil, my two brave friends, were sacrificing themselves to save me. Some particles of air still remained at the bottom of one apparatus. Instead of using it, they had kept it for me, and while they were being suffocated, they gave me life drop by drop. I wanted to push back the thing; they held my hands, and for some moments I breathed freely. I looked at the clock; it was eleven in the morning. It ought to be 28 March. The *Nautilus* went at a frightful pace, forty miles an hour. It literally tore through the water. Where was Captain Nemo? Had he succumbed? Were his companions dead with him? At the moment, the manometer indicated that we were not more than twenty feet from the surface. A mere plate of ice separated us from the atmosphere: could we not break it? Perhaps. In any case the *Nautilus* was going to attempt it. I felt that it was in an oblique position, lowering the stern, and raising the bows. The introduction of water had been the means of disturbing its equilibrium. Then, impelled by its powerful screw, it attacked the icefield from beneath like a formidable battering-ram. It broke it by backing and then rushing forward against the field, which gradually gave way; and at last, dashing suddenly against it, shot forwards on the icy field, that crushed beneath its weight. The panel was opened – one might say torn off – and the pure air came in in abundance to all parts of the *Nautilus*.

*   *   *   *

How I got on to the platform, I have no idea; perhaps the Canadian had carried me there. But I breathed, I inhaled the vivifying sea air. My two companions were getting drunk with the fresh particles. The other unhappy men had been so long without food, that they could not with impunity indulge in the simplest ailments that were given them. We, on the contrary, had no need to restrain ourselves; we could draw this air freely into our lungs, and it was the breeze, the breeze alone, that filled us with this keen enjoyment.

'Ah,' said Conseil, 'how delightful this oxygen is! Master need not fear to breathe it. There is enough for everybody.'

Ned Land did not speak, but he opened his jaws wide enough to frighten a shark. Our strength soon returned, and when I looked round me, I saw we were alone on the platform. The foreign seamen in the *Nautilus* were contented with the air that circulated in the interior; none of them had come to drink in the open air.

The first words I spoke were words of gratitude and thankfulness to my two companions. Ned and Conseil had prolonged my life during the last hours of this long agony. All my gratitude could not repay such devotion.

'My friends,' said I, 'we are bound one to the other for ever, and I am under infinite obligations to you.'

ON THE FRINGE

George Hall

The scene was present-day Canada, not the mystic East. Yet on the border of what mysterious domain did these two campers find themselves?

This title I have taken from my diary. Each year for five years my fellow-student Charles and I had left Montreal and gone north into the bush, in search of sun and silence and the liberation of the spirit. Charles had talked about being 'on the fringe' of civilization. And, in his convocation address to us, a learned Doctor of Philosophy had used the same phrase: we had completed our studies for the moment, he had said, and now we were 'on the fringe' of things, beginners in the subtle art of living and of learning to cope with life. It turned out that our trip – our last long trip together into the wilds – was to bring Charles and me 'on the fringe' of other experiences, and to compel us to examine new values – new to us, that is, but themselves as old as man.

The plan was simple. We were to leave the city and make for the Baskatong, a place inhabited mostly by Indians, about a hundred and thirty miles north of Ottawa, on the edge of a vast area of forest, mountainous and spangled with lakes and fast-flowing rivers. We chose our time to avoid both the mosquitoes (which would have eaten us alive in early summer) and the hunting season (when the quiet of the countryside is turned into a noisy and highly efficient slaughter-house).

We travelled in Charles's old flivver, an ancient wreck of a car which, like an old horse, had certain limitations – it would not gallop.

Our progress was slow, noisy and entirely without dignity. We had six punctures and constant trouble with the steering gear, but I note that in my diary I described this part of the journey as uneventful. Today I am worried by a squeak in the springs!

At our destination we garaged the car in a shed made of rough logs and sought out an old Indian friend, Pial, who provided a canoe and helped us to stow our gear. When all was done, we paused for Pial's ritual farewell, always the same, with the same grave courtesy and in the same words.

'You take no guns,' he said.

'No, Pial, we do not go to hunt.'

'Take care, then. Make camp near water, keep the fire bright in the darkness and sleep with one eye open. There are many bears and wolves in the bush and they are angered by the scent of a man.'

'We'll take care, Pial. On our return we'll tell you all about it. Goodbye, then.'

Pial raised his right arm in an Indian gesture, like a priest giving a blessing, and said, 'Addio, my brothers. God go with you.'

As the canoe slid silently through the water, urged on by the thrust of our paddles, Pial remained watching from the shore of the lake. The trip had really begun and now we moved out of one world and into another. This was no mere pleasure-jaunt into the country, it was, besides, a movement and a motion back in time, into a world unspoiled and a time unchanged. Nature in the English countryside is domestic, ordered and controlled. But in the vast forests of the northland the size and scale of things is intimidating, overwhelming: its silence can be threatening and acutely disturbing. Man is not master here.

For a long while we paddled in silence, heading for an inlet far away on the north shore which we knew to be the narrow mouth of a river; and, though there was no need for haste, we laboured at our task like men pursued. It was always like this. I could never quite decide whether we were hurrying to escape or to arrive, to leave something or to find something. We paddled ourselves to a standstill. It was Charles who spoke.

'What about a rest? I'm all in. My muscles have seized up.'

I agreed. A slight breeze gave us some steerage way, so we trailed our paddles to keep the canoe on course. It was very peaceful with the hot sun shining from a cloudless sky and the surface of the lake shimmering like burnished silver. In our kneeling position we relaxed as best we could and neither of us spoke. By the time we reached our destination it was late afternoon. Under the shadow of tall pine trees we found a small clearing, and there we made camp. Our immediate needs were a swim and a square meal and without wasting time we attended to both. After a dip we feasted on flapjacks made palatable with beans and bacon and washed down with strong black coffee. We were light-headed with hunger and the aroma of that meal was almost unendurable, its flavour as we ate it pure unadulterated rapture. Then we lay back bemused and bodily weary, content to relax and savour the sounds and smells of this enchanted place: the fragrant smell of the pines, and the acrid whiffs of smoke from our camp-fire; the smell of the warm earth giving back the heat of the day. Light flickered into darkness and the stars came out, brilliant against the darkness of the sky. Fire-flies sparked brightly among the trees. A loon cried out across the lake: frogs croaked and warbled in a near-by muskeg and a whip-poor-will started his night-long song.

Next morning we packed our kit and made ready for the river. But to describe the journey in detail would be tedious, and is unnecessary for this narrative. One day was very much like another. We became totally involved in the business of getting upstream as far as we would go – for this was to us entirely new territory. Once we had adjusted to the rhythm of our surroundings we tended, like the birds, to wake with the dawn and go to bed with the darkness. My mind cleared as I knew it would, anxieties slipped away and I felt an expansion of all my mental and physical powers. Each day we paddled hard, sometimes against fast-running currents but mostly through smooth, gently flowing water. When falls or rapids appeared we took to the river-bank and portaged our gear up to the higher level. The banks of the river were varied and interesting. Always there were the trees, dark masses of fir and pine, sometimes crowding down to the water's edge, sometimes receding from wide stretches of green sward or thickets of stunted shrubs. At other times we paddled through dark canyons with towering walls of bare rock, impressive but gloomy.

For ten days we headed north in this way, the only break in the routine being an occasional excursion inland, away from the river.

Once we discovered a lake, where we found large rocky outcrops and caves. There were small stone erections, cairns, evidently the work of man, but of what man and what age there was no means of telling. The caves themselves were empty, scoured clean by time and the elements. From time to time we caught glimpses of wild life: a large black bear crashing through the undergrowth followed by her shambling, half-grown cub: a few red foxes, shy and sneaky, and once a grey timber wolf who trailed us for miles.

★   ★   ★   ★

So far our trip had been interesting but uneventful: and now there was a sense of familiarity about the river and its banks, chiefly because every change was only a repetition, a variation on the same theme. It was on the fourteenth day that the change came – startling, breath-taking and entirely visual: unlooked-for because unexpected and for that reason all the more impressive.

The river had narrowed to a canyon, shut in by tall cliffs, sunless and menacing. The water was noisy and turbulent and we worked hard to keep the canoe heading against the current. Thrusting our paddles deep, with heads down and shoulders straining, we fought against the stream for more than a mile. Then, quite suddenly, we were out of the canyon into the sun and the scene that lay before us was enchanting. The river widened into a sweeping curve of shimmering water, blue with the blue of a cloudless sky. So gentle was its motion that it seemed not to move at all. The banks were green and gently sloping, 'green pastures beside still waters', and without the usual thatch of scrub and stunted bushes. In sharp contrast, and behind all this, a bare escarpment of rock rose high into the air, two hundred feet or more, scoured by wind and weather into rough shapes like the buttressed walls of an ancient fortress. Its northern end was cleft by the course of a narrow waterfall, the slender shaft of water falling sheer into a pool that had no visible outlet. We paddled quietly to the shore and beached the canoe. It was an obvious place to camp and to explore before starting out on the return journey. We lighted a fire and prepared the evening meal.

Our talk was of plans for the morrow. We decided to scale the heights to examine the plateau and what lay beyond it. Even to my untutored eye the geological formation was interesting and Charles, with his wider knowledge of these things, delivered an animated lecture on rock formations and some of the less-known peculiarities of the Laurentian highlands. By the time we turned in I had acquired a new outlook on rocks.

The night was very still, with a full moon sailing in a clear sky and, as I dropped off to sleep, I remember thinking what a waste of time it was to sleep on such a night. How long I slept I do not know, for we had given up the habit of checking time by a watch. But quite suddenly I was awake – wide awake – and listening. Faintly, but with peculiar penetration, the air all about us throbbed and moaned. It was like no sound I had ever heard before: not the voice of any animal or man: not the note of any instrument I knew. I thought for a moment of the moaning of the wind, but the night was still. Raising myself on one elbow, I tried to sense or see the direction from which it came – the whole landscape was still brilliantly lighted by the moon and every feature stood out clearly. I could see nothing; and by this time the sound had stopped. It was puzzling and vaguely disturbing. Wide awake, I clambered out of my sleeping-bag. The movement must have awakened Charles and he called to me.

'What's wrong?'

'There was a noise. It disturbed me,' I answered.

'What sort of noise?'

'Listen, there it is again!'

Once again the air pulsed with sound, rising and falling in toneless cadences. And, as we listened, the vibrations became more rapid, more intense, until at last it was like a hurricane. Such sounds belonged to violent motion, flying scud, tossing trees, roaring waves. Instead the air was still and the sky calm and clear. The roaring continued at full pitch for a long time. We were both on our feet, but stood quite still, bewildered and completely unnerved. Somewhere in the distance timber wolves began to howl, always an eerie sound in the night. Then the roaring slowly died down to a gentle, undulating moan; and then stopped. For a time we stood listening, almost afraid to move, apprehensive and half-expecting the noise to begin again. At last, when the danger seemed past, we relaxed with a sigh of relief and looked about us uncertainly. Sleep was out of the question, so we revived the dying fire and made coffee. And we talked in hushed voices, as if afraid of being overheard.

'Any idea what it was?' asked Charles.

'None at all. But I don't like it.'

'I believe you're afraid.' Charles was doing his hard-headed, un-emotional act, playing the objective scientist. 'There must be a per-fectly natural explanation, you know.'

'Maybe, but it seemed unnatural to me. This place is uninhabited. And you can't have a hurricane without wind. So what have you got?'

'Not spooks, if that's what you're thinking. This is northern Canada, remember, not the mystic East. That sort of thing doesn't happen here.'

'I'm not so sure.'

We spent the rest of the night in inconclusive speculation – which helped to pass the time. After a dip in the river and a good breakfast we were once again in high spirits and ready for a day's exploring.

Our immediate objective was the high rocks. Charles took command, leading the way towards the waterfall. There, if anywhere, he said, we might find an uneven surface of steps or crevices associated with the spring floods and water seepage. Our only hope of getting to the top depended upon some such place, for we had neither climbing boots nor ropes to scale a sheer surface, however rough. A birch-bark canoe is no fit place for hob-nailed boots; we had not foreseen needing them, either. As Charles had suggested, however, we found an irregular ravine-like cleft with sufficient foothold for our purpose, and in our light-soled canoe shoes we started to climb. It was slippery work, for the whole surface was moist with spray and covered with spongy moss, and the angle of ascent was almost vertical. I think we would not have succeeded but for the presence of small, stunted bushes which had somehow taken root in the cracks and crevices, to which we clung for support.

At the top we stood and looked about us. The plateau we had ex-pected was not there. The flat top of the escarpment was nothing more than a ledge, bare and rocky and about twenty yards wide. We could see the source of the waterfall – a small underground stream, gushing out from under the rocks. Before us and below the ground fell away to form a wide valley, rocky and encircled by trees and vegetation. Beyond this the rolling hills and the thick forest stretched away into the far distance. There was the faintest trace of a path, and this was strange. Animals, perhaps? Then we saw the smoke, a thin spiral rising slowly into the air from somewhere deep in the valley. We could smell the scent of burning wood. A man in no-man's-land? But what man? And why? My instinct was to let it alone and to go back, but Charles would have none of it. We had to take the path, down to the valley, and when we reached its floor we found our way barred by a cluster of feathered Indian spears stuck in the earth. I whispered to Charles:

'This is an Indian holy place, perhaps a burial ground, and forbidden to white men. We'd better keep out.'

'How do you know?' he asked.

'The spears,' I replied. 'That's what they mean.'

'Not any more,' he argued. 'These days Indians are civilized. They don't go in for that sort of thing.'

He by-passed the spears, pushing his way through a low thicket where he could look out on to the clearing. Uncertainly, I followed. I think we both had the same feeling of intrusion rather than of mere curiosity: our attitude became one of stealth. Charles suddenly remarked, 'This place is getting on my nerves!'

It was, but the reason was obscure. All we could see through the screening foliage was a log cabin, a stack of wood and a small fire burning in a ring of stones. On a small cultivated patch of earth there was maize and tobacco growing, and what looked like globe artichokes. There was no sign of any human being, red or white, and apart from the fire the place might have been deserted. Encouraged by the owner's absence, we stepped out into the clearing and at once discovered our mistake. The owner was there.

He was sitting cross-legged in front of an arbour or shelter that was made of woven branches, his bronzed body rigid and motionless. He had the long black hair of the Indian of a century ago and wore a thong of beaded leather around his forehead. His eyes, wide open, were apparently sightless, the lids unblinking, and although we were now in full view he made no sign of awareness. We were completely baffled. Was he asleep, or dead, or what? Was he, perhaps, praying? I had seen Buddhist monks motionless before a statue of the Buddha and Christians prostrate before a Calvary. But to the best of my knowledge Indians had no sacred images. The nearest approach to this would have been a totem pole – and these are comparatively modern innovations among a few tribes, and have no direct religious significance. In any case a man, however deep in devotion, does look alive, even alert. This man did not.

I remembered the animistic theory of dreams: how the spirit leaves the body and wanders forth alone. Life is only restored when the spirit returns. If it does not return, the man is dead. We might have been looking upon a proof of this theory. As a subject for academic study this had been fascinating to me: now, face to face with something very like it, I was in a state of mild shock.

Curiosity led us on. We took a few steps forward to where we could look into the shelter. It was occupied, and its occupant was death-dressed and bedecked in a revolting parody of life. Sitting upright on a ceremonial stool was the mummified body of a man, an Indian. It was emaciated to a condition of skin and bone, dried-up shrivelled skin, black with age and exposure; the skull grinned from a lipless mouth and stared from empty eye-sockets. Above the head and round the face hung the eagle-feathers of a magnificent war-bonnet, made elaborate with beaded head-band and the twin horns of a steer. And about the body was cast a ceremonial robe of soft white feathers. The feet were set in richly beaded moccasins; the hands, thin and claw-like, rested upon bony knees. It was impressive and at the same time repulsive.

Seeing this, we stood quite still and looked at one another, each asking the same question, 'What do you do in a case like this?' We were spared the decision.

Quite suddenly the Indian uttered a deep groan, raised his hands and arms above his head and bowed low in obeisance – or so I thought. He spoke some words we could not understand, then got to his feet, rising from the ground in one swift movement. At once he became aware of our presence and we stood eyeing one another in silence. There was nothing we could say: the rules of courtesy did not fit this situation, we did not know how to proceed. So we waited. He had the Indian's impassive expression, neither smiling nor frowning, and then he spoke – in English.

'You should not have come.'

Again I had the feeling of being an intruder, of being in the wrong. Charles was silent, for once quite out of his depth, and, knowing his

The mummified body of an Indian was sitting upright.

lack of tact, I began the explanations myself. With some hesitation I tried to tell the Indian who we were and why we were there. But he began speaking again, following his own line of thought and ignoring what I had said.

'This is not a good place for the paleface. But you are here, you have seen, and you must stay.'

I made no reply. There seemed no reason why we should stay – but apparently we had no choice. Make a dash for it, perhaps? But you do not descend a two-hundred-foot cliff with no footholds in haste: not unless you want to break your neck. Overpower the Indian? I doubted if the two of us together could have managed that. He stood there, six feet of brawn and sinew, dominating the situation; and already I was aware that his strength lay in something more than the merely physical. He had great dignity of bearing, a fine physique and a stern face – all impressive, but not sufficient to account for his strange influence on us. There was a magnetism about this man, an uncanny power to fascinate and to intimidate, and its effect was curiously unpleasant.

I searched his face while trying to control the expression on my own. He held my gaze and I found what I was looking for. An Indian's eyes are smaller, and set closer together, than the white man's: they are black and have no visible iris, and the impression they give is one of alertness, of peering about. In this man they were larger, more open, and of a soft luminosity. They looked out upon the world with steady penetration and seemed at the same time, to look beyond it. They were the eyes of a seer, a mystic, set in the head of a savage. Now I understood the significance of the trance in which we had found him. We were dealing with an unusual man. I remembered seeing this look in other eyes, and in another place, and the memory increased my fears. If they were not the eyes of a mystic, they were the eyes of a madman. I looked away and saw, at the feet of the mummy, the impedimenta of the Indian witch-doctor – a pair of eagle's wings, the skin of a lizard and a human bone decorated with feathers. There was a mask, too, like a wild beast's head.

That day was, perhaps, the strangest in my life. The valley was hot and airless and we sought what shade we could under the fringe of trees. All around was the familiar Canadian countryside in all its beauty, my perception of it heightened, no doubt, by our predicament, and my love of it seemed greater than ever. And yet I saw it through a veil of unreality as things are seen in dreams: I was in it yet no longer a part of it.

The atmosphere was tense and unrelaxed. The Indian played host as to expected but unwelcome guests, showing neither pleasure nor amiability. As the day passed, a sense of purpose became evident in his behaviour: what that purpose was we did not know. It was clear that he did not mean us to leave. He fasted all day and was silent most of the time. We ate the lunch we had brought and he gave us water to drink. Now and then he talked in stilted English, telling us something of the course of his life: of a boyhood spent on a reserve far to the east; of how his father and five brothers with their families fled the reserve, determined to break the white man's yoke and to live wild. The years that followed seemed to have been beset by misfortune – the tribe dwindled, for the squaws were barren, and the children died from something he called the 'white man's sickness'. At last only he and his father remained, the keepers of the graves of their people. Here in his bitterness against the white man he raised his voice and his speech ran off into the jumbled heavy-sounding phrases of his native tongue. He took a step forward, towering over us in anger with clenched fists and arms half-raised; then checked himself, dropped his hands to his sides and walked away.

★   ★   ★   ★

The afternoon was exhausting and interminable. To an observer, had there been one, the scene must have looked like a tableau frozen into permanent immobility. In the shadow of the cabin the Indian sat rigidly, watching us. Charles and I sprawled under the trees, hungry, hot and half-stupefied by the growing sense of our incapacity. We wanted to talk, to discuss our predicament, to behave normally. But this was no normal situation. We were not equipped to deal with it. I had read enough of pagan rites and ceremonies to write a book: now I was discovering the difference between academic knowledge and reality and the experience was most unpleasant. And slowly, like a growing obsession, my mind held one thought – of the scapegoat, upon whom was laid the sins of the people, thrust forth into the wilderness to be devoured by wild beasts. It was absurd, highly improbable, fantastic. Yet here we were, not knowing enough to be sure and knowing too much to be comfortable.

Only one event broke the monotony of the afternoon. Towards sundown a large timber wolf ambled into the clearing, paused, sniffing the air, then came loping across to where we lay. He sniffed us from head to foot, baring his fangs as he did so. Then, at a word from the Indian, he lay on the ground at the feet of his master, his long nose resting on his outstretched paws. It began to grow dark and we fell asleep from sheer mental and nervous exhaustion.

What followed can be described but cannot, I think, be explained. I once met a man from the East who had seen the Indian rope-trick in the open square of a native village. He was convinced, and believed what he had seen. A study of this phenomenon has resulted in the theory that it never really happens, that it is, in fact, mass hypnosis. The events of that night were comparable to this. I am still certain of the experience but quite incapable of explaining it.

We awoke to the unnerving roar of the previous night: the throbbing sound of air in violent motion and now more intense, closer at hand. And this time we saw the source. The Indian stood high on a rock outlined against the night sky whirling about him a giant bull-roarer: that implement of wood and cord, which savage tribes manipulate to ward off – or call up – powerful spirits.

'So that was it!' Charles seemed relieved, and in the noise we could talk in whispers. 'I told you there was a perfectly natural explanation.'

'Yes, but it doesn't help now.'

'Why does he do it?'

'He's summoning the spirits of the dead.'

We had no time to say more, for at that moment the Indian ceased his whirling and came down into the clearing. He walked over to where we were sitting and stood for a long moment looking at us, his eyes shining, his whole body tense and gleaming like polished bronze in the firelight. We sat on the ground like children, gazing upwards into his face. It was entirely without expression and his voice, when he spoke, was toneless . . .

'My people come to see you. You do not move. You do not speak.'

63

He moved away backwards, step by step, slowly and with hands raised and pointing directly at us. His direction was towards the arbour. There he turned, made an obeisance and taking up the devil-mask, put it on his head. Sitting cross-legged before the dead chief he placed a small round object on his knees. It was a drum, shaped like a deep tambourine, and with his right hand he began to beat upon the skin. At first the rhythm seemed irregular and uncertain and I had a growing feeling of apprehension as my senses struggled to catch the pattern. Then the rhythm quickened, melting into a low, throbbing note, that rippled and pulsed like the ripple of running water. And suddenly all tension ceased within me. With a sigh I relaxed, listening and staring, empty of both thought and feeling.

I was aware of the dancing firelight which dappled the darkness with bright flames; of the bright sky all around lighted by a moon still hidden from us by rocks and trees, I was aware that the wolf was nowhere to be seen. Later, much later, I realized that I had been completely unaware of Charles sitting by my side. I was, indeed, to use an old phrase, *held in thrall* – and I had the odd sensation of seeing all this from *outside myself*.

Then they came, out of the shadows and into the firelight, a silent procession, moving without motion of hand or foot, round and round the fire in a melancholy ritual, eight men each wearing the war-bonnet and robe of the Indian brave. Out in the night the wolf howled and gibbered, and always the drum throbbed and the drummer moaned and swayed from side to side. These were the forms of men, yet without detail of feature or of human face. They were ghosts and their effect on me was one of overwhelming sadness. And almost before I was aware of it they had gone, melting into the darkness. Only the Indian, with his hideous mask, remained to give reality to this fantastic moment.

It was quiet now. The drumming had ceased and the Indian, moving like a sleep-walker, took off the mask and stretched himself upon the ground, prostrate before the old man. He moaned softly as a man, might moan in his sleep, then raised himself up to sit cross-legged as we had first seen him, his gaze fixed intently upon the dead face and sightless eyes of the chief. And there began a confused murmuring of words and phrases, almost inaudible. Only one phrase was clear to me and he repeated it again and again.

'I must go to my father, I must go to my father.'

Like a man falling asleep in the middle of speech he then lapsed into a trance-like state, rigid, upright, but apparently without life. Perhaps he had gone to his father – for he seemed not to be with us. It is difficult to write of this experience without seeming to over-dramatize it. Yet the drama was inherent in the fact; and in my own highly suggestible state the impact was overwhelming. This was the shadow-land between life and death, the no-man's-land that men inhabit only in their dreams.

I was brought back to reality when Charles gripped my arm and said in a loud whisper, 'We've had enough of this, we must get away – and this is the time.' His grip tightened on my arm.

I glanced at the Indian, fearful that he might hear and come back to consciousness again. He made no move. His eyes were still wide open, fixed and staring but not seeing, not comprehending. Clearly he was in a condition that is deeper than sleep and I knew that Charles was right.

'What do we do?' I asked vaguely.

Charles rose to his feet. 'Leave him to me,' he said. 'I'll fix him.'

Quickly he moved towards the log cabin and went inside, while I stood, still gazing fearfully at the Indian. When Charles came out he had in his hands a coil of rope and a Winchester repeater. The sight of the gun bothered me.

'You can't shoot him!' I whispered.

'I don't want to. I'm going to tie him up. But if he comes to in the process and turns nasty I won't answer for the consequences. I've had enough and we're getting out of here. Hold the gun and stand by me. And don't panic.'

Stealthily we approached the Indian and stood close behind him, waiting. Nothing happened. He was completely unconscious of our presence.

It was all over in a few minutes. A running noose slid over the Indian's arms, pinning them to his sides. The rest of the rope was wound about his legs and forearms, then around his neck, where the last knot was tied. He was trussed up tightly in a sitting position and would have a hard time freeing himself. This onslaught raised no response. Like a man under deep hypnosis he apparently had no bodily sensations. We fled as fast as we could, following the path by which we had come – helped, mercifully, by the full moon. And we took with us the rifle: we might still have the wolf to reckon with and for this we would need the gun. You cannot parley with a timber wolf nor can you bind him with ropes. The gun we would leave at the top of the waterfall for the Indian to find when he got himself loose. But we reached the falls without being molested and only then did we pause to take stock of our position.

The climb was a nightmare experience and I slipped and slithered all over the place. But between the small shrubs to which I clung, and Charles holding my heels and putting my feet into the right places, we made it at last. Once down I experienced a feeling of intense relief. It was wonderful to be back in the sane world of ordinary things.

Looking about me I was again aware of the beauty and fascination of this place, silent under the moon. But there could be no lingering. Quickly we stowed our gear into the canoe and headed down the river, through the dark canyon with its turbulent water and out into a widening stream, calm and slow-moving and tree-lined banks and the comfort of the commonplace.

We paddled on until, overcome by weariness, we found a small clearing and there we made camp. Weariness lay upon me like a sickness, every muscle ached, every nerve was on fire and my head throbbed with pain. We made coffee and tried to eat but the effort was too much and, hungry as we were, we gave it up and crawled into our sleeping-bags. I slept, soundly, a deep and dreamless sleep, and when I awoke the sun was high in the sky. It was mid-morning and a beautiful day, to me as beautiful as the first day of creation, and this mood I carried with me on our leisurely journey downstream. We discussed our strange adventure at great length but to very little purpose.

Later that year I discussed the matter with a friend at the university, a Professor of Anthropology. He was interested and together we made copious notes. I was curious about many things and I knew that he would have the answer to at least some of them.

Was the Indian mad? Probably not. It was more probable that he was in his right mind – the mind, that is, of a savage – but living in the wrong times. Obsessed? Yes, for in most primitive beliefs there is a strong strain of obsession, hence the power of the witch-doctor and the element of overemphasis. Tribal religions are always fanatical.

Why would he not tell us his name or the name of his tribe? Because the name has strong magical and mystical qualities; it is powerful magic and must not be uttered to the uninitiated or the outsider. I recalled that this had been true of the ancient Hebrews, who had named God in an unpronounceable word of four consonants, the Holy Name that could not be uttered.

And had we really seen the ghosts of braves long dead or was this simply another case of hypnosis? My friend declined to answer this, saying rather drily, 'I'm an anthropologist, not a psychiatrist. In my subject there is ample evidence to support your story but, I fear, no explanation.' And so we left it.

I set down the facts of the event as it occurred. What more can I do?

THE MIRACLE OF UMANARSUK

Ralph Barker

Captain Robert E. Coffman, 32 year old ferry pilot from Baton Rouge, Louisiana, reacted automatically as the port engine of the obsolete Hampden medium-bomber, veteran of a hundred raids over Hitler's Germany, gave a choking, splurging cough. But although his hands moved expertly to adjust throttles and controls, he experienced a moment of near-asphyxiation as his diaphragm tautened. They were halfway across the Denmark Strait, between Iceland and Greenland, heading west on the second leg of the long northern route from Britain to Canada. And they were past the point of no return. The date was 14 October 1943.

In the next instant there was a grinding cacophony of loose machinery, of nuts and bolts and cylinders and plugs suddenly deranged, like a vast marching column thrown out of step. Then with one more screeching attempt to regain its rhythm the engine seized.

Coffman fought for altitude. The crippled Hampden, separated from the nearest airfield by the peaks of the Greenland mountains, was plunging seawards. He tugged at the control-stick and employed all his skill to keep the Hampden on a straight course. But they were still losing height.

They had left Reykjavik nearly three hours earlier on the 800-mile hop to Bluie West, on the southwest coast of Greenland. Up till now the old Handley-Page Hampden – destined for use at an air training school in British Columbia – had behaved perfectly. They had climbed to 12,000 feet, levelled off, and settled down to the five-hour trip.

Isolated up in the nose was Ted Greenaway, the 23 year old navigator. He was a Canadian, from Camrose, Alberta, and he had left a wife, Ruth, and a baby daughter Diane in Montreal. Behind Coffman, at the radio, was another Canadian, 22 year old Ron Snow, from Digby, Nova Scotia. Tall, dark and powerfully built, he enjoyed film-star good looks.

They had reached one of the 'skip' zones in which radio communication fluctuated and then went dead. Snow had sent his last position message to Iceland as their signals began to fade.

To Bob Coffman, a spare husk of a man, slow of speech but of great inner strength, the hopelessness of their situation was starkly apparent. He was one hour's flying from the Greenland coast. It might just be possible to keep going that long, but he knew that he would then be faced with a barrier of mountains 10,000 feet high. To get to Bluie West he would have to fly over those mountains. But there was no chance at all of holding the plane above that height. Already they were down to 9,000 feet. Neither was there any possibility of flying south of the mountains to make an approach on a different line. He simply didn't have enough fuel.

All the time the drag of the port engine was making itself increasingly felt. There was no mechanism for feathering it. As they continued to lose height, Coffman could foresee only two possible outcomes. 'We'll get as far as we can,' he drawled, 'and if we can't make the coast we'll come down in the sea.'

In the nose, Greenaway was pin-pointing their position, making swift calculations of range, speed and altitude. Snow, although still getting no answer from the ground, began sending an SOS. There was just a chance it might be picked up.

For the next fifty minutes Coffman held the Hampden on course, steering for the Greenland coast. Once they hit the coast they might be able to turn and follow it southwards until they found a place to land. But his muscles ached intolerably with the strain of holding the Hampden level, and their airspeed fell off until the aircraft fluttered at a point barely above the stall. Then suddenly the starboard wing flicked over and the unwieldy bomber spun downwards, out of control.

Coffman watched the altimeter needle unwinding with remorseless speed. The unwelcome prospect of a ditching rapidly deteriorated into the imminent threat of a bale-out they could scarcely hope to survive. But as the falling aircraft spiralled with surprising grace, he kept up a tense running commentary on their plight.

Greenaway, staring straight down at the icy waters below, was thrown violently forward as the aircraft spun down, crushing his leg against the navigation table. He thrust himself back from the nose, knowing as he did so that if Coffman couldn't stop the spin nothing would save him. Snow gripped the morse key frantically as the gravitational force thrust him forward, putting all his strength into a last effort to send an SOS.

'Get your parachutes on,' called Coffman. For once his Southern drawl showed signs of acceleration. 'Get the hatches open. Get ready to jump.' But the vicious force of the spin pinned Greenaway and Snow where they were.

The wiry Coffman gathered up all his physical resources into one last herculean effort to check the spin. Pushing forward with all his might on the stick, jamming both feet down on the port rudder, he willed the aircraft to respond. They were below 1,000 feet when he finally pulled out.

If he lost control again there would be no time to recover. Straight ahead were the mountains of Greenland, throwing a long skirt of ice down into the sea. The hem of the skirt was fringed with icebergs and ice islands, still packed almost solid up to eight miles out. It was an uneven, unpredictable surface, impossible to alight on. Coffman decided to set the Hampden down in the water at the edge of the ice fringe.

He kept up his running commentary as he brought the Hampden down almost to sea level. The ice-formation looked even more frightening here than it had from above. There were miles of loose pack-ice and innumerable icebergs, varying in size from cottages to vast blocks of flats.

Coffman throttled back gently until the Hampden guttered along like a dying flame. Then suddenly his stomach came up into his throat as the aircraft dropped like a stone. For a moment he thought he had held off too high – and then the belly of the Hampden struck the water like a great flat oar and the propellers fought for life, churning up the sea in showers of spray.

The nose of the Hampden sank deep and the windscreen was submerged, so that he could hear the water crashing against the fuselage above his head. He grabbed at the escape hatch and climbed out, followed by Greenaway, who had meanwhile snatched up the bag of emergency rations. Snow was struggling out of the top of the rear hatch. The bomb-bay had burst on impact and the Hampden was quickly filling with water.

'There's the dinghy!' shouted Snow.

None of them had given a thought to the dinghy, which had been packed in the wing and had inflated on impact. They waded out on to the wing and climbed in. As they did so the Hampden began to settle alarmingly. It was less than a minute since the ditching.

'Cut the rope!' shouted Greenaway.

Coffman fumbled hurriedly for the dinghy knife. As he severed the last strand the Hampden rolled to the right and sank nose first without any suction, the tips of the twin tail unit disappearing last of all.

The narrowness of their escape stunned them into silence. It was some time before they took stock of their position.

'Did you get the SOS out, Ron?' asked Coffman.

'I sent it,' said Snow, 'but I don't know if anyone picked it up.'

'They'll be looking for us anyway,' said Greenaway. 'I pin-pointed our position before we ditched and we were right on track.'

'In that case,' said Coffman, 'we'd better try to steer the same course now until we reach the coast. What's in that emergency bag?'

Greenaway turned the bag out into the well of the dinghy. There was a Very pistol and 27 cartridges. There were three small containers, one for each man. In each container were 45 malted milk tablets, four squares of barley sugar, some chewing gum, and a phial of benzedrine tablets. And there were 12 pints of water, a first aid kit, a yellow distress flag, and a small square metal mirror with an attachment for use as a heliograph.

Several broken planks of wood were floating on the surface from the wrecked bomb-bay. 'Grab a piece of wood each,' ordered Coffman, 'they'll be better than these canvas paddles.'

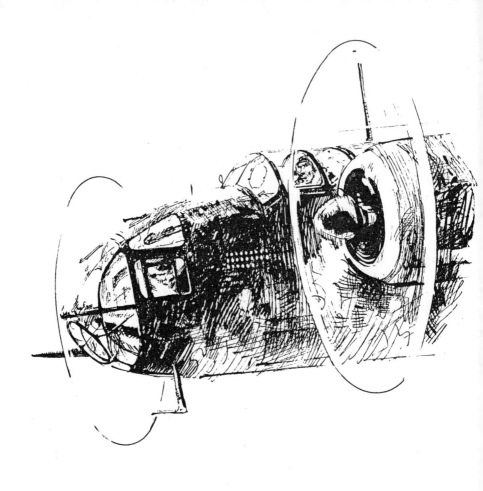

Suddenly, the aircraft dropped like a stone.

They settled down into a sort of triangle in the dinghy, two paddling and one with a larger splinter of wood fending off the pack-ice. For a long time they were obsessed by the danger of a sharp piece of ice puncturing the dinghy, but once they had got their weight properly distributed they were able to steer a fairly straight course.

'Do you think we'll see any shipping?'

'I doubt it. It's getting late in the year. Look at the pack-ice. Not much chance, I'd say.'

There was a full moon, silvering the evening sky, and the chill crispness of the air intensified as daylight faded. The night was heralded by the bright, restless eyes of a million stars.

Before them lay a scene of such entrancing beauty that in spite of their plight they felt uplifted with awe and wonderment. Around them was mile after mile of delicately cut ice, sparkling like row upon row of brilliantly-lit crystal chandeliers. Huge skyscraper icebergs, luminous in the moonlight, lifted and rolled across their path like great ships, crashing blindly into each other with thunderous reverberation and shedding their mass with a noise like a million tons of falling masonry. And all the time, supporting the magnificent tympany of the crashing icebergs, was the wood-wind and strings of the smaller bergs jostling each other in the icefield, and the tinkling cymbals of the ever-freezing pack-ice.

It was a scene, they realized, that must be almost unique. Few other men could have seen it.

They paddled throughout the night, taking turns to rest, and the barrage of ice-artillery quietened as the night wore on. The noises were the same, but the volume was attenuated. When morning came there was not a berg in sight. They had passed right through the icefield as it drifted along the coast.

Contrasting with the eerie beauty of the night in the icefield, the morning revealed a scene of utter desolation. Towering up ahead of them lay the smooth white dome of the icecap, throwing its challenge down to the sea in a succession of barren glaciers and precipitous crevasses. There would be nothing to succour them there. The little yellow dinghy, turned white in the night with encrusted ice, tossed unsteadily in the swift coastal currents. Suddenly they realized they were bearing down on a huge black rock, perhaps 500 feet high, that

73

lay between them and the shore.

The dinghy was running dangerously fast, caught in the racing rapids that swirled round the foot of the rock. The threat of capsizing was obvious. 'Look out!' they warned each other. Just as the dinghy touched the rock they jumped for it.

Coffman and Snow landed easily, hardly getting their feet wet, but Greenaway, not so well placed in the swirling dinghy when they struck, and troubled by the leg he had injured as the aircraft spun down, found himself up to the hips in icy water. He staggered forward and threw himself on to the rock. Each man had brought a portion of the emergency kit with him, and this hampered them as they fought to lift themselves clear of the lashing eddies of water. They scrambled up on to a ledge, then collapsed with exhaustion. They had been paddling almost continuously for twenty hours.

The crisp, clear night had been succeeded by a fine day. They took their boots and socks off and put them in the sun to dry. Then they examined their meagre supply of cigarettes. Every packet was soaked. They lifted the sodden tubes out of the packets and lay them on the rock to dry.

All this time they scanned the sky for searching aircraft. 'They'll have started looking this morning,' said Coffman. 'We should see something soon.' Even so they decided to ration themselves severely, sharing out the malted milk tablets and barley sugar, and their ration of aircrew chocolate, on the basis that they might not be found for perhaps a week. 'We must make our water last out too,' said Coffman. 'We'll restrict it to a pint a day between the three of us.'

'Listen!' shouted Greenaway. 'An aircraft!' And in a few moments they saw it, high over the icecap, coming their way. When it was six or seven miles distant they began firing the Very pistol. Snow, fretting at having nothing to attract attention with, picked up the heliograph and pointed it towards the aircraft, trying to get a flash in it from the sun. But the sun was behind him.

The aircraft flew high overhead and then turned away along the coast. It was a waste to fire any more of their cartridges. They had clearly not been seen. Snow, facing the sun now, went on experimenting with the heliograph. But soon the aircraft disappeared from view.

An uneasy, oppressive silence gripped them. The plane must surely have been looking for them. What better chance would they have of being seen?

A storm was bearing down towards them from the north, completing their gloom. Soon they were almost blinded by hail and sleet, the wind beat against the rock with gale force, and the ledge they were sheltering on was continually swamped. 'We shall have to climb higher,' said Coffman. 'We'll drag the dinghy up with us.'

As they climbed they looked for a cave into which they could crawl. All they found was a hole in a rock too narrow to enter. They climbed still further, until they were 100 feet above the sea. Here they found a ledge wide enough to hold the dinghy, and they collapsed again, utterly exhausted.

'We've got to find some shelter from this wind and sleet,' said Coffman. 'Otherwise we just won't last.' Exposure, he knew, would kill them far more quickly than hunger or thirst. 'Let's try turning the dinghy over. Then we can crawl underneath.' Soon they were huddled together under the upturned dinghy. It sheltered them completely.

For the next two days there was a continuous blizzard of sleet and snow. Even under the dinghy their clothing became soggy and they were soaked right through to the skin. The blizzard was followed by forty eight hours of sub-zero weather in which their flying clothing froze on them like suits of mail.

Greenaway's feet and legs began to give him excruciating pain. Already the hours of exposure were taking effect.

They knew that as long as this weather kept up the search would be postponed, even called off. But on the fifth day they heard an aircraft. At the first sound of engines their vitality returned with a rush. There was no sun so the heliograph was useless, but they fired the Very pistol several times. They caught a glimpse of the plane through the murk after it had passed over them, but they knew they had not been seen.

'If we could climb to the top of the rock,' said Coffman, 'we could plant the distress flag up there. It might show up well.'

Greenaway was too ill to move, so Coffman and Snow began the ascent. The rock was mostly bare, but in some places it was thinly coated with ice and snow. Coffman, too, was having trouble with his feet. They were already beginning to show signs of frostbite. Snow forged ahead, Coffman following more slowly. Thus they continued to climb, digging their flying boots into the occasional foothold and finding pieces of bare rock to grip with their hands. Snow had lost his flying helmet in the ditching, and his ears stung unbearably in the biting wind, but he still kept on.

After an ascent of some 300 feet the two men reached a jutting overhang just below the summit. Snow pulled himself up and planted the flag.

The two men looked across at the vast ice-cap, and then directly below to where the racing waters dashed and eddied between the rock and the shore. There was no sign of a living thing, not even a sea-bird. The rock they had climbed was a barren crag absolutely bare of vegetation. They began to feel their way back to the dinghy.

The three men lay for hour after hour in the slush under the dinghy, paralysed into a queer illusion of comfort, talking, telling their life stories, even telling jokes. After a time they slit the trousers of their flying clothing and thrust their legs together for warmth.

Coffman and Snow took turns at rubbing Greenaway's feet to try to restore the circulation. Even the heels were black now. Yet Greenaway was the brightest and most optimistic of all. He talked of his wife and child as though he were simply away on a short trip and would be back with them in a day or so.

Coffman's thin Southern blood was particularly affected by the cold, but he too never let up. Before joining the ferry service he had never seen snow in his life.

It was on the eighth day after the ditching that they saw the ship, steaming away from the tip of Greenland, heading south. The weather was clear. Coffman immediately began firing the Very pistol. He fired it at five-minute intervals for the next half-hour. By that time the ship was out of sight.

They had forgotten now that they were hungry. They had even ceased to talk about food. They still had a little water, and to eke this out they grabbed handfuls of snow whenever they got out from under the dinghy. But for most of the time they stayed in the semi-darkness of the upturned dinghy. They were too weak to go far.

Lying for hour after hour on the bare rock, their bodies became tender and raw. Bones that had once been well covered now protruded, and they did not know where to put themselves to relieve the pain.

Three more times they moved the dinghy to try to find a more comfortable spot. Always it seemed to be better for an hour or two, and then it became even more unendurable.

Worse than anything else was the thought that no one knew what had happened to them. 'One day,' said Coffman, 'when the shipping lanes are clear again, someone will find us. If we had something to write on we could leave some sort of record.' They searched their pockets, but the only scraps of paper they could find were soaked to a pulp, and their fingers were so numb with cold that they couldn't grip a pencil.

Their talk was of superficial, trivial things, having no bearing on their plight. They noticed that each of them had a second Christian name beginning with the letter E, and in their fevered state this assumed great significance. It was as though some dramatic coincidence had linked them indissolubly together. They derived great comfort from it.

Faced as they were with the imminence of death, not one of them spoke his deepest thoughts. Speech now was spasmodic and did not amount to conversation. For long periods they were silent, lapsing into a coma or hovering on the brink of unconsciousness. But in each man there remained the instinct to prolong life, to postpone the end as long as possible.

In their nightmarish dreams they saw great quantities of liquid and gargantuan meals. A seal which they had seen on the first day in the dinghy returned in their dreams to mock them, still tantalisingly out of reach.

At sunrise on the tenth day they again heard an aircraft. They struggled out from under the dinghy and began shouting and waving excitedly. Then they remembered the Very pistol. The cloud base was low and they hardly saw the aircraft, but they fired several cartridges up into the mist. At length they realized that the sound of engines had long since disappeared.

Once again they crawled back under the dinghy. All hope was now gone. It was just a question of how long they could last.

Back at Ferry Command Headquarters in Montreal the search, which had been going on intermittently all the time, was finally abandoned at this point, and the three were officially presumed dead. Greenaway's wife packed up her belongings and sent them back to Alberta.

Then she booked seats for herself and her baby on the next day's train.

On the eleventh day Coffman became much weaker and it seemed that he might be the first to go. Greenaway's feet were swollen and blackened but he was maintaining his spirits with wonderful stoicism.

'Water,' croaked Coffman. 'Water.'

There was still a little water left and Snow crawled out to get it. He picked up the can and turned back towards the dinghy. As he did so, something out to sea caught his eye. It was a ship.

He stared for a moment in utter disbelief. Then he blinked. The ship was still there. For several days now they had been imagining things. This must be another hallucination. He tried to get a grip on himself. The ship seemed quite close, only a few miles off shore. It couldn't be true.

He put the water-can down and pushed his way under the dinghy. Coffman and Greenaway still lay there in a semi-conscious state. Now that the ship was cut off from his view he almost ceased to believe in it himself. He spoke gently to the others.

'I must be seeing things,' he said, 'but I swear there's a ship out there. It's lying at anchor. It's absolutely still.'

They lifted the dinghy to one side and looked out to sea. For a moment they saw nothing as their eyes blinked in the pale northern light and they strove to refocus. Then they saw it, a small two-masted vessel, looking as though it had been painted into the landscape while they slept.

'It's a ship! A ship!' They gripped each other frantically in anxious confirmation, searching each other's eyes for the truth, afraid to believe the evidence of their own senses.

'Do you think they've seen us?'

'Of course they have!'

'They must have done!'

'Fire the Very pistol! We're saved!'

The sight of the ship, besides giving them a great resurgence of energy and vitality, had affected them all emotionally. Their eyes filled with tears, and they wept uncontrollably. Not a word of self-pity had passed between them, but now they were overwhelmed by it. Helping to support each other, they knelt together on the narrow ledge of rock. Openly and unashamedly they prayed.

Coffman fired the Very pistol. Snow operated the heliograph. For the first time since that first morning on the rock the sun was shining. But there was no answering flare.

The vessel off-shore was a 260-ton sealing ship, the Norwegian *Polar Bjorn* (Polar Bear). Beset by engine trouble, she had come in fairly close to the shore to shelter while the crew carried out repairs. She was the last ship making passage along the east coast of Greenland for the year. Only her engine defects had caused her to come in so close.

All her crew were out of sight in the engine room. Two passengers, US Army men returning from a radio station in the north-east, were resting in their bunks. There was no look-out on board as Coffman began to load and fire his last few flares.

The mood of the three marooned men changed from ecstasy to doubt and misgiving as their signals remained unanswered, and finally to desperation. It seemed that the ship on which their last hopes rested had been abandoned. There was no sign of life on board.

For the next three hours they knelt there in the sunshine, praying continually. There was only one prayer they all knew and they chanted it together unceasingly, uncomprehendingly, as children recite a memorized lesson. 'Our Father, which art in heaven . . .' they chanted, right through to the end, and then straight back to the beginning again, hundreds and hundreds of times, as though rescue depended absolutely on their maintaining an unbroken stream of prayer. It was agonized prayer, pleading prayer, frenzied prayer, the praying of men who have suffered and become resigned to death, only to be tortured with first buoyant hope and then black despair.

On board the *Polar Bjorn*, one of the US Army men, a major, came up on deck to take a closer look at the rugged Greenland coastline. He ran his eye down from the great icecap to the fissured fringe, noticing the black rock close inshore. He studied his map. It must be Umanarsuk.

Up at the weather base he had learned a little Eskimo and he translated it haltingly. 'Shaped like a great heart.' Yes, he could see that it was probably heart-shaped.

The rock was almost bare of snow and ice, and yet something bright seemed to be reflecting back at him. He looked again. He might be mistaken, but again he thought he saw a glint from something shiny, some polished piece of rock caught by the sun.

On the rock, Snow and Greenaway were still operating the helio-graph. Coffman was about to fire the last Very cartridge.

The American major saw a puff of sea mist or sea spray, and then the glint of a ptarmigan wheeling in the sun. But when he saw the object fall vertically like a stone into the sea, he felt sure it wasn't a sea-bird. He focused his binoculars on the rock and was almost blinded by a flash from the heliograph.

The major knew well enough that the Germans had established weather posts on this coast to transmit information to U-Boats. It was possible that there was a U-Boat in the vicinity and that these signals were directing it on to the *Polar Bjorn*. He went below to warn the Norwegian skipper.

Had the engines been ready the Norwegians would very probably have put on steam and cleared the area as soon as possible. But the engineers still had work to do. 'Let's go over there and find out,' suggested the American major. 'We'll take some tommy-guns. We'll soon blast them out.'

A boat was lowered, manned by three Norwegians and the American major, all heavily armed. They kept the rock covered all the way. But as they approached within hailing distance they dropped their guns. They were staring at three helpless, kneeling figures who were holding on to each other for support, muttering a prayer which had become gibberish, yet which had somehow sustained them for four tormented hours.

The rescued men were taken at once back to the ship, but before they could be given as much as a hot drink they collapsed. They did not regain consciousness for many hours.

The rescue was called at the time the 'Miracle of Umanarsuk'. The coincidence of the last ship getting engine trouble in exactly the right place, on the first sunny day for eleven days, with the three survivors, at the extreme limits of exposure, attracting notice with their last Very signal, was indeed miraculous.

A radio message announcing the rescue was transmitted at once by the *Polar Bjorn*. A telegram from Ferry Command reached Ruth Greenaway as she left her apartment in Montreal with Diane to catch the train for Alberta and home.

Greenaway's frostbite was so serious that he spent the next twelve

months in hospital. Coffman and Snow recovered more quickly.
The Greenaways eventually had seven children. Ron Snow had five.
'We had a Ferry Command reuinion in Montreal in June 1971,'
[writes Ron Snow] 'and believe me I don't think anyone slept more
than a few hours – they didn't want to miss a thing. They came from
all over – the United States, France, Britain, Canada. Ted Greenaway
was unable to make it, but he promised to attend the next one, planned
for 1976. Bob Coffman drove up with his wife from Natchez, Missis-
sippi, and he is still in good shape – one great guy, on the ground or in
the air. But he talks slower than ever.'

ISLAND OF OLD DESIRE

Peter Knight

Whenever I recall the strange island, which is like to be daily for so long as I live, there comes into my mind the picture of my first encounter with Martin Venables.

It was a bitter cold day in February, of the year 1785, when armed with my uncle's letter I climbed through a succession of floors inhabited by attorneys and smelling of old parchment and metal deed boxes, to a topmost set of rooms that looked down upon the City, with near at hand the burial ground of St Dunstan's-in-the-West. Here, an untidy manservant informed me, having relieved me of my letter, that Mr Venables could not see me for a while and that I must please to wait.

Now as I have said the weather was intensely cold, and there was no fire in the outer room in which I found myself. I thought of the little my uncle had told me concerning Mr Venables' projected voyage, a voyage which, it seemed, was to yield my long-awaited chance of going to sea. Well, thought I, if my uncle is right I shall be colder still before many weeks are past. But for the present it occurred to me that I needed an occupation to drive the chill out of my bones while I waited.

Through a closed door I thought I could hear voices engaged in earnest conversation – Mr Venables, I judged, and one other. The talk sounded as though it might go on for some time, and very soon I ceased to pay attention. It was now my hand lighted upon the cricket ball in the pocket of my surtout.

Ours had been a great school for cricket, and though I had left it now, being seventeen, it was my whim that the leathern ball should be my constant companion at all seasons. I missed the regular matches, but a friend had introduced me to a meeting of the famous club of gentlemen who played at Mr Thomas Lord's ground in St Marylebone and I found a game myself whenever I could.

Chiefly it was as a bowler I was ambitious to excel, and this, to my view, called for practice at all times of the year and in as many places as possible. Even in the narrow yard of my uncle's house in St James', where I had lived when not at school since my parents' death, I was by way of being a menace to the servants and the pot plants, striving for hours a day to learn every secret of the vagaries of the ball's behaviour, trying sundry variations of grip on the leather globe, trying experimentally how I might use my fingers on the stitches to give it speed and spin.

And now, awaiting the momentous meeting, with a leaden sky outside and nothing greener to be seen than a dim, distant prospect of the Surrey hills across the river, I fell to tossing my leather charm idly about, while I thought with half my mind.

If you shifted the grip of your fingers a trifle, just so, at the moment you let the ball go . . . the ball dropped with a noisy 'plop' into a basket that was evidently intended for rubbish, and I wondered as I scrabbled for it what the shabby manservant would think if he came back and caught me . . . Martin Venables was verging on sixty, my uncle had said, and had made a fortune from the law. He was adept at various obscure languages and had travelled a good deal besides . . . And now Mr Venables designed to fit out a vessel for a voyage of exploration of which my uncle, though they had been at university together and been fairly friendly ever since, knew nothing save that it was to be in northern waters . . .

I was a tolerably good marksman, I considered, having twice taken three wickets with as many successive balls, a feat that by tradition entitles a fellow to the gift of a new hat from the other side. Perhaps it

was rather more speed that I needed, if I could find the trick of it . . .
And Mr Venables had a fancy to carry an extra man among his ship's
complement, someone in whom a knowledge of seamanship was not
needful so much as some qualities beyond those of the common sailor,
so that he could keep an intelligible record of the voyage when they
came home . . .

It seemed that on my uncle's commendation Mr Venables believed I
might meet these conditions. So now I was to meet him; and the great
question was: Would he approve me?

I flung the ball again, and was gratified to see it describe a graceful
parabola the length of the room and dive into the basket as accurately
as a rabbit into its burrow . . .

I had been informed that the vessel was a barquentine, by name the
True Fortune, of some 300 tons and now lying in the Scottish port of
Leith. She would carry a crew of some fifteen, of whom a number
had been recruited by Mr Venables himself on the advice of certain
ship-owning friends, while the sailing-master he had engaged, one
Captain Runacres, was to find the rest.

This much my uncle could tell me. But where was the ship to go,
and what was she to do that would require a chronicler, as it seemed
was needed? The North Pole, the mysterious North-West Passage
round the uttermost tip of the Americas, buried treasure – these were
all possibilities on which I speculated in hopeful exhilaration.

At least I should have my long-cherished wish and go to sea; anything would be better than the university which I had dreaded, where
(unless they played cricket in summer) it would be nothing save
lectures and dry books. And in a few minutes now . . .

Suddenly I stood stock still in utter consternation. The ball, which I
was carelessly tossing from one hand to the other as one sometimes does
with a Christmas apple or orange, had taken an abrupt dive towards
the window, and there was a sharp tinkle of broken glass.

My embarrassment was great; but it was some slight consolation that
the offending missile – a treasure I valued – dropped back upon the
carpet instead of falling outside. The inner door opened as I stooped to
pick it up, and a personage who could be none other than my prospec-
tive employer came in.

Straightening myself with a mighty red face, I saw that Martin

Venables was a slight, pale man who looked every day of his sixty years, very plainly dressed and, I thought at once, no very likely person to choose the hazards of the northern ocean for a journey in late middle age. He glanced quizzically, with lifted eyebrows, from the cricket ball in my hand to the shattered pane through which the February air blew bitingly.

'I'm prodigious sorry, sir,' I said shame-facedly. 'I am Philip Carnforth, at your service. It seems a scurvy thing to make a cock-shy of your chamber. But the truth is that having nothing to do' – The effort to explain my childish behaviour made me stammer.

'Say no more, Mr Carnforth,' he interrupted with a smile that impressed me as both genial and gentle. 'I am in hopes we shall find plenty of occupation for you presently' – he said this meaningly, and I saw he had my uncle's letter in his hand – 'and a broken window is soon mended. You will allow me to present you to Captain Joshua Runacres, to whose skill, under God, we are to be beholden for – who knows how long to come?'

He turned to the man who had emerged from the inner chamber at his heels. 'Here, Captain, is Mr Philip Carnforth, who makes havoc with a sphere while we essay only to explore one.'

My heart fairly leapt at his words, for it sounded singularly as though my appointment were decided already. But as Runacres cast his eye over me my spirits fell. It was a shrewd, small, calculating eye, which to my instant view seemed oddly out of accord with the rest of his appearance, which struck me as both crafty and swaggering.

'Indeed, Mr Venables!' said he. 'Is our young friend thinking of putting his ambitions to the test of Northern gales?'

He looked with a suspicion of a smile about his wide, thin mouth over the fine clothes I had put on for the occasion. I was glad to think that at any rate he could find no fault with my physique. But with the quick sensitivity of seventeen years I could have sworn his lean, tanned face held a sneer. I felt a furious regret for the window I had broken like a schoolboy, which was beyond anything I had felt under Mr Venables' scrutiny, and it is from this, our very first meeting, that I date my dislike of the Captain.

'Come, come, Runacres, we shall see, we shall see!' said Mr Venables deprecatingly, his hand on the other's gilt-braided sleeve. 'But you

85

have business, I know. I am glad to have your assurance that all progresses well, and we shall meet later.'

Captain Runacres suffered himself to be piloted to the outer door, which I was not sorry to see close behind him. Then, ushered into the inner room, I faced the queerest interview I could have conceived.

It was a large apartment, with a cheerful fire and well lined with books, most of which I could make out from their bindings to be very old. I found myself, however, paying much less attention to my surroundings than to the man who faced me across a paper-littered table.

Martin Venables asked me first a deal of particulars about myself – what I had wanted to do with my life, whether I had studied geography and in particular ancient history, to which he appeared to attach an odd importance, and what I looked for from a sea life.

'I will wager, now,' said he, regarding me with a quaint lift of his white eyebrows, 'that you have dreams of making a fortune.'

'Yes, I supposed so,' I told him with a smile, and he sighed.

'*Et ego in Arcadia* – or in regions much less idyllic. And after all, I have found at the last . . .'

A strange, far-away look came into his kindly eyes, as though for the present he had forgotten me and the purpose of our meeting, and he fell to talking of himself – how he had become a rich man by his profession but it had brought him no contentment but only taught him, in his childless old age, the hollowness of life.

As his speech grew more earnest and his look more intense, I made out that he cherished some obsession about a sort of earthly paradise where all greed and struggle could be forgotten and a man like himself could find his true heart's desire. He talked like a man with a vision, and more than once he used a singular phrase, '*insula felix*', 'a happy island' – that left me sorely puzzled. I might have thought him a little mad, but to my relief he came back to practical questions and I had the impression he was summing me up shrewdly, and not unfavourably.

The upshot was that at the end of an hour I had agreed terms by which I was to join the *True Fortune* for a cruise of indeterminate duration, my duties being to keep the archives of the expedition as his secretary and to make myself generally as useful as I could. It was not till I was descending the dusty stairs, my cricket ball in my pocket and the broken pane apparently quite forgotten, that I remembered I was no wiser concerning the real object of the voyage than I had been at the beginning.

It was many weeks later, we being then in about the 65th parallel of latitude – I will not be more precise – and among the drifting ice when I came by chance on a clue.

I had elected to stand my watches with the regular crew. It was about four bells in the middle watch, a clear night and fair weather. I was standing betwixt the bulwark and a deckhouse that stood for'ard of the mizzen mast, listening to the weird crepitation of the ice against the forefoot and wondering why the stars shone so much brighter in that frozen air. Suddenly, startling my ear amid the surrounding stillness, I heard a voice.

My watch-mates were all for'ard; the voice came pretty clearly from the deckhouse, which had a little lattice for ventilation above the door, and it sounded like a man quoting from written words:

'The island lifteth herself most comely from the ice, like Queen Cleopatra rising from a couch of silver and pearl. In the midst is a tall hill where is the gold. But beyond lieth a most warm and clement valley, and here, so sweet and perfumed is the air that our men cried out in delight like children upon holiday, and each man – I know not how – felt his heart lifted and his cares and bitterness wafted quite away . . .'

Now Captain Joshua Runacres berthed in the deckhouse; it was his watch below just now, and, as the voice broke off, I thought for a moment that he must have been talking to himself. But instantly after, I caught the sound of another voice, which I recognized as that of Saul Sweeting, the *True Fortune*'s carpenter.

I could not make out what he said, but now came Runacres' voice again. '. . . A true bearing, shipmate, and a landfall soon – maybe tonight or tomorrow.' The voice ended on a laugh; the other said something more. A moment later I was crouching in the shadow of the bulwarks as Saul Sweeting came out of the deckhouse with, I thought, a kind of swagger and strode off for'ard.

I had dodged from sight instinctively, for on the instant I found myself thinking hard. It seemed odd that the Captain should be laughing and sharing confidences at night time in his cabin with a fellow who was really no more than a fo'c'sle hand. But now I recollected that the carpenter was one of the men Runacres himself had brought with him to join the crew, real hang-dog-looking creatures whom I had thought all along contrasted unfavourably with Mr Venables' hearty, good-humoured portion of our complement.

Above all were the words he had been reading. Incomprehensible though they had been, they associated themselves irresistibly with Martin Venables' reference to 'insula felix'. And here, it seemed, was a landfall we were to sight very shortly! It was evident to me that Runacres and his midnight friend from the fo'c'sle knew more of the goal of our voyage than I did.

Now from the time we had sailed from the port of Leith, I had found my first dislike of the Captain growing on me. It was not that the man was openly uncivil, but he had made his contempt of me as a land-lubber quite apparent. He resented me, too, for standing, as he saw it, in a privileged position with Mr Venables.

I suppose my feeling towards the sailing-master formed a fruitful soil for my sudden suspicion to grow on, but the upshot was that, when I joined Mr Venables at breakfast next morning – the master being then on deck – I made haste to tell him what I had overheard.

His immediate response was a singular one. He stared at me with consternation in his look, plainly taken utterly aback and thinking rapidly. Then he started up from the table and, crossing to a little chest that stood laden with books in a corner of the cabin, he unlocked it with a key he took from an inner pocket, rummaged quickly among the contents, and then, stooping down, made a close scrutiny of the lock and the woodwork around it.

'Philip,' said he, turning to me with a small book in his hand, 'I am about to admit you to an old man's confidence – as I perceive, now that I know you better, I might have done some time since. Do you recall that, about the time we were abreast of the Faroes, Master Sweeting, the carpenter, came below here to repair the deadlight upon one of the ports and was left some while to himself? He repaired it to some purpose. My private bureau has been forced and ransacked!'

'What's taken, sir?' I demanded, and he handed me the little book.

'I must assume, from what you said just now, they were anxious for a sight of this volume. Captain Runacres, no doubt, observed it in my chambers in London and guessed its nature, for I will swear I never uttered an incautious word.'

'But what is it, sir?'

'You may see for yourself,' he went on, and his voice shook. 'I ask your pardon for having kept you under a ban with the rest, but an old man is loath to have his secret dreams abraded by the comments and thoughts of the world. There, if I am not grievously mistaken, is the one veritable record of the fabled *insula felix*.

Examining the book, I found it was a mere handful of yellow sheets like the withered leaves of a tree, inscribed in faded, foreign-looking writing but in the English tongue. Almost the first thing my eye lighted on was the passage I had overheard the Captain recite in the deckhouse, word for word. On the last leaf were certain bearings of latitude and longitude.

'You have never heard, I take it,' Venables pursued as I stared, 'of the island called Estotiland which geographers have never been able to place upon the map? Or of Thule the Blessed, or of the Fortunate Island which St Brendan found in the distant sea?' I remembered certain oblique questions he had put to me at our first conference in London and since, as he went on in a voice oddly hushed:

'I have long held that these were no mere fables but fables embodying a truth – that somewhere there lay a land, a real land but happy and benignant beyond the thoughts of worldly men, a land as one might say beyond the world, where all our restlessness might be hushed and all mankind's unutterable dreams and longings through countless aeons of time might find fulfilment in the lightest breath of its air. Well, I believe that I have found it. That manuscript in your hand is a translation of a portion of a ship's log of Carlo Minetti, a gentleman adventurer of Venice who voyaged in Arctic regions in the 15th century. I have failed to find much account of him or of any other record he may have left. This fragment came by chance into my hands in Norway a year ago, and I have sworn since that if God granted me life I should find the place.'

'But Captain Runacres has the bearing, since he spoke of a landfall within a few hours,' said I. He shook his head as I handed him back the book.

'The bearing merely. I did not show him the whole. You will think me an odd enthusiast, Philip, but you observe some mention of gold in that document of old Minetti's. An accursed metal! . . . I have seen what gold can do to men's souls in my time, and believe me, I had rather lose a Golconda than that the island which the ancients cherished like the memory of a lost paradise should become a prize for covetous men to struggle for! But now –' He shrugged.

'It's gold the Captain is thinking of, I'll wager – him and his friends among the crew!' I said with assurance. 'Most likely, if he were to find it, he'd plan to find the money to bring his own expedition to colonize the island for the Bank of England.'

Venables wrung his hands almost like a man in pain saying, 'Yet for me – to walk the world even with empty pockets but with the glory of rediscovering a lost Eden! . . . Ah, heaven, can you conceive what they would make of it, those others?'

He broke off. A shout of 'Land-ho!' had sounded from the deck. Swiftly replacing the log in its locked drawer Venables darted for the companion, I following hard at his heels.

All hands save the man at the wheel had ranged themselves along the starboard bulwarks. For an instant I made sure I saw Runacres in whispered colloquy with Sweeting and one or two others by the main-mast, and I felt more sure than ever that he had brought his recruits aboard for some purpose of his own. Next moment he was swaggering and smirking at Venables' side.

'We have hit our target prettily, it seems,' says he. 'I'm puzzled, though, by the way the ice thins out to landward. We shall be able to sail clear in with this breeze.'

Some five miles off a long shape caught the morning sun, but was strangely wreathed in a vapour that looked oddly like some emanation of its own. Venables' look as he faced the Captain betrayed nothing of what I had revealed, but his eyes were puckered in puzzlement.

'Warm water, and a mist . . .' said he. 'I had not expected this. The island is surely volcanic.'

'Been simmering quietly for a thousand years, must like,' said Runacres. 'Do you design to go ashore immediately, sir?'

And now beneath his accustomed swagger I observed the man was a-twitch with inward excitement, and his little eyes darted for'ard and aft and then towards the island in a way that made me wonder.

'Yes,' Venables replied, 'I think, Captain, that I must claim the honour, with Mr Carnforth here. When you have brought the ship to anchor you will doubtless follow, but for the present you will allow me my whim.'

'And very right and proper, Mr Venables,' said Runacres with a chuckle. 'I will give orders for the gig to be got away.'

As the ship crept nearer through open water I could clearly distinguish the 'tall hill' where Minetti had said the gold was, and lower hills beyond that might be the boundary of the happy valley. It was little I foresaw how brief was to be our acquaintance with the spot that had been the focus of the old lawyer's imaginings, or how cataclysmic was to be its ending.

The Captain had levelled a spyglass at the hill, but he was brisk about his duties as the *True Fortune*, dropping her sails like folded wings, slackened way a hundred yards from a low, grey, rocky coast fringed with shingle on which, as I saw with keen surprise, no ice lay. Even as the anchor plunged, the gig was dropped at the quarter and Martin Venables and I clambered in.

'I'll stand by in the boat,' said Runacres, as he dropped into the sternsheets. 'I shall be at your orders, sir, when you require me,' to which Venables, his eyes ranging the shore eagerly, merely nodded. It was then I noticed, half unconsciously, that the men who rowed us were two of the Captain's own hands. The Captain himself, I noticed also, seemed to be hugging a sort of secret fervour of excitement, and I saw his hands were restless on the gunwales.

I cannot say my first impression of the legendary island was at all that of an earthly paradise, it looked so different from Minetti's description; but there were other matters that powerfully gripped my attention. The strange mist was far thicker than I had expected and had a queer, sulphurous smell. I was baffled, too, by an odd, distant sound like intermittent thunder heard far off. Great clouds of sea birds sped across the heaven above our heads, and I wondered whether it was just our presence that disturbed them or if they were startled by that ominous noise.

Leaving Runacres and the two hands in the gig, Venables and I advanced up an escarpment of loose rock and had soon lost sight of them behind a screen of giant boulders.

'Volcanic,' Venables muttered as if to himself. 'We might expect changes, Philip, after so many centuries. And yet . . . the very heart of a thousand legends!'

He fell silent then, and I did not speak. I could see his hands were trembling, but his eyes as he gazed at the waste of grey, empty stone were as those of a man enchanted, rapt. So he remained for perhaps half an hour, while I tried to conceive what he must be thinking, and wondered more urgently with each moment at the muffled thunder-sounds that at intervals broke the stillness.

Once I heard a sound that could not be thunder but was plainly that of musket shots. They must have come from the ship, and I was still guessing that someone on board had taken a shot at the sea birds when the tinkle of a trodden pebble close behind me made me turn quickly.

Captain Runacres stood there, a venomous grin on his swarthy face and a great knife in his hand.

Mr Venables had swung round also, so that the knife which had been in the act of plunging at his back passed harmlessly over his shoulder. Next instant with a blow of my fist I had struck it from Runacres' grasp.

It is singular how absolute comprehension can spring to a man's mind in a single flash. As the Captain fell back snarling I saw as plainly as if it were written before me that he had never meant Venables to leave the island to which he had piloted him, but that he was to die here, and doubtless myself as well, while the Captain returned to England with a story of our accidental death, to claim the glory and wealth of discovery.

Runacres let the knife lie, but he had a pistol now in his hand, and suddenly it came to me that Venables and I had brought no arms ashore with us. Venables spoke chokingly, like a man awakened abruptly from a dream.

'Is this murder, Captain?' says he, and there seemed no power of sight in his incredulous eyes.

'You fool!' rapped out Runacres, and added an oath. 'Here is your blessed island, and I wish you joy of it, for you will never leave it alive, you or your pampered landlubber here! There are my own men to

Runacres stood grinning venomously, a great knife in his hand.

take me off when I've done with you, ay, and the ship's mine by now – I can trust my lads for that!'

So this was the meaning of the musket shots I had heard; they must have been the signal for both open mutiny and treacherous murder. In the self-same moment I thought of the one thing I could do, weaponless though we were. I had remembered my cricket ball in my pocket.

Runacres had fallen back a few yards among the rocks like a conqueror with all the island at his disposal, and was pointing the pistol at Venables dominatingly from the vantage point of a slight eminence. I measured my distance and hurled the ball like a thunderbolt straight at his grinning head.

My hours of practice did not fail me. The ball struck him full in the forehead, and he clapped his two hands to his head, tottered, fell like a tree, and lay still. I had no time, however, to savour my success, for there came a singular thing to divert my attention.

For a moment the ball had lain where it fell. But now, as I eyed it, I thought it moved again as if by some weird inward power of its own. In another moment I was certain. After another halt the ball was rolling towards me over the rocky floor where we were standing, like a billiard ball on a tilted table.

'Mr Venables! Don't you see?' I shouted, grasping him by the arm as he stood stupefied. 'The island is moving!'

And then it was upon us. There came a succession of rending crashes, and I had a bewildering sensation that the whole island was bursting asunder behind us. Enveloped in a rush of sulphurous mist I saw huge boulders and pieces of rock hurtling through the darkened air. A fragment struck me on the shoulder and Venables' white hair, his wig having fallen off, was thick in an instant with stinking dust.

But it was a larger mass that fell clean upon Captain Runacres' prostrate body and left him flattened and unseemly as a crushed toad. And Venables cast one half-unseeing glance at him before, with my arm supporting him, we were stumbling for the shore with *insula felix* torn by the earthquake's frenzy in our rear.

★　　★　　★　　★

A wave of the Captain's pistol, which I had retrieved, persuaded the frightened fellows in the gig to take us off. Amid a bombardment of fragments, hot and fierce as bombshells, from the rocking land, we regained the barquentine somewhat fearfully, to find muskets and cutlasses out there but all controlled under the keen eye of Mr Harkness, the mate, and Runacres' hands sullenly grouped for'ard like beaten men.

It seemed that mutiny had indeed been raised under the command of Saul Sweeting, but to the credit of English seamen I was glad to find it had been but a half-hearted affair and the loyal hands had got it swiftly under control with little bloodshed. It was a very penitent half-dozen mutineers who now vowed fealty and their willingness to return to their duty under the command of Mr Harkness.

The ship was hastily sailed a mile off shore and there re-anchored, while we watched the awful spectacle of rock and hill and still unexplored land sink bodily, like a vast dying water-beast, below the engulfing sea. Martin Venables, beside me at the bulwark, regarded the last stages of the catastrophe like a man in a trance. But there was a contented light in his dazed eyes as he laid his trembling hand upon my shoulder.

'Thus it goes for ever, Philip – the island, as I conceive, of an aeon of fables. And it is fitting. I have cherished a dream and I have seen it fade – borne down with its legendary beauty by the gross weight of its gold, lest the land of old desire should become a pole of contention for grasping mortals . . .'

He turned to me from the prospect of troubled water and fume and the advancing ice. 'But for you, Philip – ah, youth ever carries its *insula felix* with it, and there are fair territories yet for you to explore.'

RED INDIANS ON THE WARPATH

R. M. Ballantyne

Joe Blunt and Dick Varley along with Henri the French-Canadian and the dog Crusoe have been on a hunting-expedition on the prairie and after many dangerous encounters with wild animals and Red Indians, the hunters decide to return home to the Mustang Valley. But more danger lies ahead . . .

The sun had arisen, and his beams were just tipping the summits of the Rocky Mountains, causing the snowy peaks to glitter like flame, and the deep ravines and gorges to look sombre and mysterious by contrast, when Dick and Joe and Henri mounted their gallant steeds, and, with Crusoe gambolling before, and the two pack-horses trotting by their side, turned their faces eastward.

Crusoe was in great spirits. He was perfectly well aware that he and his companions were on their way home, and testified his satisfaction by bursts of scampering over the hills and valleys. Doubtless he thought of Dick Varley's cottage, and of Dick's mild, kind-hearted mother. Undoubtedly, too, he thought of his own mother, Fan, and felt a glow of filial affection as he did so.

Dick, too, let his thoughts run away in the direction of *home*. Sweet word! Those who have never left it cannot, by any effort of imagination, realize the full import of the word 'home'. Dick was a bold hunter; but he was young, and this was his first expedition. Oftentimes, when sleeping under the trees and gazing dreamily up through the branches at the stars, had he thought of home, until his longing heart began to yearn to return. He repelled such tender feelings, however, when they became too strong, deeming them unmanly, and sought to turn his mind to the excitements of the chase; but latterly his efforts were in vain. He became thoroughly homesick, and while admitting the fact to himself, he endeavoured to conceal it from his comrades. He thought that he was successful in this attempt. Poor Dick Varley! As yet he was sadly ignorant of human nature. Henri knew it, and Joe Blunt knew it. Even Crusoe knew that something was wrong with his master, although he could not exactly make out what it was. But Crusoe made memoranda in the notebook of his memory. He jotted down the peculiar phases of his master's new disease with the care and minute exactness of a physician, and, we doubt not, ultimately added the knowledge of the symptoms of homesickness to his already well-filled stores of erudition.

It was not till they had set out on their homeward journey that Dick Varley's spirits revived, and it was not till they reached the beautiful prairies on the eastern slopes of the Rocky Mountains, and galloped over the greensward towards the Mustang Valley, that Dick ventured to tell Joe Blunt what his feelings had been.

'D'ye know, Joe,' he said confidentially, reining up his gallant steed after a sharp gallop, 'd'ye know I've bin feelin' awful low for some time past.'

'I know it, lad,' answered Joe, with a quiet smile, in which there was a dash of something that implied he knew more than he chose to express.

Dick felt surprised, but he continued: 'I wonder what it could have bin. I never felt so before.'

''Twas homesickness, boy,' returned Joe.

'How d'ye know that?'

'The same way as how I know most things – by experience an' obsarvation. I've bin homesick myself once, but it was long, long agone.'

Dick felt much relieved at this candid confession by such a bronzed veteran, and, the chords of sympathy having been struck, he opened up his heart at once, to the evident delight of Henri, who, among other curious partialities, was extremely fond of listening to and taking part in conversations that bordered on the metaphysical, and were hard to be understood. Most conversations that were not connected with eating and hunting were of this nature to Henri.

97

'Hom'sik,' he cried, 'veech mean bin' sik of hom'! Hah! Dat is fat I am always be, ven I goes hout on de expedition. Oui, vraiment.'

'I always packs up,' continued Joe, paying no attention to Henri's remark – 'I always packs up an' sots off for home when I gits homesick. It's the best cure; an' when hunters are young like you, Dick, it's the only cure. I've knowed fellers a'most die o'homesickness, an' I'm told they *do* go under altogether sometimes.'

'Go onder!' exclaimed Henri. 'Oui, I vas all but die myself ven I fust try to git away from hom'. If I have not git away, I not be here today.'

Henri's idea of homesickness was so totally opposed to theirs that his comrades only laughed, and refrained from attempting to set him right.

'The fust time I wos took bad with it wos in a country somethin' like that,' said Joe, pointing to the wide stretch of undulating prairie, dotted with clusters of trees and meandering streamlets, that lay before them. 'I had bin out about two months, an' wos makin' a good thing of it, for game wos plenty, when I began to think somehow more than usual o' home. My mother wos alive then.'

Joe's voice sank to a deep, solemn tone as he said this, and for a few minutes he rode on in silence.

'Well, it grew worse and worse. I dreamed o' home all night an' thought of it all day, till I began to shoot bad, an' my comrades wos gittin' tired o' me; so says I to them one night, says I: "I give out, lads; I'll make tracks for the settlement tomorrow." They tried to laugh me out of it at first, but it was no go, so I packed up, bid them good day, an' sot off alone on a trip o' five hundred miles. The very first mile o' the way back I began to mend, and before two days I wos all right again.'

Joe was interrupted at this point by the sudden appearance of a solitary horseman on the brow of an eminence not half a mile distant. The three friends instantly drove their pack-horses behind a clump of trees, but not in time to escape the vigilant eye of the Redman, who uttered a loud shout, which brought up a band of his comrades at full gallop.

'Remember, Henri,' cried Joe Blunt, 'our errand is one of *peace*.'

The caution was needed, for in the confusion of the moment Henri was making preparation to sell his life as dearly as possible. Before another word could be uttered, they were surrounded by a troop of about twenty yelling Blackfeet Indians. They were, fortunately, not a war party, and, still more fortunately, they were peaceably disposed, and listened to the preliminary address of Joe Blunt with exemplary patience; after which the two parties encamped on the spot, the council fire was lighted, and every preparation made for a long palaver.

We will not trouble the reader with the details of what was said on this occasion. The party of Indians was a small one, and no chief of any importance was attached to it. Suffice to say that the pacific overtures made by Joe were well received, the trifling gifts made thereafter were still better received, and they separated with mutual expressions of goodwill.

Several other bands which were afterwards met with were equally friendly, and only one war party was seen. Joe's quick eye observed it in time to enable them to retire unseen behind the shelter of some trees, where they remained until the Indian warriors were out of sight.

The next party they met with, however, were more difficult to manage, and, unfortunately, blood was shed on both sides before our travellers escaped.

It was at the close of a beautiful day that a war party of Blackfeet were seen riding along a ridge on the horizon. It chanced that the prairie at this place was almost destitute of trees or shrubs large enough to conceal the horses. By dashing down the grassy wave into the hollow between the two undulations, and dismounting, Joe hoped to elude the savages, so he gave the word; but at the same moment a shout from the Indians told that they were discovered.

'Look sharp, lads! Throw down the packs on the highest point of the ridge,' cried Joe, undoing the lashings, seizing one of the bales of goods, and hurrying to the top of the undulation with it; 'we must keep them at arm's length, boys – be alive! War parties are not to be trusted.'

Dick and Henri seconded Joe's efforts so ably that in the course of two minutes the horses were unloaded, the packs piled in the form of a wall in front of a broken piece of ground, the horses picketed close beside them, and our three travellers peeping over the edge, with their rifles cocked, while the savages – about thirty in number – came sweeping down towards them.

'I'll try to git them to palaver,' said Joe Blunt; 'but keep yer eye on 'em, Dick, an' if they behave ill, shoot the *horse* o' the leadin' chief. I'll throw up my left hand as a signal. Mind, lad, don't hit human flesh till my second signal is given, and see that Henri don't draw till I git back to ye.'

So saying, Joe sprang lightly over the slight parapet of their little fortress, and ran swiftly out, unarmed, towards the Indians. In a few seconds he was close up with them, and in another moment was surrounded. At first the savages brandished their spears and rode round the solitary man, yelling like fiends, as if they wished to intimidate him; but as Joe stood like a statue, with his arms crossed, and a grave expression of contempt on his countenance, they quickly desisted, and, drawing near, asked him where he came from, and what he was doing there.

Joe's story was soon told; but instead of replying, they began to shout vociferously, and evidently meant mischief.

'If the Blackfeet are afraid to speak to the Paleface, he will go back to his braves,' said Joe, passing suddenly between two of the warriors and taking a few steps towards the camp.

Instantly every bow was bent, and it seemed as if our bold hunter were about to be pierced by a score of arrows, when he turned round and cried:

'The Blackfeet must not advance a single step. The first that moves his *horse* shall die. The second that moves *himself* shall die.'

To this the Blackfeet chief replied scornfully: 'The Paleface talks with a big mouth. We do not believe his words. The Snakes are liars; we will make no peace with them.'

While he was yet speaking, Joe threw up his hand; there was a loud report, and the noble horse of the savage chief lay struggling in death agony on the ground.

The use of the rifle was little known at this period among the Indians of the far west, and many had never heard the dreaded report before, although all were aware, from hearsay, of its fatal power. The fall of the chief's horse, therefore, quite paralysed them for a few moments, and they had not recovered from their surprise when a second report was heard, a bullet whistled past, and a second horse fell. At the same moment there was a loud explosion in the camp of the Palefaces, a white cloud enveloped it, and from the midst of this a loud shriek was heard, as Dick, Henri, and Crusoe bounded over the packs with frantic gestures.

At this the gaping savages wheeled their steeds round, the dismounted horsemen sprang on behind two of their comrades, and the whole band dashed away over the plains as if they were chased by evil spirits.

Meanwhile Joe hastened towards his comrades in a state of great anxiety, for he knew at once that one of the powder-horns must have been accidentally blown up.

'No damage done, boys, I hope?' he cried on coming up.

'Damage!' cried Henri, holding his hands tight over his face. 'Oh, oui, great damage – moche damage; me two eyes be blowed out of dere holes.'

'Not quite so bad as that, I hope,' said Dick, who was very slightly singed, and forgot his own hurts in anxiety about his comrade. 'Let me see.'

'My eye!' exclaimed Joe Blunt, while a broad grin overspread his countenance. 'Ye've not improved yer looks, Henri.'

This was true. The worthy hunter's hair was singed to such an extent that his entire countenance presented the appearance of a universal frizzle. Fortunately the skin, although much blackened, was quite uninjured – a fact which, when he ascertained it beyond a doubt, afforded so much satisfaction to Henri that he capered about shouting with delight, as if some piece of good fortune had befallen him.

The accident had happened in consequence of Henri having omitted to replace the stopper of his power-horn, and when, in his anxiety for Joe, he fired at random amongst the Indians, despite Dick's entreaties to wait, a spark communicated with the powder-horn and blew him up. Dick and Crusoe were only a little singed, but the former was not disposed to quarrel with an accident which had sent their enemies so promptly to the rightabout.

This band followed them for some nights, in the hope of being able to steal their horses while they slept; but they were not brave enough to venture a second time within range of the death-dealing rifle.

★   ★   ★   ★

There are periods in the life of almost all men when misfortunes seem to crowd upon them in rapid succession, when they escape from one danger only to encounter another, and when, to use a well-known expression, they succeed in leaping out of the frying-pan at the expense of plunging into the fire.

So was it with our three friends upon his occasion. They were scarcely rid of the Blackfeet, who found them too watchful to be caught napping, when, about daybreak one morning, they encountered a roving band of Camanchee Indians, who wore such a warlike aspect that Joe deemed it prudent to avoid them if possible.

'They don't see us yit, I guess,' said Joe, as he and his companions drove the horses into a hollow between the grassy waves of the prairie, 'an' if we only can escape their sharp eyes till we're in yonder clump o' willows, we're safe enough.'

'But why don't you ride up to them, Joe,' inquired Dick, 'and make peace between them and the Palefaces, as you ha' done with other bands?'

'Because it's o' no use to risk our scalps for the chance o' makin' peace wi' a rovin' war party. Keep yer head down, Henri! If they git only a sight o' the top o' yer cap, they'll be down on us like a breeze o' wind.'

'Ha, let dem come!' said Henri.

'They'll come without askin' yer leave,' remarked Joe, dryly.

Notwithstanding his defiant expression, Henri had sufficient purdence to induce him to bend his head and shoulders, and in a few minutes they reached the shelter of the willows unseen by the savages. At least so thought Henri, Joe was not quite sure about it, and Dick hoped for the best.

In the course of half an hour the last of the Camanchees was seen to hover for a second on the horizon, like a speck of black against the sky, and then to disappear.

Immediately the three hunters vaulted on their steeds and resumed their journey; but before that evening closed they had sad evidence of the savage nature of the band from which they had escaped. On passing the brow of a slight eminence, Dick, who rode first, observed that Crusoe stopped and snuffed the breeze in an anxious, inquiring manner.

'What is't, pup?' said Dick, drawing up, for he knew that his faithful dog never gave a false alarm.

Crusoe replied by a short, uncertain bark, and then bounding forward, disappeared behind a little wooded knoll. In another moment a long, dismal howl floated over the plains. There was a mystery about the dog's conduct which, coupled with his melancholy cry, struck the travellers with a superstitious feeling of dread, as they sat looking at each other in surprise.

'Come, let's clear it up,' cried Joe Blunt, shaking the reins of his steed, and galloping forward. A few strides brought them to the other side of the knoll, where, scattered upon the torn and bloody turf, they discovered the scalped and mangled remains of about twenty or thirty human beings. Their skulls had been cleft by the tomahawk and their breasts pierced by the scalping-knife, and from the position in which many of them lay it was evident that they had been slain while asleep.

Joe's brow flushed and his lips became tightly compressed as he muttered between his set teeth: 'Their skins are white.'

A short examination sufficed to show that the men who had thus been barbarously murdered while they slept had been a band of trappers or hunters, but what their errand had been, or whence they came, they could not discover.

Everything of value had been carried off, and all the scalps had been taken. Most of the bodies, although much mutilated, lay in a posture that led our hunters to believe they had been killed while asleep; but one or two were cut almost to pieces, and from the blood-bespattered and trampled sward around, it seemed as if they had struggled long and fiercely for life. Whether or not any of the savages had been slain, it was impossible to tell, for if such had been the case, their comrades, doubtless, had carried away their bodies. That they had been slaughtered by the party of Camanchees who had been seen at daybreak was quite clear to Joe; but his burning desire to revenge the death of the white men had to be stifled, as his party was so small.

Long afterwards it was discovered that this was a band of trappers who had set out to avenge the death of a comrade; but God, who has retained the right of vengeance in his own hand, saw at to frustrate their purpose, by giving them into the hands of the savages whom they had set forth to slay.

As it was impossible to bury so many bodies, the travellers resumed their journey, and left them to bleach there in the wilderness; but they rode the whole of that day almost without uttering a word.

Meanwhile the Camanchees, who had observed the trio, and had ridden away at first for the purpose of deceiving them into the belief that they had passed unobserved, doubled on their track, and took a long sweep in order to keep out of sight until they could approach under the shelter of a belt of woodland towards which the travellers now approached.

The Indians adopted this course instead of the easier method of simply pursuing so weak a party, because the plains at this part were bordered by a long stretch of forest into which the hunters could have plunged, and rendered pursuit more difficult, if not almost useless. The detour thus taken was so extensive that the shades of evening were beginning to descend before they could put their plan into execution. The forest lay about a mile to the right of our hunters, like some dark mainland, of which the prairie was the sea and the scattered clumps of wood the islands.

'There's no lack o' game here,' said Dick Varley, pointing to a herd of buffaloes which rose at their approach and fled away towards the wood.

'I think we'll ha' thunder soon,' remarked Joe. 'I never feel it onnatteral hot like this without lookin' out for a plump.'

'Ha, den ve better look hout for one goot tree to get b'low,' suggested Henri. 'Voilà!' he added, pointing with his finger towards the plain; 'dere am a lot of wild hosses.'

A troop of about thirty wild horses appeared, as he spoke, on the brow of a ridge, and advanced slowly towards them.

'Hist!' exclaimed Joe, reining up. 'Hold on, lads. Wild horses! My rifle to a pop-gun there's wilder men on t'other side o' them.'

'What mean you, Joe?' inquired Dick, riding close up.

'D'ye see the little lumps on the shoulder o' each horse?' said Joe. 'Them's Injun's *feet*; an' if we don't want to lose our scalps we'd better make for the forest.'

Joe proved himself to be in earnest by wheeling round and making straight for the thick wood as fast as his horse could run. The others followed, driving the pack-horse before them.

The effect of this sudden movement on the so-called 'wild horses' was very remarkable, and to one unacquainted with the habits of the Camanchee Indians must have appeared almost supernatural. In the twinkling of an eye every steed had a rider on its back, and before the hunters had taken five strides in the direction of the forest, the whole band were in hot pursuit, yelling like furies.

The manner in which these Indians accomplish this feat is very singular, and implies great activity and strength of muscle on the part of the savages.

The Camanchees are low in stature, and usually are rather corpulent. In their movements on foot they are heavy and ungraceful, and they are, on the whole, a slovenly and unattractive race of men. But the instant they mount their horses they seem to be entirely changed, and surprise the spectator with the ease and elegance of their movements. Their great and distinctive peculiarity as horsemen is the power they have acquired of throwing themselves suddenly on either side of their horse's body, and clinging on in such a way that no part of them is visible from the other side save the foot by which they cling. In this manner they approach their enemies at full gallop, and, without rising again to the saddle, discharge their arrows at them over the horses' backs, or even under their necks.

This apparently magical feat is accomplished by means of a halter of horsehair, which is passed round under the neck of the horse and both ends braided into the mane, on the withers, thus forming a loop which hangs under the neck and against the breast. This being caught by the hand, makes a sling, into which the elbow falls, taking the weight of the body on the middle of the upper arm. Into this loop the rider drops suddenly and fearlessly, leaving his heel to hang over the horse's back to steady him, and also to restore him to his seat when desired.

By this stratagem the Indians had approached on the present occasion almost within rifle range before they were discovered, and it required the utmost speed of the hunters' horses to enable them to avoid being overtaken. One of the Indians, who was better mounted than his fellows, gained on the fugitives so much that he came within arrow range, but reserved his shaft until they were close on the margin of the wood, when, being almost alongside of Henri, he fitted an arrow to his bow. Henri's eye was upon him, however. Letting go the line of the

At the same moment the savage disappeared behind his horse.

pack-horse which he was leading, he threw forward his rifle; but at the same moment the savage disappeared behind his horse, and an arrow whizzed past the hunter's ear.

Henri fired at the horse, which dropped instantly, hurling the astonished Camanchee upon the ground, where he lay for some time insensible. In a few seconds pursued and pursuers entered the wood, where both had to advance with caution, in order to avoid being swept off by the overhanging branches of the trees.

Meanwhile the sultry heat increased considerably, and a rumbling noise, as if of distant thunder, was heard; but the flying hunters paid no attention to it, for the led horses gave them so much trouble, and retarded their flight so much, that the Indians were gradually and visibly gaining on them.

'We'll ha' to let the packs go,' said Joe, somewhat bitterly, as he looked over his shoulder. 'Our scalps'll pay for't, if we don't.'

Henri uttered a peculiar and significant *hiss* between his teeth, as he said: 'P'r'aps ve better stop and fight!'

Dick said nothing, being resolved to do exactly what Joe Blunt bid him; and Crusoe, for reasons best known to himself, also said nothing, but bounded along beside his master's horse, casting an occasional glance upwards to catch any signal that might be given.

They had passed over a considerable space of ground, and were forcing their way at the imminent hazard of their necks through a densely clothed part of the wood, when the sound above referred to increased, attracting the attention of both parties. In a few seconds the air was filled with a steady and continuous rumbling sound, like the noise of a distant cataract. Pursuers and fugitives drew rein instinctively, and came to a dead stand; while the rumbling increased to a roar, and evidently approached them rapidly, though as yet nothing to cause it could be seen, except that there was a dense, dark cloud overspreading the sky to the southward. The air was oppressively still and hot.

'What can it be?' inquired Dick, looking at Joe, who was gazing with an expression of wonder, not unmixed with concern, at the southern sky.

'Dun'no, boy. I've bin more in the woods than in the clearin' in my day, but I niver heerd the likes o' that.'

'It am like t'ondre,' said Henri; 'mais it nevair do stop.'

This was true. The sound was similar to continuous uninterrupted thunder. On it came with a magnificent roar that shook the very earth, and revealed itself at last in the shape of a mighty whirlwind. In a moment the distant woods bent before it, and fell like grass before the scythe. It was a whirling hurricane, accompanied by a deluge of rain such as none of the party had ever before witnessed. Steadily, fiercely, irresistibly it bore down upon them, while the crash of falling, snapping, and uprooting trees mingled with the dire artillery of that sweeping storm like the musketry on a battlefield.

'Follow me, lads!' shouted Joe, turning his horse and dashing at full speed towards a rocky eminence that offered shelter. But shelter was not needed. The storm was clearly defined. Its limits were as distinctly marked by its Creator as if it had been a living intelligence sent forth to put a belt of desolation round the world; and, although the edge of devastation was not five hundred yards from the rock behind which the hunters were stationed, only a few drops of ice-cold rain fell upon them.

It passed directly between the Camanchee Indians and their intended victims, placing between them a barrier which it would have taken days to cut through. The storm blew for an hour, then it travelled onward in its might, and was lost in the distance. Whence it came and whither it went none could tell, but far as the eye could see on either hand an avenue a quarter of a mile wide was cut through the forest. It had levelled everything with the dust; the very grass was beaten flat; the trees were torn, shivered, snapped across, and crushed; and the earth itself in many places was ploughed up and furrowed with deep scars. The chaos was indescribable, and it is probable that centuries will not quite obliterate the work of that single hour.

While it lasted, Joe and his comrades remained speechless and awe-stricken. When it passed, no Indians were to be seen. So our hunters remounted their steeds, and, with feelings of gratitude to God for having delivered them alike from savage foes and from the destructive power of the whirlwind, resumed their journey towards the Mustang Valley, and home.

NORTH FACE

Walter Unsworth

The little aeroplane seemed dwarfed by the enormous scale of the ice-draped mountain wall. Behind the controls crouched Colonel Ernst Udet, one of Germany's crack fighter aces from the First World War, a man noted for his cool daring. Besides him in the cockpit was Fritz Steuri, one of Grindelwald's most experienced mountain guides.

Udet needed all his skill on this bizarre mission. Time after time he took the plane right in towards the immense limestone wall until it seemed he would crash into it. Suddenly Steuri grabbed the pilot's arm and pointed towards the face.

Udet could just make out the figure of a man, knee-deep in snow, apparently waiting for something or somebody on that terrible mountain face. The pilot immediately veered away. He and Steuri had seen all they needed to see. The man on the mountain was dead. He had been standing in that grotesque position for a month: frozen to death.

At 2 a.m. on the morning of 21 August 1935, Max Seldmayer and Karl Mehringer of Munich had set out to climb the Eigerwand, biggest and most fearsome of the great Alpine faces. The natives who had given the mountain this name centuries before, had chosen well. On all sides it is a steep and difficult peak, awesome of aspect, but on one side in particular, where the north-west face frowns down on to Grindelwald, it is particularly savage: a great concave shield of rock and ice, 6,000 feet in height, as though some ancient giant had chopped away a slice of the mountain in anger. And the mountain in its turn roared revenge, for down this tremendous face poured avalanches and rockfalls. To even consider climbing it was regarded by many as the ultimate in folly.

Such a face, of course, held an irresistible attraction for the young climbers of Munich. Where others had shown the way on the Matterhorn and Grandes Jorasses, new tigers looked towards the final goal – for surely this was the last great Alpine problem?

Hans Lauper had climbed the Nordwand in 1932, but to the young climbers from Munich his route, though admittedly difficult, skirted the main problem. The real test lay further to the right, directly up the concave cauldron of the Eigerwand.

In order to understand the story of the attempts on the Eigerwand it is first of all necessary to know something of the structure of this remarkable face. The lower third consists of shelving limestone on which the snow lies in ribbons. Most people would regard this as steep rock but in fact it offers few difficulties to experienced climbers.

The first real obstacle is a high band of rock which runs across the face, perpendicular and even overhanging on the left, but more broken, though still steep, on the right where it joins the base of a steep side wall known as the Rote Fluh. This First Band, as it is called, contains two windows from the Jungfrau Railway which runs in a tunnel through the Eiger – the so-called Eigerwand Station, which looks out over the middle of the Face and a gallery window at a somewhat lower level below the Rote Fluh.

Above the First Band is the First Icefield, then another steep wall – the Second Band – above which is the large and steep Second Icefield.

So far the structure has been one of walls and shelves like some grotesque wedding cake, but the final third is quite different. It rises much more steeply, splaying out to right and left like a huge fan, and having as its base a small hanging glacier known as the Spider, because of the couloirs radiating out from it like legs.

Above the great wall the snows of the Summit Icefield lead to the top of the Eiger at 13,042 feet. In all, the Face is about 6,000 feet in height: the largest in the Alps.

Seldmayer and Mehringer were the first to try and climb the Eigerwand, though others before them had looked at it and turned away. At first they made excellent progress, climbing straight up the centre of the Face, watched by excited tourists and sceptical guides who had stationed themselves at the telescope of the Kleine Scheidegg Hotel, from where a good view of the Face can be obtained. That night – 21 August – the two Munich climbers bivouacked at 9,500 feet, having climbed 2,600 feet in the first day.

The next day, however, they made much slower progress because they were faced by the First Band. So steep was this that stones from the Face fell far outside the climbers, who were forced to haul up their sacks because of the difficulties. Nevertheless, that night they bivouacked at the top of the First Icefield – the conquest of the First Band was really quite an achievement.

On 23 August the two men could be seen moving slowly across the Second Icefield, often holding their rucksacks over their heads, as if to protect themselves from falling stones (there were no climbing helmets in those days!). Then the mists began to close in, and that night the weather broke. Seldmayer and Mehringer bivouacked somewhere on the exposed icefield.

The Eiger was living up to its reputation as a bad-weather mountain. For some unaccountable reason storms seem to gather round this peak even when the valley is bathed in sunshine, and sudden storms are as much feared by the Eiger climbers as are the falling stones and avalanches. For the whole of 24 August the storm raged round the mountain and even at the Kleine Scheidegg the temperature dropped to eight degrees below zero.

About noon on the 25th the mists lifted and the watchers at the telescope could see the two Germans moving towards the Flat Iron. They had not climbed far during the past twenty-four hours but incredibly they were still alive. The mist closed in again and fresh snow avalanches could be heard pouring down the cliffs.

They were never seen alive again. Though Seldmayer's brother arrived at Grindelwald and the mountain rescue expert Gramminger, the weather never once relented and there was nothing they could do. Not until three weeks later, when Udet flew so close to the Face, was the final outcome known. Seldmayer and Mehringer were the first of the Eigerwand's many victims.

The death of Seldmayer and Mehringer drew attention to the Eigerwand and by the start of the following season there were several parties ready to challenge the mountain. The newspapers, too, were interested and reporters hung around the Kleine Scheidegg Hotel seeking interviews from those likely to attempt the climb. By the beginning of July, two Germans, Herbst and Teufel, had already looked at the Face and sensibly retreated, much to the disgust of the reporters, but their place was taken by four remarkable young men: Edi Rainer and Willi Angerer from Austria and Anderl Hinterstoisser and Toni Kurz of Bavaria. All four were expert mountaineers, and they promised the reporters a good story.

In fact they rather enjoyed the publicity which the Eigerwand was attracting and, provoked by the journalists, they made some boasts which appeared as headlines – 'We must have the Wall or it must have us!' they declared. 'If we die,' said the handsome young Toni Kurz, 'you'll find the photographs in the rucksack!' Many mountaineers were shocked by these statements, but the truth is that the four men were very young and easily swayed by the sensation-seeking reporters.

On Monday, 6 July, Angerer and Rainer set off up the Face. They had studied the route taken by Seldmayer and Mehringer and decided that it was too direct – the idea of a frontal assault on the First Band did not appeal to them. Instead they went further to the right, where the Band was more broken, to the foot of the Rote Fluh. Here they bivouacked before coming down next day, declaring that conditions on the Face were not satisfactory for an assault.

Kurz and Hinterstoisser also made a reconnaissance during which the latter fell 120 feet, but was fortunate enough to land in deep, soft snow and escape uninjured.

The two Germans were in fact soldiers of the 100th Jäger Regiment on leave from their camp at Bad Reichenhall. When their Commanding Officer, Colonel Konrad, heard of their escapades he at once telephoned Grindelwald forbidding them to attempt the climb, but he was too late.

On Saturday, 18 July, the attempt was begun, the two ropes climbing separately at first, only combining at the foot of the Rote Fluh. They discovered that the broken part of the First Band could be climbed by means of a strenuous pitch, now known as the Difficult Crack, and this led them into an area of bare limestone slabs up which it was impossible to climb.

Their only chance of success was to traverse for over 100 feet to the left in order to gain the First Icefield but the traverse looked desperately thin. Anderl Hinterstoisser was the best rock climber of the four and he was pushed into the lead. He edged across the rock delicately, fixing pitons wherever he could and threading the rope through them so as to form a sort of handrail for the others. At last he reached the other side, and one by one his companions joined him.

When everyone was safely across, Hinterstoisser drew in the rope – and in so doing sealed their fate! Unknown to him, the traverse he had just made cannot be reversed *unless a rope is left in position.*

Not that they had any thought of retreat. The weather was fair and they made rapid progress up the First Icefield. On the rocks of the Second Band, however, the Austrian pair seemed to be in trouble. They stopped climbing and the Germans, who were in the lead, discovered that Angerer had been hit by a falling stone. They dropped down a rope to the injured man and pulled him up the difficult rocks, but this took so much time that they were forced to bivouac for the night.

There is no doubt that had Hinterstoisser and Kurz pressed on alone they might have been successful, for they were incredibly tough and skilful climbers. However, for better or worse, they had joined the Austrians and they had no thought of deserting them, though the latter must have urged them to go on whilst they themselves retreated.

No doubt all this was argued out in their bivouac that night, but the result was that next day both ropes continued the climb, across the big, steep, Second Icefield. Time and again Hinterstoisser and Kurz were forced to wait for the two Austrians, and it was nightfall when they reached the Flat Iron, just a short distance below the place where Karl Mehringer had frozen to death a year previously.

On Monday, 20 July, the Germans started up at 7 a.m. and reached the grotesquely named Death Bivouac, but the Austrians did not follow. It seemed that the injured Angerer was feeling worse. Hinterstoisser and Kurz climbed down again and there was a long conference as to their next move. Eventually it was decided that all should retreat.

They climbed down the Second Icefield quickly enough using the steps they had cut on the previous day, but the rocks of the Second Band took them hours to negotiate and darkness fell as they arrived at the top of the First Icefield. Once more they spent a night out on that awful wall.

On the morning of the 21st they descended the icefield and arrived at the traverse, only to discover, to their dismay, that it was impossible to reverse it. All morning they tried, each in turn, except the injured Angerer. As the weather deteriorated they were faced with the prospect of descending 600–700 feet of unknown rock.

Meanwhile, a railway worker called Albert von Allmen had been standing on the gallery of the Jungfrau railway window, listening to the climbers calling to one another. To Albert they seemed to be very near and directly overhead, so he shouted up. The climbers yodelled back and cried, 'All's well!' Albert expected them to arrive at his window any moment so he went into his little office in the railway tunnel and put on the kettle so that he could welcome them with a cup of tea.

But the kettle boiled and the tea was made, and there was still no sign of the climbers. Albert went out again to look for them. This time there were no yodels – just a lone voice crying, 'Help! Help!' It was the voice of young Toni Kurz.

At once the railwayman dashed into his cabin and telephoned for help. By sheer chance, three well-known guides, Hans Schlunegger, Christian and Adolf Rubi, were helping a film company to shoot scenes of the railway and the moment they were told of the affair they called for ropes and set off for the window. As guides they could not stand by whilst a fellow climber called for help – even though the Chief Guide of Grindelwald had warned all Eigerwand climbers not to expect help in case of accident.

From the window, the three guides traversed out on to the Eigerwand until they were about 300 feet below young Kurz. In a shouted conversation he rapidly explained what had happened. Hinterstoisser had unroped to explore the way down, had slipped and fallen to his death. Rainer too had come to grief and so had the injured Angerer, who was strangled by the rope and was hanging below Kurz. Within a few terrible minutes the Eigerwand had taken a savage revenge.

It was evening and there was nothing the guides could do. Already ice was forming on the rocks and it would be difficult enough to get back to the railway window.

'Can you last out the night?' they called.

'No! No!' screamed Kurz. 'Don't leave me!'

With his pitiful cries ringing in their ears, the guides retreated.

The night was bitterly cold. Kurz hung from his piton. Icicles eight inches long formed on the points of his crampons. He lost his left glove, and his hand and arm, exposed to the elements, gradually froze solid.

Incredibly, he was still alive next morning and his voice sounded as strong as ever. The three guides had been joined by another, Arnold Glatthard, but they could not reach the injured German. Kurz insisted that they could only reach him from above, but the rocks were now so icy that this was not possible.

Even so, the four guides had managed to climb to within 130 feet of Kurz, defying the icy rocks and the falling stones which periodically hummed down the Face. They asked him to let down a line to them, but he had none, and their attempts to shoot one up to him by means of rockets failed miserably.

To most men such a failure would have spelt the end of all hope, but Toni Kurz did not intend to give in without a fight. Despite the incredible hardships he had suffered, he was able to climb down to the body of the unfortunate Angerer and cut through the rope with his ice-axe, thus giving himself several extra feet. Grotesquely, Angerer's body remained where it was, frozen to the rock.

Kurz patiently began unravelling the spare rope, using one hand and his teeth. The three strands, tied together, would be sufficient to reach the guides below him . . . *it took Kurz five hours to do this.*

An avalanche came down, sweeping Angerer's body off the cliff, cascading like a waterfall over Kurz and the guides. When it had passed, Kurz was still there, still unravelling his one chance of rescue.

At last he managed to tie the strands into one long thin cord and lowered it to the guides. They tied on a rope which Kurz hauled up, but to everyone's dismay the rope was too short! Hurriedly the guides tied on another rope to the first.

With the amazing fortitude and patience he had shown throughout his ordeal, Toni Kurz made ready to abseil down the rope to safety. His injured arm made things very difficult, but after an hour of manoeuvring he began to descend. Foot by foot he slid down the rope and then, by the cruellest stroke of fortune, his abseil sling jammed in the knot which held the two ropes together!

By stretching up the guides could almost touch the soles of his boots. They could see now the terrible state he was in; a horrible travesty of a man, with his left arm swollen and sticking out at right-angles from his body and his face purple with frostbite. He was mumbling incoherently as he fiddled unsuccessfully with the knot.

'Try man! Keep trying!' the guides called desperately.

But for Toni Kurz the time for trying was over. He had fought for his life as few men have ever fought, but the Eigerwand had won in the end. Suddenly his voice became strong again. 'I'm finished!' he cried, and he swung lifeless from the rope.

★ ★ ★ ★

The Eigerwand tragedy of 1936 shocked the climbing world, and the Swiss Government, sensitive to public opinion, hurriedly placed a ban on any further attempts, though they withdrew it when it was pointed out that such a ban was virtually impossible to enforce. Nevertheless it was made quite plain to everyone that the Eigerwand was beyond the pale, and that no attempts would be made to rescue climbers who found themselves in difficulties on the Face.

Not that this warning had the slightest effect. At the beginning of the 1937 season the ace climbers from Italy, Austria and Germany gathered round the Kleine Scheidegg. The reporters, too, gathered, no doubt hoping for another dramatic tragedy with which to thrill their readers, but the real climbers were wise to them by this time and kept out of their way, and only a few sensation-seekers who carried ropes, and bragged about what they were going to do, looked for publicity.

The fact that the Eigerwand had been the death of so many good climbers, however, did have a sobering effect on the newcomers. They realized that this Face was more dangerous than anything yet attempted and that every attempt should be made to discover as much as possible about it before starting to climb it. Suddenly, Lauper's route of 1932 was remembered – surely this old climb would be an easy way of examining the Face at close quarters?

On 6 July the two Italian guides Giuseppe Piravano and Bruno Detassis climbed the Lauper Route, and found it much more difficult than they had bargained for. Conditions were bad, Piravano was injured by an avalanche, and it took all Detassis's skill and courage to get his companion to the safety of the Mittellegi Hut

Nine days later two climbers from Salzburg, Primas and Gollackner, also started up the Lauper Route. Conditions were even worse than they were for the Italians, but the two Austrians did not carry much in the way of provisions or equipment since they had no intention of completing the climb – they simply wanted to get a close look at the Eigerwand. Unfortunately for them, they found the Lauper Route so difficult that they were unable to retreat. They were forced into a series of terrible bivouacs and on 18 July the nineteen-year-old Gollackner died from exposure. His companion was more fortunate – he was rescued after spending five days on the mountain.

On the same day that the Austrians set out on their ill-fated climb, 15 July, a thirty-one-year-old German, Andreas Heckmair, was quietly leaving Grindelwald for home. He, too, had come to climb the Eigerwand, but his experience told him that the Face would not be in condition for many days and he could not afford the wait. Not for him the 'climb at all costs' way of thinking – Andreas Heckmair was a man who could weigh the prospects of success at a glance. He made up his mind to return the following year with perhaps better luck.

Also on the 15th, as Heckmair was leaving Grindelwald, two of his fellow countrymen, Vörg and Rebitsch, were just arriving. Both were acknowledged masters of north-wall climbing, especially the well-built and athletic Ludwig Vörg, who was known throughout the Eastern Alps as 'the Bivvy King' because of his ability to make a comfortable bivouac under the most appalling conditions. He had recently climbed the 7,000 feet sheer west face of Ushba in the Caucasus, and both he and Rebitsch were among the top rank of climbers.

On the 19th Rebitsch and Vörg set out to search for Primas and Gollackner who had not been seen for the last four days. Like the others, they found the Lauper Route difficult and they were forced to make a desperate traverse to the left across the steep slopes of the Mittellegi Ridge. They bivouacked on the open slopes below the hut and the next day arrived just in time to witness the rescued Primas being brought in by the guides. Rebitsch and Vörg volunteered to bring down the body of poor Gollackner.

It took the two Germans a week to recover from their rescue activities, but on the 27th they were ready to attempt the Eigerwand.

This was to be no rushed affair, for like the departed Heckmair, Rebitsch and Vörg were old hands at north-wall climbing and they knew every trick of the game. Their first concern was to build up a sort of base camp above the lower section of the Face, at the start of the serious climbing, and so they set out heavily laden, with no intention of going higher for the time being. Two other German climbers, Liebl and Rieger, had generously given up their own attempt to assist them.

As the four men toiled up the endless shelves of broken limestone, they suddenly came upon a grim warning. There was the mangled body of Anderl Hinterstoisser lying where it had fallen during the tragedy of 1936. Rebitsch and Vörg took their loads to the foot of the Rote Fluh, then returned to base. Temporarily their plans for the climb were abandoned, for once again it was their duty to bring down the remains of a dead comrade.

Two days later they set out with more supplies, but had no intentions of going too high because the weather looked stormy. The bad weather did not materialize, however, and the two men found themselves climbing rapidly to the foot of the Rote Fluh, which they reached by noon. Since there was still plenty of daylight left, they decided to explore further and soon came to the Difficult Crack.

The rock of the crack was polished and slippery, so they took off their nailed boots and climbed the pitch in bare feet! Soon they came across Hinterstoisser's pitons hammered into the rock the year before, and they realized at once that the delicate traverse to the left at this point was the key to the Face. They crossed it without trouble and christened it the Hinterstoisser Traverse, but they did not make the same mistake as their predecessor – they left a permanent handrail of rope across the tricky rock.

Just beyond the traverse, Rebitsch and Vörg came upon a perfect little niche for a bivouac, which they called the Swallow's Nest, and here they dumped their gear, returning to Kleine Scheidegg before dark.

This was really a tremendous performance and it demonstrated that a competent pair of climbers could go beyond the Hinterstoisser Traverse and return quite safely in the course of a single day.

Unfortunately, for weeks after that the weather was bad. The two men did some other climbs whenever there was a reasonable break, but it was never sufficiently settled for them to attempt the Eigerwand. One by one the other Eiger hopefuls drifted away, until by the second week of August only Rebitsch and Vörg remained. The reporters, convinced that the season's attempts had ended, also left the scene.

On 11 August the two Germans began their attempt on the Eigerwand. By 10.30 am they were at their first supply point below the Rote Fluh. They carried gear from it to the Swallow's Nest, then returned for more, finally bivouacking at the Nest at 5 pm.

Next day they were quickly away and by 7 pm had reached Death Bivouac where they half expected to discover Mehringer's frozen corpse and were relieved to find it had gone. They could have bivouacked, but preferred instead to cross the Third Icefield to the great Ramp which was such an obvious line of attack. On the way, however, they were caught in a hailstorm and forced to bivouac on the icefield.

On the following morning the weather signs were so bad that they decided to retreat, and by evening they were once more established in the Swallow's Nest. Next day they came down and departed for home.

Their performance on the Face had been quite remarkable. They had crossed the Hinterstoisser Traverse several times in both directions, they had been higher than any previous party, and they had retreated with complete assurance. Rebitsch and Vörg had conclusively shown that the Eigerwand could be climbed, if tackled by experienced climbers.

The season of 1938 opened disastrously with the death of two young Italians, Sandri and Menti, who foolishly tried the Face in June, before good weather could be expected. They did not even reach the Difficult

Crack before they fell to their deaths.

Among the Germans there had been something of a reshuffle caused by Rebitsch being chosen as deputy leader of an expedition to Nanga Parbat in the Himalaya. Vörg had to seek a new partner, and his choice happily fell on Andreas Heckmair, the vastly experienced and skilful climber who had already played a part in the attempts on the Grandes Jorasses. As a team they were superb: Vörg, fit and strong, an athlete through and through; Heckmair, thin, stern-countenanced and looking older than his thirty-two years. For a climb such as the Eigerwand it would have been difficult at that time to choose a better combination.

During the discussions about the proposed attempt it became apparent that both men saw the problem in the same light. The Eigerwand was something special, something bigger and more serious than other nordwands and therefore only likely to be climbed by the best climbers using the finest equipment. The two things went together – but Heckmair and Vörg were as destitute as usual, with no money to spare for expensive gear.

By a stroke of good fortune a sponsor came forward at the last moment: a man who sympathized with their aims and ambitions and was willing to support them with money. Suddenly the two Germans found they could have any gear they required and they set about equipping themselves for the climb.

Another thing which worried them, however, was the pressure of newspaper reporters at the Kleine Scheidegg. Once it became common knowledge that Vörg was returning for another attempt, the reporters would pounce on them and harry them mercilessly. Remembering the bad feeling which Kurz and his companions had roused in 1936, Heckmair and Vörg wanted to have nothing to do with the Press. But how to get to the Face, and stay there for days on end, without being recognized? Their ruse was simple: because all the Eigerwand climbers were penniless they lived in tents and bivouacs on the meadows below the mountain, and it was on these that the newsmen concentrated. Heckmair and Vörg, with their new-found affluence, stayed in a small hotel at the Kleine Scheidegg, pretending to be tourists! Their presence went completely undetected.

Meanwhile, others had appeared to take part in the struggle for the

Eigerwand, and in particular two teams of Austrians, Fraissl and Brankowski from Vienna and Heinrich Harrer and Fritz Kasparek. They concentrated on 'training climbs' such as the Mittellegi Ridge and the Mönch north face in order to get to know the condition of the mountains. Kasparek and Harrer then took a sack of provisions to the foot of the Rote Fluh, and on the morning of 21 July began their attempt in earnest. As they climbed the lower pitches they could hear another party behind them, and they knew it would be Fraissl and Brankowski.

They quickly reached the gear they had dumped and now heavily laden – one sack weighed fifty-five pounds – they made their way towards the Difficult Crack. Suddenly they stopped in surprise, for there, bivouacking in a cave, were two strangers. Heckmair and Vörg, eluding everybody, had started the climb on the previous afternoon! Soon all six climbers were gathered together at the bivouac cave. The question was, who was to continue – six on the Eigerwand at once was considered too many. Generously, Heckmair and Vörg volunteered to go down, using as an excuse the onset of doubtful weather. After all their preparation it must have been a bitter disappointment.

The four Austrians watched the Germans begin their descent and then turned to continue the climb. Despite their loads, Kasparek and Harrer quickly outpaced the other two. Fraissl and Brankowski, as it happened, were having trouble – they had been hit by stonefall before reaching the Difficult Crack and had decided to retire. Though they did not know it at the time, Harrer and Kasparek had the climb to themselves!

They made very good time, although they were forced to sack-haul at the Difficult Crack and they found the Hinterstoisser Traverse coated in ice. At the Swallow's Nest they left a supply of gear in case of retreat and then pushed on up the Second Band. That night they bivouacked at the foot of the Second Icefield.

On the morning of 22 July the two Austrians continued on their way, climbing up the steep ice of the Second Icefield. Kasparek had only old-fashioned ten-point crampons to help him, but poor Harrer had no crampons at all. They had to cut careful steps all the way, trying at the same time to ignore the sinister whine of falling stones.

As they reached the top of the icefield they looked down and saw two climbers almost running up the steps they had just made. Already, the Austrians had realized that Fraissal and Brankowski must have retreated – the two who now approached could only be Heckmair and Vörg. And so it proved. The Germans, on learning that Kasparek and Harrer were alone on the Face, had literally raced up to join them.

Because of their superior equipment and greater experience, the German pair went in front, with Heckmair leading. Kasparek and Harrer followed as a separate team.

The Flat Iron and Death Bivouac were passed, and for the first time ever the climbers found themselves on the huge Ramp, a series of icy slabs sloping diagonally across the Face. The climbing was difficult and Kasparek gave a sudden warning cry as his foot slipped. He slithered and then dropped fifty feet, but Harrer held him firm on the rope. Fortunately Kasparek escaped with nothing worse than an injured hand. They all bivouacked for the night at the top of the Ramp.

Above the Ramp, the climb entered into a huge icy chimney which was obviously going to prove difficult. Inch by inch Andreas Heckmair wriggled up it until, just as it seemed he might succeed, his hold gave way and he fell, to be held dangling from a well-placed piton.

At his second attempt he was more successful, and before long all four men were together again looking at the next formidable obstacle: a thirty feet bulge of green ice.

There was no way round this forbidding pitch and the four men looked at one another in consternation. On no other climb had they ever met anything so remotely difficult: how does one climb ice which is overhanging? Heckmair began his attempt.

At first he banged an ice piton into the underside of the bulge and swung up on it, using a rope loop or sling. He next had to rely on some brittle icicles hanging from the bulge, but the moment he put his weight on these they snapped off and he pitched from the ice, once again saved by his piton.

Fortunately he was uninjured and he went at the problem again. This time he discovered a fragile column of ice which he could use as a handle whilst he leant away from the bulge. It gave him just enough room to cut some handholds and pull himself round the lower part of the obstacle. How he managed to balance, the others could only guess, but balance he did whilst he cleverly hammered home a piton into the top of the ice. He put his rope through the piton and with the others

Kasparek gave a sudden cry as his foot slipped.

pulling he managed to hoist himself further. A few smart blows with the axe on top of the bulge, a mighty heave, and he was up!

Heckmair had made a remarkable lead, but it was doubtful whether, of the second pair, either Kasparek or Harrer could lead it with their inferior footwear, so the Germans dropped down a rope with which to pull them up. The four men remained united for the remainder of the climb.

They now realized that the Ramp and Chimney had taken them too far to the left and that it was essential to traverse right towards the centre of the Face, where the hanging glacier of the Spider awaited them. This they managed along an airy ledge, now known as the Traverse of the Gods, and before long they were climbing up the steep central rib of the Spider itself.

At precisely this moment the weather changed and one of those sudden storms for which the Eiger is notorious flung its fury against the North Face. Hail and snow lashed the four climbers as they struggled up the Spider and then, it seemed, the whole world came apart. Torrents of snow roared down from the upper slopes of the mountain, cascading into the natural funnel of the Spider and breaking like huge waves over the trapped men. It seemed certain that they would be either swept from the Face or suffocated under the terrible press of snow, but when at last the avalanche was over, they were still there, hanging grimly on to their ice-axes, heads bowed against the storm.

That night, as they bivouacked on the upper rim of the Spider icefield, they were thankful to be still alive. The next day, they knew, would be one of victory or disaster.

To escape from the clutches of the Spider it was necessary for them to climb one of its 'legs', which are really gullies leading to the summit snowfield. None are easy, and as Heckmair led off next morning, they were all in doubt about the outcome. The storm had not abated. The flurries of snow whipped into their faces, making it impossible to see, and the rocks were coated with ice.

The climbing was so difficult that there was seldom room for more than two to stand together, and consequently the party was spread out, with communication almost impossible due to the storm.

At one point there was near disaster. Heckmair fell off, tumbled into Vörg who was holding the rope for him, and knocked his companion off too. Using their axes and crampons both managed to stop themselves from sliding very far, which was just as well, for when they climbed back to their stance they discovered they had pulled their belay piton completely out!

It now became a race against time. They knew they were within striking distance of the top and they had no desire to spend another night bivouacking in a blizzard. From above, during breaks in the gale, they occasionally heard shouts, but they did not reply because they were in no immediate danger and their shouts might have been misinterpreted as cries for help. The men shouting were, in fact, their friends Fraissl and Brankowski, and the guide Hans Schlunegger, who had come to search for them. These gallant friends returned to the valley convinced the party was lost!

At last the four weary men came to the summit snows of the Eiger, but even at this stage the mountain had not done with them. The storm had made the snow deep and soft and likely to avalanche, and it was only by exercising extreme caution that they managed to climb it safely. In fact, so blind were they due to the storm that the leaders almost walked over the opposite edge of the mountain!

At 3.30 pm on 24 July 1938, Heckmair, Vörg, Kasparek and Harrer reached the summit of the Eiger having climbed the notorious Eigerwand. They staggered down the easy slopes of the normal route, down, down, like weary automatons until the storm gave way to mist.

Suddenly, in front of them, a young boy appeared out of the mist. He looked awestruck for a moment and then he gasped, 'Have you come off the Face?'

'Yes,' they said wearily. 'Off the Face.'

The boy let out a yell and went running down the slopes. 'They're coming! They're coming! They've done it!' he cried.

The reporters had been beaten to the news after all.

BATTLE OF THE WITCHDOCTORS

H. Rider Haggard

Allan Quartermain's native name was 'Macumazahn' which means 'he who sleeps with one eye open'. Here he tells of his first meeting with the wily old witchdoctor Indaba-zimbi . . .

Among the Kaffirs was an old fellow named Indaba-zimbi, which, being translated, means 'tongue of iron'. I suppose he got this name from his strident voice and exhaustless eloquence. This man was a great character in his way. He had been a noted witch-doctor among a neighbouring tribe, and I met him under the following circumstances...

Two years before my father's death I had occasion to search the country round for some lost oxen. After a long and useless quest it occurred to me that I had better go to the place where the oxen were bred by a Kaffir chief, whose name I forget, but whose kraal was about fifty miles from our station. There I journeyed, and found the oxen safe at home. The chief entertained me handsomely, and on the following morning I went to pay my respects to him before leaving, and was somewhat surprised to find a collection of some hundreds of men and women sitting round him anxiously watching the sky in which the thunder-clouds were banking up in a very ominous way.

'You had better wait, white man,' said the chief, 'and see the rain-doctors fight the lightning.'

I inquired what he meant, and learned that this man, Indaba-zimbi, had for some years occupied the position of wizard-in-chief to the tribe, although he was not a member of it, having been born in the country now known as Zululand. But a son of the chief's, a man of about thirty, had lately set up as a rival in supernatural powers. This irritated Indaba-zimbi beyond measure, and a quarrel ensued between the two witch-doctors that resulted in a challenge to trial by lightning being given and accepted. These were the conditions. The rivals must await the coming of a serious thunderstorm, no ordinary tempest would serve their turn. Then, carrying assegais in their hands, they must take their stand within fifty paces of each other upon a certain patch of ground where the big thunderbolts were observed to strike continually, and by the exercise of their occult powers and invocations to the lightning, must strive to avert death from themselves and bring it on their rival. The terms of this singular match had been arranged a month previously, but no storm worthy of the occasion had arisen. Now the local weather-prophets believed it to be brewing.

I inquired what would happen if neither of the men were struck, and was told that they must then wait for another storm. If they escaped the second time, however, they would be held to be equal in power, and be jointly consulted by the tribe upon occasions of importance.

The prospect of being a spectator of so unusual a sight overcame my desire to be gone, and I accepted the chief's invitation to see it out. Before mid-day I regretted it, for though the western heavens grew darker and darker, and the still air heralded the coming of the storm, yet it did not come. By four o'clock, however, it became obvious that it must burst soon – at sunset, the old chief said, and in the company of the whole assembly I moved down to the place of combat. The kraal was built on the top of a hill, and below it the land sloped gently to the banks of a river about half a mile away. On the hither side of the bank was the piece of land that was, the natives said, 'loved of the lightning.' Here the magicians took up their stand, while the spectators grouped themselves on the hillside about two hundred yards away – which was, I thought, rather too near to be pleasant. When we had sat there for a while my curiosity overcame me, and I asked leave of the chief to go down and inspect the arena. He said I might do so at my own risk. I told him that the fire from above would not hurt white men, and went to find that the spot was a bed of iron ore, thinly covered with grass, which of course accounted for its attracting the lightning from the storms as they travelled along the line of the river. At each end of this iron-stone area were placed the combatants, Indaba-zimbi facing the east, and his rival the west, and before each there burned a little fire made of some scented root. Moreover they were dressed in all the paraphernalia of their craft, snakeskins, fish bladders, and I know not what beside, while round their necks hung circlets of baboons' teeth and bones from human hands. First I went to the western end where the chief's son stood. He was pointing with his assegai towards the advancing storm, and invoking it in a voice of great excitement.

'Come, fire, and lick up Indaba-zimbi!

Hear me, Storm Devil, and lick Indaba-zimbi with your red tongue!

Spit on him with your rain!

Whirl him away in your breath!

Make him as nothing – melt the marrow in his bones!

Run into his heart and burn away the lies!

Show all the people who is the true Witch Finder!

Let me not be put to shame in the eyes of this white man!'

Thus he spoke, or rather chanted, and all the while rubbed his broad chest – for he was a very fine man – with some filthy compound of medicine or *mouti*.

After a while, getting tired of his song, I walked across the iron-stone, to where Indaba-zimbi sat by his fire. He was not chanting at all, but his performance was much more impressive. It consisted in staring at the eastern sky, which was perfectly clear of cloud, and every now and again beckoning at it with his finger, then turning round to point with the assegai towards his rival. For a while I looked at him in silence. He was a curious wizened man, apparently over fifty years of age, with thin hands that looked as tough as wire. His nose was much sharper than is usual among these races, and he had a queer habit of holding his head sideways like a bird when he spoke, which, in addition to the humour that lurked in his eye, gave him a most comical appearance. Another strange thing about him was that he had a single white lock of hair among his black wool. At last I spoke to him:

'Indaba-zimbi, my friend,' I said, 'you may be a good witch-doctor, but you are certainly a fool. It is no good beckoning at the blue sky while your enemy is getting a start with the storm.'

'You may be clever, but don't think you know everything, white man,' the old fellow answered, in a high, cracked voice, and with something like a grin.

'They call you Iron-tongue,' I went on; 'you had better use it, or the Storm Devil won't hear you.'

'The fire from above runs down iron,' he answered, 'so I keep my tongue quiet. Oh, yes, let him curse away, I'll put him out presently. Look now, white man.'

I looked, and in the eastern sky there grew a cloud. At first it was small, though very black, but it gathered with extraordinary rapidity.

This was odd enough, but as I had seen the same thing happen before it did not particularly astonish me. It is by no means unusual in Africa for two thunderstorms to come up at the same time from different points of the compass.

'You had better get on, Indaba-zimbi,' I said, 'the big storm is coming along fast, and will soon eat up that baby of yours,' and I pointed to the west.

'Babies sometimes grow to giants, white man,' said Indaba-zimbi, beckoning away vigorously. 'Look now at my cloud-child.'

I looked; the eastern storm was spreading itself from earth to sky, and in shape resembled an enormous man. There was its head, its shoulders, and its legs; yes, it was like a huge giant travelling across the heavens. The light of the setting sun escaping from beneath the lower edge of the western storm shot across the intervening space in a sheet of splendour, and, lighting upon the advancing figure of cloud, wrapped its middle in hues of glory too wonderful to be described; but beneath and above this glowing belt his feet and head were black as jet. Presently, as I watched, an awful flash of light shot from the head of the cloud, circled it about as though with a crown of living fire, and vanished.

'Aha,' chuckled old Indaba-zimbi, 'my little boy is putting on his man's ring,' and he tapped the gum ring on his own head, which natives assume when they reach a certain age and dignity. 'Now, white man, unless you are a bigger wizard than either of us you had better clear off, for the fire-fight is about to begin.'

I thought this sound advice.

'Good luck go with you, my black uncle,' I said. 'I hope you don't feel the iniquities of a misspent life weighing on you at the last.'

129

'You look after yourself, and think of your own sins, young man,' he answered, with a grim smile, and taking a pinch of snuff, while at that very moment a flash of lightning, I don't know from which storm, struck the ground within thirty paces of me. That was enough for me, I took to my heels, and as I went I heard old Indaba-zimbi's dry chuckle of amusement.

I climbed the hill till I came to where the chief was sitting with his indunas, or headmen, and sat down near to him. I looked at the man's face and saw that he was intensely anxious for his son's safety, and by no means confident of the young man's powers to resist the magic of Indaba-zimbi. He was talking in a low voice to the induna next to him. I affected to take no notice and to be concentrating my attention on the novel scene before me; but in those days I had very quick ears, and caught the drift of the conversation.

'Hearken!' the chief was saying, 'if the magic of Indaba-zimbi prevails against my son I will endure him no more. Of this I am sure, that when he has slain my son he will slay me, me also, and make himself chief in my place. I fear Indaba-zimbi. *Ou!*'

'Black One,' answered the induna, 'wizards die as dogs die, and, once dead, dogs bark no more.'

'And once dead,' said the chief, 'wizards work no more spells,' and he bent and whispered in the induna's ear, looking at the assegai in his hand as he whispered.

'Good, my father, good!' said the induna, presently. 'It shall be done tonight, if the lightning does not do it first.'

'A bad lookout for old Indaba-zimbi,' I said to myself. 'They mean to kill him.' Then I thought no more of the matter for a while, the scene before me was too tremendous.

The two storms were rapidly rushing together. Between them was a gulf of blue sky, and from time to time flashes of blinding light passed across this gulf, leaping from cloud to cloud. I remember that they reminded me of the story of the heathen god Jove and his thunderbolts. The storm that was shaped like a giant and ringed with the glory of the sinking sun made an excellent Jove, and I am sure that the bolts which leapt from it could not have been surpassed even in mythological times. Oddly enough, as yet the flashes were not followed by thunder. A deadly stillness lay upon the place, the cattle stood silently on the hillside, even the natives were awed to silence. Dark shadows crept along the bosom of the hills, the river to the right and left was hidden in wreaths of cloud, but before us and beyond the combatants it shone like a line of silver beneath the narrowing space of open sky. Now the western tempest was scrawled all over with lines of intolerable light, while the inky head of the cloud-giant to the east was continually suffused with a white and deadly glow that came and went in pulses, as though a blood of flame was being pumped into it from the heart of the storm.

The silence deepened and deepened, the shadows grew blacker and blacker, then suddenly all nature began to moan beneath the breath of an icy wind. On sped the wind; the smooth surface of the river was ruffled by it into little waves, the tall grass bowed low before it, and in its wake came the hissing sound of furious rain.

Ah! the storms had met. From each there burst an awful blaze of dazzling flame, and now the hill on which we sat rocked at the noise of the following thunder. The light went out of the sky, darkness fell suddenly on the land, but not for long. Presently the whole landscape grew vivid in the flashes, it appeared and disappeared, now everything was visible for miles, now even the men at my side vanished in the blackness. The thunder rolled and cracked and pealed like the trump of doom, whirlwinds tore round, lifting dust and even stones high into the air, and in a low, continuous undertone rose the hiss of the rushing rain.

I put my hand before my eyes to shield them from the terrible glare, and looked beneath it towards the lists of iron-stone. As flash followed flash, from time to time I caught sight of the two wizards. They were slowly advancing towards one another, each pointing at his foe with the assegai in his hand. I could see their every movement, and it seemed to me that the chain lightning was striking the iron-stone all round them.

Suddenly the thunder and lightning ceased for a minute, everything grew black, and, except for the rain, silent.

'It is over one way or the other, chief,' I called out into the darkness.

'Wait, white man, wait!' answered the chief, in a voice thick with anxiety and fear.

Hardly were the words out of his mouth when the heavens were lit

The chief's son seemed to be wrapped in the lightning.

up again till they literally seemed to flame. There were the men, not ten paces apart. A great flash fell between them, I saw them stagger beneath the shock. Indaba-zimbi recovered himself first – at any rate when the next flash came he was standing bolt upright, pointing with his assegai towards his enemy. The chief's son was still on his legs, but he was staggering like a drunken man, and the assegai had fallen from his hand.

Darkness! then again a flash, more fearful, if possible, than any that had gone before. To me it seemed to come from the east, right over the head of Indaba-zimbi. At that instant I saw the chief's son wrapped, as it were, in the heart of it. Then the thunder pealed, the rain burst over us like a torrent, and I saw no more.

The worst of the storm was done, but for a while the darkness was so dense that we could not move, nor, indeed, was I inclined to leave the safety of the hillside where the lightning was never known to strike, and venture down to the iron-stone. Occasionally there still came flashes, but, search as we would, we could see no trace of either of the wizards. For my part, I believed that they were both dead. Now the clouds slowly rolled away down the course of the river, and with them went the rain; and now the stars shone out in their wake.

'Let us go and see,' said the old chief, rising and shaking the water from his hair. 'The fire-fight is ended, let us go and see who has conquered.'

I rose and followed him, dripping as though I had swum a hundred yards with my clothes on, and after me came all the people of the kraal.

We reached the spot; even in that light I could see where the iron-stone had been split and fused by the thunderbolts. While I was staring about me, I suddenly heard the chief, who was on my right, give a low moan, and saw the people cluster round him. I went up and looked. There, on the ground, lay the body of his son. It was a dreadful sight. The hair was burnt off his head, the copper rings upon his arms were fused, the assegai handle which lay near was literally shivered into threads, and, when I took hold of his arm, it seemed to me that every bone of it was broken.

The men with the chief stood gazing silently, while the women wailed.

'Great is the magic of Indaba-zimbi!' said a man, at length. The

133

chief turned and struck him a heavy blow with the kerrie in his hand.

'Great or not, thou dog, he shall die,' he cried, 'and so shalt thou if thou singest his praises so loudly.'

I said nothing, but thinking it probable that Indaba-zimbi had shared the fate of his enemy, I went to look. But I could see nothing of him, and at length, being thoroughly chilled with the wet, starting back to my waggon to change my clothes. On reaching it, I was rather surprised to see a strange Kaffir seated on the driving-box wrapped up in a blanket.

'Hullo! come out of that,' I said.

The figure on the box slowly unrolled the blanket, and with great deliberation took a pinch of snuff.

'It was a good fire-fight, white man, was it not?' said Indaba-zimbi, in his high, cracked voice. 'But he never had a chance against me, poor boy. He knew nothing about it. See, white man, what comes of presumption in the young. It is sad, very sad, but I made the flashes fly, didn't I?'

'You old humbug,' I said, 'unless you are careful you will soon learn what comes of presumption in the old, for your chief is after you with an assegai, and it will take all your magic to dodge that.'

'Now you don't say so,' said Indaba-zimbi, clambering off the waggon with rapidity; 'and all because of this wretched upstart. There's gratitude for you, white man. I expose him, and they want to kill me. Well, thank you for the hint. We shall meet again before long,' and he was gone like a shot, and not too soon, for just then some of the chief's men came up to the waggon.

On the following morning I started homewards. The first face I saw on arriving at the station was that of Indaba-zimbi.

'How do you do, Macumazahn?' he said, holding his head on one side and nodding his white lock. 'I hear you are Christians here, and I want to try a new religion. Mine must be a bad one seeing that my people wanted to kill me for exposing an impostor.'

A FAMILY OF CASTAWAYS

J. R. Wyss

The storm had lasted for six days – and even then, far from subsiding, it seemed to gather even greater fury. We were carried far out of our course towards the southeast, and it became quite impossible for the captain to take any reckonings, or to determine our position. The masts had snapped and had been thrown overboard, and the ship began to leak terribly. Everyone on board gave themselves up for lost, and fell on their knees, begging God to have mercy on them in their terrible plight. My wife and my four young sons gathered close to me.

Suddenly above the terrible din of the storm I heard the welcome cry: 'Land! Land!' At the selfsame moment the ship shuddered violently and there was a long and terrible rending of the timbers. The waves beat furiously over us, and I realized that the ship had wedged itself firmly between the rocks.

'All is lost; lower the boats!' cried a voice, which I recognized as the captain's. At first we could scarcely believe it. Then, 'Lost!' cried the children, throwing themselves, terrified, into my arms. I was desperately anxious to reassure them as much as I could, so I exclaimed:

'Try to be calm, boys – after all, land is not far off. God will surely show us some way of saving ourselves. I will go up on deck and see what can be done.'

But when I gained the deck I found myself battered half senseless by the tremendous seas which were already sweeping the ship. The spray completely blinded me and I had to grope my way to a fairly sheltered position before I could look around me at all. Then I saw that all the lifeboats had already been launched, and that the crew had left the ship. Just at that moment a sailor cut loose the last boat. They had forgotten us!

I called out, I screamed to them, but my voice was drowned in the roar of the tempest, and I saw to my horror that we had been abandoned with the wreck.

In the midst of all our troubles I was relieved to see that the ship had so wedged itself among the rocks that the poop was high in the air. This meant that our cabin was well above water level. At the same time, through the driving rain and spray, I could make out a lowlying coast away to the southward, which, desolate though it looked, seemed suddenly the most desirable place in the world.

I made my way back to my family, trying to sound as calm as I could – though I was really more afraid than I had ever been before.

'Cheer up!' I cried. 'All is not lost yet! Part of the ship is still well above the water-line. By tomorrow the seas will probably have gone down a little, and we shall be able to get ashore somehow.'

This put the boys in good spirits, and they accepted my assurances quite unquestioningly, with all the confidence of youth.

I could see that my wife fully appreciated how finely our lives hung in the balance, but at the same time I knew that her trust in God was as steadfast as ever. 'We have a terrible night ahead of us,' she said. 'Let us have something to eat; food will strengthen our bodies and fortify our spirits.'

So night fell. The storm still beat down upon the ship as furiously as ever. Every moment I feared that she would fall to pieces.

My wife prepared a simple meal which the boys ate ravenously. Then the younger ones went to bed, but Fritz, the eldest, the only one who fully realized the gravity of the situation, sat up with us.

'Papa,' he said, 'I have been trying to think of some way of reaching land. If only we could find some way of supporting my mother and my brothers in the water, you and I could swim ashore without assistance.'

'Your idea is a good one,' I said. 'Let us try putting it into practice.'

We collected a pile of empty cork barrels, large enough to keep a person afloat. These we put ready so that they could be fastened in pairs under the arms of each of the children and of my wife at a moment's notice. This done, we tied round our waists some knives, rope, flints, and a few other necessities which we should need when we reached land, so that we should be all ready to swim for our lives, should the ship go to pieces during the night.

Then Fritz, who was very tired, went to bed. But my wife and I kept watch till daybreak.

We passed the hours in prayer and in making all kinds of plans. How thankful we were when morning dawned! I noticed that the storm was subsiding. As soon as it was light I went up on deck. The wind had lulled a good deal and the seas were going down. The sun was just rising, and the horizon was clearing rapidly.

I felt suddenly more cheerful, and called my wife and children to come on deck. The younger boys were most surprised when they found we were all alone on the ship.

'Where have the sailors gone?' they asked. 'Why didn't they take us with them? What in the world will happen to us now?'

'Our companions were so panic-stricken that they scarcely knew what they were doing,' I explained. 'They sailed away without remembering us, leaving us alone to God's protection. But look, the sky is clear and land is not far off; perhaps our abandonment may prove a blessing in disguise. Let us try to think out a plan of action. God helps those who help themselves, remember.'

Fritz, as adventurous as ever, still wanted us to try swimming to land; but Ernest, my second son, who was about twelve years old, an intelligent but rather nervous boy, was terrified of doing this, and proposed that we should build a raft instead.

I pointed out that such a raft, besides taking a long time to construct, would be very difficult to steer, even if we had all the right materials handy, and so we abandoned the idea.

'Well,' I said, 'before we do anything else, let us explore the ship thoroughly; while we are doing that we can all try to think out the best way of getting ashore. Afterwards, we will reassemble on the deck, bringing with us anything useful that we have found.'

Everyone set off in different directions on a tour of discovery. I went to the store-room, to see for myself what food and water we had on board. Fritz visited the ammunition-room, and brought back guns, pistols, powder, and shot. Ernest explored the carpenter's shop, and came out with a bundle of tools and nails. Little Francis, the youngest, who was only six years old, but who was anxious to help too, showed us a box of fish-hooks and lines that he had found. Fritz and Ernest teased him about them, but I praised his good sense, for I knew we might soon have to exist on the fish we could catch. As for Jack, my third son, a bright boy of ten, he went straight for the captain's cabin. As he opened the door, two huge dogs sprang at him. Hunger had made them quite tame, however, and they allowed Jack to lead them along by the ears.

My wife told me she had found a cow, an ass, two goats, six sheep, a ram, and a sow. She had fed them all, but only just in time, for the poor beasts had had nothing to eat or drink for two days.

'All these things will be most useful,' I said. 'Except for Jack's dogs, which are bound to eat more than they are worth themselves.'

'But, Papa, I thought they would help us with our hunting when we get ashore,' he objected.

'Very true,' I agreed. 'But, remember, we are not on dry land yet. Have *you* any idea how we can get there?'

'Well,' said he, 'why can't we sit ourselves in some of the big tubs here, and float ourselves ashore that way? I have often gone sailing in a tub on Grandpapa's pond at home in Switzerland.'

'Why, that is a splendid idea!' I cried. 'Quickly, let us get the saw, the hammer, and the nails, and see what we can do.'

So we all went down into the hold, where I had already noticed several empty casks floating about .We managed to hoist four of them on to the lower deck, which was just above the level of the water. The casks were strongly made and hooped with iron, and were just right for our purpose. With Fritz's help I sawed each one in two.

We now had eight tubs. Then I looked out a long, flexible plank, and we placed the eight tubs along it, in a line, leaving a piece of plank protruding beyond the tubs at each end, to act as a sort of keel. Next we nailed the tubs first to the plank, and then to each other, to make them firmer, and then we nailed two other planks along the sides of the tubs. The result was a rough sort of boat divided into eight compartments. I was confident that it was fit to sail a short distance, provided that the sea was calm.

But, unfortunately, when our boat was finished, it was so heavy, that, try as we could, we were quite unable to launch it.

I called for a screw-jack, and Fritz, who had seen one about somewhere, ran to fetch it. Then I slid some wooden rollers under the boat, and, with the help of the screw-jack, we managed to get it moving.

Then I fastened a rope to the boat, tying the free end to the wreck itself. We put more rollers underneath, and applied the screw-jack hard. To our delight, the boat rushed into the sea – indeed, had I not taken the precaution of fastening it to our ship with a rope, it would have sailed right out of reach. At first the boat did not float quite upright, but by putting some heavy articles into the tubs to act as ballast, it regained its equilibrium. The boys were thrilled with it, and wanted to embark at once. However, I could see that it was not yet safe enough, for the least movement was liable to overturn it. Then I remembered the floats which Red Indians use for steadying their boats, and I decided to apply the same principle to our little ship.

So I took two spars, which I fixed at the stem and stern of my boat, in such a way as to enable us to turn them to right or left, as we required. To each of these I attached a small empty cask, which served to keep the float steady. The boat now floated upright and evenly. It only remained for us to decide the best way of getting clear of the wreck; so I got into one of the tubs and steered the boat towards an opening in the wreckage, then, with a hatchet and saw, I cut my way out, and that done, we set about making some oars.

It was very late when we finished work and it was obviously impossible to try to reach land that evening. This meant staying another night on the wreck, although we knew only too well that it might start breaking up at any moment. We all ate a hearty supper, for which we were more than ready, for we had been so busy, that we had hardly had time to eat all day.

I did not go to bed myself until I had put ready the boys' swimming-jackets, so that they should be ready to swim for their lives if the necessity arose. Then I advised my wife to put on one of the sailor's clothes, for these would be much more practical than her own under the present circumstances. After a little hesitation she agreed, and she soon appeared dressed like one of the young midshipmen. She felt rather awkward at first, but I complimented her on her appearance and cheered her up by reminding her that we should be going ashore next day. She went to her hammock, and slept peacefully.

The night passed without incident.

★　　★　　★　　★

By daybreak we were all wide awake; we were much too excited to sleep well. After morning prayers, I called the children together. 'We are now, God willing, going to try to reach a place of safety,' I said. 'First of all we must feed the animals and leave them enough food to last them several days. I hope we shall be able to come back for them later. Now, get yourselves ready, and collect everything we can take with us that is likely to be useful on shore.'

I made sure that we took with us some guns, a barrel of powder, and other ammunition, three pairs of pistols, and a bullet mould with some lead. Each of us had a game-bag well stocked with food. I took some soup-cakes, biscuits, an iron pot, some knives, hatchets, saws, fishing-lines, and so on, as well as sufficient canvas to make a tent. We collected so many things that we were forced to leave some behind, although I managed to pack many in instead of the ballast which I had originally placed in the tubs.

When all was ready we stepped bravely into our tubs. The hens cackled a mournful farewell. I suddenly decided that we would be wise to take the poultry with us, together with the ducks and pigeons: 'For even if we cannot feed them, they can feed us,' I said. So we put ten hens and two cocks in a tub and covered it with a wooden grating. As for the geese, ducks, and pigeons, I let them loose, and hoped they would manage to fly or swim ashore. The boys were already sitting in their tubs when my wife arrived carrying a heavy sack which she threw into the tub occupied by little Francis. I paid no particular attention to this at the time, thinking she had put it there simply to act as a more comfortable seat for the child.

As soon as we were all settled in, I cut the mooring-rope, and we began to row towards land. The tide was coming in, and I counted on it to help our rowing. The children gazed longingly at the land ahead, and we strained every nerve to reach it, but for quite a long time all our efforts were in vain. The boat spun round and round without making any headway at all, until at last I found the right method of steering.

In the first tub was my wife, in the second was little Francis; Fritz had the third. The two centre ones contained the powder, the guns, the canvas, the tools, food, and live-stock. Jack occupied the sixth, Ernest the seventh, and I came last, and did my best to steer. Each of us wore our cork life-jackets, in case of accident. The dogs were too big for us to take on board; but as soon as they saw us start off they began to whine, and then leaped into the sea and swam after us. Turk was an English dog, Flora a Danish one. I was afraid that they would not be able to swim so far, and was terrified lest they should try to jump into the boat and capsize us all. But whenever they got tired they simply rested their paws on the floats or on the barrels, and so kept up with us without very much effort.

The sea was getting calmer all the time, the sky was cloudless, and the sun bright. We moved steadily along with the incoming tide. Around us floated all the debris of the wreck, and Fritz and I both managed to seize a barrel of provisions and tow it after us.

Our voyage, though rather slow, was eventually successful. As we neared the shore it lost something of its former desolate appearance. Fritz, whose sight was very keen, picked out some palm-trees. Ernest, who was inclined to be greedy, was delighted at the idea of some coconuts, and declared that the trees were larger and better than any he had ever seen in Europe.

'How exciting it all is!' exclaimed little Francis.

I was sorry I had not thought of bringing the captain's telescope; but Jack produced a small one from his pocket and handed it to me. I studied the land ahead, searching for a likely landing-place. The coast directly in front of us looked very barren indeed, but it seemed more inviting towards the left. However, a strong current was forcing us nearer the rocks on the barren side. All at once we spotted a small creek which our geese and ducks were obviously making for. Relying on their instinct, I steered our boat into this bay, and soon I reached a place where the bank was low and where there was just sufficient water to float us.

The elder boys leaped ashore at once. Francis, who had been wedged in his tub like a potted herring, had to be helped out.

'And the coconuts, Papa?' asked little Francis.

'Yes,' I replied, smiling, 'Fritz has very good eyesight, and he was not mistaken. I can see some trees over there. You shall have your coconuts by and by.'

The dogs, who had got ashore first, jumped around us, barking joyfully. Even the ducks, geese, and pigeons seemed glad to see us, while the penguins screamed at us from the nearby rocks, and a host of startled flamingoes wheeled about our heads. But the dreadful din was very welcome, for it meant that we should not be short of food, so long as there were so many sea-birds here to catch and eat.

First, we knelt down and thanked God for saving us from the wreck. Then we began unloading the boat. We set the hens free, and then looked for a suitable spot where we could pitch our tent. We made a framework by using the poles from the floats. I drove the first pole into the ground, and on the top of this I nailed the other pole, at an angle, wedging the end into a cleft in the cliff above us. Over this we stretched our canvas, and fixed the ends to the ground with pegs. Fritz fastened hooks to the sides, so that we could close the entrance at night.

Then I told the children to collect as much dry grass and moss as they could find, for our beds. While they were doing this, I built a stone hearth a little way from our tent, and had soon kindled some dry drift-wood into a blazing fire.

My wife put a pot of water on the flames. As soon as it began to boil I dropped in five or six cakes of dried soup, and my wife, helped by little Francis, began cooking our dinner.

Meanwhile Fritz, who had loaded the guns, took one and set off along the river-bank. Ernest remarked that hunting on a desert island was never very interesting. He wandered away to the right along the beach, while Jack turned off to the left among the rocks in search of mussels. As for me, I went to find the two casks which we had taken in tow as we sailed ashore, but I found that though the place where we had landed was suitable for beaching a boat, it would not do for landing heavy casks. While I was thinking of a way of getting round this problem, I heard Jack yelling at the top of his voice. Seizing a hatchet, I ran to help him, and I found him standing in a pool up to his knees, with an enormous lobster gripping him tightly by the leg.

'Papa!' he shouted, half triumphant, half terrified. 'Come here quickly; I have caught something really enormous!'

'All right, then, bring it here.'

'I can't,' he admitted, 'it has caught *me*.'

I couldn't help laughing to see the captor taken captive like this. As I waded into the water the lobster let go and tried to escape; but I stunned him with a blow from my hatchet, and dragged him ashore.

After this, we ate the soup, constructed a rough shelter, then slept . . .

★   ★   ★   ★

I awoke at cock-crow, and immediately called my wife so that I could discuss the day's plans with her.

'Sometimes,' I confided, 'there seem to be so many dangers and difficulties ahead of us that my courage almost fails me! It is absolutely essential that we visit the wreck again, soon, unless we want to lose all the cattle; and there are a lot of things on board which would be very useful to us here. On the other hand, we have a great deal to do on shore, too; and first and foremost we ought to set about building ourselves a more permanent kind of home.'

In the end we agreed that my wife should remain on shore with the younger children, and that Fritz, being the eldest and the strongest, should come to the wreck with me. I went to wake the children, shouting to them: 'Get up, get up! It is broad daylight, and we have lots to do today! You ought to be ashamed of yourselves, letting the sun find you still in bed!'

Meanwhile the dogs lay quietly beside us, making no attempt to join in the meal.

I realized for the first time that they had not come through the previous night's adventures unscathed. There were many traces of jackals' teeth on their necks.

My wife suggested that we should dress their wounds with butter, washed first in fresh water so as to extract the salt. In a few days the bites were completely healed.

'If only we could find some spiked collars on board the ship,' said Fritz. 'They would help to protect the dogs; for you may be sure the jackals are bound to come back again, now that they have discovered us, and next time they may succeed in hurting the dogs really badly.'

'Oh,' cried Jack, 'I will soon make them some fine collars, if Mamma will help me.'

'With all my heart,' replied his mother. 'I will certainly help you. We will see what you can do.'

'Now,' said I, 'it is high time we set to work. Come along, Fritz; your mother and I have agreed that you and I shall go back to the wreck today, to see what we can salvage. Your brothers will stay here with your mother, and I know I can rely on them to be obedient.'

Later, while Fritz was getting the boat ready, I set to work to construct a flagstaff on some rising ground ground near the beach, and I fastened to it a piece of white canvas to serve as a signal between the wreck and the shore. It was arranged that it should be lowered in case of danger, and that three or four shots should bring us back to land immediately. I warned my wife that we would probably have to stay on the wreck all night, as there would be so much for us to do there. She agreed to this, though not without some hesitation, and she stipulated that, to be on the safe side, we should sleep in our tub-boat, and not on the wreck itself.

We took nothing with us but our guns and ammunition, relying upon the stores already on board for our food. We left the shore in silence, sad at the thought of leaving our loved ones all alone yet again. Fritz rowed whilst I steered. When we were some distance from the shore, I noticed a current, caused by the force of the river flowing into the sea, which I thought would help us on our way. I was right. I steered into it, and it carried us along so easily that for three-quarters of the voyage we had to make scarcely any effort of our own. We arrived safely at the vessel, and entered it by the opening which we had made when we left it, and then we made our boat fast. As soon as we got out of the tub, Fritz ran straight to the deck where the cow was tethered. All the animals were delighted to see us, though it was quite obvious that they had not suffered from any lack of food during our absence.

We stood and watched for a few minutes, and then we gave all the animals fresh food and water, then decided to have something to eat ourselves, to give us strength for all the work we had before us.

While we ate we discussed what job we should tackle first. Fritz suggested that we should first make a sail for our boat.

'But why do you want to do that straight away?' I asked. 'There are a hundred much more important things to do first, surely.'

'Perhaps,' he said, 'but while we were sailing out I noticed that the wind was blowing strongly in our faces, but that the current was strong enough to carry us along in spite of it. Now, I thought, when we go back the current will be against us, but the wind will be in our favour. Our boat will be very heavy once we have loaded so many things into it, and I do not think I shall be strong enough to row us back alone without the help of a sail.'

'Now I understand,' I said laughingly. 'You mean you want to save yourself some work! But, to be serious, what you say is reasonable enough. You will certainly not be strong enough to row us back to shore on your own; and if I were to leave the rudder and row too, it would be dangerous; so we will do as you suggest.'

I first found a spar which looked as if it would make a good mast, and then another thinner one, upon which I could hoist the sail. Fritz bored a hole in the plank, into which we could 'step' the mast, and then I went to the sail-room and cut out a large triangular piece of canvas, which I rigged on to the mast in such a way that I could raise or lower it as I wanted.

While I was fixing the sail, Fritz took the telescope, and had a good look at the shore. He came back and said that all seemed quiet there, and at the same time he handed me a little red streamer to use as our flag. I smiled a little, but to please Fritz I attached the flag to the mast-head.

'Papa,' said Fritz, 'your sail will make my part of the work a great deal easier; now you ought to think of yourself, and do something which will help you steer more safely and accurately.

'That is not a bad idea at all,' I smiled; and I set about fixing to each end of the boat two thick pieces of rope, into which I fastened an oar so that it could be steered either way.

All these tasks took a considerable time, and I realized that we could not reach the shore before nightfall at earliest, unless we were to return empty-handed, with the main part of our mission unaccomplished. We had arranged with my wife that we would hoist a flag if we intended remaining on board, and the red streamer was ideal for the purpose.

We spent what was left of the day in emptying the ballast from our boat and filling it with things that would be useful to use on the island. Even the Vandals could hardly have pillaged a ship more thoroughly! Foreseeing that we might have to live on our own on the island for a very long time, I gave first preference to all the articles which would be most useful; this meant making ample provision for powder and bullets to serve us in hunting and to defend us against possible attacks by wild beasts.

All sorts of things which we had first set aside as worthless now seemed absolutely indispensable.

Our ship had originally been sent out to establish a colony in the South Seas, and there were a large number of things on board which are not generally found on such ships. With so much to choose from, selection was very difficult. We took knives and forks, spoons, and kitchenware, all of which we needed urgently. In the captain's cabin we found some silver tureen-covers, some pewter plates and spoons, and a hamper of excellent wine. We put all these in our tubs. From the galley we took roasting jacks, kettles, frying-pans, pots and saucepans, and also a quantity of Westphalia hams, sausages, some sacks of maize and other grain, and a few potatoes. We worked at top speed, because the ship seemed in such a precarious state that we feared she might heel over at any moment.

Fritz reminded me how hard our beds were in the tent; so I went to find some hammocks and blankets. Fritz himself, who could never possess too many weapons, took another gun, a sword, a barrel of powder, and a hunting-knife. To all these we added a barrel of sulphur, some matches and some rope, and a roll of canvas. Our little boat was now so heavily laden and riding so deep in the water, that I believe it would have been quite unsafe to set out in her had not the sea been very calm.

Night fell very suddenly and it was no use trying to get back to the island in the dark. We could see a large fire burning on the rocks, and so we knew that all was well at home. We in our turn hung up the great ship's lanterns to assure them of our safety. Two shots from the shore told us that they had seen the light and understood the signal.

After praying fervently for the safety of every one of us, we went to sleep in our tubs, wearing our life-jackets, so as to be ready in case of any alarm.

★　　★　　★　　★

Next morning, even before it was light enough to see the coast distinctly, I was up on deck, looking through my telescope at our tent. My family were obviously still asleep. Meanwhile Fritz prepared breakfast. Very soon I was delighted to see my wife come out of the tent and look anxiously towards the wreck. I immediately hoisted the signal we had agreed on the day before, and in answer we received three dips from the flag on the beach. I was anxious no longer, for I knew now that all had been quiet on shore during the night.

'Fritz,' I said, 'now that we are certain that the others are managing quite well without us, I think we should try to think of some way of getting the animals ashore. Otherwise, with the wreck shifting as it is, they are liable to perish any time.'

'Well,' said Fritz, 'why can't we build a raft and float them ashore on that?'

'It would be far too difficult to build,' I answered. 'And how in the world could we get the cow, the donkey, and the sow on to such a raft; and even if we got them on to it, how could we keep them on it? A raft might be suitable for the sheep and the goats, but it would not do for the rest. You must think again.'

'I know!' cried Fritz. 'We can throw the sow into the sea and make her swim. Her own fat will keep her afloat, and if we tie a rope round her neck we can tow her after us, behind the boat.'

'That is all very well as far as the sow is concerned,' I said. 'But tell me, what shall we do with the sheep and the goats? They are really more use to us than the sow.'

'Well, let us make them swimming-jackets something like ours,' suggested the boy. 'Then they will swim after us like fish, and we can tow them along like the sow.'

'Excellent!' I cried. 'That is a real brain-wave! Let us try it out here and now!'

We ran to the sheep pen and picked out one of the young sheep. We fastened two floats to its sides, and threw it into the sea. I watched

147

the wretched creature disappear under the water; it sank like a stone, and I thought it would never come up again. But at last it rose to the surface, nodding its head very dismally, and began to swim. When it grew exhausted, it merely had to remain motionless, and it then floated along quite effortlessly.

I was delighted. 'Now we shall be able to get them all ashore!' I cried. 'We shall be able to save the lot! But just at the moment, I am most concerned about getting this poor old sheep back on to the ship again!'

Fritz wanted to dive into the sea after it. But I made him first put on his life-jacket, and then he let himself down gently into the water. Taking a rope he threw it round the sheep's neck, and drew the animal back towards the ship, and then pulled it out of the water. It seemed none the worse for its experience.

I took four empty casks, tying them together in pairs with a large piece of canvas. We proposed passing this canvas underneath the bellies of the cow and the ass, so that they would swim along supported by a cask on either side. I added a leather thong, stretching from the casks across the breasts and haunches of the animals, to make the whole contraption quite secure. We had much more trouble when we came to deal with the sow, for we had decided that she had better have a jacket too, in spite of her own ample fat. It was not until we had put a string through her nose that we were able to keep her still enough to fit her with her swimming-jacket.

The sheep and the goats gave us less trouble, and very soon we had the whole herd assembled on the upper deck ready to start. We fastened a rope round the horn or the stomach of each animal, attaching the other end to a large piece of wood, which would make it easier for us to guide them and drag them behind us once we were in the boat.

Now everything was ready. We dragged the donkey to the edge of the ship, and gave him a hearty push into the sea. He fell with a mighty splash and sank at once, but very soon he bobbed to the surface, and swam along so expertly between his casks that we were full of admiration. It was now the cow's turn, and as she was far more important to us than the donkey, I was far more anxious about her. As soon as the donkey was some distance from the ship, we launched the cow equally successfully, and she began swimming to land as calmly as could be.

We gave the donkey a hearty push into the sea.

We treated the sheep and the goats in the same way, and at last only the sow was left. She caused us a lot of bother. In the end we managed to float her like the others, and she was so enraged by the whole affair that she beat the water quite wildly and was in fact the first to reach the shore.

There was not a moment to lose. We jumped into our boat and cut the moorings, and were soon sailing amongst our animals. We were able to pick up all their guiding ropes without much difficulty, and attach them to the stern of the boat, and in this way we dragged the whole herd towards land, greatly helped by a favourable breeze, which made our sail billow bravely.

We soon realized that without the sail our voyage would have ended disastrously, for the animals were a colossal drag upon our little boat, and we would never have been able to reach the shore by rowing alone. But, as it was, by the end of a quarter of an hour we had already made considerable headway.

We were very proud of our success, and amazed at the speed we were making. We sat down on our cargo, and ate a hearty dinner; then I scanned the shore in the hope of seeing the rest of the family. Before leaving the wreck I had noticed that they had started on an expedition farther inland, but since then I had seen no sign of them.

However, all our efforts to save our animals would have been futile if not Fritz had not spied in time the danger which was now threatening us. All of a sudden he called out: 'Good gracious, we are finished! An enormous fish is just about to attack us!'

'What do you mean, finished?' I cried, half angry and half terrified. 'Get ready, and as soon as he is near enough, fire at him.'

We seized our guns, loaded each with two bullets, and stood ready to face the fish. He came at us from the stern of the boat and swam at a tremendous rate towards one of the sheep. Then Fritz fired, so accurately that the bullets lodged in the monster's head. He dived and disappeared. Now and then he floated to the surface again, and we could see the shining underside of his belly; but a trail of blood stained the water all round him. I looked round carefully with my telescope, trying to see if he were likely to attack again.

'Don't worry, he has had enough,' said Fritz proudly.

However, I bade Fritz reload his gun so as to be ready for any new emergency, for I was sure the fish was a shark, and I did not think it very likely that it was the only one in the area. Fortunately my fears were without foundation, and we were left in peace.

I resumed my steering, and the wind carried us straight to our little bay. We entered it easily, lowered the sail, and soon reached a spot where the animals could wade ashore. I cut their cords, they leaped gladly on to dry land, and in a few moments our little boat was back at its moorings.

None of the family appeared, however, and I began to feel rather anxious; for night was falling fast, and I had no idea which way they had gone. But it was not long before we heard their voices in the distance, and we soon saw them all running towards us, my wife a little way behind the children.

When all the excitement had died down a little, we gave them a detailed account of our expedition. My wife could scarcely believe that we had really managed to bring all the animals ashore.

I admitted that I had fairly addled my brain, trying to think of a way of landing them, without any success.

'Yes,' said Fritz, smiling broadly, 'this was all my idea.'

'That is quite true,' I said. 'It was indeed all his idea, and we have him to thank for it.'

My wife thought that we both deserved their thanks for saving such a valuable cargo. Francis was delighted with the little red flag that fluttered from our mast. Ernest and the others jumped into the boat, and admired the mast, the sail, and the flag, and insisted on our explaining how we had managed to make them all. Jack, who was not so interested in the workings of the ship, slipped away along the shore to the animals, and started taking the swimming-jackets off the sheep and the goats. He went into fits of laughter when he saw the donkey desperately trying to rid himself of his two casks, and tried to help him too. The donkey refused to allow this, however, but Jack managed to clamber on his back, and came riding towards us at a great speed, kicking and smacking the animal to make him go faster. We all laughed at the comical sight they made, and when I helped Jack to jump down, I was very surprised to notice that he was wearing a belt of yellow skin, into which he had thrust a pair of pistols.

'Where on earth did you pick up this bandit's rig-out?' I asked.

'I made it myself,' he replied. 'And now, look at the dogs.'

Then I noticed that each of the dogs was wearing a similar sort of collar, studded with nails, the points sticking outwards, so that their throats were well protected.

'These are splendid,' I said. 'And did you make them all?'

'Yes,' said Jack, 'though Mamma helped me a little with the sewing.'

His mother confirmed this, and added that she had taken good care to bring her needles and thread ashore with her. I thanked them both for all their hard work. I could see that Fritz was rather annoyed to see that Jack had skinned his jackal and cut his beautiful hide into pieces without his permission, to provide the material for the belt and collars; but he hid his resentment as much as he could.

As I saw that no preparations had been made for supper yet, I told Fritz to bring me the Westphalia ham which was still in one of our tubs. The whole family looked at me in astonishment, but Fritz was soon back, carrying the ham.

'How splendid!' they cried. 'A real ham! And how good it looks!'

'Ah,' said my wife, 'but if you have to wait for your supper until that ham is cooked, you will have to wait a very long time indeed. However, I have a dozen turtle's eggs here which I picked up on our walk to-day. I can very soon make an omelette with them, for, thank goodness, we have plenty of butter now.'

'The turtle's eggs,' remarked Ernest, who was always anxious to give his knowledge an airing, 'are easily recognized by their round shape; and they are as soft to the touch as damp parchment. We found them buried in the sand, close to the sea.'

'I see,' I said. 'But how exactly did you manage to spot them?'

'Oh, all that belongs to the history of our little expedition,' said my wife, 'and when you have time to listen, I will tell you about it. But just now I think we had better see about the supper.'

'Very well,' I said. 'Go and cook our omelette, and after supper, as our dessert, we will listen to the story of your adventures. As for our ham, I assure you that it tastes very nice raw, for we have already tried it that way on the wreck; but I don't doubt that it will be better cooked. Meanwhile, while supper is cooking, I will go and take the swimming-jackets from the rest of the animals. The children had better come and help me.'

The boys all came with me to the seashore and the work of unharness-
ing the rest of the animals did not take long. The sow was the only one
who proved difficult. She refused to let any of us get near her. Then
Ernest thought of sending the dogs after her, and in a few moments
they had seized her firmly by each ear, forcing her to halt, squealing
dreadfully. We then released her from the casks, as we had the others,
and made our way back to the tent.

My wife had made the omelette, and was waiting for us.

Our supper looked really magnificent, all set out on a table-cloth,
which was spread over the end of the butter-cask. This my wife had
laid with the spoons, forks, and plates which we had brought from the
ship. We had an excellent meal, with cheese, biscuits, and a delicious
omelette. The dogs, hens, pigeons, sheep, and goats came round to
pick up the pieces we left; but the geese and the ducks preferred to
dabble in a small pond near by, in which they had discovered plenty
of worms and a kind of small crab.

We had a very merry little banquet, and when it was over I told Fritz
to fetch me a bottle of the canary wine we had found in the captain's
cabin, for already I felt we had great hopes of surviving on our island.

IN THE SHADOW OF THE BLACK STONE

John Buchan

Richard Hannay offers refuge to a stranger called Franklin P. Scudder – then the drama begins . . . Scudder is murdered, and Hannay discovers the dead man's pocket book which tells of a threat to world peace and incriminates a gang of spies who go by the name of the Black Stone. Within minutes of his friend's death, Hannay is plunged into a situation of political intrigue fraught with danger. Wrongly suspected of murder he finds himself shadowed by the Black Stone who want to retrieve Scudder's notebook at all costs.

Having fled from the murder scene, Hannay (the story-teller) has crashed a stolen car and is now on the desolate moors of Galloway with the Black Stone and the police hot on his heels. Dressed in the clothes of a Scottish roadman, 'Mr Turnbull', he had dodged through their net once – but now that net threatens to close even tighter . . .

I woke very cold and stiff about an hour after dawn. It took me a little while to remember where I was, for I had been very weary and had slept heavily. I saw first the pale blue sky through a net of heather, then a big shoulder of hill, and then my own boots placed neatly in a blaeberry bush. I raised myself on my arms and looked down into the valley, and that one look set me lacing up my boots in mad haste.

For there were men below, not more than a quarter of a mile off, spaced out on the hillside like a fan, and beating the heather.

I crawled out of my shelf into the cover of a boulder, and from it gained a shallow trench which slanted up the mountain face. This led me presently into the narrow gully of a burn, by way of which I scrambled to the top of the ridge. From there I looked back, and saw that I was still undiscovered. My pursuers were patiently quartering the hillside and moving upwards.

Keeping behind the skyline I ran for maybe half a mile, till I judged I was above the uppermost end of the glen. Then I showed myself, and was instantly noted by one of the flankers, who passed the word to the others. I heard cries coming up from below, and saw that the line of search had changed its direction. I pretended to retreat over the skyline, but instead went back the way I had come, and in twenty minutes was behind the ridge overlooking my sleeping place. From that viewpoint I had the satisfaction of seeing the pursuit streaming up the hill at the top of the glen on a hopelessly false scent.

I had before me a choice of routes, and I chose a ridge which made an angle with the one I was on, and so would soon put a deep glen between me and my enemies. The exercise had warmed my blood, and I was beginning to enjoy myself amazingly. As I went I breakfasted on the dusty remnants of the ginger biscuits.

I knew very little about the country, and I hadn't a notion what I was going to do. I trusted to the strength of my legs, but I was well aware that those behind me would be familiar with the lie of the land, and that my ignorance would be a heavy handicap. I saw in front of me a sea of hills, rising very high towards the south, but northwards breaking down into broad ridges which separated wide and shallow dales. The ridge I had chosen seemed to sink after a mile or two to a moor which lay like a pocket in the uplands. That seemed as good a direction to take as any other.

My stratagem had given me a fair start – call it twenty minutes – and I had the width of a glen behind me before I saw the first heads of the pursuers. The police had evidently called in local talent to their aid, and the men I could see had the appearance of herds or gamekeepers. They hallooed at the sight of me, and I waved my hand. Two dived into the glen and began to climb my ridge, while the others kept their own side of the hill. I felt as if I were taking part in a schoolboy game of hare and hounds.

But very soon it began to seem less of a game. Those fellows behind were hefty men on their native heath. Looking back I saw that only three were following direct, and I guessed that the others had fetched a circuit to cut me off. My lack of local knowledge might very well be my undoing, and I resolved to get out of this tangle of glens to the pocket of moor I had seen from the tops. I must so increase my distance as to get clear away from them, and I believed I could do this if I could find the right ground for it. If there had been cover I would have tried a bit of stalking, but on these bare slopes you could see a fly a mile off. My hope must be in the length of my legs and the soundness of my wind, but I needed easier ground for that, for I was not bred a mountaineer. How I longed for a good Afrikander pony!

I put on a great spurt and got off my ridge and down into the moor before any figures appeared on the skyline behind me. I crossed a burn, and came out on a highroad which made a pass between two glens. All in front of me was a big field of heather sloping up to a crest which was crowned with an odd feather of trees. In the dyke by the roadside was a gate, from which a grass-grown track led over the first wave of the moor.

I jumped the dyke and followed it, and after a few hundred yards – as soon as it was out of sight of the highway – the grass stopped and it became a very respectable road, which was evidently kept with some care. Clearly it ran to a house, and I began to think of doing the same. Hitherto my luck had held, and it might be that my best chance would be found in this remote dwelling. Anyhow there were trees there, and that meant cover.

I did not follow the road, but the burnside which flanked it on the right, where the bracken grew deep and the high banks made a tolerable screen. It was well I did so, for no sooner had I gained the hollow than, looking back, I saw the pursuit topping the ridge from which I had descended.

After that I did not look back; I had no time. I ran up the burnside, crawling over the open places, and for a large part wading in the shallow stream. I found a deserted cottage with a row of phantom peat-stacks and an overgrown garden. Then I was among young hay, and very soon had come to the edge of a plantation of wind-blown firs. From there I saw the chimneys of the house smoking a few hundred yards to my left. I forsook the burnside, crossed another dyke, and almost before I knew I was on a rough lawn. A glance back told me that I was well out of sight of the pursuit, which had not yet passed the first lift of the moor.

The lawn was a very rough place, cut with a scythe instead of a mower, and planted with beds of scrubby rhododendrons. A brace of black-game, which are not usually garden birds, rose at my approach. The house before me was the ordinary moorland farm, with a more pretentious whitewashed wing added. Attached to this wing was a glass veranda, and through the glass I saw the face of an elderly gentleman meekly watching me.

I stalked over the border of coarse hill gravel and entered the open veranda door. Within was a pleasant room, glass on one side, and on the other a mass of books. More books showed in an inner room. On the floor, instead of tables, stood cases such as you see in a museum, filled with coins and queer stone implements.

There was a kneehole desk in the middle, and seated at it, with some papers and open volumes before him, was the benevolent old gentleman. His face was round and shiny, like Mr Pickwick's, big glasses were stuck on the end of his nose, and the top of his head was as bright and bare as a glass bottle. He never moved when I entered, but raised placid eyebrows and waited on me to speak.

It was not an easy job, with about five minutes to spare, to tell a stranger who I was and what I wanted and to win his aid. I did not attempt it. There was something about the eye of the man before me, something so keen and knowledgeable, that I could not find a word. I simply stared at him and stuttered.

'You seem in a hurry, my friend,' he said slowly.

I nodded towards the window. It gave a prospect across the moor through a gap in the plantation, and revealed certain figures half a mile off struggling through the heather.

'Ah, I see,' he said, and took up a pair of field-glasses through which he patiently scrutinized the figures.

'A fugitive from justice, eh? Well, we'll go into the matter at our leisure. Meantime I object to my privacy being broken in upon by the clumsy rural policeman. Go into my study, and you will see two doors facing you. Take the one on the left and close it behind you. You will be perfectly safe.'

And this extraordinary man took up his pen again.

I did as I was bid, and found myself in a little dark chamber which smelt of chemicals, and was lit only by a tiny window high up in the wall. The door had swung behind me with a click like the door of a safe. Once again I had found an unexpected sanctuary.

157

All the same I was not comfortable. There was something about the old gentleman which puzzled and rather terrified me. He had been too easy and ready, almost as if he had expected me. And his eyes had been horribly intelligent.

No sound came to me in that dark place. For all I knew the police might be searching the house, and if they did they would want to know what was behind this door. I tried to possess my soul in patience, and to forget how hungry I was.

Then I took a more cheerful view. The old gentleman could scarcely refuse me a meal, and I fell to reconstructing my breakfast. Bacon and eggs would content me, but I wanted the better part of a flitch of bacon and half a hundred eggs. And then, while my mouth was watering in anticipation, there was a click and the door stood open.

I emerged into the sunlight to find the master of the house sitting in a deep armchair in the room he called his study, and regarding me with curious eyes.

'Have they gone?' I asked.

'They have gone. I convinced them that you had crossed the hill. I do not choose that the police should come between me and one whom I am delighted to honour. This is a lucky morning for you, Mr Richard Hannay.'

As he spoke his eyelids seemed to tremble and to fall a little over his keen grey eyes. In a flash the phrase of Scudder's came back to me, when he had described the man he most dreaded in the world. He had said that he 'could hood his eyes like a hawk.' Then I saw that I had walked straight into the enemy's headquarters.

My first impulse was to throttle the old ruffian and make for the open air. He seemed to anticipate my intention, for he smiled gently, and nodded to the door behind me.

I turned, and saw two menservants who had me covered with pistols.

He knew my name, but he had never seen me before. And as the reflection darted across my mind I saw a slender chance.

'I don't know what you mean,' I said roughly. 'And who are you calling Richard Hannay? My name's Ainslie.'

'So?' he said, still smiling. 'But of course you have others. We won't quarrel about a name.'

He regarded me with a curious eye.

I was pulling myself together now, and I reflected that my garb, lacking coat and waistcoat and collar, would at any rate not betray me. I put on my surliest face and shrugged my shoulders.

'I suppose you're going to give me up after all, and I call it a damned dirty trick. My God, I wish I had never seen that cursed motor car! Here's the money and be damned to you,' and I flung four sovereigns on the table.

He opened his eyes a little. 'Oh no, I shall not give you up. My friends and I will have a little private settlement with you, that is all. You know a little too much, Mr Hannay. You are a clever actor, but not quite clever enough.'

He spoke with assurance, but I could see the dawning of a doubt in his mind.

'Oh, for God's sake stop jawing,' I cried. 'Everything's against me. I haven't had a bit of luck since I came on shore at Leith. What's the harm in a poor devil with an empty stomach picking up some money he finds in a bust-up motor car? That's all I done, and for that I've been chivvied for two days by those blasted bobbies over those blasted hills. I tell you I'm fair sick of it. You can do what you like, old boy! Ned Ainslie's got no fight left in him.'

I could see that the doubt was gaining.

'Will you oblige me with the story of your recent doings?' he asked.

'I can't, guv'nor,' I said in a real beggar's whine. 'I've not had a bite to eat for two days. Give me a mouthful of food, and then you'll hear God's truth.'

I must have showed my hunger in my face, for he signalled to one of the men in the doorway. A bit of cold pie was brought and a glass of beer, and I wolfed them down like a pig – or rather, like Ned Ainslie, for I was keeping up my character. In the middle of my meal he spoke suddenly to me in German, but I turned on him a face as blank as a stone wall.

Then I told him my story – how I had come off an Archangel ship at Leith a week ago, and was making my way overland to my brother at Wigtown. I had run short of cash – I hinted vaguely at a spree – and I was pretty well on my uppers when I had come on a hole in a hedge, and, looking through, had seen a big motor car lying in the burn. I had poked about to see what had happened, and had found three sovereigns lying on the seat and one on the floor. There was nobody there or any sign of an owner, so I had pocketed the cash. But somehow the law had got after me. When I had tried to change a sovereign in a baker's shop, the woman had cried on the police, and a little later, when I was washing my face in a burn, I had been nearly gripped, and had only got away by leaving my coat and waistcoat behind me.

'They can have the money back,' I cried, 'for a fat lot of good it's done me. Those perishers are all down on a poor man. Now, if it had been you, guv'nor, that had found the quids, nobody would have troubled you.'

'You're a good liar, Hannay,' he said.

I flew into a rage. 'Stop fooling, damn you! I tell you my name's Ainslie, and I never heard of anyone called Hannay in my born days. I'd sooner have the police than you with your Hannays and your monkey-faced pistol tricks ... No, gov'nor, I beg pardon, I don't mean that. I'm much obliged to you for the grub, and I'll thank you to let me go now the coast's clear.'

It was obvious that he was badly puzzled. You see he had never seen me, and my appearance must have altered considerably from my photographs, if he had got one of them. I was pretty smart and well dressed in London, and now I was a regular tramp.

'I do not propose to let you go. If you are what you say you are, you will soon have a chance of clearing yourself. If you are what I believe you are, I do not think you will see the light much longer.'

He rang a bell, and a third servant appeared from the veranda.

'I want the Lanchester in five minutes,' he said. 'There will be three to luncheon.'

Then he looked steadily at me, and that was the hardest ordeal of all.

There was something weird and devilish in those eyes, cold, malignant, unearthly, and most hellishly clever. They fascinated me like the bright eyes of a snake. I had a strong impulse to throw myself on his mercy and offer to join his side, and if you consider the way I felt about the whole thing you will see that that impulse must have been purely physical, the weakness of a brain mesmerized and mastered by a stronger spirit. But I managed to stick it out and even to grin.

'You'll know me next time, guv'nor,' I said.

'Karl,' he spoke in German to one of the men in the doorway, 'you will put this fellow in the storeroom till I return, and you will be answerable to me for his keeping.'

I was marched out of the room with a pistol at each ear.

★   ★   ★   ★

The storeroom was a damp chamber in what had been the old farmhouse. There was no carpet on the uneven floor, and nothing to sit down on but a school form. It was black as pitch, for the windows were heavily shuttered. I made out by groping that the walls were lined with boxes and barrels and sacks of some heavy stuff. The whole place smelt of mould and disuse. My jailers turned the key in the door, and I could hear them shifting their feet as they stood on guard outside.

I sat down in that chilly darkness in a very miserable frame of mind. The old boy had gone off in a motor to collect two ruffians who had interviewed me yesterday. Now, they had seen me as the roadman, and they would remember me, for I was in the same rig. What was a roadman doing twenty miles from his beat, pursued by the police? A question or two would put them on the track. Probably they had seen Mr Turnbull, and then the whole thing would be crystal clear. What chance had I in this moorland house with three desperadoes and their armed servants?

I began to think wistfully of the police, now plodding over the hills after my wraith. They at any rate were fellow-countrymen and honest men, and their tender mercies would be kinder than these ghoulish aliens. But they wouldn't have listened to me. That old devil with the eyelids had not taken long to get rid of them. I thought he probably had some kind of graft with the constabulary. Most likely he had letters from Cabinet Ministers saying he was to be given every facility for plotting against Britain. That's the sort of owlish way we run our politics in the Old Country.

The three would be back for lunch, so I hadn't more than a couple of hours to wait. It was simply waiting on destruction, for I could see no way out of this mess. I wished that I had Scudder's courage, for I am free to confess I didn't feel any great fortitude. The only thing that kept me going was that I was pretty furious. It made me boil with rage to think of those three spies getting the pull on me like this. I hoped that at any rate I might be able to twist one of their necks before they downed me.

The more I thought of it the angrier I grew, and I had to get up and move about the room. I tried the shutters, but they were the kind that lock with a key, and I couldn't move them. From the outside came the faint clucking of hens in the warm sun. Then I groped among the sacks and boxes. I couldn't open the latter, and the sacks seemed to be full of things like dog-biscuits that smelt of cinnamon. But, as I circumnavigated the room, I found a handle in the wall which seemed worth investigating.

It was the door of a wall cupboard – what they call a 'press' in Scotland – and it was locked. I shook it, and it seemed rather flimsy. For want of something better to do I put out my strength on that door, getting some purchase on the handle by looping my braces round it. Presently the thing gave with a crash which I thought would bring in my warders to inquire. I waited for a bit, and then started to explore the cupboard shelves.

There was a multitude of queer things there. I found an odd Vesta or two in my trouser pockets and struck a light. It went out in a second, but it showed me one thing. There was a little stock of electric torches on one shelf. I picked up one, and found it was in working order.

With the torch to help me I investigated further. There were bottles and cases of queer-smelling stuffs, chemicals no doubt for experiments, and there were coils of fine copper wire and hanks and hanks of a thin oiled silk. There was a box of detonators, and a lot of cord of fuses. Then away at the back of a shelf I found a stout brown cardboard box, and inside it a wooden case. I managed to wrench it open, and within lay half a dozen little grey bricks, each a couple of inches square.

I took up one, and found that it crumbled easily in my hand. Then I smelt it and put my tongue to it. After that I sat down to think. I hadn't been a mining engineer for nothing, and I knew lentonite when I saw it.

With one of these bricks I could blow the house to smithereens. I had used the stuff in Rhodesia and knew its power. But the trouble was that my knowledge wasn't exact. I had forgotten the proper charge and the right way of preparing it, and I wasn't sure about the timing. I had only a vague notion, too, as to its power, for though I had used it I had not handled it with my own fingers.

But it was a chance, the only possible chance. It was a mighty risk, but against it was an absolute black certainty. If I used it the odds were, as I reckoned, about five to one in favour of my blowing myself into the tree-tops; but if I didn't I should very likely be occupying a six-foot hole in the garden by the evening. That was the way I had to look at it. The prospect was pretty dark either way, but anyhow there was a chance, both for myself and for my country.

The remembrance of little Scudder decided me. It was about the beastliest moment of my life, for I'm no good at these cold-blooded resolutions. Still I managed to rake up the pluck to set my teeth and choke back the horrid doubts that flooded in on me. I simply shut off my mind and pretended I was doing an experiment as simple as Guy Fawkes' fireworks.

I got a detonator, and fixed it to a couple of feet of fuse. Then I took a quarter of a lentonite brick, and buried it near the door below one of the sacks in a crack of the floor, fixing the detonator in it. For all I knew half those boxes might be dynamite. If the cupboard held such deadly explosives, why not the boxes? In that case there would be a glorious skyward journey for me and the German servants and about an acre of the surrounding country. There was also the risk that the detonation might set off the other bricks in the cupboard, for I had forgotten most that I knew about lentonite. But it didn't do to begin thinking about the possibilities. The odds were horrible, but I had to take them.

I ensconced myself just below the sill of the window, and lit the fuse. Then I waited for a moment or two. There was dead silence – only a shuffle of heavy boots in the passage, and the peaceful cluck of hens from the warm out-of-doors. I commended my soul to my Maker, and wondered where I would be in five seconds.

A great wave of heat seemed to surge upwards from the floor, and hang for a blistering instant in the air. Then the wall opposite me flashed into a golden yellow and dissolved with a rending thunder that hammered my brain into a pulp. Something dropped on me, catching the point of my left shoulder.

And then I think I became unconscious.

My stupor can scarcely have lasted beyond a few seconds. I felt myself being choked by thick yellow fumes, and struggled out of the debris to my feet. Somewhere behind me I felt fresh air. The jambs of the window had fallen, and through the ragged rent the smoke was pouring out to the summer noon. I stepped over the broken lintel, and found myself standing in a yard in a dense and acrid fog. I felt very sick and ill, but I could move my limbs, and I staggered blindly forward away from the house.

A small mill-lade ran in a wooden aqueduct at the other side of the yard, and into this I fell. The cool water revived me, and I had just enough wits left to think of escape. I squirmed up the lade among the slippery green slime till I reached the mill-wheel. Then I wriggled through the axle hole into the old mill and tumbled on to a bed of chaff. A nail caught the seat of my trousers, and I left a wisp of heather-mixture behind me.

The mill had been long out of use. The ladders were rotten with age, and in the loft the rats had gnawed great holes in the floor. Nausea shook me, and a wheel in my head kept turning, while my left shoulder and arm seemed to be stricken with the palsy. I looked out of the window and saw a fog still hanging over the house and smoke escaping from an upper window. Please God I had set the place on fire, for I could hear confused cries coming from the other side.

But I had no time to linger, since this mill was obviously a bad hiding-place. Anybody looking for me would naturally follow the lade, and I made certain the search would begin as soon as they found that my body was not in the storeroom. From another window I saw that on the far side of the mill stood an old stone dovecot. If I could get there without leaving tracks I might find a hiding-place, for I argued that my enemies, if they thought I could move, would conclude I had made for open country, and would go seeking me on the moor.

I crawled down the broken ladder, scattering chaff behind me to cover my footsteps. I did the same on the mill floor, and on the threshold where the door hung on broken hinges. Peeping out, I saw that between me and the dovecot was a piece of bare cobbled ground, where no footmarks would show. Also it was mercifully hid by the mill buildings from any view from the house. I slipped across the space, got to the back of the dovecot and prospected a way of ascent.

That was one of the hardest jobs I ever took on. My shoulder and arm ached like hell, and I was so sick and giddy that I was always on the verge of falling. But I managed it somehow. By the use of out-jutting stones and gaps in the masonry and a tough ivy root I got to the top in the end. There was a little parapet behind which I found space to lie down. Then I proceeded to go off into an old-fashioned swoon.

I woke with a burning head and the sun glaring in my face. For a long time I lay motionless, for those horrible fumes seemed to have loosened my joints and dulled my brain. Sounds came to me from the house – men speaking throatily and the throbbing of a stationary car. There was a little gap in the parapet to which I wriggled, and from which I had some sort of prospect of the yard. I saw figures come out – a servant with his head bound up, and then a younger man in knicker-bockers. They were looking for something, and moved towards the mill. Then one of them caught sight of the wisp of cloth on the nail, and cried out to the other. They both went back to the house, and brought two more to look at it. I saw the rotund figure of my late captor, and I thought I made out the man with the lisp. I noticed that all had pistols.

For half an hour they ransacked the mill. I could hear them kicking over the barrels and pulling up the rotten planking. Then they came outside, and stood just below the dovecot, arguing fiercely. The servant with the bandage was being soundly rated. I heard them fiddling with the door of the dovecot, and for one horrid moment I fancied they were coming up. Then they thought better of it, and went back to the house.

All that long blistering afternoon I lay baking on the roof-top. Thirst was my chief torment. My tongue was like a stick, and to make it worse I could hear the cool drip of water from the mill-lade. I watched the course of the little stream as it came in from the moor, and my fancy followed it to the top of the glen, where it must issue from an icy fountain fringed with cool ferns and mosses. I would have given a thousand pounds to plunge my face into that.

I had a fine prospect of the whole ring of moorland. I saw the car speed away with two occupants, and a man on a hill pony riding east. I judged they were looking for me, and I wished them joy of their quest.

But I saw something else more interesting. The house stood almost on the summit of a swell of moorland which crowned a sort of plateau, and there was no higher point nearer than the big hills six miles off. The actual summit, as I have mentioned, was a biggish clump of trees – firs mostly, with a few ashes and beeches. On the dovecot I was almost on a level with the tree-tops, and could see what lay beyond. The wood was not solid, but only a ring, and inside was an oval of green turf, for all the world like a big cricket field.

I didn't take long to guess what it was. It was an aerodrome, and a secret one. The place had been most cunningly chosen. For suppose anyone were watching an aeroplane descending here, he would think it had gone over the hill beyond the trees. As the place was on the top of a rise in the midst of a big amphitheatre, any observer from any direction would conclude it had passed out of view behind the hill. Only a man very close at hand would realize that the aeroplane had not gone over but had descended in the midst of the wood. An observer with a telescope on one of the higher hills might have discovered the truth, but only herds went there, and herds do not carry spy-glasses. When I looked from the dovecot I could see far away a blue line which I knew was the sea, and I grew furious to think that our enemies had this secret conning-tower to rake our waterways.

Then I reflected that if that aeroplane came back the chances were ten to one that I would be discovered. So through the afternoon I lay and prayed for the coming of darkness, and glad I was when the sun went down over the big western hills and the twilight haze crept over the moor. The aeroplane was late. The gloaming was far advanced when I heard the beat of wings and saw it vol-planing downward to its home in the wood. Lights twinkled for a bit and there was much coming and going from the house. Then the dark fell and silence.

Thank God it was a black night. The moon was well on its last quarter and would not rise till late. My thirst was too great to allow me to tarry, so about nine o'clock, so far as I could judge, I started to descend. It wasn't easy, and half way down I heard the back door of the house open, and saw the gleam of a lantern against the mill wall. For some agonizing minutes I hung by the ivy and prayed that who-ever it was would not come round by the dovecot. Then the light dis-appeared, and I dropped as softly as I could on to the hard soil of the yard.

I crawled on my belly in the lee of a stone dyke till I reached the fringe of trees which surrounded the house. If I had known how to do it I would have tried to put that aeroplane out of action, but I realized that any attempt would probably be futile. I was pretty certain that there would be some kind of defence round the house, so I went through the wood on hands and knees, feeling carefully every inch before me. It was as well, for presently I came on a wire about two feet from the ground. If I had tripped over that, it would doubtless have rung some bell in the house and I would have been captured.

A hundred yards farther on I found another wire cunningly placed on the edge of a small stream. Beyond that lay the moor, and in five minutes I was deep in bracken and heather. Soon I was round the shoulder of the rise, in the little glen from which the mill-lade flowed. Ten minutes later my face was in the spring, and I was soaking down pints of the blessed water.

But I did not stop till I had put half a dozen miles between me and that accursed dwelling.

ROWING ACROSS THE ATLANTIC

Tom McClean

On 17 May 1969, Tom McClean set off from St John's, Newfoundland, in his 20 foot Yorkshire dory Super Silver *in an attempt to row across the Atlantic single-handed. After 44 days at sea, life becomes a continual struggle against fatigue and loneliness . . .*

On Monday, 30 June, I reluctantly wrote in my log thirteen words that I hated to read: 'I must confess that, at last, I am beginning to feel worn down.' To even admit it was like wringing a confession by torture from me. But the facts had to be faced and, if possible, dealt with.

The winds were still light. Little more than breezes, in fact. But for the last three days they had been switching back and forth like a yo-yo. Northerly one day, south the next and that morning I had woken to a south-easterly. Not to be able to proceed in the one vital direction had become sheer frustration. I knew I must have passed the halfway mark and yet I could not convince myself that I had.

My mental condition was still patchy and, although I stuck to my timetable like a drowning man clutching at a straw, it was difficult to shake off the tormenting idea that I was actually heading back to Newfoundland. I actually began wondering whether or not I should consider seeking help if things became too bad. If things got to that pitch I would have to ask for aid from the next ship I spotted or call up assistance on the radio. But judging from the number of ships I had seen it could be days or weeks before another came along.

As *Silver* slid through the grey waters I totted up the for-and-against scorecard. The side for giving up totted up in rapid-fire style. I had

169

been at continuous full stretch now for just on six weeks. Every muscle, every nerve, every sinew and every tiny brain cell had been strained without let-up with the single object of keeping myself alive. I was a mass of aches, bruises, blisters, salt sores and a couple of agonizing boils had begun to erupt on the back of my neck. I was filthy and itchy to such a degree that I felt as scabrous as a mangy cat.

The rowing was becoming more difficult, and sleep, even during these calm nights, was transformed into fitful restlessness. And I was going off my food. The only thing I really fancied the last two or three days was canned fruit.

And the salt! The ever-present salt. I was caked with the stuff. Practically everything in the boat was covered in a thin white crust. It was in my hair, my nose, my eyes, under my clothes and I could not get rid of the taste.

That was the case for giving up. I had to ask myself, could it get worse? The only answer was not only that it could, but would. But if I decided to surrender what could I do about it? The answer was just as obvious. Nothing.

That was the case against giving up. That and the fact that despite my discomfort there was still a little voice inside me telling me I was not beaten yet. I had to be sure that I could hang on and would. I wondered, if it were possible to be granted just one wish, what would I ask for? I decided that right then it would be a pair of braces. My oilskin trousers kept slipping down in Chaplinesque style because the elastic waistband had perished. I had tried tying them up with a piece of string, but it did not work at all well.

Not a very imaginative wish, perhaps. Even a little crazy. But it served to help me resist wishing for the impossible – the feel of land under my feet. But my feet were not yet really ready for the land. Although by this time I was able to pull my sea-boots over a couple of pairs of socks, they were still too tight. The swelling had decreased until my feet looked almost normal size once again. But that was about the only normal thing about them. They still had that pickled look and they were still stinging and painful. They were, however, quite obviously on the mend and that was all that mattered.

The hours slipped by, virtually uncounted and unheeded. They merely acted as markers for my vital timetable which I hoped would help me nurse my mind and body back to strength.

On Tuesday I managed to work out a rough position. I made it 50°30′ N, 28°43′ W. Maybe it was not pinpoint accurate, but it must have been as near as possible under the circumstances. I was over the halfway mark at last and truly on the home run. There could be no thought of giving up now.

Looking back on that moment I now realize, with some surprise, that the discovery that I was over the halfway mark caused very little excitement. If it had happened a week or ten days before I would have felt like throwing a party. My elation would have known no bounds and it would have been a moment of congratulations to both *Silver* and myself.

I had been looking forward to that moment ever since I left St Johns. It had been the big goal, the massive target which had kept me going through the most severe experience of my life. Yet when it came it brought only a slight sense of relief. I am only thankful that it was enough to bolster my determination with the sort of cynical resignation used by most servicemen to describe the early period of their careers: 'Cheer up! The first three years are the worst!'

It was without cynicism, however, that I recalled reading, some time ago, the prayer of a sailor's mother. I believe it was written in the Victorian age, but I cannot remember the author's name. It ran:

> O Heaven, my child in mercy spare!
> O God, where'er he be;
> O God, my God, in pity spare
> My boy tonight at sea!

How corny that verse sounds now. How real it sounded halfway across the Atlantic. Under those conditions the strongest heart, I feel, would wonder if it was to be spared.

It has been said that sharks, like vultures, can sense the dying and travel many miles to attend the feast at the wake. I think it must be true. At 2 pm on Wednesday 2 July I saw my first shark. It slid alongside silently and without warning. I was emptying my after-lunch tea leaves over the side when I saw the sinister grey shape keeping pace with *Silver*. I knew there were sharks in the Atlantic. I had, of course, expected to see them. But this first meeting was so sudden I nearly dropped my tea-mug over the side. He was so close, I swear I could have reached over and touched him.

Once I had got over the shock of his sudden appearance I watched him for a few minutes swimming alongside and all I could think of at first was: 'My God, but he looks bloody ominous.'

I looked round on all sides of *Silver*, expecting to see triangular fins cutting through the water. God knows what I really expected to see, but in that first wild moment I thought the sea would be littered with them and all heading for *Silver* like U-boats zooming in for the kill. To my surprise, and great relief, there was not another shark to be seen.

One shark, however, was more than enough for me. This one kept me company for seven hours. First he would appear on one side of *Silver*, then on the other. At times he would disappear from view for five or ten minutes, but then suddenly swim back into sight again. He swam alongside *Silver*, ahead, astern and underneath. There were times when he came so close that I could hear him scraping the boat.

When he first appeared on the scene I sensed a chill of apprehension such as I had never quite felt before. And it did not begin to wear off until at least an hour had passed. I suppose that one can get used to practically anything in time, even a shark.

What, I asked myself, does one do about a shark which appears bent on much more than just a passing acquaintanceship? I tried chucking old tins over the side, hoping he might choke on them. Like a true gourmet he completely ignored them, disdaining even to honour them with a sniff. Should I, perhaps, try throwing so much food over the side that he would eventually become so full that he would swim away and forget me as a possible delicacy? I had no idea, however, how much food it would take to fill a shark and, in any case, I was going to need it myself.

Hours later, it seemed, it dawned on me that I couldn't possibly feed every shark that came along. It annoyed me to find that my mind was still churning over in such a ponderous manner. That shark had shaken me more than I had thought possible. But I had nothing else to do. The winds were still light and I figured that trying to think of ways to get rid of my unwanted companion was as good mental exercise as anything else.

Wild ideas, some just plain stupid, were examined with care and gone through step by step. It did not matter how unworkable they were so long as they kept me thinking.

I toyed with the notion of making a hook out of one of the rowlocks, baiting it with a paste of biscuits and porridge cake and trying to catch the blighter. The fact that I didn't even have a file with which to fashion the hook did not stop me working out the best way of shaping a rowlock for the purpose. I even went to the extent of planning how to shape it into a barbed hook.

I planned an ambush. The basis of this was to tempt him close to *Silver*'s side with titbits and then to spear him with one of the oars after fashioning the shaft end into a point with my clasp knife. At one stage, recalling a Tarzan film I had once seen in which Lex Barker had wrestled with an alligator before stabbing it to death, I flamboyantly thought of jumping over the side and tackling him with my knife. Needless to say, I didn't bother to work that one out. The only logical conclusion was that one day *Silver* would be found empty and drifting.

Finally I ran out of ideas. The last one was to give the shark a name. At least it would make the situation seem a little more chummy. I dubbed him 'Bluey'. Nevertheless, I was glad to see the last of him at about 9 pm. He sped off to the west and I watched him until his fin was out of sight. I heaved a sigh and said: 'Cheerio, Bluey, don't bother to call again.'

But he did. Bluey showed up again the next day. At least, I assumed it was the same shark. He slid on to the scene just as before, silent and sinister. It was about midday and I had been rowing for several hours. I don't know how long he had been keeping an eye on me, but as I was shipping the oars to prepare my lunch I spotted him about two yards off *Silver*'s port side and just about a foot beneath the water, grey, vicious and apparently ravenously hungry. And again he kept pace as *Silver* drifted before a 15 to 20 mph wind. I scanned the water to see if he had brought any of his friends along this time, but again he was alone. Maybe he figured I was big enough only for a meal for one. I watched him nosing along as I ate, not too heartily I must admit, my curry lunch.

With a pathetic spot of bravado I waved my spoon at him and said: 'That's right, Bluey, just hang around until you think I'm fattened enough for your liking.' Even as I spoke I shuddered as my imagination

173

vividly presented me with a picture of Bluey grabbing me by an arm with his jaws. I knew I was brooding far too much on Bluey. If I went on like that I really would begin believing that I was about to end up as sharkbait. In an effort to forget him I tested my lifeline radio.

As I had not yet succeeded in picking up a ship's operator, I made my call without too much enthusiasm. Almost mechanically I mouthed my little message: 'Atlantic row-boat *Super Silver* here. Come in, please.'

I had repeated it several times when I heard a faint voice: 'Sailing ship fifty miles to your north.'

Almost jumping with excitement, I shouted at the top of my voice: 'Hello, hello there. Atlantic row-boat *Super Silver* here. Come in, please.'

Again that faint voice. And again the same message: 'Sailing ship fifty miles to your north.' He repeated it several times. I cut in with: '*Super Silver* here. Are you mistaking me for a sailing ship? This is row-boat *Super Silver* . . . row-boat *Super Silver*. Do you read me, please?'

He obviously did not read me, for all I heard was another message about a sailing ship. I gave up trying to tell him differently and switched off. And when I looked over the side Bluey was still with me. The sheer persistence of the brute was unnerving. He did not disappear until dark. Even then I could imagine him slipping quietly alongside *Silver* and just waiting, waiting, waiting . . . for me.

I woke on Saturday, 5 July, to a wind from the east. It built up to forty miles an hour and, although it was from the east and causing me to lose precious distance, I blessed it. For Bluey did not appear. He had no doubt headed for the calm of deeper water. The wind lasted all day and there was nothing for me to do except heave out the sea anchor. I stayed in my shelter all morning, trying to build up my strength. I dozed off and on most of the day turning and twisting on the hard floorboards.

My discomfort, as I tried to rest on those boards, was a result of the clinging inertia which had possessed me with increasing danger over the past two weeks. My air bed was no longer inflated. A week before, the constant rubbing against other articles in the shelter, as *Silver* rolled and pitched her way through the sea, had worn a hole right through the side. I had forgotten to bring a repair outfit with me. My desultory attempt to patch it with Elastoplast and Bostik lasted a few hours only. A sudden hiss of escaping air and it was as flat as a pancake within a few seconds. It had been like that ever since and I hadn't bothered to try patching it up again.

An insignificant mishap, perhaps. And certainly of no importance in terms of my safety. But it was yet another illustration of the risk, lurking like a submerged iceberg, which could rip the bottom out of my adventure simply by allowing myself to drift into a stupid state of not caring. These little incidents drummed home again and again the inescapable fact that if anything goes wrong in a lone adventure of this sort there is nobody to blame but yourself.

I had reminded myself of this before. I had to keep reminding myself. There had been moments when the temptation to lie back and say: 'Well, I've done all I can, now it is up to luck, or fate or God' had been almost unbearable. Yet I had been able to pat myself on the back and say that I had fought against that – and fought well.

By lunchtime it came to me with a knock-out impact that for the first time I had given up the fight without knowing that I had done so. I had been lying in my shelter all morning bemoaning my luck, kidding myself that I was not giving in and wallowing in self-congratulations for having fought the good fight so well. The whole morning had gone without my once remembering my timetable; without my once making the conscious effort of prodding myself into even the most ineffectual action; without my once remembering what I had to do simply to stay alive.

The dawning realization of the chilling truth jolted me psychologically as nothing else had done so far on the trip. I was literally panting with anxiety as I scrambled out of the shelter. I tried to stand and drag in great heaving breaths of that Atlantic air to steady myself.

But I could not. Whether from the effort or shock I don't know, but my knees were trembling so much I just could not keep my feet. It was not just a quivering type of tremble. Seized by rapid shakes which seemed to be moving my kneecaps at least two or three inches and sending shuddering jerks along the muscles of my calves and thighs, I found that my legs were completely uncontrollable.

I sat down on my rowing seat, legs outstretched as far as possible and clamped a hand over each knee. I sat there with my eyes shut, rocking slightly backward and forward until the fit of shakes died away.

One thing was crystal clear at that point. I had to get into action, and quickly. My mind, however, was not so clear. My thinking mechanism was hampered by a haze of such improbabilities, impossibilities and wishful dreaming that I think I was like the amateur mountain climber who, having got so far, made the mistake of looking down. I just wanted to stay put. To cling on to the one spot which seemed so safe.

If I moved would I fall? If I moved would those damned knees start jerking about again? If I moved . . . if? I had to move. Slowly I opened my eyes and looked at my hands. Even more slowly I eased their grip on my knees. Nothing happened. I shook each leg in turn. Again nothing happened. The trembling had stopped. Gingerly I got to my feet, expecting the whole ghastly business to start again. It did not.

I felt as much like eating as jumping over the side, but it was the handiest thing to start. I went about my preparation for lunch in such a deliberate fashion that it was almost like moving in slow-motion. 'God almighty,' I told myself, 'if you get into a state like this again it is you who will be cooked.'

The aroma of cooking curry that day, usually so mouth-watering for me, became a repellent odour. I had been off my food for a couple of days but I never dreamt I would see the day when the smell of curry would actually make me feel sick. The more I thought about it, the more it affected me. It swirled around my head in great choking waves until I thought it would actually stick in my hair. The first spoonful produced such a bout of nausea I had to force myself to swallow it. Food was vitally important to me at that stage. I knew I had to eat that dish of curry even if it took me the rest of the day to get it down.

Without a doubt it was the worst meal of the trip. And as I sat there literally willing myself to spoon, swallow, spoon, swallow, Bluey popped up again. Mealtimes were like a magnet to him. There he was suddenly alongside *Silver* again, just a few inches below the surface with that evil fin cutting its own narrow wake in the water. In an almost mesmerized state, I sat watching him until my curry had grown cold. I started eating again, stuffing the cold mess into my mouth with haste. All I wanted to do now was finish it. And all the time I watched that shark.

Thinking that the hot bite of a dehydrated curry block might give him a bit of gyp in his belly and drive him off, I threw one over the side. He did not even give it a glance. As if to demonstrate his contempt of that feeble effort, he changed course, sliding head-on towards *Silver*'s beam. Something, his fin, back or tail, rasped along her bottom as he passed underneath to take up his shadowing position on the other side.

Then I realized that this time Bluey had not come alone. At first glance the sea around me seemed alive with those dreaded grey fins. At second glance I counted only five. *Only* five? Five or fifty-five, what did it matter? For some reason which I could not fathom, none of them approached as close as Bluey – if, indeed, it was the same shark. Maybe it was my imagination, but I was convinced that it was one and the same, I told myself I could make out marks on his body, the shape of his head, his length, etc., all of which, as far as I was concerned, made a positive identification.

'Christ,' I told myself, 'this bloody sardine is getting you down. If you don't watch out you'll be giving him a free meal – yourself.'

I had already taken photographs of him. I did that the first day he appeared. I started another snapping session then, as if to show him who had the upper hand. I snapped him from a standing position, from a sitting position, from the stern, from the bow.

To blazes with him. I was on my way home and I was going to get there, Bluey or no Bluey and with or without his companions. And, I shouted at him, 'I'll make it even if you follow me all the way.'

★   ★   ★   ★

When darkness fell I tried to forget the hauntings of Bluey and his chums. I hoped that by morning they would have sheered off, leaving me once again in solitary state. There were so many things for me to consider that I desperately needed some time completely free of diversion, shock or danger.

Most important of all was, just how was I getting along? The wind had been from the east for two days. Despite the fact that I knew I had put in quite a deal of rowing in the past couple of weeks, my mental state had been so persistently patchy that I had taken no count of the hours and only a very rough check of the direction. How much ground had I lost?

Under the beam of my flashlight I had a look at the compass before turning in. Sure enough, I was heading west. Nothing during this journey has been so morale-sapping as those times when the wind has you heading willy-nilly in the wrong direction.

I groaned and then cut myself short. I had been doing too much groaning. Severely I told myself, 'That is the first step to giving up the ghost.' Giving myself a mental shake, I placed myself under two strict orders as I bedded down:

1. Snap out of the lethargy which is clogging you both mentally and physically.

2. Get *Silver* heading in the right direction and get as much distance under your belt as soon as possible.

I tried to introduce a military crispness and urgency into those orders. As I stretched my aching bones out on the hard boards of *Silver*, I kept repeating them until I dropped off into a troubled sleep. At three o'clock in the morning a crack of thunder which seemed to have made a direct hit on *Silver* shook me wide awake. There had not been much in the way of fair weather on this trip, but this was the first thunderstorm I had run into.

There was no more sleep for me that night. The storm lasted three hours. I do not think I have ever known anything quite so fantastically fierce. *Silver* seemed to rattle with every clap of thunder. The noise from the skies filled the entire space between sea and sky, rolling and echoing in the blackness until it seemed as if some unseen monster must be hurtling towards me at breakneck speed. And in between the thunder I could hear the sea swishing and surfing as it built itself up in a fury to match the rage overhead. The wind came whistling in, developing itself – it seemed to me almost with glee – into a continuous savage scream. And it came from the east, pushing me yet further and further away from home.

Every now and then the thick, choking, booming blackness was split by great streaks of forked lightning. It cleaved its way from sky to sea in vast electric sparks like the side-effects of some monumental scientific experiment being carried out by crazed gods and going hopelessly wrong.

The fierce storm made Silver rattle with every thunderclap.

The lightning was perhaps the most comforting and most frightening part of the storm. Comforting because each streak lit up the sea for split seconds and it was a blessing to find even fractional relief from the blindness of the night. And frightening because each fork seemed to be working its way closer and closer to *Silver*. Each streak of power was so hostile that I felt it must surely sizzle and steam as it dug its way down into the dark waters. Little *Silver* wouldn't stand a chance if she was struck . . . just a puff of smoke and a few black ashes as our epitaph.

Silver had begun to buck and pitch with growing violence. There was something almost supernatural about that alien night as I clung to the seat and listened to the boiling savagery around me. Then the rain began. It fell in sheets from the beginning. Pouring down, drumming on *Silver*'s turtle-decking and pecking with throbbing persistence at my head and shoulders. The almost biblical-style tempest was now complete.

I was wearing two sets of waterproof clothing and I pulled both hoods tightly over my ears to cut out the noise. But there was no escape. I realized that if I sat out in the open much longer I ran the chance of becoming scared. There was only one remedy: a spot of the old ostrich treatment. I dived into my shelter and tucked myself as far up in one corner as I could get. One consoling thought I hugged to myself as I sat there in the darkness – it was 100 per cent certain that Bluey would no longer be in attendance.

I was right. By daybreak the storm had begun to fade, but the rain continued to lash down and there was not a sign of Bluey or any of his chums. I had not felt so chuffed for days. The wind had dwindled to a mere 25 mph, but it was still from the east. Monday, 7 July, was the third day on the trot of easterlies. For a moment I felt the lethargic depression of the previous day creeping in. Then I remembered my orders of the night before.

That easterly wind had to be beaten somehow. I hauled in the sea anchor and started rowing head-on to the wind. The sheer uselessness of such effort was not lost on me. But I stuck at it, driven on by the perverse fit of cussedness which I hoped to make a substitute for the spirit of lethargy. I rowed for three hours, knowing full well that I was getting nowhere. Every time I began wondering how long the easterlies would last I chased the thought out of my mind by the simple formula of saying: 'It can't last for ever.'

By mid-afternoon I had to give up. The sea was running high again and *Silver* was shipping water in dangerous quantities. I had to stand by the pumps at least twice in every hour. But I was glad to be there. I was being forced to fight again. The pumping sessions made me realize just how much punishment I had taken. My muscles were stretched to torture point, but the pain was a blessing as it stung me into sharp awareness for the first time in over two weeks.

My concern about the easterlies was banished the next morning when I woke to a 20 mph west wind. By ten o'clock it had risen to about 40 mph and *Silver* was zipping along so beautifully in the right direction I almost cried with joy. After lunch the wind dropped, but I didn't care, it was still from the west. Feeling that I could not afford to waste even a second, I began another crushing session of rowing. I kept at it until dark without even stopping for tea.

I clawed my way through the first two hours of rowing, ignoring the pain as my back creaked with each movement and my arms felt as if they would drop off. For most of the time my eyes were tight shut and my teeth so tightly clenched that my jaws ached. Then suddenly I was through that curtain of agony and rowing automatically, insensitive to the demands I was making on my physical strength. What was driving me? I wish I had known the answer. With almost clinical detachment I examined myself as I bent backward, forward, backward, forward, plodding on and on and not daring to stop.

One thing was clear. I was not out there striving for anyone or anything. Success or failure meant nothing to anyone else but myself. Strangely, I had to remind myself that I had decided this was the only way for me to make something of myself; to make the world notice me even if only for a short time; to make a place for the name of McClean on the lists of those who have dared and won. But however I wrapped it up there was no getting away from the fact that I was doing it for myself. For money too? I admitted that had also come into my calculations. What about pride? Yes, that even more than money.

Whichever way I looked at it, I kept coming up with the same question: 'Am I being just bloody selfish?' And there was always the same answer – 'Yes, you are. But you're stuck with it now.' There was no doubt that this habit of handing out self-lectures every now and then was a real lifeline. I daresay the lads back at camp would have had a chuckle if they had known. They would have said that it was a foregone conclusion that I would talk to myself if there was nobody else around.

My worries about being delayed by easterlies completely vanished on Wednesday, 9 July. That morning marked the beginning of twelve days of westerly winds almost without a break. I didn't know it at the time, but it was really the start of the last lap.

It was also a great day for a very different reason. An examination of my feet showed that they had almost fully recovered from the rigours of the Labrador Current. Those frozen days seemed such a long way off, yet I felt that I could remember any minute of them. I resolved that never again would I go through anything like that and, as if to seal the vow, my seaboots slipped over my feet with ease.

I stood up as excited as a child on his first visit to the circus. I stamped each foot in turn and danced a little jig of joy. Perhaps the most curious sensation was that of feeling fully dressed for the first time in weeks. It was incredible that a pair of rubber boots could create such a change in my mood.

The rash of salt sores on my neck, wrists and backside showed no signs of lessening. The blisters on my hands still built up one on another. My muscles ached so much that if I moved to relieve the pain in one point it cropped up somewhere else. The boils on the back of my neck felt like mountains. And trying to sleep had become a nightmare. My shoulders had started to give me so much pain at night that it was impossible to lie on my side for more than a few seconds. After towing or pumping sessions my hands felt as if they would never open fully again. There were times when there seemed to be no power at all in the fingers.

There had been moments when I wondered just how far the limits of human endurance could take me. Yet once those sea-boots were on my feet, none of the agony, the pain or the worry seemed to matter any more. If my feet were on the mend, then the rest of my body would catch up before long. The sea-boots and the westerly wind were exactly the ingredients for the tonic I needed. Maybe I looked a mess, maybe I was a mess, but I was on top once more and I didn't intend to fall off again.

That evening the sun showed itself and a following light rain shower created a huge rainbow which arched right across the sea and *Silver* was heading right through it. To me it was the gateway to home. Home! Harvest-time on the Venns' farm was not too far off. John had sent me a telegram before I left St Johns, saying: 'Don't forget to make it in time for the harvest.' I was now sure that I would do just that.

But how far? How long? How many more storms? How many more hours of rowing? And, more important, how many more chances would the Atlantic grant me?

This, however, was not the moment for cares or for thinking of what might be. This was a moment to think of other things and there was plenty to think about – a walk in the hills, a beer with the lads, of things I had done, of things I hoped to do. All the good things, all the happy times. All the things which add up to a sailor's dream of home. I knew for sure that the fire was back in my belly at last. Nothing except final disaster could lick me now.

It occurred to me that up to now all my prayers on this trip had been a plea for help in moments of trouble. Surely now was the moment for a prayer of thanks. Heartfelt and humble thanks for the help which had reached me without being requested.

At five-thirty on the morning of Thursday, 10 July, I was wakened by the drone of a plane overhead. To me it was the sound of land. By the end of the day I realized that I was in an area where I would hear planes several times during the day and night. But two days passed without my being able to sight even a wing-tip. The grey cloudy skies had dogged me almost all the way were still with me. Yet I never failed to stare upwards whenever I heard a plane, trying to follow the direction of the sound until it was out of earshot.

The days were passing with unflagging monotony. Wake up, eat, row, eat, row, tidy up *Silver*, pump, row, pump, sleep: over and over again the same routine, one day following another almost without change except for the speed of the wind. But my buoyant mood was still with me. It was going to take more than a spot of boredom to get me down from here on. I had worked out an estimated position on Saturday, 12 July. It was 52°06' N, 20° W. I made that just 720 miles from Ireland. The whiff of home was well and truly in my nostrils.

Sleep was out of the question. I was too excited for that. Whatever had happened, whatever could happen, I was sure I was going to make it. I had to do something and the only real exertion open to me was to row. I had rowed steadily through most of the day. Admittedly, I had been looking forward to supper and getting my head down. Now I could not bear the thought of missing a single valuable minute.

Throughout the night I stayed at the oars, rowing as if I would reach land by the morning. I stopped only for tea and a shot of rum at about 2 pm. About an hour later I saw the lights of a ship heading east. Almost at the same moment I became aware of a shining ghostlike shape darting about in the water. I watched it switch from side to side of *Silver*. Apart from my tea breaks that was the only time I shipped my oars. I don't know how long I watched, but I think I was mesmerized for a while.

Then I realized it was a large fish glowing with the phosphorous which sparkled like tinsel glitter over the surface. I had no idea of what it was. Maybe, I thought, Bluey has returned to haunt me. But whatever it was, it was both beautiful and spooky. It hung around for about ten minutes and then suddenly vanished. One minute it was there bursting through the water like a shooting star, leaving dancing fire in its wake. The next second, nothing. I suppose it must have dived, having tired of its game with *Silver*.

For a few seconds I sat staring at the spot where it had disappeared. I was sorry to see it go, for those ten minutes had been quite the most beautifully entertaining of the trip. It had been like a cabaret show, made all the more welcome because it had been so unexpected. I was glad that I had decided to row through the night. And I rowed on.

By dawn I was bone weary, but I was happy. So happy, in fact, that my appetite returned in a rush. I breakfasted on porridge, tea and biscuits and marmalade, and then crawled into my shelter for a couple of hours' sleep.

A couple of hours was a complete underestimation. That night row had taken far more out of me than I had thought. I did not wake until three o'clock in the afternoon. Strangely enough, I couldn't have picked a better day to sleep if I could have forecast the weather ahead with pin-point accuracy.

It was a completely calm day. The Atlantic was barely ruffled by the mildest breeze. Yet even the term breeze is too strong to describe that peaceful day. Zephyr is the perfect word. The *Oxford Dictionary* defines it as 'the west wind personified'. How true, how true. Throughout the day it never blew harder than between two and three miles per hour, and I took full advantage of it. After a hurried meal I rowed through the afternoon until about five-thirty in the most perfect rowing conditions I had yet encountered. *Silver* and I floated along.

And there was to be a perfect end to a perfect day. Just before five-thirty I spotted a ship which I thought might be the weather ship *Juliet* which was on station somewhere in the area I had entered. But she was steaming eastwards and was, I was sure, too far away to spot me. But this time I was taking no chances on being overlooked. It was the first ship I'd had a chance to stop and I was anxious to get a message to my friends back home.

I lit a flare and, standing on the seat, waved it above my head. But that ship showed no signs of seeing me. I tied a red anorak to the telescopic radio mast and raised it as far as it would go. Again there were no signs of recognition.

Then I fired one of my radar flares which rise to 2,000 feet and explode, shooting out a shower of fine metallic dust which should be picked up by a ship's radar. It worked. She changed course and bore down on me. As she steamed slowly past on my port side, there was a shout from the deck: 'Are you all right?' I yelled back: 'Yes, I'm okay. All I want is my position and to ask your skipper to radio a message back to Lloyd's in London.'

It was the SS *Hansa*, on her way to Deptford, London, with a cargo of newsprint for the Express Newspapers. I waved my chart above my head as she inched past me. Then the *Hansa* stopped and I rowed alongside. The captain climbed down from the bridge to the midships deck and shouted down: 'Your position is 52° 24′ N, 20° 26′ W.'

I scribbled it on a blank page in my log-book and then passed up my message and several rolls of films which I asked him to pass on to the *Sunday Express* when he got to Deptford. Then he asked if I wanted to come aboard, have a bath or just have a drink. I refused them all with thanks.

'How about food and water?' he shouted. 'Are you okay for supplies?'

'I am absolutely fine, thanks,' I shouted. 'I don't need a thing now I've got my position.'

With that the captain shouted: 'Okay. Keep clear of my propellers.' He gave me time to row off before starting his engines and heading for Blighty. I watched her for a few minutes, feeling a little wistful. But it did not last for long. When I checked the position he had given me I found I was only ten degrees from the Irish coast. And I made that no more than 600 miles.

The smell of the land was with me with a vengeance.

Three days later Tom McClean survived a near disaster when Super Silver *capsized. After baling out the dory, he continued rowing and finally came ashore at Blacksod Bay, Ireland, on 27 July 1969.*

THE WILD WASTE-PAPER

Norman Hunter

It was Mrs Flittersnoop, the Professor's housekeeper, who started it all, really. And once you started anything in Professor Branestawm's house you never knew where it would finish or even if it ever would. She was dusting the Professor's desk one evening while he was having some breakfast over night, so that he could get up early the next morning to do something important. And on the desk she noticed a little bottle marked 'Cough Mixture'. At least it was off the desk and in the waste-paper basket before she noticed it really.

'Dear, dear,' she said, 'how careless of him to leave things about. And no cork in it either. Well, well, that saves picking it up again, anyway.' And she dusted the rest of the dust off the inkstand and went to bed, leaving the bottle where it had fallen, with its contents leaking out all over the waste-paper in the basket.

★   ★   ★   ★

The clock in Professor Branestawm's bedroom struck ten to seven the next morning, because it was one of the Professor's own inventions, and because that was the time.

'That sounds like Tuesday,' said the Professor, falling out of sleep

187

and out of bed almost at the same time. In a moment he had whistled for a cup of tea. In another moment he had dressed himself with his usual scrupulous carelessness. In five more moments he had put on his five pairs of spectacles, four pairs for different purposes, and the fifth pair for looking for the others with when he lost them.

'Now, let me see,' said the Professor, taking a sip of his morning tea and wishing it wasn't so hot. 'What did I get up early for today?' He pulled his near-sighted glasses down from his forehead and looked for the note he had made on his shirt-cuff the day before.

'Bother it!' he exclaimed. There was no note there. Tuesday was his clean shirt day. There was no time to be lost. Any moment now the laundry man might come and take his note away.

'Mrs Flittersnoop!' he called, and leaving the most of his tea untouched he ran downstairs about two at a time, but without stopping to count them.

He had no sooner reached the bottom than the study door was flung open with a crash, and Mrs Flittersnoop, the housekeeper, rushed out screaming. And well she might, for after her, flip flap, flop-a-crumple, came an awful misshapen white sort of thing with squiggly blue marks all over it. Just like a severely enlarged grocer's bill, which was what it actually was, only you're not supposed to know yet.

'Great gear boxes!' exclaimed the Professor, making a guess at what had happened and getting it right first time. 'Stop, hands up, get away, not today thank you, down sir,' said the Professor to the floppy thing as he ran after it. But it didn't seem to understand any of that sort of talk, so just as the three of them came tearing out into the garden he picked up a clothes-prop and hit it somewhere near the middle, whereupon it crumpled up all of a heap. The next minute a spare gust of wind caught it and whisked it away over the tree tops and out of sight.

'Oh, Professor, Professor,' wailed Mrs Flittersnoop, looping herself round his neck and going all pale round the eyes. 'I'm so frightened. Whatever was it? Came at me like a wild thing, it did, as soon as I got inside the door. And me turned forty this twelvemonth. It's a shame, that's what it is.'

'No, it isn't,' said the Professor, who was thinking of something else. 'Pick up a stick and come back to the study.'

Back they went, the Professor very excited and his nose twitching

Suddenly Mrs Fluttersnoop rushed out screaming.

like anything. Mrs Flittersnoop, very scared and nervous, but determined to go wherever the Professor went, for safety.

Then the Professor opened the door a crack, and they peeped in.

'Coo,' said Mrs Flittersnoop.

'Hum,' said the Professor.

The sight that met their eyes was enough to make anyone coo and hum, and make a lot of other astonished noises, too, for that matter. The most unlikely things were going on inside the waste-paper basket. The pieces of waste-paper seemed to have had something that didn't agree with them, for they were swelling up and growing bigger every moment. One huge yellow-coloured monster like a gigantic sort of sponge was almost out of the basket. Others were slowly waving crumpled papery legs about in the air as if seeking for a foothold.

'Oh! Oh! What's happening? Oh! stop them, Sir,' cried Mrs Flittersnoop. But the Professor turned on her sharply.

'It's your own fault, you careless person,' he said severely. 'What did you upset in the waste-paper basket last night? Now then . . .'

The overloaded, overcrowded waste-paper basket started creaking and groaning like anything.

'P-p-pup-pup-please, Professor, I never – that is, it wasn't, I mean I didn't, how could I? . . .'

'Be quiet,' said the Professor. 'There are interesting developments about to take place.'

'Bang!' They took place. The waste-paper basket burst with a noise like a gun going off, and the swollen-up, monstrous, terrible-looking waste-paper came oozing and leaping out into the room in the most threatening manner imaginable.

'Most educational,' said the Professor, looking through all his pairs of glasses one after the other, while the Housekeeper fainted and came to again three times without stopping.

'Look out,' she screamed suddenly, pointing frantically into the room.

A huge piece of grown-up postcard, with its gigantic stamp glaring like an enormous fierce eye, had climbed up the curtains and was staring down at them. Then suddenly all the wild waste-paper seemed to rally, and it all came rushing at the door, bobbing over the carpet, the pieces rustling against each other with a noise like a thousand burst water-pipes.

'Run,' cried the Professor, and they ran. They ran like old boots, and like cats on hot bricks, and like everything that is rapid and frantic, and after them, bobbety rustle-ty crumple-ty whoosh, came the wild waste-paper. Huge, terrifying, gigantic,. with paper arms waving and ink-smudged faces snarling.

'The pear tree,' gasped the Professor as they reached the vegetable garden. 'Quick, up, only safe place. Waste-paper can't climb trees – at least not pear trees – at least hope not – hurry!'

He picked Mrs Flittersnoop up with a sudden burst of strength that was quite unnatural to him and threw her into the branches, where fortunately her apron caught on some twigs, then casting a hurried glance backwards he scrambled up after her and soon they were perched on the topmost branches, swaying in the wind, and wishing nothing of the kind had happened . . .

Out of the kitchen door came their paper pursuers, helter skelter, crumple rumple, over the lawn and piled themselves up at the foot of the tree still rattling and crackling, and seeming to be growing still bigger.

'Now, look where you've landed us,' said the Professor.

'Me!' she protested. 'Me, indeed – that I never.'

'Yes you ever,' said the Professor. 'Didn't you knock a bottle into the waste-paper basket last night?'

'Yes, but that was cough mixture,' she said.

'Cough mixture my grandfather's second cousin,' growled the Professor. 'What do I want with cough mixture? That was my special selected elixir of vitality, or life-giver, a marvellous liquid whose secret it has taken me more than a life-time to discover. It brings to life anything it touches, and the only thing that will stop it is paregoric cough mixture. That's why I put it in a cough mixture bottle; otherwise the bottle would be six times as big as the house by now.'

'But-b-b-b-,' began the Housekeeper.

'You see what it's done. Brought the waste-paper to life. Lucky for you the paper soaked it all up, or the whole houseful of furniture would be chasing us by now. Yes, yes,' he raised one hand, and in doing so nearly fell out of the tree. 'I know what you're going to say;

why didn't I put a cork in. Well, I didn't put a cork in because the elixir is ruined if you keep the air away from it. Nothing can live without air. Hullo, what's happening?'

A movement among the pieces of paper had attracted his attention. Two of the smaller pieces had detached themselves from the crumpling mass and gone rolling and hopping back to the house.

'They're going back,' cried Mrs Flittersnoop excitedly. 'Perhaps the stuff is wearing off. Shoo!' she cried. But none of the other pieces went.

'Don't be silly,' said the Professor. 'That elixir won't wear off for thirty years or so. Wait, I'm going to drop lighted matches on them and set them on fire.'

He fumbled in his pockets, and then remembered he had left his matches on the bedroom candlestick.

'Tut tut,' he said, 'what a nuisance.' Then remembering that his memory wasn't very good, he fumbled a bit more and found he hadn't left them on the candlestick after all. They were in the lining of his waistcoat. He struck one, and leant as far out as he could, with the Housekeeper clinging frantically to his coat-tails to stop him falling. Then the match went out.

'Tut tut,' he said again. He struck another match and dropped it at once. But the match hadn't lit, so that was no good.

'Tut tut as before,' he said, and struck another. And this time he dropped it well alight. Down and down dropped the little flaming stick like a miniature beacon of hope, or an imitation sky rocket coming down, or even like a lighted match being dropped out of a pear tree.

'Ah-h-h,' went the Professor and the Housekeeper both together, but neither of them in time.

Then 'Oh-h-h,' they went, for just as the match was about to drop into the midst of the puffed-up awful wild waste-paper, what must it do but go and catch on a branch and stay there till it flickered and died out.

The Professor was just going to strike another match when Mrs Flittersnoop pulled him back by his coat-tails.

'Look, they're coming back,' she gasped.

And so they were. The two pieces of wild waste-paper that had gone into the house were hurrying out again. And they were carrying something that glinted and shone in the sunlight.

'Exceptional,' said the Professor. 'They're bringing a saw from the tool-shed. Surely they can't know what a saw is. Now, can it have anything to do with what's written on the paper? Would the elixir make a butcher's bill know a saw if it saw it, and if so does that mean that the gas bill which I threw away yesterday, and which I see below us, may explode at any moment?'

The Professor stopped thinking to scratch his head, then he went on thinking again. But he didn't have time to think much because all at once the tree began to shake and shiver, and above the crumpling rustling noise of the mad paper came the hoarse rasp of the saw. The paper monstrosities were starting to cut the tree down.

'Help!' shrieked Mrs Flittersnoop when she realized what was happening. 'Oh, do something – do something, Professor!' she moaned, shaking like a jelly and going all different colours.

But the Professor hadn't been listening to what she had said. He was busy studying the scene below through his long-sighted glasses, and making notes in several different languages on an ample pear he had picked.

The tree shook more and more as the sharp saw bit deeper and deeper into the trunk. Mrs Flittersnoop gave up talking to the Professor, and got more and more frightened. She began to think the silliest things, such as 'if you fall out of a pear tree is it a pear drop?'

'Amazing intelligence,' said the Professor. 'They've done it.'

They had. The tree gave a convulsive shiver and down it crashed, falling with such violence that the Professor and his housekeeper were flung over the fence into the next garden.

'Hullo!' said the next-door man, coming out of his potting shed with a dahlia seed in his hand.

He hadn't time to say any more, for over the fence, for all the world like a lot of huge crazy sponges, came the wild waste-paper. They rushed at the Professor and the Housekeeper and the next-door man, and there was such a scrimmage and a dust up, and a goodness knows what, as nobody has ever seen since.

Bravely the Professor grappled with the first piece, and tore it to shreds. But each shred swelled up and became a separate monstrous thing. The Housekeeper was struggling inside an envelope. The next-door man was all wrapped up in a circular about corn cure, though he'd never had corns in his life.

And in another second there would have been no more Professor or Housekeeper or next-door man. And the wild waste-paper would have had the upper hand, and everything would have been awful. But just at that very exact moment the piece of gas bill the Professor was fighting stepped on the edge of a bonfire the next-door man had been having.

'Poof!' went the flames, and the gas bill flashed up and disappeared in a handful of ash, setting fire to the corn cure circular as it did so. Then the envelope with the Housekeeper in caught fire and soon the whole crumply crowd of frightful paper monsters was blazing and crackling away like a furnace.

'Oh, my eyebrows,' cried the Housekeeper. 'They're gone – singed off.'

'And, oh, my dahlia seed,' wailed the next-door man. 'It's fried, baked, and toasted, so it is. I'll never grow any dahlias from that now.'

The Professor mopped his forehead with the Housekeeper's apron.

'Thank goodness for your bonfire,' he gasped. 'If it hadn't been for that . . .' He stopped, leaving the others to fill in the missing words.

ANTARCTIC ODYSSEY

Sir Ernest Shackleton

When the Endurance *was crushed by pack-ice in latitude 69° South on 17 October 1915, Sir Ernest Shackleton and his men had to abandon their attempt to cross Antarctica – their main concern now being survival.*

For months they existed precariously on the sea ice before making their way to the uninhabited Elephant Island, 570 miles southeast of Cape Horn. Shackleton decided to try and reach South Georgia (800 miles to the northeast) in an ordinary ship's boat, the James Caird *with some of his crew in an attempt to mount a relief operation to save the rest of his men.*

The decision made, I walked through the blizzard with Worsley and Wild to examine the *James Caird*. The 20-foot boat had never looked big; she appeared to have shrunk in some mysterious way when I viewed her in the light of our new undertaking. She was an ordinary ship's whaler, fairly strong, but showing signs of the strains she had endured since the crushing of the *Endurance*. Where she was holed in leaving the pack was, fortunately, above the water-line and easily patched. Standing beside her, we glanced at the fringe of the storm-swept, tumultuous sea that formed our path. Clearly our voyage would be a big adventure. I called the carpenter and asked him if he could do anything to make the boat more seaworthy. He first enquired if he was to go with me, and seemed quite pleased when I said, 'Yes'. He was over fifty years of age and not altogether fit, but he had a good knowkedge of sailing boats and was very quick. McCarthy said that he could contrive some sort of covering for the *James Caird* if he might use the lids of the cases and the four sledge-runners. He proposed to complete the covering with some of our canvas, and he set about making his plans at once . . .

The weather was fine on 23 April, and we hurried forward our preparations. It was on this day I decided finally that the crew for the *James Caird* should consist of Worsley, Crean, McNeish, McCarthy, Vincent, and myself. A storm came on about noon, with driving snow and heavy squalls. Occasionally the air would clear for a few minutes, and we could see a line of pack-ice, five miles out, driving across from west to east. This sight increased my anxiety to get away quickly. Winter was advancing, and soon the pack might close completely round the island and stay our departure for days or even for weeks. I did not think that ice would remain around Elephant Island continuously during the winter, since the strong winds and fast currents would keep it in motion. We had noticed ice and bergs going past at the rate of four or five knots. A certain amount of ice was held up about the end of our spit, but the sea was clear where the boat would have to be launched.

Worsley, Wild, and I climbed to the summit of the seaward rocks and examined the ice from a better vantage-point than the beach offered. The belt of pack outside appeared to be sufficiently broken for our purposes, and I decided that, unless the conditions forbade it, we would make a start in the *James Caird* on the following morning. Obviously the pack might close at any time. This decision made, I spent the rest of the day looking over the boat, gear, and stores, and discussing plans with Worsley and Wild.

Our last night on the solid ground of Elephant Island was cold and uncomfortable. We turned out at dawn and had breakfast. Then we launched the *Stancomb Wills* and loaded her with stores, gear, and ballast, which would be transferred to the *James Caird* when the heavier boat had been launched. The ballast consisted of bags made from blankets and filled with sand, making a total weight of about 1,000 lbs. In addition we had gathered a number of boulders and about 250 lbs of ice, which would supplement our two casks of water.

The stores taken in the *James Caird*, which would last six men for one month, were as follows:

30 boxes of matches.
6½ gallons paraffin.
1 tin methylated spirit.
10 boxes of flamers.

1 box of blue lights.
2 Primus stoves with spare parts and prickers.
1 Nansen aluminium cooker.
6 sleeping bags.
A few spare socks.
Few candles and some blubber-oil in an oil bag.
Food:
   3 cases sledging rations.
   2 cases nut food.
   2 cases biscuits.
   1 case lump sugar.
   30 packets of Trumilk.
   1 tin of Bovril cubes.
   1 tin of Cerebos salt.
   36 gallons of water.
   250 lbs of ice.
Instruments:
   Sextant.
   Binoculars.
   Prismatic compass.
   Sea-anchor.
   Charts.
   Aneroid.

The swell was slight when the *Stancomb Wills* was launched and the boat got under way without any difficulty; but half an hour later, when we were pulling down the *James Caird*, the swell increased suddenly. Apparently the movement of the ice outside had made an opening and allowed the sea to run in without being blanketed by the line of pack. The swell made things difficult. Many of us got wet to the waist while dragging the boat out – a serious matter in that climate. When the *James Caird* was afloat in the surf she nearly capsized among the rocks before we could get her clear, and Vincent and the carpenter, who were on the deck, were thrown into the water. This was really bad luck, for the two men would have small chance of drying their clothes after we had got under way. Hurley, who had the eye of the professional photographer for 'incidents', secured a picture of the upset, and I firmly believe that he would have liked the two unfortunate men to remain in the water until he could get a 'snap' at close quarters; but we hauled them out immediately, regardless of his feelings.

The *James Caird* was soon clear of the breakers. We used all the available ropes as a long painter to prevent her drifting away to the northeast, and then the *Stancomb Wills* came alongside, transferred her load, and went back to the shore for more. As she was being beached this time the sea took her stern and half filled her with water. She had to be turned over and emptied before the return journey could be made. Every member of the crew of the *Stancomb Wills* was wet to the skin. The watercasks were towed behind the *Stancomb Wills* on this second journey, and the swell, which was increasing rapidly, drove the boat on to the rocks, where one of the casks was slightly stove in. This accident proved later to be a serious one, since some sea-water had entered the cask and the contents were now brackish.

By midday the *James Caird* was ready for the voyage. Vincent and the carpenter had secured some dry clothes by exchange with members of the shore party (I heard afterwards that it was a full fortnight before the soaked garments were finally dried), and the boat's crew was standing by waiting for the order to cast off. A moderate westerly breeze was blowing. I went ashore in the *Stancomb Wills* and had a last word with Wild, who was remaining in full command, with directions as to his course of action in the event of our failure to bring relief, but I practically left the whole situation and scope of action and decision to his own judgment, secure in the knowledge that he would act wisely. I told him that I trusted the party to him and said goodbye to the men. Then we pushed off for the last time, and within a few minutes I was aboard the *James Caird*. The crew of the *Stancomb Wills* shook hands with us as the boats bumped together and offered us the last good wishes. Then, setting our jib, we cut the painter and moved away to the northeast. The men who were staying behind made a pathetic little group on the beach, with the grim heights of the island behind them and the sea seething at their feet, but they waved to us and gave three hearty cheers. There was hope in their hearts and they trusted us to bring the help that they needed.

I had all sails set, and the *James Caird* quickly dipped the beach and its line of dark figures. The westerly wind took us rapidly to the line of pack, and as we entered it I stood up with my arm round the mast,

The James Caird dipped the beach and its dark figures.

directing and steering, so as to avoid the great lumps of ice that were flung about in the heave of the sea. The pack thickened and we were forced to turn almost due east, running before the wind towards a gap I had seen in the morning from the high ground. I could not see the gap now, but we had come out on its bearing and I was prepared to find that it had been influenced by the easterly drift. At four o'clock in the afternoon we found the channel, much narrower than it had seemed in the morning but still navigable. Dropping sail, we rowed through without touching the ice anywhere, and by 5.30 pm we were clear of the pack with open water before us. We passed one more piece of ice in the darkness an hour later, but the pack lay behind, and with a fair wind swelling the sails we steered our little craft through the night, our hopes centred on our distant goal. The swell was very heavy now, and when the time came for our first evening meal we found great difficulty in keeping the Primus lamp alight and preventing the hoosh splashing out of the pot. Three men were needed to attend to the cooking, one man holding the lamp and two men guarding the aluminium cooking-pot, which had to be lifted clear of the Primus whenever the movement of the boat threatened to cause a disaster. Then the lamp had to be protected from water, for sprays were coming over the bows and our flimsy decking was by no means water-tight. All these operations were conducted in the confined space under the decking, where the men lay or knelt and adjusted themselves as best they could to the angles of our cases and ballast. It was uncomfortable, but we found consolation in the reflection that without the decking we could not have used the cooker at all.

The tale of the next sixteen days is one of supreme strife amid heaving waters. The sub-Antarctic Ocean lived up to its evil winter reputation. I decided to run north for at least two days while the wind held and so get into warmer weather before turning to the east and laying a course for South Georgia. We took two-hourly spells at the tiller. The men who were not on watch crawled into the sodden sleeping bags and tried to forget their troubles for a period; but there was no comfort in the boat. The bags and cases seemed to be alive in the unfailing knack of presenting their most uncomfortable angles to our rest-seeking bodies. A man might imagine for a moment that he had found a position of ease, but always discovered quickly that some unyielding point was impinging on muscle or bone. The first night aboard the boat was one of acute discomfort for us all, and we were heartily glad when the dawn came and we could set about the preparation of a hot breakfast.

This record of the voyage to South Georgia is based upon scant notes made day by day. The notes dealt usually with the bare facts of distances, positions, and weather, but our memories retained the incidents of the passing days in a period never to be forgotten. By running north for the first two days I hoped to get warmer weather and also to avoid lines of pack that might be extending beyond the main body. We needed all the advantage that we could obtain from the higher latitude for sailing on the great circle, but we had to be cautious regarding possible ice-streams. Cramped in our narrow quarters and continually wet by the spray, we suffered severely from cold throughout the journey. We fought the seas and the winds and at the same time had a daily struggle to keep ourselves alive. At times we were in dire peril. Generally we were upheld by the knowledge that we were making progress towards the land where we would be, but there were days and nights when we lay to, drifting across the storm-whitened seas and watching with eyes interested rather than apprehensive the uprearing masses of water, flung to and fro by Nature in the pride of her strength. Deep seemed the valleys when we lay between the reeling seas. High were the hills when we perched momentarily on the tops of giant combers. Nearly always there were gales. So small was our boat and so great were the seas that often our sail flapped idly in the calm between the crests of two waves. Then we would climb the next slope and catch the full fury of the gale where the wool-like whiteness of the breaking water surged around us. We had our moments of laughter – rare, it is true, but hearty enough. Even when cracked lips and swollen mouths checked the outward and visible signs of amusement we could see a joke of the primitive kind. Man's sense of humour is always most easily stirred by the petty misfortunes of his neighbours, and I shall never forget Worsley's efforts on one occasion to place the hot aluminium stand on top of the Primus stove after it had fallen off in an extra heavy roll. With his frost-bitten fingers he picked it up, dropped it, picked it up again, and toyed with it gingerly as though it were some fragile article of lady's wear. We laughed, or rather gurgled with laughter.

The wind came up strong and worked into a gale from the northwest on the third day out. We stood away to the east. The increasing seas discovered the weaknesses of our decking. The continuous blows shifted the box-lids and sledge-runners so that the canvas sagged down and accumulated water. Then icy trickles, distinct from the driving sprays, poured fore and aft into the boat. The nails that the carpenter had extracted from cases at Elephant Island and used to fasten down the battens were too short to make firm the decking. We did what we could to secure it, but our means were very limited, and the water continued to enter the boat at a dozen points. Much baling was necessary, and nothing that we could do prevented our gear from becoming sodden. The searching runnels from the canvas were really more unpleasant than the sudden definite douches of the sprays. Lying under the thwarts during watches below, we tried vainly to avoid them. There were no dry places in the boat, and at last we simply covered our heads with our Burberrys and endured the all-pervading water. The baling was work for the watch. Real rest we had none. The perpetual motion of the boat made repose impossible; we were cold, sore, and anxious. We moved on hands and knees in the semi-darkness of the day under the decking. The darkness was complete by 6 pm, and not until 7 am of the following day could we see one another under the thwarts. We had a few scraps of candle, and they were preserved carefully in order that we might have light at meal-times. There was one fairly dry spot in the boat, under the solid original decking at the bows, and we managed to protect some of our biscuits from the salt water; but I do not think any of us got the taste of salt out of our mouths during the voyage.

The difficulty of movement in the boat would have had its humorous side if it had not involved us in so many aches and pains. We had to crawl under the thwarts in order to move along the boat, and our knees suffered considerably. When a watch turned out it was necessary for me to direct each man by name when and where to move, since if all hands had crawled about at the same time the result would have been dire confusion and many bruises. Then there was the trim of the boat to be considered. The order of the watch was four hours on and four hours off, three men to the watch. One man had the tiller-ropes, the second man attended to the sail, and the third baled for all he was worth.

Sometimes when the water in the boat had been reduced to reasonable proportions, our pump could be used. This pump, which Hurley had made from the Flinder's bar case of our ship's standard compass, was quite effective, though its capacity was not large. The man who was attending the sail could pump into the big outer cooker, which was lifted and emptied overboard when filled. We had a device by which the water could go direct from the pump into the sea through a hole in the gunwale, but this hole had to be blocked at an early stage of the voyage, since we found that it admitted water when the boat rolled.

While a new watch was shivering in the wind and spray, the men who had been relieved groped hurriedly among the soaked sleeping-bags and tried to steal a little of the warmth created by the last occupants; but it was not always possible for us to find even this comfort when we went off watch. The boulders that we had taken aboard for ballast had to be shifted continually in order to trim the boat and give access to the pump, which became choked with hairs from the moulting sleeping-bags and fineskoe. The four reindeer-skin sleeping-bags shed their hair freely owing to the continuous wetting, and soon became quite bald in appearance. The moving of the boulders was weary and painful work. We came to know every one of the stones by sight and touch, and I have vivid memories of their angular peculiarities even today. They might have been of considerable interest as geological specimens to a scientific man under happier conditions. As ballast they were useful. As weights to be moved about in cramped quarters they were simply appalling. They spared no portion of our poor bodies. Another of our troubles, worth mention here, was the chafing of our legs by our wet clothes, which had not been changed now for seven months. The insides of our thighs were rubbed raw, and the one tube of Hazeline cream in our medicine-chest did not go far in alleviating our pain, which was increased by the bite of the salt water. We thought at the time that we never slept. The fact was that we would doze off uncomfortably, to be aroused quickly by some new ache or another call to effort. My own share of the general unpleasantness was accentuated by a finely developed bout of sciatica. I had become possessor of this originally on the floe several months earlier.

Our meals were regular in spite of the gales. Attention to this point was essential, since the conditions of the voyage made increasing calls upon our vitality. Breakfast, at 8 am, consisted of a pannikin of hot hoosh made from Bovril sledging ration, two biscuits, and some lumps of sugar. Lunch came at 1 pm, and comprised Bovril sledging ration, eaten raw, and a pannikin of hot milk for each man. Tea, at 5 pm, had the same menu. Then during the night we had a hot drink, generally of milk. The meals were the bright beacons in those cold and stormy days. The glow of warmth and comfort produced by the food and drink made optimists of us all. We had two tins of Virol, which we were keeping for an emergency; but, finding ourselves in need of an oil-lamp to eke out our supply of candles, we emptied one of the tins in the manner that most appealed to us, and fitted it with a wick made by shredding a bit of canvas. When this lamp was filled with oil it gave a certain amount of light, though it was easily blown out, and was of great assistance to us at night. We were fairly well off as regarded fuel, since we had $6\frac{1}{2}$ gallons of paraffin.

A severe southwesterly gale on the fourth day out forced us to heave to. I would have liked to have run before the wind, but the sea was very high and the *James Caird* was in danger of broaching to and swamping. The delay was vexatious, since up to that time we had been making sixty or seventy miles a day, good going with our limited sail area. We hove to under double-reefed mainsail and our little jigger, and waited for the gale to blow itself out. During that afternoon we saw bits of wreckage, the remains probably of some unfortunate vessel that had failed to weather the strong gales south of Cape Horn. The weather conditions did not improve, and on the fifth day out the gale was so fierce that we were compelled to take in the double-reefed mainsail and hoist our small jib instead. We put out a sea-anchor to keep the *James Caird's* head up to the sea. This anchor consisted of a triangular canvas bag fastened to the end of the painter and allowed to stream out from the bows. The boat was high enough to catch the wind, and, as she drifted to leeward, the drag of the anchor kept her head to windward. Thus our boat took most of the seas more or less end on. Even then the crests of the waves often would curl right over us and we shipped a great deal of water, which necessitated unceasing baling and pumping. Looking out abeam, we would see a hollow like a tunnel formed as the crest of a big wave toppled over on to the swelling body of water. A thousand times it appeared as though the

James Caird must be engulfed; but the boat lived. The southwesterly gale had its birthplace above the Antarctic Continent, and its freezing breath lowered the temperature far toward zero. The sprays froze upon the boat and gave bows, sides, and decking a heavy coat of mail. This accumulation of ice reduced the buoyancy of the boat, and to that extent was an added peril; but it possessed a notable advantage from one point of view. The water ceased to drop and trickle from the canvas, and the spray came in solely at the well in the after part of the boat. We could not allow the load of ice to grow beyond a certain point, and in turns we crawled about the decking forward, chipping and picking at it with the available tools.

When daylight came on the morning of the sixth day out we saw and felt that the *James Caird* had lost her resiliency. She was not rising to the oncoming seas. The weight of the ice that had formed in her and upon her during the night was having its effect, and she was becoming more like a log than a boat. The situation called for immediate action. We first broke away the spare oars, which were encased in ice and frozen to the sides of the boat, and threw them overboard. We retained two oars for use when we got inshore. Two of the fur sleeping-bags went over the side; they were thoroughly wet, weighing probably 40 lbs each, and they had frozen stiff during the night. Three men constituted the watch below, and when a man went down it was better to turn into the wet bag just vacated by another man than to thaw out a frozen bag with the heat of his unfortunate body. We now had four bags, three in use and one for emergency use in case a member of the party should break down permanently. The reduction of weight relieved the boat to some extent, and vigorous chipping and scraping did more. We had to be very careful not to put axe or knife through the frozen canvas of the decking as we crawled over it, but gradually we got rid of a lot of ice. The *James Caird* lifted to the endless waves as though she lived again.

About 11 am the boat suddenly fell off into the trough of the sea. The painter had parted and the sea-anchor had gone. This was serious. The *James Caird* went away to leeward, and we had no chance at all of recovering the anchor and our valuable rope, which had been our only means of keeping the boat's head up to the seas without the risk of hoisting sail in a gale. Now we had to set the sail and trust to its holding.

While the *James Caird* rolled heavily in the trough, we beat the frozen canvas until the bulk of the ice had cracked off it and then hoisted it. The frozen gear worked protestingly, but after a struggle our little craft came up to the wind again, and we breathed more freely. Skin frost-bites were troubling us, and we had developed large blisters on our fingers and hands. I shall always carry the scar of one of these frost-bites on my left hand, which became badly inflamed after the skin had burst and the cold had bitten deeply.

We held the boat up to the gale during that day, enduring as best we could discomforts that amounted to pain. The boat tossed interminably on the big waves under grey, threatening skies. Our thoughts did not embrace much more than the necessities of the hour. Every surge of the sea was an enemy to be watched and circumvented. We ate our scanty meals, treated our frost-bites, and hoped for the improved conditions that the morrow might bring. Night fell early, and in the lagging hours of darkness we were cheered by a change for the better in the weather. The wind dropped, the snow-squalls became less frequent, and the sea moderated. When the morning of the seventh day dawned there was not much wind. We shook the reef out of the sail and laid our course once more for South Georgia. The sun came out bright and clear, and presently Worsley got a snap for longitude. We hoped that the sky would remain clear until noon, so that we could get the latitude. We had been six days out without an observation, and our dead reckoning naturally was uncertain. The boat must have presented a strange appearance that morning. All hands basked in the sun. We hung our sleeping-bags to the mast and spread our socks and other gear all over the deck. Some of the ice had melted off the *James Caird* in the early morning after the gale began to slacken, and dry patches were appearing in the decking. Porpoises came blowing round the boat, and Cape pigeons wheeled and swooped within a few feet of us. These little black-and-white birds have an air of friendliness that is not possessed by the great circling albatross. They had looked grey against the swaying sea during the storm as they darted about over our heads and uttered their plaintive cries. The albatrosses, of the black or sooty variety, had watched with hard, bright eyes, and seemed to have a quite impersonal interest in our struggle to keep afloat amid the battering seas. In addition to the Cape pigeons an occasional stormy petrel flashed overhead. Then there was a small bird, unknown to me, that appeared always to be in a fussy, bustling state, quite out of keeping with the surroundings. It irritated me. It had practically no tail, and it flitted about vaguely as though in search of the lost member. I used to find myself wishing it would find its tail and have done with the silly fluttering.

We revelled in the warmth of the sun that day. Life was not so bad, after all. We felt we were well on our way. Our gear was drying, and we could have a hot meal in comparative comfort. The swell was still heavy, but it was not breaking and the boat rode easily. At noon Worsley balanced himself on the gunwale and clung with one hand to the stay of the mainmast while he got a snap of the sun. The result was more than encouraging. We had done over 380 miles and were getting on for halfway to South Georgia. It looked as though we were going to get through.

The wind freshened to a good stiff breeze during the afternoon, and the *James Caird* made satisfactory progress. I had not realized until the sunlight came how small our boat really was. There was some influence in the light and warmth, some hint of happier days, that made us revive memories of other voyages, when we had stout decks beneath our feet, unlimited food at our command, and pleasant cabins for our ease. Now we clung to a battered little boat, 'alone, alone – all, all alone; alone on a wide, wide sea.' So low in the water were we that each succeeding swell cut off our view of the sky-line. We were a tiny speck in the vast vista of the sea – the ocean that is open to all and merciful to none, that threatens even when it seems to yield, and that is pitiless always to weakness. For a moment the consciousness of the forces arrayed against us would be almost overwhelming. Then hope and confidence would rise again as our boat rose to a wave and tossed aside the crest in a sparkling shower like the play of prismatic colours at the foot of a waterfall. My double-barrelled gun and some cartridges had been stowed aboard the boat as an emergency precaution against a shortage of food, but we were not disposed to destroy our little neighbours, the Cape pigeons, even for the sake of fresh meat. We might have shot an albatross, but the wandering king of the ocean aroused in us something of the feeling that inspired, too late, the Ancient Mariner. So the gun remained among the stores and sleeping-bags in the narrow quarters beneath our leaking deck, and the birds followed us unmolested.

The eighth, ninth, and tenth days of the voyage had few features worthy of special note. The wind blew hard during those days, and the strain of navigating the boat was unceasing; but always we made some advance towards our goal. No bergs showed on our horizon, and we knew that we were clear of the ice-fields. Each day brought its little round of troubles, but also compensation in the form of food and growing hope. We felt that we were going to succeed. The odds against us had been great, but we were winning through. We still suffered severely from the cold, for, though the temperature was rising, our vitality was declining owing to shortage of food, exposure, and the necessity of maintaining our cramped positions day and night. I found that it was now absolutely necessary to prepare hot milk for all hands during the night, in order to sustain life till dawn. This meant lighting the Primus lamp in the darkness and involved an increased drain on our small store of matches. It was the rule that one match must serve when the Primus was being lit. We had no lamp for the compass and during the early days of the voyage we would strike a match when the steersman wanted to see the course at night; but later the necessity for strict economy impressed itself upon us, and the practice of striking matches at night was stopped. We had one water-tight tin of matches. I had stowed away in a pocket, in readiness for a sunny day, a lens from one of the telescopes, but this was of no use during the voyage. The sun seldom shone upon us. The glass of the compass got broken one night, and we contrived to mend it with adhesive tape from the medicine-chest. One of the memories that comes to me from those days is of Crean singing at the tiller. He always sang while he was steering, and nobody ever discovered what the song was. It was devoid of tune and as monotonous as the chanting of a Buddhist monk at his prayers; yet somehow it was cheerful. In moments of inspiration Crean would attempt 'The Wearing of the Green'.

On the tenth night Worsley could not straighten his body after his spell at the tiller. He was thoroughly cramped, and we had to drag him beneath the decking and massage him before he could unbend himself and get into a sleeping-bag. A hard north-westerly gale came up on the eleventh day (5 May) and shifted to the southwest in the late afternoon. The sky was overcast and occasional snow-squalls added to the discomfort produced by a tremendous cross-sea – the worst, I thought, that we had experienced. At midnight I was at the tiller and suddenly noticed a line of clear sky between the south and south-west. I called to the other men that the sky was clearing, and then a moment later I realized that what I had seen was not a rift in the clouds but the white crest of an enormous wave. During twenty-six years' experience of the ocean in all its moods I had not encountered a wave so gigantic. It was a mighty upheavel of the ocean, a thing quite apart from the big white-capped seas that had been our tireless enemies for many days. I shouted, 'For God's sake, hold on! It's got us.' Then came a moment of suspense that seemed drawn out into hours. White surged the foam of the breaking sea around us. We felt our boat lifted and flung forward like a cork in breaking surf. We were in a seething chaos of tortured water; but somehow the boat lived through it, half full of water, sagging to the dead weight and shuddering under the blow. We baled with the energy of men fighting for life, flinging the water over the sides with every receptacle that came to our hands, and after ten minutes of uncertainty we felt the boat renew her life beneath us. She floated again and ceased to lurch drunkenly as though dazed by the attack of the sea. Earnestly we hoped that never again would we encounter such a wave.

The conditions in the boat, uncomfortable before, had been made worse by the deluge of water. All our gear was thoroughly wet again. Our cooking stove had been floating about in the bottom of the boat, and portions of our last hoosh seemed to have permeated everything. Not until 3 am, when we were all chilled almost to the limit of endurance, did we manage to get the stove alight and make ourselves hot drinks. The carpenter was suffering particularly, but he showed grit and spirit. Vincent had for the past week ceased to be an active member of the crew, and I could not easily account for his collapse. Physically he was one of the strongest men in the boat. He was a young man, he had served on North Sea trawlers, and he should have been able to bear hardships better than McCarthy, who, not so strong, was always happy.

The weather was better on the following day (6 May), and we got a glimpse of the sun. Worsley's observation showed that we were not more than a hundred miles from the northwest corner of South

Georgia. Two more days with a favourable wind and we would sight the promised land. I hoped that there would be no delay, for our supply of water was running very low. The hot drink at night was essential, but I decided that the daily allowance of water must be cut down to half a pint per man. The lumps of ice we had taken aboard had gone long ago. We were dependent upon the water we had brought from Elephant Island, and our thirst was increased by the fact that we were now using the brackish water in the breaker that had been slightly stove in in the surf when the boat was being loaded. Some sea-water had entered at that time.

Thirst took possession of us. I dared not permit the allowance of water to be increased since an unfavourable wind might drive us away from the island and lengthen our voyage by many days. Lack of water is always the most severe privation that men can be condemned to endure, and we found, as during our earlier boat voyage, that the salt water in our clothing and the salt spray that lashed our faces made our thirst grow quickly to a burning pain. I had to be very firm in refusing to allow any one to anticipate the morrow's allowance, which I was sometimes begged to do. We did the necessary work dully and hoped for the land. I had altered the course to the east so as to make sure of our striking the island, which would have been impossible to regain if we had run past the northern end. The course was laid on our scrap of chart for a point some thirty miles down the coast. That day and the following day passed for us in a sort of nightmare. Our mouths were dry and our tongues were swollen. The wind was still strong and the heavy sea forced us to navigate carefully, but any thought of our peril from the waves was buried beneath the consciousness of our raging thirst. The bright moments were those when we each received our one mug of hot milk during the long, bitter watches of the night. Things were bad for us in those days, but the end was coming. The morning of 8 May broke thick and stormy, with squalls from the northwest. We searched the waters ahead for a sign of land, and though we could see nothing more than had met our eyes for many days, we were cheered by a sense that the goal was near at hand. About ten o'clock that morning we passed a little bit of kelp, a glad signal of the proximity of land. An hour later we saw two shags sitting on a big mass of kelp, and knew then that we must be within ten or fifteen miles of the shore. These birds are as sure an indication of the proximity of land as a lighthouse is, for they never venture far to sea. We gazed ahead with increasing eagerness, and at 12.30 pm, through a rift in the clouds, McCarthy caught a glimpse of the black cliffs of South Georgia, just fourteen days after our departure from Elephant Island. It was a glad moment. Thirst-ridden, chilled, and weak as we were, happiness irradiated us. The job was nearly done.

We stood in towards the shore to look for a landing-place, and presently we could see the green tussock-grass on the ledges above the surf-beaten rocks. Ahead of us and to the south, blind rollers showed the presence of uncharted reefs along the coast. Here and there the hungry rocks were close to the surface, and over them the great waves broke, swirling viciously and spouting thirty and forty feet into the air. The rocky coast appeared to descend sheer to the sea. Our need of water and rest was well-nigh desperate, but to have attempted a landing at that time would have been suicidal. Night was drawing near, and the weather indications were not favourable. There was nothing for it but to haul off till the following morning, so we stood away on the starboard tack until we had made what appeared to be a safe offing. Then we hove to in the high westerly swell. The hours passed slowly as we waited the dawn, which would herald, we fondly hoped, the last stage of our journey. Our thirst was a torment and we could scarcely touch our food; the cold seemed to strike right through our weakened bodies. At 5 am the wind shifted to the northwest and quickly increased to one of the worst hurricanes any of us had ever experienced. A great cross-sea was running, and the wind simply shrieked as it tore the tops off the waves and converted the whole seascape into a haze of driving spray. Down into valleys, up to tossing heights, straining until her seams opened, swung our little boat, brave still but labouring heavily. We knew that the wind and set of the sea was driving us ashore, but we could do nothing. The dawn showed us a storm-torn ocean, and the morning passed without bringing us a sight of the land; but at 1 pm, through a rift in the flying mists, we got a glimpse of the huge crags of the island and realized that our position had become desperate. We were on a dead lee shore, and we could gauge our approach to the unseen cliffs by the roar of the breakers against the sheer walls of rock. I ordered the double-reefed mainsail to be set in the hope that we might claw off, and this attempt increased the strain upon the boat. The *Caird* was bumping heavily, and the water was pouring in everywhere. Our thirst was forgotten in the realization of our imminent danger, as we baled unceasingly, and adjusted our weights from time to time; occasional glimpses showed that the shore was nearer. I knew that Annewkow Island lay to the south of us, but our small and badly marked chart showed uncertain reefs in the passage between the island and the mainland, and I dared not trust it, though as a last resort we could try to lie under the lee of the island. The afternoon wore away as we edged down the coast, with the thunder of the breakers in our ears. The approach of evening found us still some distance from Annewkow Island, and, dimly in the twilight, we could see a snow-capped mountain looming above us. The chance of surviving the night, with the driving gale and the implacable sea forcing us on to the lee shore, seemed small. I think most of us had a feeling that the end was very near. Just after 6 pm, in the dark, as the boat was in the yeasty backwash from the seas flung from this iron-bound coast, then, just when things looked their worst, they changed for the best. I have marvelled often at the thin line that divides success from failure and the sudden turn that leads from apparently certain disaster to comparative safety. The wind suddenly shifted, and we were free once more to make an offing. Almost as soon as the gale eased, the pin that locked the mast to the thwart fell out. It must have been on the point of doing this throughout the hurricane, and if it had gone nothing could have saved us; the mast would have snapped like a carrot. Our backstays had carried away once before when iced up and were not too strongly fastened now. We were thankful indeed for the mercy that had held that pin in its place throughout the hurricane.

We stood off shore again, tired almost to the point of apathy. Our water had long been finished. The last was about a pint of hairy liquid which we strained through a bit of gauze from the medicine-chest. The pangs of thirst attacked us with redoubled intensity, and I felt that we must make a landing on the following day at almost any hazard. The night wore on. We were very tired. We longed for day. When at last the dawn came on the morning of 10 May there was practically no wind, but a high cross-sea was running. We made slow progress towards the shore. About 8 am the wind backed to the northwest and threatened another blow. We had sighted in the meantime a big indentation which I thought must be King Haakon Bay, and I decided that we must land there. We set the bows of the boat towards the bay and ran before the freshening gale. Soon we had angry reefs on either side. Great glaciers came down to the sea and offered no landing-place. The sea spouted on the reefs and thundered against the shore. About noon we sighted a line of jagged reef, like blackened teeth, that seemed to bar the entrance to the bay. Inside, comparatively smooth water stretched eight or nine miles to the head of the bay. A gap in the reef appeared, and we made for it. But the fates had another rebuff for us. The wind shifted and blew from the east right out of the bay. We could see the way through the reef, but we could not approach it directly. That afternoon we bore up, tacking five times in the strong wind. The last tack enabled us to get through, and at last we were in the wide mouth of the bay. Dusk was approaching. A small cove, with a boulder-strewn beach guarded by a reef, made a break in the cliffs on the south side of the bay, and we turned in that direction. I stood in the bows directing the steering as we ran through the kelp and made the passage of the reef. The entrance was so narrow that we had to take in the oars, and the swell was piling itself right over the reef into the cove; but in a minute or two we were inside, and in the gathering darkness the *James Caird* ran in on a swell and touched the beach. I sprang ashore with the short painter and held on when the boat went out with the backward surge. When the *James Caird* came in again three of the men got ashore, and they held the painter while I climbed some rocks with another line. A slip on the wet rocks twenty feet up nearly closed my part of the story just at the moment when we were achieving safety. A jagged piece of rock held me and at the same time bruised me sorely. However, I made fast the line, and in a few minutes we were all safe on the beach, with the boat floating in the surging water just off the shore. We heard a gurgling sound that was sweet music in our ears, and, peering around, found a stream of fresh water almost at our feet. A moment later we were down on our knees drinking the pure ice-cold water in long draughts that put new life into us. It was a splendid moment.

After reaching South Georgia, Shackleton and his men hauled themselves over a *10,000 ft range of icy rock to reach the whaling station on the far side of the island.*

Here a boat was commandeered and after four valiant attempts they finally made it back to Elephant Island to rescue their stranded comrades on 30 August 1916.

THE 'OLD MAN' OF
THE SEA

Thor Heyerdahl

Thor Heyerdahl, five companions and a green parrot put to sea on a balsa-wood raft called Kon-Tiki. With the aid of a solitary sail they hoped to drift along the south equatorial current to the Polynesian Islands of the Pacific some 4,000 miles away.

Floating on a raft only 30 cm above the waves they had many close encounters with the inhabitants of the sea . . .

After a week or so the sea grew calmer, and we noticed that it became blue instead of green. We began to go west-northwest instead of due northwest, and took this as the first faint sign that we had got out of the coastal current and had some hope of being carried out to sea.

The very first day we were left alone on the sea we had noticed fish round the raft, but were too much occupied with the steering to think of fishing. The second day we went right into a thick shoal of sardines, and soon afterwards an eight-foot blue shark came along and rolled over with its white belly uppermost as it rubbed against the raft's stern, where Herman and Bengt stood barelegged in the seas, steering. It played round us for a while, but disappeared when we got the hand harpoon ready for action.

Next day we were visited by tunnies, bonitos and dolphins, and when a big flying fish thudded on board we used it as bait and at once pulled in two large dolphins (dorados) weighing from 20 to 35 lbs each. This was food for several days. On steering watch we could see many fish we did not even know, and one day we came into a school of porpoises which seemed quite endless. The black backs tumbled about, packed close together, right in to the side of the raft, and sprang up here and there all over the sea as far as we could see from the masthead. And the

215

nearer we came to the equator, and the farther from the coast, the commoner flying fish became. When at last we came out into the blue water where the sea rolled by majestically, sunlit and sedate, ruffled by gusts of wind, we could see them glittering like a rain of projectiles, shooting from the water and flying in a straight line till their power of flight was exhausted and they vanished beneath the surface.

If we set the little paraffin lamp out at night flying fish were attracted by the light and, large and small, shot over the raft. They often struck the bamboo cabin or the sail and tumbled helpless on the deck. For, unable to get a take-off by swimming through the water, they just remained lying and kicking helplessly, like large-eyed herrings with long breast fins. It sometimes happened that we heard an outburst of strong language from a man on deck when a cold flying fish came unexpectedly at a good speed slap into his face. They always came at a good pace and snout first, and if they caught one full in the face they made it burn and tingle. But the unprovoked attack was quickly forgiven by the injured party, for this, with all its drawbacks, was a maritime land of enchantment where delicious fish dishes came hurtling through the air. We used to fry them for breakfast, and whether it was the fish, the cook, or our appetites, they reminded us of fried troutlings once we had scraped the scales off.

The cook's first duty when he got up in the morning was to go out on deck and collect all the flying fish that had landed on board in the course of the night. There were usually half a dozen or more, and one morning we found twenty-six fat flying fish on the raft. Knut was much upset one morning because, when he was standing operating with the frying pan, a flying fish struck him on the hand instead of landing right in the cooking fat.

Our neighbourly intimacy with the sea was not fully realized by Torstein till he woke one morning and found a sardine on his pillow. There was so little room in the cabin that Torstein was lying with his head in the doorway and, if anyone inadvertently trod on his face when going out at night, he bit him in the leg. He grasped the sardine by the tail and confided to it understandingly that all sardines had his entire sympathy. We conscientiously drew in our legs so that Torstein should have more room the next night, but then something happened which caused Torstein to find himself a sleeping-place on the top of all the kitchen utensils in the wireless corner.

It was a few nights later. It was overcast and pitch dark, and Torstein had placed the paraffin lamp just by his head, so that the night watches should see where they were treading when they crept in and out over his head . . . About four o'clock Torstein was woken by the lamp tumbling over and something cold and wet flapping about his ears. 'Flying fish,' he thought, and felt for it in the darkness to throw it away. He caught hold of something long and wet that wriggled like a snake, and let go as if he had burned himself. The unseen visitor twisted itself away and over to Herman, while Torstein tried to get the lamp alight. Herman started up too, and this made me wake thinking of the octopus which came up at night in these waters. When we got the lamp alight, Herman was sitting in triumph with his hand gripping the neck of a long thin fish which wriggled in his hands like an eel. The fish was over three feet long, as slender as a snake, with dull black eyes and a long snout with a greedy jaw full of long sharp teeth. The teeth were as sharp as knives and could be folded back into the roof of the mouth to make way for what it swallowed. Under Herman's grip a large-eyed white fish, about eight inches long, was suddenly thrown up from the stomach and out of the mouth of the predatory fish, and soon after up came another like it. These were clearly two deep water fish, much torn by the snake-fish's teeth. The snake-fish's thin skin was bluish violet on the back and steel blue underneath, and it came loose in flakes when we took hold of it.

Bengt too was woken at last by all the noise, and we held the lamp and the long fish under his nose. He sat up drowsily in his sleeping bag and said solemnly:

'No, fish like that don't exist.'

With which he turned over quietly and fell asleep again.

Bengt was not far wrong. It appeared later that we six sitting round the lamp in the bamboo cabin were the first men to have seen this fish alive. Only the skeleton of a fish like this one had been found a few times on the coast of South America and the Galapagos Islands; ichthyologists called it *Gempylus*, or snake mackerel, and thought it lived at the bottom of the sea at a great depth, because no one had ever seen it alive. But if it lived at a great depth, thus must at any rate be by day, when the sun blinded the big eyes. For on dark nights *Gempylus*

The visitor was obviously hoping for a tasty tit-bit.

was abroad high over the surface of the seas; we on the raft had experience of that.

A week after the rare fish had landed in Torstein's sleeping bag, we had another visit. Again it was four in the morning, and the new moon had set so that it was dark, but the stars were shining. The raft was steering easily, and when my watch was over I took a turn along the edge of the raft to see if everything was ship-shape for the new watch. I had a rope round my waist, as the watch always had, and, with the paraffin lamp in my hand, I was walking carefully along the outermost log to get round the mast. The log was wet and slippery, and I was furious when someone quite unexpectedly caught hold of the rope behind me and jerked till I nearly lost my balance. I turned round wrathfully with the lantern, but not a soul was to be seen. There came a new tug at the rope, and I saw something shiny lying writhing on the deck. It was a fresh *Gempylus*, and this time it had got its teeth so deep into the rope that several of them broke before I got the rope loose. Presumably the light of the lantern had flashed along the curving white rope, and our visitor from the depths of the sea had caught hold in the hope of jumping up and snatching an extra long and tasty tit-bit. It ended its days in a jar of formalin.

The sea contains many surprises for him who has his floor on a level with the surface, and drifts along slowly and noiselessly. A sportsman who breaks his way through the woods may come back and say that no wild life is to be seen. Another may sit down on a stump and wait, and often rustlings and cracklings will begin, and curious eyes peer out. So it is on the sea too. We usually plough across it with roaring engines and piston strokes, with the water foaming round our bows. Then we come back and say that there is nothing to see far out on the ocean.

Not a day passed but we, as we sat floating on the surface of the sea, were visited by inquisitive guests which wriggled and waggled about us, and a few of them, such as dolphins and pilot fish, grew so familiar that they accompanied the raft across the sea and kept round us day and night.

When night had fallen, and the stars were twinkling in the dark tropical sky, the phosphorescence flashed around us in rivalry with the stars, and single glowing plankton resembled round live coals so vividly that we involuntarily drew in our bare legs when the glowing pellets were washed up round our feet at the raft's stern. When we caught them we saw that they were little brightly shining species of shrimp. On such nights we were sometimes scared when two round shining eyes suddenly rose out of the sea right alongside the raft and glared at us with an unblinking hypnotic stare – it might have been the Old Man of the Sea himself. These were often big squids which came up and floated on the surface with their devilish green eyes shining in the dark like phosphorous. But sometimes they were the shining eyes of deep water fish which only came up at night and lay staring, fascinated by the glimmer of light before them. Several times, when the sea was calm, the black water round the raft was suddenly full of round heads two or three feet in diameter, lying motionless and staring at us with great glowing eyes. On other nights balls of light three feet and more in diameter would be visible down in the water, flashing at irregular intervals like electric lights turned on for a moment.

We gradually grew accustomed to having these subterranean or submarine creatures under the floor, but nevertheless we were just as surprised every time a new version appeared. About two o'clock on a cloudy night, on which the man at the helm had difficulty in distinguishing black water from black sky, he caught sight of a faint illumination down in the water which slowly took the shape of a large animal. It was impossible to say whether it was plankton shining on its body, or if the animal itself had a phosphorescent surface, but the glimmer down in the black water gave the ghostly creature obscure, wavering outlines. Sometimes it was roundish, sometimes oval or triangular, and suddenly it split into two parts which swam to and fro under the raft independetly of one another. Finally there were three of these large shining phantoms wandering round in slow circles under us. They were real monsters, for the visible parts alone were some five fathoms long, and we all quickly collected on deck and followed the ghost dance. It went on for hour after hour, following the course of the raft. Mysterious and noiseless, our shining companions kept a good way beneath the surface, mostly on the starboard side, where the light was, but often they were right under the raft or appeared on the port side. The glimmer of light on their backs revealed that the beasts were bigger than elephants, but they were not whales, for they never came up to breathe. Were they giant ray-fish which changed shape when they turned over on their sides? They took no notice at all if we held the light right down on the surface to lure them up, so that we might see what kind of creatures they were. And like all proper goblins and ghosts, they had sunk into the depths when the dawn began to break.

We never got a proper explanation of this nocturnal visit from the three shining monsters, unless the solution was afforded by another visit we received a day and a half later in the full midday sunshine. It was 24 May, and we were lying drifting on a leisurely swell in exactly 95° west by 7° south. It was about noon, and we had thrown overboard the guts of two big dolphins we had caught early in the morning. I was having a refreshing plunge overboard at the bows, lying in the water, keeping a good look out and hanging on to a rope-end, when I caught sight of a thick brown fish, six feet long, which came swimming inquisitively towards me through the crystal-clear sea water. I hopped quickly up on to the edge of the raft and sat in the hot sun looking at the fish as it passed quietly, when I heard a wild war-whoop from Knut, who was sitting aft behind the bamboo cabin. He bellowed 'Shark!' till his voice cracked in a falsetto, and as we had sharks swimming alongside the raft almost daily without creating such excitement, we all realized that this must be something extra special, and flocked astern to Knut's assistance.

Knut had been standing there, washing his pants in the swell, and when he looked up for a moment he was staring straight into the biggest and ugliest face any of us had ever seen in the whole of our lives. It was the head of a veritable sea monster, so huge and so hideous that if the Old Man of the Sea himself had come up he could not have made such an impression on us. The head was broad and flat like a frog's, with two small eyes right at the sides, and a toadlike jaw which was four or five feet wide and had long fringes hanging drooping from the corners of the mouth. Behind the head was an enormous body ending in a long thin tail with a pointed tail fin which stood straight up and showed that this sea monster was not any kind of whale. The body looked brownish under the water, but both head and body were thickly covered with small white spots. The monster came quietly, lazily swimming after us from astern. It grinned like a bulldog and lashed gently with its tail. The large round dorsal fin projected clear of the water and sometimes the tail fin as well, and when the creature was in the trough of the swell the water flowed about the broad back as though washing round a submerged reef. In front of the broad jaws swam a whole crowd of zebra-striped pilot fish in fan formation, and large remora fish and other parasites sat firmly attached to the huge body and travelled with it through the water, so that the whole thing looked like a curious zoological collection crowded round something that resembled a floating deep water reef.

A 25 lbs dolphin, attached to six of our largest fish-hooks, was hanging behind the raft as bait for sharks, and a swarm of pilot fish shot straight off, nosed the dolphin without touching it, and then hurried back to their lord and master, the sea king. Like a mechanical monster it set its machinery going and came gliding at leisure towards the dolphin which lay, a beggarly trifle, before its jaws. We tried to pull the dolphin in, and the sea monster followed slowly, right up to the side of the raft. It did not open its mouth, but just let the dolphin bump against it, as if to throw open the whole door for such an insignificant scrap was not worth while. When the giant came right up to the raft, it rubbed its back against the heavy steering oar, which was just lifted up out of the water, and now we had ample opportunity of studying the monster at the closest quarters – at such close quarters that I thought we had all gone mad, for we roared stupidly with laughter and shouted over-excitedly at the completely fantastic sight we saw. Walt Disney himself, with all his powers of imagination, could not have created a more hair-raising sea monster than that which thus suddenly lay with its terrific jaws along the raft's side.

The monster was a whale shark, the largest shark and the largest fish known in the world today. It is exceedingly rare, but scattered specimens are observed here and there in the tropical oceans. The whale shark has an average length of 50 feet, and according to zoologists it weighs 15 tons. It is said that large specimens can attain a length of 65 feet, and a harpooned baby had a liver weighing 600 lbs, and a collection of three thousand teeth in each of its broad jaws.

The monster was so large that when it began to swim in circles round us and under the raft its head was visible on one side while the whole of its tail stuck out on the other. And so incredibly grotesque, inert and stupid did it appear when seen full-face that we could not help shouting with laughter, although we realized that it had strength enough in its tail to smash both balsa logs and ropes to pieces if it attacked us. Again and again it described narrower and narrower circles just under the raft, while all we could do was to wait and see what might happen. When out on the other side it glided amiably under the steering oar and lifted it up in the air, while the oar-blade slid along the creature's back. We stood round the raft with hand harpoons ready for action, but they seemed to us like toothpicks in relation to the heavy beast we had to deal with. There was no indication that the whale shark ever thought of leaving us again; it circled round us and followed like a faithful dog, close to the raft. None of us had ever experienced or thought we should experience anything like it; the whole adventure with the sea monsters swimming behind and under the raft, seemed to us so completely unnatural that we could not really take it seriously.

In reality the whale shark went on circling us for barely an hour, but to us the visit seemed to last a whole day. At last it became too exciting for Erik, who was standing at a corner of the raft with an eight-foot hand harpoon, and encouraged by ill-considered shouts, he raised the harpoon above his head. As the whale shark came gliding slowly towards him, and had got its broad head right under the corner of the raft, Erik thrust the harpoon with all his giant strength down between his legs and deep into the whale shark's gristly head. It was a second or two before the giant understood properly what was happening. Then in a flash the placid half-wit was transformed into a mountain of steel muscles. We heard a swishing noise as the harpoon line rushed over the edge of the raft, and saw a cascade of water as the giant stood on its head and plunged down into the depths. The three men who were standing nearest were flung about the place head over heels and two of them were flayed and burnt by the line as it rushed through the air. The thick line, strong enough to hold a boat, was caught up on the side of the raft but snapped at once like a piece of twine, and a few seconds later a broken-off harpoon shaft came up to the surface two hundred hards away. A shoal of frightened pilot fish shot off through the water in a desperate attempt to keep up with their old lord and master, and we waited a long time for the monster to come racing back like an infuriated submarine; but we never saw anything more of the whale shark.

THE DESERT ROAD

David Newman

When David Newman decided to drive to Nigeria in his Ford Zephyr, he knew there'd be great risks involved especially as he planned to drive across the almost trackless wastes of the Sahara Desert on the way.

The heat is like a hammer blow between the eyes. Every movement is deliberate self-flagellation. The sun has grown fiercer every step of the way from Morocco, and now I am exposed to its full Saharan fire.

It hangs in the sky motionless, like some remorseless instrument of torture. Nothing mitigates its unremitting intensity. I long for the sight of even one small cloud in the sky, but nothing breaks the monotony of that burning dome.

I shelter from the wind, and the heat from the sun is almost exactly balanced by the reflected heat from the sand. A breeze would bring instant relief, I am positive, but the wind comes like a blast from a steel furnace.

All around the desert dances in total light. My face muscles ache from screwing up the eyes. My eyes feel as though they will never open wide again.

I am even denied the luxury of sweating. I look down at my arms and instead of blessed drops of perspiration all I see are tiny circlets of salt. The sweat has dried as soon as it appeared.

Mirages tremble in the distance. Flat sheets of water miles across are surrounded by low hills and trees. I even see boats plying back and forth.

And I am so alone.

Around me the country is flat. A thorn bush here and there casts no shadows. A rock projects, but it merely draws attention to the flatness around it.

The *piste*★ to Abadla was level and clearly marked but heavily corrugated. I drove fast to minimize the effect of the bumps, and I arrived there just before lunch.

Forty or fifty soldiers lived in this hellish wilderness, under canvas, and thought of nothing but returning to France. They had heard that 'some mad Englishman' was on his way, and received me with open arms. Cans of beer sprayed foam into the sand. A huge lunch was prepared in the mess tent, and glass after glass of wine was poured down my throat. They told me, and I almost believed them, that wine was the best thing for the desert.

An hour later I drove – hiccuping – along a stretch of blissful tarmac road which the soldiers were laying. It lasted for five miles and ended abruptly, pitching me once more on to desert tracks.

The shaking the car received convinced me that something would have to give soon. At frequent intervals I hoisted myself out of the driving seat and peered all around to make sure nothing was working loose. Already I was thinking I would be content if the car lasted merely as far as Tindouf. Nigeria seemed a century and a whole world away.

The terrain was firm sand and compacted stones, but a fine dust filled the car and covered everything with a thick white film. I doused a cloth in water and bound it round my nose and mouth. I drank great draughts of warm, muddy water, but it tasted better than champagne. Each time I took the water bottle from my lips its level had dropped by a quart, and seconds later I was thirsting for more.

The terrain changed. The sand and stones became low hills with jagged rocks lurching upwards. Then they flattened again and irregular patches of deep soft sand swept groping fingers towards me. I zigzagged frantically to avoid their embrace.

During the afternoon I passed some miles from what I took to be a mining installation in the distance. Tall derricks and gantries crisscrossed on the skyline.

The tracks now became indistinct and confusing, and my instruments told me I should have reached Hamaguir. I had no indication that I was

★ *piste* = track.

on the right road. But I was well over a hundred miles from Colomb Bêchar, and moving quickly.

The splendid map I had bought in London showed no roads at all in these parts. This area was marked quite simply 'The Sahara Desert'. Well that was accurate enough anyway.

By four o'clock I was convinced that I had missed Hamaguir – my first reporting station. It must have been that cluster I took for a mining camp. But I had no intention of turning back. Every foot covered in the Sahara was an achievement, and I did not want to go over the same ground twice.

I decided to press on for Tinfouchi, and hope that the Hamaguir sentries had possibly seen me pass.

The thermometer in the car read 130 degrees. The clock had stopped, and there was a growing banging noise from somewhere in the back. My wrists ached from the constant battle with the steering wheel.

Now I began to worry. The thirst, which cracked my throat, the dust which caked my eyes, the heat, which lay on me like a rock, combined to drain my energy and thought. I was no longer certain which direction I was going. And I wished the authorities had not been so mad as to let me through.

A plank of wood lay by the track, roughly fashioned in the shape of an arrow. Painted on it was the word 'Tindouf'. Some thoughtful traveller must have put it there, and I thanked him. I was evidently heading in the right direction at least.

I got out to investigate the banging. The clamps on the exhaust pipe had worked loose and it was battering itself to shreds on the underside of the car. I bound it up with wire, but a few miles further the banging started again. I ignored it. An exhaust pipe has no purpose in the desert. It is useful in civilisation to minimize engine noise, and direct the waste gases away from the passers by, but I was not likely to see many passers-by, in the next few thousand miles.

The terrain changed again. Now I was driving through gently sloping hillocks and smooth boulders.

As I rounded a band between two small hillocks I saw my first trans-Saharan *camion*. It was a magnificent sight. It was as big as a steam engine, with fourteen gargantuan wheels each standing higher than the roof of my car. Underneath, it cleared the desert by a good five feet.

These juggernauts alone make it possible for the French to colonize the desert. With their Sahara-hardened crews of eight or ten, they lumber along desert trails, urging their way through virtually anything.

At the front an engine, which appeared large enough to run a power station, was exposed to the air to keep it as cool as was possible. The cabin was like a small lounge, with bunks stretching along behind the driver's seat. The back was crammed with stores to keep alive the men in desert outposts.

To these men the Sahara is a bitch-goddess. They love her, they hate her, they respect her. By their love and their hate they come to know her – or at least they come to know that they cannot ever know her, for she is ever changing. The tracks they travel at one time, they can be sure will not be there when they pass again. The wind will shift and cover them, and the men must find another way. And they are not immune to her misfortunes.

This one, for example, had broken down. The *camion* had struck a large bounder with too much force, and several of the rods and arms of the front suspension were bent. Some of the crew were busy dismantling it to straighten them, while others were preparing food in the now cooling evening.

I drew up beside them, and asked if I could be of assistance.

The crew were clearly astounded to see me, but after they got over their shock of seeing an Englishmen and a car appear from the desert, they each in turn shook me by the hand, and offered me beer from their cooler.

The driver, a blond giant, with hands like buckets, gave me some advice about the route ahead, warning me to be careful over some particularly bad patches. He expected to be on the move again in about six hours, so I had that much insurance behind me.

'Don't try and drive too much in the dark,' he warned, grinning cheerfully, 'it is very easy to go astray, and no one would ever find you again.' With this comforting thought in my ears I drove on.

A few miles later I saw another rough sign pointing off to the left. It said: 'Col. Robert.'

Two thoughts prompted me to follow it. One was that Colonel Robert might be an interesting character, the other was that signs in the desert are so few and far between that it is worth following all of them.

As I rounded the bend I saw my first camion.

The *piste* indicated by the sign was narrow and rocky. The car bounced from one obstacle to the next up a track that got steeper and steeper. Finally it became impossible. I stopped the car, turned round with difficulty and returned to my correct route. I never did find out who Colonel Robert was or is, but imagined then that the track must have led to his grave.

It wasn't until a couple of years afterwards that it suddenly struck me that '*Col*' is a perfectly good French word meaning 'mountain pass'.

I was very cross with myself for having been diverted in this way, but it was much cooler now, and I pressed on into the increasing gloom. The tracks were clear enough in front of me but the patches of sand were hard to see. Twice I sailed through deep patches of soft sand, the engine racing, and struck firm ground just in time. The third time I tried to avoid one patch, saw another in front of me, changed my mind, and with the engine pinking and clattering sank up to the axles in the desert.

After struggling with the shovel for one hour exactly the wheels seemed to be free of sand, and my hands skinless.

I wondered whether I should take the sand-mats down from the car roof, but they seemed well secured up there. They were heavy, and it was going to be too much bother to unload them.

I drove forward three feet and stuck again.

There was about ten yards of powdery sand ahead of me. I pondered again whether I should take the sand-mats down. If I had taken them down straight away I could easily have got through, but I had a lot to learn yet.

I resolved to wait until the *camion* caught up with me, when the driver would give me a tow. I had covered 185 miles of stinking desert, and I was moderately pleased. I lit the night light, opened a bottle of wine and wrote up my log.

The wine made me feel very happy indeed, and around eight o'clock I fell asleep.

With a grinding and a snorting and a roaring the *camion* arrived – a brightly-lit brontosaurus – just before midnight. '*Attention, oui,*' said the driver clambering down. 'You were driving in the dark. What did I tell you?'

My head was swimming still, from the wine I had drunk, and I had been too tired to make any supper. But the driver and his crew rallied round, stood me on terra firma, and drove off with headlights cutting a great swathe into the blue-blackness.

It was now bitterly cold. After the fearsome heat of the day this cold felt like the depth of an Arctic winter. I would not have been surprised to see the frost forming on the ground, or ice choking the radiator.

I wrapped my sleeping bag in blankets and snuggled down inside it. There was an absolute silence. Nothing stirred. The moon, pale and lovely, cast a serene flattering light on the desert. Lines that were harsh and jagged in the sun became soft and caressing. I blew a cloud of cigarette smoke at the moon, eased my weary, sand-blown limbs, and began to enjoy my complete solitude. My first day in the desert was ended and already I was beginning to fall under its spell. I slept soundly.

As the sun rose over the swelling sand dunes I coughed and coughed. Black phlegm filled my throat, a relic no doubt of the dust that had filled the car all the time I drove. For five full minutes I lay and coughed, and hawked and spat.

My bread was dehydrated, and hard as stone. It softened with a little water, and I made breakfast with it and a tin of sardines. Then with the sand beginning to warm again I drove off. Tinfouchi was 100 miles away, and I wanted to catch the *camion*. I would feel a whole lot safer with him behind me.

The *piste* was clear and sandy, but had deep ruts carved in it by the *camions*. Their high wheel-base left a ridge in the centre of the track that was often far too high for my car. I either made an encircling movement if I saw the ridge soon enough, or else put my foot down hard and bulldozed my way through. After thirty miles or so I burst a tyre.

A quick wheel change and I was off again into a region of great sand dunes. From the top of a dune I could see them undulating into the distance, like a vast petrified ocean. They seemed to have encircled me completely within what seemed like seconds.

I found what appeared to be a possible way out, a kind of pass, deep with soft sand and rutted with tracks. There was about 100 feet of loose ground, but with a centre ridge that would have lifted my car off its wheels and left them dangling.

For twenty minutes I drove round the dunes trying to find another way. I saw none.

There was nothing for it but to try and clear that ridge. I would clear the approach to the pass, then lay sand-mats which, if I drove at them hard enough, should lift me into the air for a short way. The car's momentum should enable it to bulldoze the rest of the way.

I started digging. The blisters that formed on my hand the previous day now broke and skinned. Soon little drops of blood forced their way through. There was no sign of any sweat at all and I became so exhausted I could do no more. I looked at my watch. I had been digging for ninety minutes, and I seemed to have made no impression at all.

I glowered at the narrow pass, my chest heaving. If my plan did not work the car would be wrecked, and that would be the end of my journey.

For nearly an hour I drove round again in ever widening circles, searching for another way out. I seemed as though I was in a maze. I would see what looked like an opening, and drive towards it, only to find yet another obstacle behind it.

Once I stopped the car and got out to look at a possible exit. It didn't appear to lead anywhere but I walked past it and on a little way. Then I turned to look at the car.

A flutter of panic seized me. The car was miles away, a tiny blue smudge near the horizon. Now soon I had forgotten the advice not to wander from my vehicle. The car bobbed and weaved a little in the heat undulations from the sand.

I took a grip of myself, and forced myself with enormous deliberation step by step back to it. I felt dizzy. I felt sick and frightened.

Finally I slumped behind the wheel and almost sobbed.

I decided to return to the pass, which clearly was my only hope. But which way was the damned pass? Which way should I go? It all looked so much the same.

I began driving round and round again in circles. I looked up at the sun, trying to recall where it was when I was digging. A sharp pain shot from my eyes through to the back of my head, as I did so. I came on the pass by chance, just as I least expected it. It was almost a sanctuary.

For half an hour I rested, trying to summon enough strength to tackle the shovel again. I forced myself out to work, and laid the sand-mats in what seemed the best position. I reversed the car for three hundred yards and sat there working up the courage to hurl my car at them.

The engine fired enthusiastically. I let in the clutch and we surged forward. We picked up speed. Change to second. Faster and faster. Quickly into third. The needle flickering around seventy. The front wheels touched the mats and we soar across the pass. The rear wheels dig soft sand, and I have cleared the pass by about six yards.

I sat there shaking. I don't know whether it was from emotion or fright. I do know that the elation I felt was greater than any I had experienced on a race track.

A few hundred yards away was a tree. I've no notion how a tree came to grow in this waterless waste. It was quite dead and stony hard. I spread a tarpaulin over its skeleton and rested in the shade. After I had cooked some lunch on the primus, for my further diversion I set a can on a heap of sand and emptied my revolver at it. Three out of six bullets passed through the can from a distance of 25 yards.

My flickering nerves calmed after this relaxation, and I moved off. Within half a mile I was stuck again.

I wound bandages round my hands and started digging again. This time I had learnt my lesson, and the sand-mats were laid right away. Again I was exhausted. Again I rested. Again I moved off.

Now I came to a large flat plain. The ground was packed hard, like the Utah salt flats, and I sped across five miles of it in as many minutes. For seven miles further the *piste* became cruel and rocky, and I could go no farther than five miles an hour. I kept out of trouble by concentrating for every foot of the way.

I was gaining speed again when I rounded a dune, and without any warning foundered in a foot-deep depression.

I was used to the drill now. Out of the car, out with the shovel, dig like hell.

The pounds of excess fat which I had stored away on my body were dropping away fast. And try as I would I could not control the amount of water I drank. The quarts gurgled down my throat at this stop alone. The bandages on my hands were trapping sand, and seemed to be doing more harm than good so I tore them off, and found that by gripping the shovel more firmly I could lessen the rubbing.

As I paused to suck in great gulps of the burning air, which seared my pharynx on the way down, I was sure I could hear voices, and then the noise of a hammer striking steel.

An hour later I laid down my shovel and walked round the dune. There, not two hundred yards from where I was stuck was the *camion*, with its crew stretched out underneath its belly, sleeping through the hottest part of the day. I ran towards them shouting with glee, as though they were dear friends I had not seen in years.

Two of the crew came to help me out of my difficulty. The driver laughed at my experiences, and advised me that whenever the *piste* divided into two, as round a dune, to take the lefthand track. It was invariably the best one.

With the comforting assurance that the *camion* was once more behind me, I made to go. As I did so the driver came towards me and took my hand in his great fist.

'I like to shake you hand,' he said, gritting his teeth on the unfamiliar English sounds as though they were iron filings. 'You good for Sahara.'

For another three hours I made steady progress – sticking in the sand twice, but digging out easily. A tyre burst, and a second went flat. I was clearly not going to make Tinfouchi by nightfall.

As I was checking over the car after the last tyre change, I heard the whine of the *camion* engine getting closer. When it eventually came into sight I thought the driver had gone mad. The desert all round for several miles was flat with firm sand and compacted stones, and the *camion* was swerving first in one direction and then the other, making turns so tight that it looked as though it must capsize. It was going nearly flat out – at about forty mph – and one of the crew was standing on the running board.

Then I saw the reason, a gazelle. The graceful creature was bounding away from the monster truck in terror, turning and twisting desperately to shake it off. Finally it lay down on the ground, exhausted. The man on the running board jumped down ahd despatched the beast with a knife.

There were many gazelle in this region of the Sahara. Heaven knows how they managed to live. They would live for months at a time simply by nibbling the dried-up thorn bushes, drawing their noisture from there. Their flesh however – as I was later to discover – was sweet and tender, and fresh meat is hard to come by in the desert.

The *camion* crew presented me with the horns, and set about skinning the animal and preparing a fire to cook it immediately. No meat would keep fresh for more than an hour in those conditions. I declined their invitation to share in the feast as I was by now well past the twenty-one hours time limit that had been set me between reporting posts.

The flat, firm terrain continued for some miles as the sun disappeared in a blinding blaze of glory over the horizon. I followed the wheel tracks in front of me, but they became hard to distinguish in the fading light. They spread out and fanned in different directions, and I would follow first one set and then another.

I glanced at the compass. The needle pointed steadily south as I followed one set of vehicle tracks, then it slowly swung round until it was pointing ninety degrees away.

'My God, I'm driving round in circles,' I murmured. I stopped and got out to examine the tracks. They were everywhere. I knew I must be somewhere near Tinfouchi, but in which direction was it?

I started driving round in every increasing circles, until three hours later I spotted the lights of a fort in the distance.

I cheered, and dashed towards them. Suddenly the desert in front of me dropped away to a black emptiness. I slammed on the brakes, thanked God for the brake-booster, and stopped a few feet short of a sheer precipice.

At a more gentle place I circumnavigated the escarpment and found my way to the entrance of the post. It was protected by a barbed wire compound and a sign saying '*Attention – Mines*'. So I stopped.

Two officers strode out of the post to greet me. They saluted solemnly as they approached and asked to see my papers. They scanned each sheet with pedantic precision. They had, said one, been expecting me all day.

I was sorry, but I had been lost, and had spent the past three hours running round in circles looking for the place.

They knew, they said dourly, they had watched my headlights in the distance. Tinfouchi, they explained was a punishment camp, a military glasshouse, where the bad boys of the Saharan army were sent to expiate their crimes in a man-devized purgatory. I would therefore not be allowed into the camp at night. I could however bed down within the barbed wire compound, in a corner which was clear of mines.

The welcome was chilly and correct, and I was glad I didn't walk in my sleep.

I prepared a meal on the edge of my minefield. I was worn out and tired, but starving. Potato, onion and corned beef hash, bread and tinned cheese, coffee and a little wine, filled the gap.

Some of the soldiers, members of staff evidently, wandered out to chat with me. They were clearly delighted to see a new face from the outside world.

The occupants of this gloomy place also suffered from an absolute prohibition on the drinking of alcohol, so they were thrice-delighted when I broke open a couple more bottles of wine and passed them round. By the time they had smoked most of my cigarettes as well, they had assured me of unlimited quantities of free fuel and oil the next day, plus a visit to the fort stores.

I didn't get to bed until two, and then the glacial night and wind-driven sand forced me to take my sleeping bag into the car where I stretched out as best I could on the front seat. I passed a thoroughly uncomfortable five hours of near-sleep.

In the morning the commandant came out to introduce himself. He apologized for not having welcomed me personally the previous night, but they had very very strict rules there. I saw over his shoulder platoons of men being marched at the double backwards and forwards in another compound.

The commandant told me I could have as much petrol as I needed – but it was not of the best grade.

Every nut and bolt on the car seemed to have worked loose during the previous two days' drive. Tightening them up from now on would have to be a daily task. As I drove back on to the *piste* leading to Tindouf at mid-day I saw my friends in the *camion* arrive. We exchanged waves.

Tindouf, which was as close to Agadir as to me now, was only 290 miles away. But the first thirty miles of that was as rugged as any I had crossed yet. I don't think I got out of first gear for three hours. I crawled over razor-edged rocks, and deep gullies. The wind had blown the sand into little wavelets, so that I was constantly bucking and rearing as in a small boat in a high sea. But my previous day's experiences had been all to the good.

Slowly over rocks, fast over sand and these corrugations. Never take your foot off the accelerator when you hit bad sand, and above all don't change your mind at the last minute about which track you are going to take. When you bog down in soft sand get the mats out right away, no matter how comfortably stored they may be.

Now I was driving over a high plain with a firm surface, and gentle undulations. The surface was rent occasionally with gullies of soft sand, but I was getting almost expert in avoiding them. The heat was, if anything, worse. It was 150 degrees in the sun – there was no shade to measure it in.

The wind came to plague me. It whipped over the rolling waves of sand, carrying armfuls of it about two or three feet above ground. This stung and burnt as it struck me. The whine of the wind was incessant and maddening.

At times I could swear I could hear voices close behind me. Or I could hear dogs barking, or children crying. At times I heard the sea, or snakes, or other vehicles. Each time it was the wind.

I would stop and peer round and the wind would bite and blister and run away over the rolling plains laughing with ghostly glee.

Tiny twisting sandstorms danced around me as the wind eddied and rushed here and there. The whole desert was alive and writhing under the blistering heat.

The tufts of hair that premature baldness has left me were matted with sand. My now flourishing beard stiff and encrusted with crystals of it. As I hit a patch of soft sand the front wheels would swivel left and right, and the car would twist like a bronco trying to throw its rider.

By six-thirty I had covered 130 miles with one brief stop. I stopped once more to let the sun go down, and thrilled again to the magnificent Saharan sunset. The wind dropped. It became enjoyably cool. The dunes turned an opulent gold, and the gullies filled with deep blue shadow. The lakes too and the air around me turned to gold. It faded gradually. The sky became a velvet black, and the desert under the stars and moon a pale grey-blue. The whole effect was breath-taking.

I sat behind the wheel unwilling to break the stilling effect of this theatrical display. The horizon played a fading diminuendo of chromatic chords, and sensation returned.

My back ached. My blistered hands throbbed. A desert sore, caused by the lack of fresh food and vitamins, was ripening on my arm. I was filthy. My muscles were ragged from lack of sleep. But I determined to keep going.

236

RAID ON ENTEBBE

Tony Williamson

Flight 139 bound for Paris from Tel Aviv was hijacked with 258 passengers on board and taken to Entebbe – into the hands of terrorists, Ugandan soldiers and the treacherous custody of President Idi Amin.

Over half the hostages were released as a number of the hijackers' demands were met, but it was no coincidence that the hundred or so who remained captive were all of Jewish extraction and were to be used in a macabre blackmail game by the Palestinian and Baader Meinhof terrorists.

Daily, the iniquitous President Amin visited the hostages in his large black Mercedes to reassure them of his 'protection', but after a week of hardship, fear and illness the Ugandan dictator's words rang hollow.

The outlook for the hostages looked bleak, for surely there could be no chance of rescue as they were guarded day and night by fanatical terrorists and 120 Ugandan soldiers. Besides, the nearest Israeli troops were over 2,000 miles away.

Nevertheless, at least one of the hostages lived in hope of a miracle. . . .

Benji was playing with a friend. Suddenly, with a very serious expression, he said that they were going to be rescued. Sarah looked at him in surprise, struck by the gravity of the boy.

'What do you mean?' asked the friend.

Benji frowned, looking puzzled. 'I don't know. I just have a feeling that we're going to be rescued.'

The friend was sceptical, but Benji persisted. 'We'll be rescued by the army,' he said. 'I just know we will.'

Sarah felt close to tears. She did not have the heart to tell him that such a rescue was impossible. Their soldiers were more than 2,000 miles away and this was a hostile country. To Benji it was simple. The commandos would come and take them home. But to Sarah Davidson it was an impossible dream.

At that every moment, three Hercules were taking off from Sharm el-Sheikh. The commandos were on their way . . .

★　　★　　★　　★

It was midnight in Uganda, eleven o'clock in Tel Aviv.

Nadia Israel was trying to get to sleep, her young aunt, Nina, already asleep beside her.

Jean-Jacques Maimoni was sitting by the window, looking across the tarmac, watching the soldiers leaning on their guns and talking idly with each other.

Sarah Davidson wanted to get to sleep, but Benji and Ron were cheerfully planning to play all night.

Captain Bacos was with his crew, most of them asleep. They had been talking quietly about tomorrow and what it would bring. He looked around the dimly-lit room, relieved that the worst of the sickness appeared to be over.

By the window Jean-Jacques Maimoni got to his feet and went to his mattress in the centre of the room, picking his way carefully among the sleeping families. He lay down and closed his eyes. He was asleep almost immediately.

Across the airfield, less than a mile away, the modern terninal and control tower were brightly lit, the guards oblivious to the fact that in the darkness Israeli agents were moving silently into position. Explosive charges, taped to telephone and telex cables, were primed and ready to be detonated.

And 30,000 feet above Entebbe two generals were watching a glowing radar screen. Beyond them the telecommunications men were hunched over their transmitters. Below, skimming the waters of Lake Victoria, were three giant Hercules.

The time was one minute past midnight. . . .

★　　★　　★　　★

'This is El Al Flight 166 with the prisoners from Tel Aviv,' said the

Israeli pilot in a quiet, laconic voice. 'Can I have permission to land?'

The C130 was three minutes from touchdown showing clearly on the glide path in the Entebbe Control Tower. What did not show was the fact that there were two aircraft, side by side, coming in over Lake Victoria.

There were three air traffic controllers on duty at Entebbe, and they were completely bewildered by the sudden inexplicable chain of events. Badrew Muhindi and Tobias Rwengeme were trying to locate the African Airways flight from Nairobi which had vanished from their radar screens, while Lawrence Mawenda was endeavouring to contact the Civil Aviation Director, Peter Kalanzi, and getting no reply.

In desperation the air traffic controllers grabbed telephones and tried to call Kampala for instructions, but every line was dead. They could only watch with numbed disbelief, as two aircraft came out of the night and touched down on the main runway. They were not civil aircraft at all but huge, camouflaged military transports.

Across the airfield, hidden by rising ground, the third of the giant Hercules was touching down on the disused runway. The pilot, using the brilliantly-lit old terminal as a beacon and switching on his landing lights at the last possible moment, placed the C130 firmly on the pot-holed runway and reversed the four powerful Allison D22A turboprops. The Hercules had the shortest landing distance for any aircraft in the world of comparable size, and less than thirty seconds after touchdown it was turning off the runway and taxi-ing towards the old terminal.

Inside, Lieut.-Colonel Yonatan ('Yoni') Netanyahu took up his position beside the cargo ramp, glancing back along the crouching ranks of men. Only their eyes gleamed in the darkness. The lights had been extinguished for almost an hour now so that they were all fully accustomed to the dark.

It had been a far from pleasant journey lasting seven hours, and for much of that time they had been buffeted by head winds and storms over the Red Sea. After the first hour many of the Israeli soldiers had begun to suffer from nausea and this persisted until they were clear of the mountains of Ethiopia five hours later.

But the men were hardened soldiers and the discomfort only served to take their minds off the ever-present danger of the sea beneath them. In spite of the storms, the C130 pilots held the huge aircraft low

beneath the radar cover of the neighbouring countries. Such a manoeuvre would have been impossible had it not been for the sophisticated
flight control equipment which constantly corrected the height and
course of the aircraft. To have lifted up above the storm would have
meant revealing their positions to Egypt, Libya, Saudi Arabia and the
Sudan. Long before they reached Entebbe, the Ugandan Army would
have been on full alert and waiting for them.

Instead the giant C130s thundered through the howling winds, only
a few hundred feet above the angry sea, their engines at maximum revs
to hold a cruising speed of 350 mph. Above them, well clear of the
storm, were two squadrons of Phantom F4 fighters, armed with Side-
winder missiles. With their radar systems they were able to watch the
entire area around the Red Sea, ready to go into action the moment
Arab fighters threatened the task force below.

The pilots who flew the Hercules were among the finest in Israel's
Air Force, but for the first 1,500 miles it took all their courage and
experience to hold the giant transports in tight formation through the
turbulence. Long before they reached Ethiopia the Phantoms above
were peeling away and heading back for Israel, their range exhausted.
For the next six hours the fighter pilots would sweat it out at Sharm
el-Sheikh, ready to take off at any moment to protect the returning
aircraft.

As the Phantoms pulled out, two Boeings were falling into position
above the Hercules at a height of 33,000 feet. This was one of the
trouble spots; the last few hundred miles along the Red Sea before the
C130s could turn inland and begin cutting through the valleys and
ravines of Ethiopia. The flight plan of the Boeings, which were register-
ing as a single aircraft on the area radar, coincided with the task force
for one hour before their faster speed took them away.

The planning team had calculated that this discrepancy of speed,
some 75 miles per hour, would enable the Boeings to be above the C130s
for 300 miles before they turned inland over Ethiopia. For this period
they had calculated that the radar posts along the Red Sea would be
watching 'Flight LY 169' on course for Nairobi and would fail to
notice the brief period – less than four sweeps of a radar scope – when
the Hercules lifted up and over the first ridge of the Eritrean mountains
between Massawa and Port Sudan. A strike by radar technicians in the

Sudan was an unexpected bonus for the Israelis, who learned hours before the flight that only one out of three radar stations was being manned.

As the C130s slipped down the valleys and ravines towards Lake Rudolph on the border of Kenya, the Boeings were holding their scheduled course across Ethiopia at a height of 33,000 feet. The leading Boeing, LY 169, maintained radio contact with area traffic controllers, proceeding in a perfectly innocent fashion towards Nairobi. Only when they were descending towards the mountains beyond Nanyuki did Beni Peled's Boeing peel away and head in a wide, four hundred mile circle for Lake Victoria, timing its arrival to coincide with the C130s who had cut straight across from Lake Rudolph to Kakamega.

It was this precision flying which put the task force together in one spot in the middle of Africa at midnight local time, and the only people who had the slightest indication of what was happening were the radar operators at Nairobi Airport. Their area radar extended to Entebbe and they had watched, with some bewilderment, the unidentified Boeing approach Entebbe and then suddenly climb to 30,000 feet. When it became stationary on their radar screens they knew the Boeing was circling within the 'blind cone' above the airport. After that, the appearance of three more aircraft came as no surprise, nor did their disappearance from the screens which indicated that they had landed.

Few Kenyans had reason to like President Idi Amin. For years their countrymen in Uganda had been persecuted, and for the past year the Ugandan Radio had been making threats against Kenya, including arbitrary territorial claims involving a large section of Kenya beside Lake Victoria. Nor did the Ugandan association with the Palestinians make them more popular in Kenya, especially since, only a few months before, a Palestinian plot at Nairobi Airport had been foiled with Israeli help. It was not surprising, therefore, that at midnight on Saturday a number of Kenyans watched what was happening with a certain satisfaction.

For Colonel Netanyahu's men the problem had always been how to get close enough to the old terminal. Although discipline around the building was lax, the Israelis were under no illusions about the Palestinian reaction to an attack. They would kill as many of the hostages as possible.

The early plans, which had ranged from parachute drops in the dark to a Boeing 707 packed with commandos disguised as prisoners, had all been rejected because they did not fulfil the primary requirement of putting the Israeli force close enough to the terrorists to prevent retaliation on the hostages.

At first the tactical problems had appeared insoluble. More than a hundred well-armed Ugandan soldiers, spread around the terminal and on the roof terrace, made storming the building out of the question. A landing on the main runway, almost a mile away, would give the Ugandans ample time to take cover and open fire with automatic rifles and machine-guns. To attack across brilliantly-lit open ground, in the face of such a fusillade, would be suicidal. The Israelis would be pinned down before they got half way, and with the Ugandans in commanding positions and able to call on reserves from the nearby army camp, the chances of ever reaching the terminal were remote.

Only an overwhelming force capable of sustaining heavy casualties could make such an attack feasible, and Yoni's group was anything but that. His men numbered no more than fifty tough young commandos.

The final solution had been a plan so audacious that it would catch the Ugandans and the hijackers completely off their guard. It was the key to the entire Israeli operation and its essential element sat now between the men, gleaming in the darkness, the engine already purring as the Hercules taxied to the edge of the tarmac facing the old terminal; a large black Mercedes complete with an escort of two British Land-Rovers. In the driving seats of the Mercedes and the Land-Rovers were Israelis with blackened hands and faces. It had been decided, because Amin's Mercedes had curtained windows, that it would be unnecessary to have a fake President in the car. Instead, behind the drawn curtains, two paratroopers crouched with Galil assault rifles. In the back of the two Land-Rovers were men very similar to the President's Palestinian bodyguards.

The Hercules came to a halt, and the heavy ramp slowly lowered itself to the ground.

'Go,' said the commander.

The first Land-Rover accelerated down the ramp, out on to the brilliantly-lit tarmac followed immediately by the Mercedes and the second Land-Rover.

Gabrielle Tiedemann* and Wilfred Boese* were standing outside the door of the terminal talking to a young Ugandan officer when the C130 came to a stop five hundred yards away. They watched with some surprise as the huge aircraft swung itself round, then opened its cargo hold.

Beyond them, scattered across the tarmac in front of the terminal, Ugandan soldiers turned to face the aircraft which had come to a halt on the edge of the illuminated area. It had scarcely stopped when the ramp was coming down and the vehicles roared out on to the tarmac. Without hesitation the soldiers snapped to attention.

The escort Land-Rovers and the Mercedes swept towards them at a steady pace, the guards sitting casually in the rear of the vehicles. No one doubted the evidence clearly before them, that President Amin was arriving for another meeting with the hostages and hijackers. Those who had time to think about the giant military transport simply assumed that he had arrived from the OAU conference in Mauritius. Only Boese and Tiedemann found this unlikely, and as the Mercedes with its escorts came closer, Boese turned and went into the terminal, collecting his sub-machine-gun from where it was leaning against the wall.

By this time the convoy was among the Ugandans and coming to a stop. One soldier, close to the lead Land-Rover and some ninety yards from the terminal building, suddenly realized that the men he had assumed were Palestinians were wielding Uzi sub-machine-guns, not the Russian Kalichikofs they normally carried. With a shout of alarm he raised his gun, realizing immediately that he had seen none of these men before.

That Ugandan soldier was the first man to die at Entebbe.

Even as the first wave of gunfire broke out, Yoni's men were lunging down the ramp of the Hercules and racing for the terminal. This was the exercise they had rehearsed again and again until they could empty the aircraft and fan out into position in forty-five seconds. The training paid off. Even as the astonished Ugandans were trying to recover, Israeli commandos were racing across the tarmac, firing short bursts from the Uzi sub-machine-guns.

Around the Mercedes it was chaos. The men in the Land-Rovers

* Tiedemann & Boese: Baader Meinhof terrorists.

243

were laying down a withering fire on all sides. In the Mercedes itself
were commandos equipped with Galil assault rifles, sweeping the area
with high velocity automatic fire. In the leading Land-Rover the driver
was methodically shooting out the brilliant lights along the roof of the
terminal.

It was all too much for those Ugandan soldiers that were still on their
feet after that first, shattering, minute. They turned and ran for the
darkness, only to find Israelis coming in on either side in a flanking
movement. The attack was total and terrifying, the area in front of the
terminal already littered with wounded and dying men.

Gabrielle Tiedemann saw it all, at first with disbelief, then with rage.
She raised her pistol, aiming at the lean young men racing towards the
terminal. She fired one shot, and was then cut down by a hail of bullets
from the converging Israelis.

In the passage leading to the main hall of the terminal, Wilfred Boese
was desperately trying to find the magazine for his sub-machine-gun.
He had left it by the doorway of the room containing the hostages. The
sound of shooting and the cries of Ugandans were deafening. He was
only dimly aware of the quick bursts of fire outside the building, of the
lights beginning to go out. He found the magazine, slapped it into his
gun and cocked it. Facing him was the door to the lounge; behind him
the passage and tarmac beyond, echoing to the snarl of machine-guns.

Boese knew what he must do. He stepped into the main hall, his gun
aimed at the helpless hostages. Many of them were still asleep, others
just beginning to react to the gunfire outside. A few were starting to
cry out, huddling down on the floor. A few feet away from him was a
man he recognized as Ilan Hartuv. They stared at each other and Boese
hesitated, his finger on the trigger, a hundred helpless people before
him.

★　　★　　★　　★

Across the room Ilan Hartuv watched Boese appear in the doorway,
slapping a magazine into his gun, gazing towards them for an interminable moment, then rushing back along the passage.

Around the room men were clutching terrified wives and children,
some piling mattresses over their families. All the lights were going out

The driver was shooting out the brilliant lights.

on the tarmac outside and people began to shout in panic, trying to locate friends and relatives.

Akiva Lexer, the lawyer, looked up at the window as a soldier jumped on to the ledge and hung there, like some 'incredible angel', calling to them to be calm and lie down. But some were too bewildered to follow this advice.

Jean-Jacques Maimoni awoke to a terrifying world of noise and sprang to his feet. Uzi machine-guns chattered across the room and he fell, dying. The sounds and the terror were too much for Mrs Ida Borowitz. She jumped to her feet, in spite of the attempts of people around her to keep her on the floor, and became an immediate target in the dim light. She had no way of knowing that the Israeli soldiers believed there were terrorists in the room capable of raining death on the helpless people around them. So Mrs Borowitz, a moving shadow in the darkness, died without realizing that the impossible rescue had begun.

The Davidson family, with chaos all about them, crawled into the washroom and huddled there. They had not heard the shouts in Hebrew from outside the terminal, and Sarah was sure that this was the thing she had dreaded most of all, the systematic execution of the hostages.

Inside the main hall Pasco Cohen was lying in the darkness in a pool of blood, critically wounded. He had jumped to his feet when the firing began in an attempt to reach his family, but neither they nor his friends knew this. As the firing continued outside, the man who had survived the death camps and all the wars of Israel was fighting his last battle.

For Nadia Israel, clutching at her young aunt in the darkness, the deafening explosions of grenades and the chattering of sub-machine-guns seemed to be everywhere. She became numbed by fear and the conviction that death would come at any moment, ceased to be aware of time or even the existence of the terminal. She retreated into a limbo of the mind and would not emerge until sanity returned around her.

The confusion continued in the terminal. At the height of the firing many of the hostages still believed that the battle was between Ugandan soldiers and terrorists. Akiva Lexer remembered the words of President Amin who had promised a solution to their problem earlier that evening. He had almost made up his mind that this must be the solution he had referred to, when an Israeli soldier with a loud-hailer began to shout through the window in Hebrew, telling everyone to be calm and lie down.

The room became quiet, many of the people stunned by the realization that this was a rescue operation. Above them, on the roof terrace, there was fierce fighting. The rabble of machine-guns was punctuated by the crack of exploding grenades. The building shook, plaster falling from the ceiling.

After more than ten minutes there was a lull in the firing and a few people risked looking out of windows. In the dim light outside they saw Israeli soldiers moving in and out of shadows, crouching around the vehicles halfway across the tarmac. Beyond them the night sky was lit with an explosion on the far side of the airfield, and in the distance they could hear a major battle in progress.

Baruch Gross was in a side room with his wife, Ruth, and son, Shy. From his window he could see the body of Wilfred Boese, sprawled beside the entrance to the terminal. Beyond it were other bodies, but even as he watched there was another flurry of gunfire from the rear of the building and he crouched down on the floor again. The firing continued for fifteen minutes, diminishing finally to occasional shots, then the Israeli soldiers began moving into the room, speaking urgently to the terrified hostages lying on the floor.

'Come quickly,' they said. 'It is time to leave. Everyone come quickly.'

The Davidson family were huddled together in the darkness of the washroom. It had been quiet for more than a minute and Sarah Davidson was beginning to believe that perhaps, after all, they would survive. Suddenly the door beside her opened and she looked up to see a young Israeli soldier looking down at her and smiling broadly. He seemed no more than a boy, and as her mouth fell open in amazement he asked in a quiet, very calm voice: 'Are you all right?'

'Yes,' she said weakly. 'But what are you doing here?'

'We've come to take you home.'

'Home!' She stared at him as though he was mad. 'How can you take us home?'

The young Israeli commando grinned. 'In an aeroplane, of course.'

At that moment Sarah Davidson wanted to kiss this young boy more than anything else in the world. Instead, like so many of the bewildered people in the terminal, she simply nodded her head and rose to her feet, then gathered her children and began walking towards the door.

Outside they saw everyone milling around, moving down the passage and on to the tarmac. Many people were only half-dressed, others dazed and having to be led by friends. There seemed to be Israeli soldiers everywhere now, talking quietly, telling people to keep calm.

Nadia Isarel and her aunt were among the first to reach the passage. Outside there was more firing and Nadia flinched, holding back, but a soldier appeared beside her and gave an encouraging grin. Ahead, just beyond the door, was a Land-Rover and she ran with her aunt towards it. People were scrambling into the vehicle, some crying, others clutching at it as though this was their only link with reality. By the time Nadia reached it the vehicle was crammed with people, but the driver slapped the bonnet and told her to climb on. She threw herself on to it, holding the bonnet with her hands, looking at the young Israeli commando with bewildered disbelief. He smiled in reassurance, then drove across the tarmac until the huge Hercules loomed up out of the darkness.

As she tumbled off the Land-Rover, clutching at her aunt's hand, she saw people running out of the night from the terminal. There were doctors by the ramp, helping people on board, asking them if they had any injuries. Inside there were soldiers, some of them cheerful, but others with bloody bandages and gaunt faces. She stumbled up the ramp and into the body of the Hercules, finding a canvas seat and sitting there with shaking hands. 'We're going home,' someone said. But even now she knew it couldn't possibly be true.

The soldiers had set up a defensive circle, their weapons pointing out into the darkness as the groups of hostages ran towards the aircraft. Some were trying to locate members of their family even as they ran, others sobbed with fear as shots rattled out across the terminal.

One child, a small boy, was being led by his mother when a burst of gunfire broke out. With a scream of fear he tore himself free and stood in the middle of the tarmac with his hands over his eyes. A young Israeli soldier moved forward, gesturing for his mother to run for the plane, then scooped the child up in his arms and started after her. From the darkness there was a burst of firing and he turned, shielding the boy with his body, firing the Uzi from his hip.

All around the terminal Israeli commandos were moving through the night like cats, waiting for the slightest sign of snipers or advancing Ugandans. Others were using Galil assault rifles fitted with night sights, constantly searching the darkness. Beyond them, from the terminal, the hostages streamed in a bewildered column.

Mrs Jocelyn Monier emerged from the main hall with blood pouring down from a shrapnel wound in her thigh. She was picked up by one soldier and placed on the back of another, who took her across to the aircraft at a jogtrot. When she arrived a doctor began treating her immediately, assuring her that it was a flesh wound and not serious.

Nili Ben-Dor, the wife of the Israeli footballer, had not even had time to dress and ran for the Hercules in her bra and briefs. She was not aware of it until she was inside the aircraft where an Israeli soldier, with a sympathetic look, took off his shirt and gave it to her.

By the time the Davidsons reached the aircraft most of the firing had stopped. They climbed up the ramp and moved along the crowded fuselage, taking seats and only then beginning to relax. Their son, Benji, still had the hand of bridge in his pocket. He showed it to Sarah who stared at it for a moment, then burst into tears. She was crying for the first time since they arrived in Entebbe . . .

In the terminal Israeli commandos searched every room until they were satisfied that all the hostages had left. The bodies of Jean-Jacques Maimoni and Ida Borowitz were carried out to the aircraft, together with Pasco Cohen who was already receiving emergency treatment from a doctor. Even then it was clear that there was little hope for him.

On the aircraft soldiers counted and recounted the hostages until they were satisfied that everyone was on board. Then the Land-Rovers came up the ramp with the last of the soldiers who would travel on this aircraft.

Along the runway other commandos were spreading out, weapons sweeping the darkness in case of any attempt to fire on the Hercules as it took off. The huge aircraft taxied to the end of the old runway, switched on its lights and the turboprops roared. Within seconds it was rolling forward, gathering speed, lifting off up into the night.

It had been on the ground for just fifty-three minutes.

On the other side of the airfield, Dan Shomron* set about the

* Unit Commander Brigadier-General Dan Shamron.

complicated task of withdrawing his men. Here the aerial command post was invaluable, contacting each unit over the entire area of the airport and co-ordinating the embarkation. It was a complex, time-consuming operation, but in twenty minutes all Shomron's units were around the aircraft.

The remaining Ugandan soldiers at Entebbe were in disarray. The main terminal and control tower were a shambles, the two squadrons of Mig 21s and 17s totally destroyed and still blazing. The old terminal was littered with the bodies of terrorists and Ugandans and in the darkness more than a hundred wounded soldiers were waiting for help. An armoured column, on its way from Kampala, was still thirty minutes from Entebbe.

On the runway a C130 prepared to leave. Each unit was checked on board, the vehicles ascending the ramps with the heavy armoured car the last to enter, its machine-guns ready to fire until the last moment before the ramp finally closed. Commanders checked their men, then the Hercules started down the runway and lifted into the sky.

The last aircraft was Shomron's, its ramp closing only when its sister aircraft had vanished into the night. Ugandan soldiers were beginning to advance on the runway, realizing that the attacking force was leaving. In the control tower a Ugandan officer watched the huge aircraft thunder along the runway, and as a last resort cut off the airfield runway lights.

The pilot of the Hercules, faced with total blackness, guided the aircraft by instinct, watching the air speed indicator approaching take-off speed. At one point the C130 swerved dangerously close to the edge of the runway, but the pilot brought it back. Then it was airborne and they were safe.

Over Lake Victoria, some five hundred feet above the water, a Hercules flew towards Nairobi. Inside the cargo hold was the gleaming black Mercedes which had played such a crucial role in the assault on Entebbe. To take it back to Israel was a calculated risk, for the IDF were determined to keep this aspect of their operation secret. There had been a contingency in the plan to drop the car into Lake Victoria from the C130, a relatively simple task as the cargo hold could open in flight, but the ruse had worked so perfectly that the car was now as much a part of history as the operation itself.

Less than a week before the Model 60 Mercedes, type 220, painted black, had been rusting in a junk yard three miles north of Tel Aviv. It had been found and purchased by an army supply officer whose instructions had been to find that precise model, preferably black. The car had been taken to an IDF maintenance unit where the engine had been serviced, the car resprayed and equipped with a new set of tyres. The total cost had been less than £200, and yet now it could well be priceless.

There was no doubt in the minds of the generals that one day this particular Mercedes would take its place in a military museum. For that reason they decided not to jettison the car, but to take it back to Sharm el-Sheikh where it would remain until such time as the government decided to unveil the key to operation Entebbe. In the weeks and months that followed many fanciful stories would no doubt be written about it, but the Mercedes would remain the property of the army to whom it belonged.

★   ★   ★   ★

As the C130s thundered towards Nairobi, Beni Peled and Yekuti Adam were sending their last messages to Israel before turning to follow the Hercules.

At Military Headquarters in Tel Aviv, the message brought jubilation to the generals and ministers. The ninety-five minutes of tension would be something they would never forget; now that it was over they could hardly bring themselves to believe that all had gone so perfectly. The operation had succeeded better than their wildest dreams, and even now it was difficult to absorb the fact that they had accomplished the impossible.

There were no speeches, no congratulations. The exhilaration of knowing was enough. In General Gur's office men who had fought a hundred campaigns were lost for words. They could only grin at each other and say: 'We did it'. One man put it more fervently. 'Tonight the Lord was with the army.'

BLACK NIGHTS ON THE THAMES

Gunter Pluschow

Gunter Pluschow, a German naval lieutenant in World War I, escaped from Donington Hall in Derbyshire. He was determined to make his way back to Germany – but the British authorities were just as determined to capture him. A newspaper article warned the public to be on the look-out for the fugitive. It read:

> 'Gunter Pluschow, the German naval lieutenant, fugutive from Donington Hall, has now been at large seven days. The Chinese dragon tattooed on his left arm while on service in the East should, however, betray his identity.
>
> Further particulars of the escape with Lieutenant Treppitz, who was caught at Millwall Docks within twenty-four hours, show that last Sunday a thunderstorm raged over Donington Hall when the evening roll-call was taken. Instead of assembling with the other prisoners within the inner two rings of the wire entanglement, the two hid within the outer circle. Their names were answered by other prisoners. A wooden plank near the outer ring showed how they got across the barbed wire. . . .'

Nevertheless the intrepid lieutenant was now in London – still at large – and cunningly disguised as a dock labourer. . . .

For days I loafed about London, my cap set jauntily at the back of my head, my jacket open, showing my blue sweater and its one ornament, the gilt stud, hands in pocket, whistling and spitting, as is the custom of sailors in ports all the world over. No one suspected me, and my whole plan hinged on this, for my only safeguard against discovery lay in the exclusion of even the slightest suspicion directed against myself. If

252

anyone had paid even passing attention to me, if a policeman has asked me for my name, I could only have given my own. Therefore, it was quite superfluous that the warrants put such stress on the tattoo marks on my arm as a clue to my identity. If matters had got thus far, it would have meant that the fight was over.

On the second morning I had colossal luck! I sat on the top of a bus, and behind me two business men were engaged in animated conversation. Suddenly I caught the words, 'Dutch steamer – departure – Tilbury,' and from that moment I listened intently, trying to quell the joyful throbbings of my heart. For these careless gentlemen were recounting nothing less than the momentous news of the sailing, each morning at seven, of a fast Dutch steamer for Flushing, which cast anchor off Tilbury Docks every afternoon.

In the twinkling of an eye I was off the bus. I rushed off to Blackfriars Station, and an hour later was at Tilbury. It was midday, and the workmen were streaming into their public-houses. First I went down to the river and reconnoitred; but my boat had not yet arrived. As I still had some time before me and felt very hungry, I went into one of the numerous eating-houses specially frequented by dock-labourers. In a large room a hundred of them were gathered around long tables partaking of huge meals. I followed their example, and, by putting down 8d., received a plate heaped with potatoes, vegetables and a large piece of meat. After that I purchased a big glass of stout from the bar, and, sitting down amongst the men with the utmost unconcern, proceeded with my dinner, endeavouring to copy the table manners of the men around me, and nearly coming to grief when trying to assimilate peas with the help of a knife.

In the midst of my feast I suddenly felt a tap on the shoulder. Icy shivers ran down my back. The proprietor stood behind me and asked me for my papers. I naturally understood that he meant my identity book, and gave all up as lost. As I was unable to produce them, I was obliged to follow him, and saw to my dread that he went to the telephone. I was already casting furtive glances at the door and thinking how I could best make my escape, when the publican, who had been watching me through the glass door, returned and remarked: 'If you have forgotten your papers, I can't help you. By the by, what is your name? And where do you come from?'

I was off the bus in the twinkling of an eye.

'I am George Mine, an American, ordinary seaman from the four-masted barque *Ohio*, lying upstream. I just came in here and have paid of my dinner, but of course haven't got my papers about me.'

He remarked: 'This is a private, social-democratic club, and only members are allowed to eat here – you ought surely to know that – but if you become a member, you are welcome to come as often as you like.'

Of course I agreed at once to his proposal, and paid three shillings' entrance fee. A bit of glaring red ribbon was passed through my button-hole, and thus I became the latest member of the social-democratic trades union of Tilbury!

I returned to my table as if nothing had happened, gulped down my stout to fortify myself after the shock I had just had, but also soon left, for, to be quite frank, I had lost all my appetite and no longer cared for my food.

I now went down to the riverside, threw myself on to the grass, and, feigning sleep, kept a lynx-eyed watch.

Ship after ship went by, and my expectations rose every minute. At last, at 4 pm, with proud bearing, the fast Dutch steamer dropped anchor and made fast to a buoy just in front of me. My happiness and my joy were indescribable when I read the ship's name in white shining letters on the bow: *Mecklenburg*.

There could be no better omen for me, since I am a native of Mecklenburg-Schwerin. I crossed over to Gravesend on a ferry-boat, and from there unobtrusively watched the steamer. I adopted the careless demeanour and rolling gait of the typical Jack Tar, hands in my pockets, whistling a gay tune, but keeping eyes and mind keenly on the alert.

This was my plan: to swim to the buoy during the night, climb the hawser, creep on deck and reach Holland as a stowaway.

I soon found the basis for my operations.

After I had ascertained that nobody was paying attention to me, I climbed over a pile of wood and rubbish, and concealed myself under some planks, where I discovered several bundles of hay. These afforded me a warm resting-place, of which I made use of that and the following nights.

About midnight I left my refuge. Cautiously I clambered over the old planks and the litter strewn over the ground. The rain came down noisily, and, though I had taken my bearings during the day, it was almost impossible in the pitch-dark night to find the two barges which I had seen near the lumber pile.

Creeping on all fours, listening with straining ears and trying to pierce the surrounding blackness, I came closer to my object.

However, I perceived with dismay that the two barges which, in daytime, had been completely submerged, lay high and dry. Luckily, at the stern, a little dinghy rode on the water.

With prompt resolution I wanted to rush into the boat, but before I knew where I was I felt the ground slipping from under my feet and I sank to the hips into a squashy, slimy, stinking mass. I threw my arms about, and was just able to reach the plank, which ran from the shore to the sailing-boat, with my left hand.

It took all my strength to get free of the slime which had nearly proved my undoing, and I was completely exhausted when I at last dragged myself back to my bed of hay.

When the sun rose on the third morning of my escape, I had already returned to a bench in Gravesend Park, and was watching the *Mecklenburg* as she slipped her moorings at 7 am and made for the open sea.

All that day, as well as later on, I loafed about London. For hours, like so many other wastrels, I watched from the bridges and position of the neutral steamers, the loading and unloading of cargoes, noting their stage and progress, in order, if possible, to take advantage of a lucky moment to slip on board.

I fed all these days in some of the worst eating-houses of the East End. I looked so disreputable and dirty, often limping or reeling about like a drunkard, and put on such an imbecile stare that no one bothered about me. I avoided speech, and sharply observed the workmen's pronunciation and the way in which they ordered their food. Soon I had acquired such facility and quickness – to say nothing of amazing impudence – that I no longer even considered the possibility of being caught. In the evening I returned to Gravesend.

This time a new steamer lay at anchor in the river, the *Princess Juliana*.

I now proceeded to pay still more attention to the conformation of the riverside, so as to safeguard myself against further accidents.

At midnight I found myself at the spot I had chosen. The bank was stony and the tide just going out. I quietly discarded my jacket boots and stockings, stowed the latter, with my watch, shaving-set, etc., in my cap, and put it on, fastening it securely on my head.

After that I hid the jacket and the boots under a stone, tightened the leather belt which held my trousers, and, dressed as I was, slipped gently into the water and swam in the direction of the boat.

The night was rainy and dark. Soon I was unable to recognize the shore which I had just left, but could just make out the outline of a rowing-boat which lay at anchor. I made for it, but in spite of terrible exertions could not get any nearer. My clothes were soaked through, and, growing heavier and heavier, nearly dragged me down. My strength began to abandon me, and so strong was the current that other rowing-boats which lay at anchor seemed to shoot past me like phantoms. Swimming desperately and exerting all my strength, I tried to keep my head above the water.

Soon, though, I lost consciousness, but when I recovered it, I lay high and dry on some flat stones covered with seaweed.

A kind fate had directed me to the few stony tracts of the shore where the river makes a sharp bend, and, thanks to the quickly out-flowing tide, I lay out of the water.

Trembling and shivering with cold and exertion, I staggered along the river-bank, and after an hour I found my jacket and by boots. After that I climbed over my fence and lay down, with chattering teeth, on my couch of straw.

It was still pouring, and an icy wind swept over me. My only covering consisted of my wet jacket and my two hands, which I spread out protectively over my stomach so as to try at least to keep well and going for the next few days. After two hours, being quite unable to sleep, I got up and ran about to get a little warmer.

My wet clothes only dried when they had hung over a stove a few days later in Germany! I again went to London for the day. I hung around in several churches, where I probably created the impression that I was praying devoutly; in reality I enjoyed an occasional nap there.

I had acquired so much confidence that I walked into the British Museum, visited several picture-galleries and even frequented matinées at music-halls, without being asked questions. The pretty blonde attendants at the music-halls were especially friendly to me, and seemed to pity the poor sailor who had wandered in by chance. What amused me most was to see the glances of disgust and contempt which the ladies and the young girls used to throw at me on the top of the buses. If they had known who sat near them! Is it surprising that I should not smell sweetly considering my night's work and the wet and slimy state of my clothes? In the evening I was back at Gravesend. In the little park which overlooked the Thames I listened quietly for hours to the strains of a military band. I had definitely given up my plan to swim to the steamer, for I saw that the distance was too great and the current too strong. I decided, therefore, to commandeer unobtrusively, somehow, a dinghy in which to reach the steamer. Just in front of me I saw one which I deemed suitable for my purpose, but it was moored to a wharf over which a sentry stood guard by day and night. But the risk had to be taken. The night was very dark when, about twelve, I crept through the park and crawled up to the embankment wall, which was about six feet high. I jumped over the hedge and saw the boat rocking gently on the water. I listened breathlessly. The sentry marched up and down. Half asleep, I had taken off my boots, fastening them with the laces round my neck, and holding an open knife between my teeth. With the stealth of an Indian I let myself down over the wall, and was just able to reach the gunwale of the boat with my toes. My hands slipped over the hard granite without a sound, and a second later I dropped into the boat, where I huddled in a corner listening with breathless attention; but my sentry went on striding up and down undisturbed under the bright arc-lamps. My boat, luckily, lay in shadow.

My eyes, trained through TBD* practice, saw in spite of the pitch darkness almost as well as by day. Carefully I felt for the oars. Damn! They were padlocked! Luckily the chain lay loose, and silently I first freed the boat-hook, then one oar after the other from the chain. My knife now sawed through the two ropes which held the boat to the wall and I dipped my oars noiselessly into the water and impelled my little boat forward.

When I had entered the boat, it had already shipped a good deal of water. Now I noticed to my dismay that the water was rapidly rising. It was already lapping the thwart, and the boat became more and more

* TBD = Torpedo-boat Destroyer.

difficult to handle as it grew heavier and heavier. I threw myself despairingly on my oars. Suddenly, with a grinding noise, the keel grounded and the boat lay immovable. Nothing now was of avail, neither pulling nor rowing, nor the use of the boat-hook. The boat simply refused to budge. Very quickly the water sank round it, and after a few minutes I sat dry in the mud, but to make up for this the boat was brimful of water. I had never in my life witnessed such a change in the water-level due to the tide. Although the Thames is well known in this respect, I had never believed that possible.

At this moment I found myself in the most critical position of my escape. I was surrounded on all sides by slushy, stinking slime, whose acquaintance I had made two evenings before at the risk of my life. The very thought caused me to shudder. About 200 yards off the sentry marched up and down, and I found myself with my boat fifteen feet from the six-foot-high granite wall.

I sat reflecting coolly. One thing appeared a sheer necessity – not to be found there by the English, who might have killed me like a mad dog.

But the water was not due to rise before the next afternoon. Therefore it behoved me to muster my energy, clench my teeth, and try to get the better of the mud. I slipped off my stockings, turned up my trousers as high as I could, and then I placed the thwarts and the oars close to each other on the seething and gurgling ooze, used the boat-hook as a leaping-pole by placing its point on a board, stood on the gunwale, and, gathering all my strength to a mighty effort, I vaulted into space – but lay, alas, the next moment three feet short of the wall, and sank deep over knee into the clammy slush, touching hard bottom, however, as I did so. Now I worked myself along the wall, placed my boat-hook as a climbing-pole against it, and found myself in a few seconds on top, after which I slid into the grass of the park, where a few hours previously I had been listening to the music. Unbroken silence reigned around me. Unutterable relief flooded me, for nobody, not even the sentry, had noticed anything.

With acute discomfort I contemplated my legs. They were covered with a thick, grey, malodorous mass, and there was no water in the vicinity to clean them. But it was impossible to put on boots or stockings whilst they were in that condition. With infinite trouble I succeeded in scraping off the dirt as far as possible, and waited for the rest to dry; then only was I able to resume a fairly decent appearance.

My first plan had miscarried, but in spite of this I felt I had had such luck with it that I was ready to undertake a second venture.

I now made my way to the little bridge, which was guarded by my sentry, and, impersonating a drunken sailor, I reeled about until I gently collided with the good fellow. He, however, seemed quite used to such happenings, for remarking pleasantly, 'Hallo, old Jack! One whisky too much!' he patted me on the shoulder and let me pass.

A hundred yards farther on, and I had regained my normal demeanour. After a short search I found the place from which I had started the night before on my ill-starred swimming attempt.

It was about 2 am, and in a trice I had undressed and sprang, agile and unhampered – as God had made me – into the water. For the first time the sky was covered with clouds, and the outlines of rowing-boats, anchored at a distance of about 200 yards from the shore, appeared vague and shadowy. The water was quite unusually phosphorescent, I have only observed it to that degree in the tropics. I swam, therefore, in a sea of gold and silver. At any other time I would have admired this play of Nature immensely, but now I only felt fear that my body would flash suspiciously white in this clear golden light. At the start, all went well. But as soon as I had passed the left bend of the river, where the shore afforded some protection, I was seized by the current, and had to fight for my life with the watery elements. As I was losing my strength I reached the first boat, made a final effort and hoisted myself noisily into it. Oh, persecution of a pitiless fate! The boat was empty – no scull, no boathook with which I could have put it in motion. After a short pause I again slipped into the water and drifted on to the next boat. And this, too, was empty! And the same happened with the three next. And when I reached the last one, after I had rested a little, I again dipped into the glittering but now unpleasantly cold water. Two hours after I had started on my adventure, I again reached the place where I had left my clothes.

As I was trembling like an aspen leaf with cold and exposure, I found it particularly hard to get into my sodden and sticky togs.

Half an hour later I was back in my sleeping-place amid the hay, beginning to feel serious doubts in the existence of my lucky star!

Could I be blamed if my spirits fell a little, and if I became quite indifferent to my interests? I confess I was so discouraged that the next morning I did not find sufficient energy to leave my hiding-place in time, and only escaped over my fence after the proprietor of the timber-pile had passed close in front of my retreat several times.

But that night, after I had passed the first fishermen's huts of Gravesend, I found a small scull. I took it with me. In mid-stream, just near the landing-place of the fishing-vessels, a little dinghy bobbed on the water. Not more than twenty feet away sat their owners on a bench, so absorbed in tender flirtation with their fair ones that the good sea-folk took no heed of my appearance on the scene.

It was risky, but 'Nothing venture, nothing have,' I muttered to myself. And, thanks to my acquired proficiency, I crept soundlessly into the boat – one sharp cut, and the tiny nutshell softly glided alongside a fishing-boat, on whose quarter-deck a woman was lulling her baby to sleep.

As there were no rowlocks in the boat, I sat aft, and pushed off with all my strength from the shore. I had, however, hardly covered one-third of the distance, when the ebbtide caught me in its whirl, spun my boat around like a top and paralysed all my efforts at steering. The time had come to show my sailor's efficiency. With an iron grip I recovered control of the boat, and, floating with the tide, I steered a downstream course. A dangerous moment was at hand. An imposing military pontoon-bridge, stretching across the river, and guarded by soldiers, came across my way. Summoning cool resolution and sharp attention to my aid, looking straight ahead and only intent on my scull, I disregarded the sentry's challenge and shot through between the two pontoons. A few seconds after the boat sustained a heavy shock, and I floundered on to the anchor-cable of a mighty coal-tender. With lightning speed I flung my painter round it, and this just in time, for the boat nearly capsized. But I was safe. The water whirled madly past it, as the ebbtide, reinforced by the drop of the river, must have fully set in. I had now only to wait patiently.

My steamer lay to starboard. I wanted to bide my time until the flow of the tide made it possible for me to get across.

I was already bubbling over with cocksureness when the necessary damper was administered. Dawn was breaking, the outlines of the anchored ships became clearer and clearer. At last the sun rose, and still the water ran out so strongly that it was impossible even to contemplate getting away. Anyhow, it was impossible to carry out my flight just then. But at last, happy in the possession of the long-desired boat, I slid downstream and, after an hour, pulled up at a crumbling old bridge on the right bank of the Thames. I pushed my boat under it, took both sculls with me as a precautionary measure, and hid them in the long grass. Then I lay down close to them, and at eight o'clock I saw my steamer, the *Mecklenburg*, vanishing proudly before my eyes. My patience had still to undergo a severe test. I remained lying in the grass for the next sixteen hours, until, at eight o'clock that night, the hour of my deliverance struck.

I again entered my boat. Cautiously I allowed myself to be driven upstream by the incoming tide, and fastened my boat to the same coal-tender near which I had been stranded the night before. Athwart to me lay the *Princess Juliana* moored to her buoy.

As I had time to spare, I lay down at the bottom of my boat and tried to take forty winks, but in vain. The tide rose, and I was once more surrounded by the rushing water.

At midnight all was still around me, and when at one o'clock the boat was quietly bobbing on the flow, I cast off, sat up in my boat, and rowed, with as much self-possession as if I had been one of a Sunday party in Kiel Harbour, to the steamer.

Unnoticed, I reached the buoy. The black hull of my steamer towered high above me. A strong pull – and I was atop the buoy. I now bade farewell to my faithful swan with a sound kick, which set it off downstream with the start of the ebb. During the next few minutes I lay as silent as a mouse. Then I climbed with iron composure – and this time like a cat – the mighty steel cable to the hawse. Cautiously I leaned my head over the rail and spied about. The forecastle was empty.

I jerked myself upwards and stood on the deck.

I now crept along the deck to the capstan and hid in the oil save-all beneath the windlass.

As all remained quiet, and not a soul hove in sight, I climbed out of my nook, took off my boots, and stowed them away under a stack of timber in a corner of the fore-deck. I now proceeded to investigate in my stockinged feet. When I looked down from a corner astern the fore-deck to the cargo-deck I staggered back suddenly. Breathlessly, but without turning a hair, I remained leaning against the ventilator. Below, on the cargo-deck, stood two sentries, who were staring fixedly upwards.

After I had remained for over half an hour in this cramped position, and my knees were beginning to knock under, there tripped two stewardesses from the middle-deck. They were apparently coming off night duty. My two sentries immediately seized the golden moment, and became so absorbed in their conversation that they no longer paid any attention to what was going on around them.

The dawn was breaking, and I had to act at once if I was not to lose all I had achieved at such a price.

I let myself down along the counter on the side of the fore-deck opposite to the two loving couples, and landed on the cargo-deck. Without pausing for a moment I stepped out gently, glided past the two sentries, reached the promenade-deck safely, and, climbing up a deck-pillar, found myself shortly afterwards on the out-board side of a lifeboat.

Holding on with one hand with a grip of iron, for the Thames was lapping hungrily not 12 yards away, with my other, aided by my teeth, I tore open a few of the tapes of the boat-cover, and with a last output of strength I crept through this small gap and crouched, well hidden from curious eyes, into the interior of the boat.

And then, naturally, I came to the end of my endurance. The prodigious physical exertions, acute excitement, and last, but not least, my ravenous hunger, stretched me flat on the boards of the boat, and in the same moment I no longer knew what was going on around me.

★   ★   ★   ★

Shrill blasts from the siren woke me from a sleep which in its dreamlessness resembled death.

I prudently loosened the tapes of my boat-cover, and with difficulty suppressed a 'Hurrah!' for the steamer was running into the harbour of Flushing.

Nothing mattered any longer. I pulled out my knife, and at one blow ripped open the boat-cover from end to end; but this time on the deck side.

With a deep breath, I stood in the middle of the boat-deck, and expected to be made a prisoner at any moment.

But no one bothered about me. The crew was occupied with landing manoeuvres; the travellers with their luggage.

I now descended to the promenade-deck, where several passengers eyed me with indignation on account of my unkempt appearance and my torn blue stockings, which looked, I must say, anything but dainty.

But my eyes must have been so radiantly happy, and such joy depicted on my dirty, emaciated features that many a woman glanced at me with surprise.

I could no longer go about like this. I therefore repaired to the fore-deck, fetched my boots (my best hockey boots, kindly gifts from the English), and, though a Dutch sailor blew me up gruffly, I calmly put on my beloved boots, and wandered off to the gangway.

The steamer had made fast directly to the pier.

The passengers left the ship, bidding farewell to the Captain and the ship's officers. At first I had intended to make myself known to the Captain, in order to avoid any trouble to the Dutch Steamship Company. But more prudent counsels prevailed, and with my hands in my pocket, looking as unobtrusive as I could, I slunk down the gangway.

Nobody paid any attention to me, so I pretended to belong to the ship's crew, and even helped to fasten the hawsers. Then I mixed with the crowd, and whilst the passengers were being subjected to a strict control I looked round, and near the railings discovered a door, on which stood in large letters 'Exit Forbidden.'

There, surely, lay the way to Freedom! In the twinkling of an eye I negotiated this childishly easy obstacle, and stood without.

I was free!

I had to make the greatest effort of my life to keep myself from jumping about like a madman.

A STORY OF SURVIVAL

Mark Twain

The Clipper ship Hornet *carrying locomotives and general cargo sailed out of New York harbour on 15 January 1866.*

Three-and-a-half months later her Captain (Captain Mitchell) and crew were caught up in one of the most remarkable stories of survival ever recorded.

At seven o'clock on the morning of the 3 May, the chief mate and two men started down into the hold to draw some 'bright varnish' from a cask. The captain told him to bring the cask on deck – that it was dangerous to have it where it was, in the hold. The mate, instead of obeying the order, proceeded to draw a can full of the varnish first. He had an 'open light' in his hand, and the liquid took fire; the can was dropped, the officer in his consternation neglected to close the bung, and in a few seconds the fiery torrent had run in every direction, under bales of rope, cases of candles, barrels of kerosene, and all sorts of freight, and tongues of flame were shooting upwards through every aperture and crevice toward the deck.

The ship was moving along under easy sail, the watch on duty were idling here and there in such shade as they could find, and the listlessness and repose of morning in the tropics was upon the vessel and her belongings. But as six bells chimed, the cry of 'Fire!' rang through the ship, and woke every man to life and action. And following the fearful warning, and almost as fleetly, came the fire itself. It sprang through hatchways, seized upon chairs, table, cordage, anything, everything – and almost before the bewildered men could realize what the trouble was and what was to be done the cabin was a hell of angry flames. The mainmast was on fire – its rigging was burnt asunder! One man said all this had happened within eighteen or twenty minutes after the first alarm – two others say in ten minutes. All say that one hour after the alarm, the main and mizzenmasts were burned in two and fell overboard.

Captain Mitchell ordered the three boats to be launched instantly, which was done – and so hurriedly that the longboat (the one he left the vessel in himself) had a hole as large as a man's head stove in her bottom. A blanket was stuffed into the opening and fastened to its place. Not a single thing was saved, except such food and other articles as lay about the cabin and could be quickly seized and thrown on deck. Thomas* was sent into the longboat to receive its proportion of these things, and, being barefooted at the time, and bareheaded, and having no clothing on save an undershirt and pantaloons, of course he never got a chance afterward to add to his dress. He lost everything he had, including his logbook, which he had faithfully kept from the first. Forty minutes after the fire alarm, the provisions and passengers were on board the three boats, and they rowed away from the ship – and to some distance, too, for the heat was very great. Twenty minutes afterward the two masts I have mentioned, with their rigging and their broad sheets of canvas wreathed in flames, crashed into the sea.

All night long the thirty-one unfortunates sat in their frail boats and watched the gallant ship burn; and felt as men feel when they see a tried friend perishing and are powerless to help him. The sea was illuminated for miles around, and the clouds above were tinged with a ruddy hue; the faces of the men glowed in the strong light as they shaded their eyes with their hands and peered out anxiously upon the wild picture, and the gunwales of the boats and the idle oars shone like polished gold.

At five o'clock on the morning after the disaster, in latitude 2 degrees 20 minutes north, longitude 112 degrees 8 minutes west, the ship went down, and the crew of the *Hornet* were alone on the great deep, or, as one of the seamen expressed it, 'We felt as if somebody or something had gone away – as if we hadn't any home any more.'

Captain Mitchell divided his boat's crew into two watches and gave the third mate charge of one and took the other himself. He had saved a studding sail from the ship, and out of this the men fashioned a rude sail

* John S. Thomas, 3rd mate.

with their knives; they hoisted it, and taking the first and second mates' boats in tow, they bore away upon the ship's course (northwest) and kept in the track of vessels bound to or from San Francisco, in the hope of being picked up.

In the few minutes' time allowed him, Captain Mitchell was only able to seize upon the few articles of food and other necessaries that happened to lie about the cabin. Here is the list: Four hams, seven pieces of salt pork (each piece weighed about four pounds), one box of raisins, one hundred pounds of bread (about one barrel), twelve two-pound cans of oysters, clams, and assorted meats; six buckets of raw potatoes (which rotted so fast they got but little benefit from them), a keg with four pounds of butter in it, twelve gallons of water in a forty-gallon tierce or 'scuttle butt,' four one-gallon demi-johns full of water, three bottles of brandy, the property of passengers; some pipes, matches, and a hundred pounds of tobacco; had no medicines. That was all these poor fellows had to live on for forty-three days – the whole thirty-one of them!

Each boat had a compass, a quadrant, a copy of Bowditch's *Navigator* and a nautical almanac, and the captain's and chief mate's boat had chronometers.

Of course, all hands were put on short allowance at once. The day they set sail from the ship each man was allowed a small morsel of salt pork – or a little piece of potato, if he preferred it – and half a sea biscuit three times a day. To understand how very light this ration of bread was, it is only necessary to know that it takes seven of these sea biscuits to weigh a pound. The first two days they only allowed one gill of water a day to each man; but for nearly a fortnight after that the weather was lowering and stormy, and frequent rail squalls occurred. The rain was caught in canvas, and whenever there was a shower the forty-gallon cask and every other vessel that would hold water was filled – even all the boots that were watertight were pressed into this service, except such as the matches and tobacco were deposited in to keep dry. So for fourteen days. There were luxurious occasions when there was plenty of water to drink. But after that how they suffered the agonies of thirst!

For seven days the boats sailed on, and the starving men ate their fragment of biscuit and their morsel of raw pork in the morning, and hungrily counted the tedious hours until noon and night should bring their repetitions of it. And in the long intervals they looked mutely into each other's faces, or turned their wistful eyes across the wild sea in search of the succoring sail that was never to come.

And thought, I suppose. Thought of home – of shelter from storms – of food and drink and rest.

The hope of being picked up hung to them constantly – was ever present to them, and in their thoughts, like hunger. And in the captain's mind was the hope of making the Clarion Islands, and he clung to it many a day.

The nights were very dark. They had no lantern and could not see the compass, and there were no stars to steer by. Thomas said, of the boat, 'She handled easy, and we steered by the feel of the wind in our faces and the heave of the sea.' Dark and dismal and lonesome work was that! Sometimes they got a fleeting glimpse of the sailor's friend, the North Star, and then they lighted a match and hastened anxiously to see if their compass was faithful to them – for it had to be placed close to an iron ringbolt in the stern, and they were afraid, during those first nights, that this might cause it to vary. It proved true to them, however.

On the fifth day a notable incident occurred. They caught a dolphin! And while their enthusiasm was still at its highest over this stroke of good fortune, they captured another. They made a trifling fire in a tin plate and warmed the prizes – to cook them was not possible – and divided them equitably among all hands and ate them.

On the sixth day two more dolphins were caught.

Two more were caught on the seventh day, and also a small bonita, and they began to believe they were always going to live in this extravagant way; but it was not to be; these were their last dolphins, and they never could get another bonita, though they saw them and longed for them often afterward.

On the eighth day the rations were reduced about one half. Thus – breakfast, one fourth of a biscuit, an ounce of ham, and a gill of water to each man; dinner, same quantity of bread and water, and four oysters or clams; supper, water and bread the same, and twelve large raisins or fourteen small ones, to a man. Also, during the first twelve or fifteen days, each man had one spoonful of brandy a day, then it gave out.

This day, as one of the men was gazing across the dull waste of waters as usual, he saw a small, dark object rising and falling upon the waves. He called attention to it, and in a moment every eye was bent upon it in intensest interest. When the boat had approached a little nearer, it was discovered that it was a small green turtle, fast asleep. Every noise was hushed as they crept upon the unconscious slumberer. Directions were given and hopes and fears expressed in guarded whispers. At the fateful moment – a moment of tremendous conse-quence to these famishing men – the expert selected for the high and responsible office stretched forth his hand, while his excited comrades bated their breath and trembled for the success of the enterprise, and seized the turtle by the hind leg and handed him aboard! His delicate flesh was carefully divided among the party and eagerly devoured – after being 'warmed' like the dolphins which went before him.

The eighteenth day was a memorable one to the wanderers on the lonely sea. On that day the boats parted company. The captain said that separate from each other there were three chances for the saving of some of the party where there could be but one chance if they kept together.

The magnanimity and utter unselfishness of Captain Mitchell (and through his example, the same conduct in his men) throughout this distressing voyage, are among its most amazing features. No disposition was ever shown by the strong to impose upon the weak, and no greediness, no desire on the part of any to get more than his just share of food, was ever evinced. On the contrary, they were thoughtful of each other and always ready to care for and assist each other to the utmost of their ability. When the time came to part company, Captain Mitchell and his crew, although theirs was much the more numerous party (fifteen men to nine and seven respectively in the other boats), took only one third of the meagre amount of provisions still left, and passed over the other two thirds to be divided up between the other crews; these men could starve, if need be, but they seem not to have known how to be mean.

After the division the captain had left for his boat's share two thirds of the ham, one fourth of a box of raisins, half a bucket of buscuit crumbs, fourteen gallons of water three cans of 'soup-and-bully' beef.

The captain told the mates he was still going to try to make the Clarion Isles, and that they could imitate his example if they thought best, but he wished them to freely follow the dictates of their own judgment in the matter. At eleven o'clock in the forenoon the boats were all cast loose from each other, and then, as friends part from friends whom they expect to meet no more in life, all hands hailed with a fervent 'God bless you, boys; good-bye!' and the two cherished sails drifted away and disappeared from the longing gaze that followed them so sorrowfully.

On the afternoon of this eventful eighteenth day two 'boobies' were caught – a bird about as large as a duck, but all bone and feathers – not as much meat as there is on a pigeon – not nearly so much, the men say. They ate them raw – bones, entrails, and everything – no single morsel was wasted; they were carefully apportioned among the fifteen men. No fire could be built for cooking purposes – the wind was so strong and the sea ran so high that it was all a man could do to light his pipe.

At eventide the wanderers missed a cheerful spirit – a plucky, strong-hearted fellow, who never drooped his head or lost his grip – a staunch and true good friend, who was always at his post in storm or calm, in rain or shine – who scorned to say die, and yet was never afraid to die – a little trim and taut old rooster, he was, who starved with the rest, but came on watch in the stern sheets promptly every day at four in the morning and six in the evening for eighteen days and crowed like a maniac! Right well they named him Richard of the Lion Heart! One of the men said with honest feeling: 'As true as I'm a man, if that rooster was here today and any man dared to abuse the bird, I'd break his neck!' Richard was esteemed by all and by all his rights were respected. He received his little ration of bread crumbs every time the men were fed, and, like them, he bore up bravely and never grumbled and never gave way to despair. As long as he was strong enough, he stood in the stern sheets or mounted the gunwale as regularly as his watch came round, and crowed his two-hour talk, and when at last he grew feeble in the legs and had to stay below, his heart was still stout and he slapped about in the water on the bottom of the boat and crowed as bravely as ever! He felt that under circumstances like these America expects every rooster to do his duty, and he did it. But is it not to the high honor of that boat's crew of starving men that, tortured day and night by the pangs of hunger as they were, they refused to appease them with the blood of their humble comrade? Richard was transferred to the chief

The birds were large, but almost without meat.

mate's boat and sailed away on the eighteenth day.

The third mate does not remember distinctly, but thinks morning and evening prayers were begun on the nineteenth day. They were conducted by one of the young Fergusons, because the captain could not read the prayer book without his spectacles, and they had been burned with the ship. And ever after this date, at the rising and the setting of the sun, the storm-tossed mariners reverently bowed their heads while prayers went up for 'they that are helpless and far at sea.'

On the morning of the twenty-first day, while some of the crew were dozing on the thwarts and others were buried in reflection, one of the men suddenly sprang to his feet and cried, 'A sail! a sail!' Of course, sluggish blood bounded then and eager eyes were turned to seek the welcome vision. But disappointment was their portion, as usual. It was only the chief mate's boat drifting across their path after three days' absence. In a short time the two parties were abreast each other and in hailing distance. They talked twenty minutes; the mate reported 'all well' and then sailed away, and they never saw him afterward.

On the twenty-fourth day Captain Mitchell took an observation and found that he was in latitude 16 degrees north and longitude 117 degrees west – about a thousand miles from where his vessel was burned. The hope he had cherished so long that he would be able to make the clarion Isles deserted him at last; he could only go before the wind, and he was now obliged to attempt the best thing the southeast trades could do for him – blow him to the 'American group' or to the Sandwich Islands – and therefore he reluctantly and with many misgivings turned his prow towards those distant archipalagoes. Not many mouthfuls of food were left, and these must be economized. The third mate said that under this new program of proceedings 'we could see that we were living too high; we had got to let up on them raisins, or the soup-and-bullies, one, because it stood to reason that we warn't going to make land soon, and so they wouldn't last.' It was a matter which had few humorous features about it to them, and yet a smile is almost pardonable at this idea, so gravely expressed, of 'living high' on fourteen raisins at a meal.

The rations remained the same as fixed on the eighth day, except that only two meals a day were allowed, and occasionally the raisins and oysters were left out.

What these men suffered during the next three weeks no mortal man may hope to describe. Their stomachs and intestines felt to the grasp like a couple of small tough balls, and the gnawing hunger pains and the dreadful thirst that was consuming them in those burning latitudes became almost insupportable. And yet, as the men say, the captain said funny things and talked cheerful talk until he got them to conversing freely, and then they used to spend hours together describing delicious dinners they had eaten at home, and earnestly planning interminable and preposterous bills of fare for dinners they were going to eat on shore, if they ever lived through their troubles to do it, poor fellows. The captain said plain bread and butter would be good enough for him all the days of his life, if he could only get it.

But the saddest things were the dreams they had. An unusually intelligent young sailor named Cox said: 'In those long days and nights we dreamed all the time – not that we ever slept. I don't mean – no, we only sort of dozed – three fourths of the faculties awake and the other fourth benumbed into the counterfeit of a slumber; oh, no – some of us never slept for twenty-three days, and no man ever saw the captain asleep for upward of thirty. But we barely dozed that way and dreamed – and always of such feasts! bread, and fowls, and meat – everything a man could think of, piled upon long tables, and smoking hot! And we sat down and seized upon the first dish in our reach, like ravenous wolves, and carried it to our lips, and – and then we woke up and found the same starving comrades about us, and the vacant sky and the desolate sea!'

These things are terrible even to think of.

On the twenty-eighth day the rations were: One teaspoonful of bread crumbs and about an ounce of ham for the morning meal; a spoonful of bread crumbs alone for the evening meal, and one gill of water three times a day! A kitten would perish eventually under such sustenance.

At this point the third mate's mind reverted painfully to an incident of the early stages of their sufferings. He said there were two between-decks, on board the *Hornet*, who had been lying there sick and helpless for he didn't know how long; but when the ship took fire, they turned out as lively as anyone under the spur of the excitement. One was a 'Portyghee,' he said, and always of a hungry disposition; when all the provisions that could be got had been brought aft and deposited near the wheel to be lowered into the boats, 'that sick Portyghee watched his chance, and when nobody was looking, he harnessed the provisions and ate up nearly a quarter of a bar'l of bread before the old man caught him, and he had more than two notions to put his lights out.' The third mate dwelt upon this circumstance as upon a wrong he could not fully forgive, and intimated that the Portyghee stole bread enough, if economized in twenty-eighth-day rations, to have run the longboat party three months.

Four little flying fish, the size of the sardines of these latter days, flew into the boat on the night of the twenty-eighth day. They were divided among all hands and devoured raw. On the twenty-ninth day they caught another, and divided it into fifteen pieces, less than a teaspoonful apiece.

On the thirtieth day they caught a third flying fish and gave it to the revered old captain – a fish of the same poor little proportions as the others – four inches long – a present a king might be proud of under such circumstances – a present whose value, in the eyes of the men who offered it, was not to be found in the Bank of England – yea, whose vaults were not able to contain it! The old captain refused to take it; the men insisted; the captain said no – he would take his fifteenth – they must take the remainder. They said in substance, though not in words, that they would see him in Jericho first! So the captain had to eat the fish.

The third mate always betrayed emotion when he spoke of 'the old man.' The men were the same way; the captain is their hero – their true and faithful friend, whom they delight to honor. After the ordeal was over I said to one of these infatuated skeletons, 'But you wouldn't go quite so far as to die for him?' A snap of the finger – 'As quick as that! – I wouldn't be alive now if it hadn't been for him.'

About the thirty-second day the bread gave entirely out. There was nothing left, now, but mere odds and ends of their stock of provisions. Five days afterwards, on the thirty-seventh day – latitude 16 degrees 30 minutes north, and longitude 170 degrees west – kept off for the 'American group' – 'which don't exist and never will, I suppose,' said the third mate. They ran directly over the ground said to be occupied by these islands – that is, between latitude 16 degrees and 17 degrees north, and longitude 133 degrees to 136 degrees west. Ran over the imaginary islands and got into 136 degrees west, and then the captain made a dash for Hawaii, resolving that he would go till he fetched land, or at any rate as long as he and his men survived.

On Monday, the thirty-eighth day after the disaster, 'We had nothing left,' said the third mate, 'but a pound and a half of ham – the bone was a good deal the heaviest part of it – and one soup-and-bully tin.' These things were divided among the fifteen men, and they ate it all – two ounces of food to each man. I do not count the ham bone, as that was saved for the next day. For some time now the poor wretches had been cutting their old boots into small pieces and eating them. They would also pound wet rags to a sort of pulp and eat them.

After apportioning the hame bone, the captain cut the canvas cover that had been around the ham into fifteen equal pieces, and each man took his portion. This was the last division of food that the captain made. The men broke up the small oaken butter tub and divided the staves among themselves, and gnawed them up. The shell of the little green turtle, heretofore mentioned, was scraped with knives and eaten to the last shaving. The third mate chewed pieces of boots and spat them out, but ate nothing except the soft straps of two pairs of boots – ate three on the thirty-ninth day and saved one for the fortieth.

The men seem to have thought in their own minds of the shipwrecked mariner's last dreadful resort – cannibalism; but they do not appear to have conversed about it. They only thought of the casting lots and killing one of their number as a possibility; but even when they were eating rags and bone and boots and shell and hard oak wood, they seem to have still had a notion that it was remote.

Thomas and also several of the men state that the sick 'Portyghee,' during the five days that they were entirely out of provisions, actually ate two silk handkerchiefs and a couple of cotton shirts, besides his share of the boots and bones and lumber.

Captain Mitchell was fifty-six years old on the 12 June – the fortieth day after the burning of the ship. He said it looked somewhat as if it might be the last one he was going to enjoy. He had no birthday feast except some bits of ham canvas – no luxury but this, and no substantials save the leather and oaken bucket staves.

Speaking of the leather diet, one of the men told me he was obliged to eat a pair of boots which were so old and rotten that they were full of holes; and then he smiled gently and said he didn't know, though, but what the holes tasted about as good as the balance of the boot.

★   ★   ★   ★

At eleven o'clock on 15 June, after suffering all that men may suffer and live for forty-three days, in an open boat, on a scorching tropical sea, one of the men feebly shouted the glad tidings, 'Land ho!' The 'watch below' were lying in the bottom of the boat. What do you suppose they did? They said they had been cruelly disappointed over and over again, and they dreaded to risk another experience of the kind – they could not bear it – they lay still where they were. They said they would not trust to an appearance that might not be land after all. They would wait.

Shortly it was proven beyond question that they were almost to land. Then there was joy in the party. One man is said to have swooned away. Another said the sight of the green hills was better to him than a day's rations, a strange figure for a man to use who had been fasting for forty days and forty nights.

The land was the island of Hawaii, and they were off Laupahoehoe and could see nothing inshore but breakers. Laupahoehoe is a dangerous place to try to land. When they got pretty close to shore, they saw cabins, but no human beings. They thought they would lower the sail and try to work in with the oars. They cut the ropes and the sail came down, and then they found they were not strong enough to ship the oars. They drifted helplessly toward the breakers, but looked listlessly on and cared not a straw for the violent death which seemed about to overtake them after all their manful struggles, their privations, and their terrible sufferings. They said, 'It was good to see the green fields again.' It was all they cared for. The 'green fields' were a haven of rest for the weary wayfarers; it was sufficient; they were satisfied; it was nothing to them that death stood in their pathway; they had long been familiar to him; he had no terrors for them.

Two natives saw the boat, knew by the appearance of things that it was in trouble, and dashed through the surf and swam out to it. When they climbed aboard, there were only five yards of space between the poor sufferers and a sudden and violent death. Fifteen minutes afterward the boat was beached upon the shore, and a crowd of natives (who are the very incarnation of generosity, unselfishness, and hospitality) were around the strangers dumping bananas, melons, taro, poi – anything and everything they could scrape together that could be eaten – on the ground by the cartload; and if Mr Jones, of the station, had not hurried down with his steward, they would soon have killed the starving men with kindness. Jones and the Kanaka girls and men took the mariners in their arms like so many children and carried them up to the house, where they received kind and judicious attention until Sunday evening, when two whaleboats came from Hilo, Jones furnished a third, and they were taken in these to the town just named, arriving there at two o'clock Monday morning.

*　　*　　*　　*

Each of the young Fergusons kept a journal from the day the ship sailed from New York until they got on land once more at Hawaii. The captain also kept a log every day he was adrift. These logs, by the captain's direction, were to be kept up faithfully as long as any of the crew were alive, and the last survivor was to put them in a bottle, when he succumbed, and lash the bottle to the inside of the boat. The captain gave a bottle to each officer of the other boats, with orders to follow his example. The old gentleman was always thoughtful.

The hardest berth in that boat, I think, must have been that of provision keeper. This office was performed by the captain and the third mate; of course they were always hungry. They always had access to the food, and yet must not gratify their craving appetites.

The young Fergusons are very highly spoken of by all the boat's crew, as patient, enduring, manly, and kindhearted gentlemen. The captain gave them a watch to themselves – it was the duty of each to bail the water out of the boat three hours a day.

The chief mate, Samuel Hardy, lived at Chatham, Massachusetts; second mate belonged in Shields, England; the cook, George Washington (Negro), was in the chief mate's boat, and also the steward (Negro); the carpenter was in the second mate's boat.

To Captain Mitchell's good sense, cool judgment, perfect discipline, close attention to the smallest particulars which could conduce to the welfare of his crew or render their ultimate rescue more probable, that boat's crew owe their lives. He had shown brain and ability that make him worthy to command the finest frigate in the United States, and a genuine unassuming heroism that [should] entitle him to a Congressional Medal. I suppose some of the citizens of San Francisco who know how to appreciate this kind of a man will not let him go on hungry forever after he gets there.

ISLAND OF CRABS

Frank Bullen

There is a tiny islet on the outskirts of the Solomon Archipelago that to all such casual wanderers as stray so far presents not a single feature of interest. Like scores of others in those latitudes, it has not yet attained to the dignity of a single coconut tree, although many derelict nuts have found a lodgment upon it, and begun to grow, only to be wiped out of existence at the next spring-tide. Viewed from a balloon it would look like a silly-season mushroom, but with a fringe of snowy foam around it marking the protecting barrier to which it owes its existence, to say nothing of its growth. Yet of all places in the world which I have been privileged to visit, this barren little mound of sand clings most tenaciously to my memory, for reasons which will presently appear.

One of those devastating cyclones that at long intervals sweep across the Pacific, leaving a long swath of destruction in their wake, had overtaken the pearling schooner of which I was mate. For twenty-four hours we fled before it, we knew not whither, not daring to heave-to. The only compass we possessed had been destroyed by the first sea that broke on board. Whether it was night or day we had no notion, except by watch, and even then we were doubtful, so appalling was the darkness. Hope was beginning to revive that, as the *Papalangi* had proved herself so staunch, she might yet 'run it out,' unless she hit something.

But the tiny rag rigged forrard to keep her before it suddenly flew into threads; the curl of the sea caught her under the counter and spun her up into the wind like a teetoture. The next vast comber took her broadside-on, rolled her over, and swallowed her up. We went 'down quick into the pit.'

Although always reckoned a powerful swimmer, even among such amphibia as the Kanakas, I don't remember making a stroke. But after a horrible, choking struggle in the black uproar I got my breath again, finding myself clinging, as a drowning man will, to something big and seaworthy. It was an ordinary ship's hencoop that the skipper had bought cheap from a passenger vessel in Auckland. As good a raft as one could wish, it bore me on over the mad sea, half dead as I was, until I felt it rise high as if climbing a cataract and descend amidst a furious boiling of surf into calm, smooth water. A few minutes later I touched a sandy beach. Utterly done up, I slept where I lay, at the water's edge, though the shrieking hurricane raged overhead as if it would tear the land up by the roots.

When I awoke it was fine weather, though to leeward the infernal reek of the departing meteor still disfigured a huge segment of the sky. I looked around, and my jaw dropped. Often I had wondered what a poor devil *would* do who happened to be cast away on such a spot as this. Apparently I was about to learn. A painful pinch at my bare foot startled me, and I saw an ugly beast of a crab going for me. He was nearly a foot across, his blue back covered with long spikes, and his wicked little eyes seemed to have an expression of diabolical malignity. I snatched at a handful of his legs and swung him around my head, dashing him against the side of my coop with such vigour that his armour flew to flinders around me. I never have liked crab, even when dressed, but I found the raw flesh of that one tasty enough – it quite smartened me up. Having eaten heartily, I took a saunter up the smooth knoll of sand, aimlessly, I suppose, for it was as bare as a plate, without a stone or a shell. From its highest point, about ten feet above high-water mark, I looked around, but my horizon was completely bounded by the ring of breakers aforesaid. I felt like the scorpion within the fiery circle, and almost as disposed to sting myself to death had I possessed the proper weapon. As I stood gazing vacantly at the foaming barrier and solemn enclosing dome of fleckless blue, I was again surprised by a vicious nip at my foot. There was another huge crab boldly attacking me – me, a vigorous man, and not a sodden corpse, as yet. I felt a grue of horror run all down my back, but I grabbed at the vile thing and hurled it from me half across the island. Then I became aware of others arriving, converging upon me from all around, and I was panic-stricken. For one mad moment I thought of plunging into the sea again; but reason reasserted itself in time, reminding me that, while I had certain advantages on my side where I was, in the water I should fall a helpless victim at once, if, as might naturally be expected, these ghouls were swarming there. Not a weapon of any kind could I see, neither stick nor stone. My feelings of disgust deepened into despair. But I got little time for thought. Such a multitude of the eerie things were about me that I was kept most actively employed seizing them and flinging them from me. They got bolder, feinting and dodging around me, but happily without any definite plan of campaign among them. Once I staggered forward, having trodden unaware upon a spiky back as I sprung aside, wounding my foot badly. I fell into a group of at least twenty, crushing some of them, but after a painful struggle among those needle-like spines regained my feet with several clinging to my body. A kind of frenzy seized me, and, regardless of pain, I clutched at them right and left, dashing them to fragments one against the other, until quite a pile of writhing, dismembered enemies lay around me, while my hands and arms were streaming from numberless wounds. Very soon I became exhausted by my violent exertions and the intense heat, but, to my unfathomable thankfulness, the heap of broken crabs afforded me a long respite, the sound ones finding congenial occupation in devouring them. While I watched the busy cannibals swarming over the yet writhing heap, I became violently ill, for imagination vividly depicted them rioting in my viscera. Vertigo seized me, I reeled and fell prone, oblivious to all things for a time.

When sense returned it was night. The broad moon was commencing her triumphal march among the stars, which glowed in the blue-black concave like globules of incandescent steel. My body was drenched with dew, a blessed relief, for my tongue was leathery and my lips were split with drouth. I tore off my shirt and sucked it eagerly, the moisture it held, though brackish, mitigating my tortures of thirst. Suddenly I bethought me of my foes, and looked fearfully around. There was not

I dashed them to fragments, one against the other.

one to be seen, nothing near but the heap of clean-picked shells of those devoured. As the moon rose higher, I saw a cluster of white objects at a little distance, soon recognizable as boobies. They permitted me to snatch a couple of them easily, and wringing off their heads I got such a draught as put new life into me. Yet my position was almost as hopeless as one could imagine. Unless, as I much doubted, this was a known spot for *bêche de mer* or pearl-shell fishers, there was but the remotest chance of my rescue, while, without anything floatable but my poor little hencoop, passing that barrier of breakers was impossible. Fortunately I have always tried to avoid meeting trouble half-way, and with a thankful feeling of present wants supplied, I actually went to sleep again.

At daybreak I awoke again to a repetition of the agonies of the previous day. The numbers of my hideous assailants were more than doubled as far as I could judge. The whole patch of sand seemed alive with the voracious vermin. So much so that when I saw the approach of those horrible hosts my heart sank, my flesh shrank on my bones, and I clutched at my throat. But I could not strangle myself, though had I possessed a knife I should certainly have chosen a swift exit from the unutterable horror of my position, fiercely as I clung to life. To be devoured piecemeal, retaining every faculty till the last – I could not bear the thought. There was no time for reflection, however; the struggle began at once and continued with a pertinacity on the part of the crabs that promised a speedy end to it for me. How long it lasted I have no idea – to my tortured mind it was an eternity. At last, over-borne, exhausted, surrounded by mounds of those I had destroyed, over which fresh legions poured in ever-increasing numbers, earth and sky whirled around me, and I fell backward. As I went, with many of the vile things already clinging to me, I heard a yell – a human voice that revived my dulling senses like a galvanic shock. With one last flash of vigour I sprang to my feet, seeing as I did so a canoe with four Kanakas in it, not fifty yards away, in the smooth water between the beach and the barrier. Bounding like a buck, heedless of the pain as my wounded feet clashed among the innumerable spiky carapaces of my enemies, I reached the water, and hurled myself headlong towards that ark of safety. How I reached it I do not know, nor anything further until I returned to life again on board the *Warrigal* of Sydney, as weak as a babe and feeling a century older.

EARLY DAYS IN THE ROYAL FLYING CORPS

Captain James McCudden V.C.

About 6 May 1913, I was sent down to Jersey Brow to report to Sergeant-Major Starling for disposal. The Sergeant-Major interviewed me, and having ascertained that I possessed a fair knowledge of engines, he sent me over to Sergeant Brockbank, who was in charge of the aeroplanes of the Flying Depôt, to take charge of an engine in an aeroplane, having never seen one in my life before. However, I took charge of a 70 hp Renault, which was the motive-power of one Maurice Farman No. 223, the pilot of which was Captain Dawes.*

The sergeant now informed me that it was my job to swing the propeller, which in the case of the 'Maurice' was a most formidable-looking guillotine. I was told to practice swinging propellers on a most inoffensive little aeroplane which was standing in the corner of the same shed. This was a Caudron, equipped with a 45 hp Anzani motor, which had not been run for months. I diligently swung this propeller all the morning and achieved quite a lot of success in my efforts.

After the morning's work we went back to barracks for dinner. Meanwhile someone had been having quite an interesting time examining the engine of the Caudron, and wondering what the difference was between the tap on the right and the lever on the left, etc.

* In 1918, Col G. W. P. Dawes, DSO, Commanding Royal Air Force in the Balkans.

284

We arrived back at the sheds and went on with the afternoon's work, which consisted of rubbing rust off the multitudinous wires of the Maurice Farman. About 4.30, having nothing more to do, and desiring something to happen, I strolled over to the Caudron, which was facing the open door of the shed, with a view to some more practice in propeller swinging.

Maurice Farman No 223 was in the entrance of the same shed, completely blocking the exit. I have been told hundreds of times since that I should have examined the Caudron's switch before touching its propeller. However, as I had been turning the same propeller all the morning, I did not consider it necessary, so I took a firm hold on the propeller and gave it a hefty swing. With a terrific roar the engine started, all out, as the switch was on and the throttle full open. I had sufficient commonsense to drop flat until the lower wing had passed over me.

Now, this Caudron badly wanted to fly, even without a pilot, but the 'Maurice' standing in the doorway decided not to let it. The Caudron was very annoyed at this and determined to make a fight for it. With a heart-rending scrunch the Caudron charged the Maurice full tilt, the left wing of the Caudron binding against the lower right-hand tail boom of the Maurice, and the Caudron's right wing taking a firm hold on the Maurice's right-hand interplane struts.

Meanwhile the Caudron's propeller was doing its 1,400 revs to some purpose. As it had completely eaten up two tail booms and nearly one wing, I thought it time to curtail the Caudron's blood-thirsty career. I managed to switch off, and the engine stopped. Whilst all this was happening the surrounding atmosphere was full of blue castor oil smoke, and crowds of mechanics were rushing from all directions, armed with fire extinguishers, ladders, etc. Indeed I did hear that the local Fire Brigade turned out, complete with brass hats and other regalia.

A dead calm reigned as Major Raleigh entered the shed and proceeded to question me. I told him all that had happened, which merely elicited the order: 'Sergeant Major! Fall in two men!' and off I went to the guard-room by the shortest route.

On my way someone remarked consolingly that he didn't suppose I would get more than five years.

I was put in the guard-room opposite the officers' mess at Blenheim

Barracks. Nearly every evening in these days the Guards' Band (the Grenadiers, I think) played outside the mess, and I shall never forget my feelings in that guard-room, while outside the band played the most popular selections from the various shows. I particularly remember their playing the 'Mysterious Rag' and 'Oh! You Beautiful Doll!' these two rags at that time being at their height of popularity. Funny how these details stick in one's memory. But it wasn't an encouraging beginning for a newcomer to the RFC, was it?

I remained in this guard-room for five days, and was released under open arrest pending trial. As it was the afternoon, and a nice day, I went down to the aerodrome to work. About 5 pm I saw Lieutenant B. T. James, RE, going up alone on a silver-doped BE 2a, fitted with the first wireless experimental set. Five days in a guard-room had not allayed my desire to fly in the slightest, so I asked Mr James if he would take me up.*

With his usual good nature he said he would, and so I had my first flight, about the first week in May, 1913. I enjoyed this experience immensely, but on landing I concluded that flying was not so easy as was generally imagined. Of course I was very proud at having flown, as very few mechanics had had the privilege in those days.

However, after landing, I was sent for by the Colonel, who awarded me seven days' detention and docked me of fourteen days' pay. I leave my readers to decide whether the 'crime' fitted the punishment or not, but, of course, the evidence wasn't very conclusive either way, so off I went to the Detention Barracks at Aldershot, commonly known as the 'Glass-house,' for a week.

One doesn't waste very many minutes whilst in a detention barracks, and at the expiration of my term I rejoined the Flying Depôt a much wiser man – or boy.

*   ★   ★   ★

On 9 April I went to Gosport and on 16 April I qualified for my Royal Aero Club Certificate on a 'Longhorn' Maurice Farman, and some-

---

* Mr B. T. James was an officer of Royal Engineers, and was the pioneer of wireless telegraphy in the RFC. He had brought the science of 'wireless' in aeroplanes to a high state of efficiency before he was killed in France, after having done much gallant and distinguished services.

times sarcastically termed a 'Longhorn bullet,' but more commonly a 'mechanical cow.'

On 1 May I was posted to the Central Flying School for training as a 'scout' pilot on real scout machines which did 100 miles an hour or more. How important that sounded to me then.

I had my first 'spin' during a flight on a DH1 over the Plain with a passenger. I was at 4,000 feet, and had started a left-hand spiral when the machine suddenly began to behave funnily and felt no more like a flying machine than a red brick. I knew we were going round and round one way, but did not know why, for even then I did not know what a spin was. However, I jambed the rudder over in the opposite direction, and the machine came out with a hefty jerk and very nearly spun the other way round.

This little episode, strange to say, did not frighten me in the least, for I did not know what was really happening.

During my two months at the Central Flying School I did a good deal of instructing, and when I left for France I had put in well over one hundred hours flying, because on some days at the school we did five and six hours daily.

On 10 July 1916, I made my first war flight as a pilot. My observer was a Lieutenant Lascelles, and we patrolled from Ypres to the Bois de Biez for three hours, in order to stop hostile machines from crossing our lines. However, we did not see any, so at 8.30 we flew back to Clairmarais, which was then a long way west of the lines.

On the next day I again patrolled the same area with Lieutenant Lascelles, and again we did not see any German machines.

On the 18th five of us did a reconnaissance to Dixmude, Thielt, and Roulers, and although we saw one or two Fokkers getting height, they did not attack us.

The next evening we again did a reconnaissance to Menin, Roubaix, Tourcoing, and Lille, at 12,000 feet, but apart from severe shelling by 'Archie,' we had the whole of the sky to ourselves.

At this period the majority of the enemy 'jägdstäffeln' or chaser squadrons were on the Somme, and the only enemy pursuit machine that we ever saw was a solitary Fokker who would climb above the formation, make one dive on our rear machine, and if he did not get his target, he usually dived away as fast as he could.

On 20 July, five machines left the aerodrome at 5.30 am to do an offensive patrol. We were to rendezvous over our aerodrome at 10,000 feet; Captain Maxwell was leading.

Whilst climbing I noticed a low mist blowing down from the north-west, and by the time we had manoeuvred into our correct position in the formation, we could not see the ground. We flew east for about twenty minutes, and then turned east-southeast. As far as I could judge at this time we should have been somewhere over Lille, but as my Observer and I could not see the ground, it was difficult to say.

We flew east-southeast for about thirty minutes and then turned west. We could now occasionally see the ground, and I could see by the villages that we were over unfamiliar country. We flew west for some time and then through a gap in the mist I saw what I mistook to be the town of Bailleul; so, as the formation had now dissolved, I decided to get under the mist and follow a main road to Clairmaris.

When I got down to 2,000 feet I saw that the mist was decidedly low, and I continued to go down and ran into it at 600 feet. I still went down in an endeavour to get underneath the mist, and then just in front of and above me loomed up a large row of trees, such as always border the *Routes Nationales* of France. I at once switched on, zoomed over the trees, and trusted to my lucky star that the country was fairly clear in front. Fortunately it was, and I made some pretence of landing, finally running through a small fence, and then stopping in the back-garden of a small French farm house, just in time to bid 'Bonjour, M'sieur!' to the agitated farmers, who came running out. The machine had sustained no damage whatever in this forced landing, and so all we could do was to wait until the mist cleared.

We walked to a neighbouring village, and had a very welcome breakfast with the local Major, who told us that we were a few kilometres from St Pol; so we were about forty miles south of our area. Whilst we were at our breakfast we heard one of our machines still flying around in the mist, which was very thick indeed, trying to find a place to land. All we could do was to wish him the same good luck that had befriended us.

★　　★　　★　　★

Nothing happened of interest worth relating until 6 September, when one morning I was up at 14,000 feet on patrol between Armentières and Ypres. When about half way through the patrol, going north, I saw a two-seater approaching our lines over Messines. I at once gave chase and the German turned off east, nose down.

I got to within 400 yards, but could not gain at all, although I could just hold him for speed, so I opened fire. I fired one drum of Lewis at him, and he continued to go down while I changed drums. I then got off another drum, and still got no reply from the enemy gunner, but the German was going down more steeply now.

I put on another drum and fired it, when we had both got down to a height of 4000 feet, well east of the lines. I then turned away, and saw the German go through some clouds at 2,000 feet over Gheluve, still diving steeply.

I flew back to the aerodrome, landed, and made out my report. Three days later a report came from an agent to say that a German machine had crashed on the Menin road at Gheluve, and the time and place coincided with my combat report – so that was my first Hun.

This machine was painted all white. All the while the Hun had been going down he had gone straight, and his gunner did not fire a shot, so I think that they were a new crew learning the country and went out without a gun. In any case, this was a very easy German to get for one's first, and it bucked me up a lot.

The next day I went up at 2 pm to do an offensive patrol with Captain Latch and Lieutenant Readman. We left the ground and got height towards the line, which we crossed at 12,000 feet, over Boessinghe.

We flew east to Passchendaele, and then turned south. Over Passchendaele we received our usual dose of hate from Archie, and while dodging his bursts, I happened to see a German machine about 3,000 feet below us climbing up to us. We reached the southern limit of our offensive patrol, which at that time was Ploegsteerte, and then turned north-east.

At about 14,000 feet over Gheluvelt I saw a monoplane west of us coming towards us from the direction of Ypres. As it came closer I saw that it was our friend the solitary Fokker, to whom I have previously referred. I fired a red light to draw the attention of the rest of the patrol and then turned nose-on to the Fokker.

We both opened fire together at about 300 yards range. After firing about three shots my gun stopped, and whilst I was trying to rectify the stoppage the Fokker turned round behind me and had again opened fire.

I now did a silly thing. Instead of revving round and waiting for the other two DH's to help me, I put my engine off and dived, but not straight. The Fokker followed, shooting as opportunity offered, and I could hear his bullets coming far too close to be healthy. At one time I glanced up and saw him just a hundred feet above me following my S turns.

We got down to about 8,000 feet like this when I managed to get my gun going, so I put my engine on, and zoomed. The Fokker zoomed also, but passed above and in front of me.

Now was my opportunity, which I seized with alacrity. I elevated my gun and fired a few shots at him from under his fuselage, but my gun again stopped. The Fokker, whose pilot apparently had lost sight of me, dived steeply towards Houthem, and I followed, feeling very brave. Again I got my gun to function, but the Fokker had easily outdived me, and I last saw him re-starting his engine in a cloud of blue smoke just over his aerodrome, which was at that time Cuciave, near Menin.

My lucky star undoubtedly shone again on this day, for the Fokker had only managed to put two bullets through my machine, so I was indeed thankful, for if the German had only been a little skilful I think he would have got me. But still, this was all very good experience for me, and if one gets out of such tight corners it increases one's confidence enormously.

The next day I had quite a lot of excitement. Several Hun balloons east of Ypres were making themselves very objectionable to our front line trenches in particular, and so a strafe was organized to annoy the aforesaid balloons, which we could see quite distinctly from our aerodrome at Abeele. I left the ground at 1 pm to attack a balloon at Poelcappelle, and so off to the lines I went and crossed the trenches at about 2000 feet.

The balloon was about 2,500 feet high when I crossed, but the enemy were visibly hauling it down, and by that time I was subjected to an intense fire by everything that the enemy could fire with. I was then the only machine over the lines, so the local AA* positions were able

* AA = Anti Aircraft.

The Fokker followed, shooting as opportunity offered.

to give me their undivided attention, and they did it to some purpose too.

Black smoke seemed to be on all sides of me, and by the time I got to within half a mile of the balloon the AA fire was altogether too intense to carry on through, so I fired a drum of cartridges at the balloon at about 700 yards range to no apparent effect, and then turned south-west for the shelter of the friendly Salient.* I pushed my nose down and recrossed our trenches at 1,000 feet over Bellewarde Lake, and decided that the man who brings down a German balloon is indeed a hero.

I then returned to my aerodrome and had several patches put on the fabric of my machine. I always took a great personal interest in my machine, and I was rewarded by the knowledge that my machine was as fast and would climb as well as any in the squadron.

The same evening I decided to have another go at a balloon that was up just east of Polygon Wood. This wood at this time was a familiar landmark with its racecourse track in the centre.

I left the ground about 6 pm and flew east to Ypres and noted the height of the balloon. Then I flew direct at it for half a mile so as to get a correct compass bearing on it, as a thick layer of clouds were at 4,000 feet and I decided to use them to the best advantage. I returned to my starting place, climbed into the clouds and got above, and then flew for about six minutes according to my compass bearing.

When I considered I was over the balloon, down I went through the clouds, but the balloon was still a little way ahead, although in a direct forward line. I went into the clouds again, just as Archie went 'Wonk, wonk,' and after flying east for half a minute I came down again to have a peep.

As I came out of the clouds I nearly ran into a Hun two-seater who was coming towards me just under the clouds, apparently guarding the balloon. I at once opened fire and saw a number of my bullets strike his right-hand wings, after which he went down in a dive, but I did not follow as we were too far over the lines, and too low.

Then I looked round for the balloon, but could not see it, and as I was

* The reference is to the famous Ypres salient, which, however friendly it may have seemed to our aviators, was by no means regarded with friendly feelings by the Infantry – or PBI as they generally call themselves.

now at 2500 feet, and the local Archies were doing their best to give me some assistance in effecting a landing in Hunland, I thought it best to clear. I turned southwest for the nearest point of the line, taking into account the northeasterly wind, and made for Ploegsteert Wood. I simply went through a devil of a time with Archies, for they just put up a barrage in front of me and I kept on having to turn at right angles, and once I turned completely east again.

I at last got close to the lines and made a dive for it. At last I got over at 1,000 feet and breathed a sigh of intense relief. I now had a look round and saw the balloon that I was going to attack just being hauled out of the clouds.

My machine had been badly hit too, and the base of one shell went through a spar of my right-hand lower wing, which was wobbling about like a jelly. I flew the remainder of my way back to the aerodrome at about 65 mph, so as not to impose too great a strain on the wing with the broken spar, and landed safely, after an hour's concentrated excitement. I was very glad to get down, and since then I have never liked Hun balloons.

On the evening of the 23rd I was on offensive patrol with Mr Curlewis, and we were over Menin at about 13,000 feet when suddenly my engine spluttered and finally stopped. I had finished my petrol. I turned west gliding, but could not see much of the ground west of me as the evening sun was low and the usual haze was over the ground. However, I hoped to make the Ypres Salient at least, and when I got down to 7000 feet I could see Ypres. By the time I was over Ypres I had 2,000 feet to spare, and so picked out a landing place near Elverdinghen and managed to land on a small strip of cut corn safely, but just missing a big shell-hole by a matter of inches. I had perched near a battery, so I went over to the battery and telephoned my Squadron for petrol and oil.

The tender and mechanics arrived soon after dark and so we left things for the morning. The battery commander had just arrived from England, and was very afraid indeed that owing to my landing near his battery the Germans would shell him out of that position.

That night I made my bed under the wing of my machine and went to sleep about 11 pm. I was awakened about 1 am by the stentorian voice of, apparently, a battery sergeant, who was directing all the personnel of a battery near by to fire unlimited rounds of ammunition Hunlandwards. I forget now what words he used, but in the clearing of a wood where my machine lay, his voice sounded uncommonly like a drill instructor's. Star shells were going up everywhere, and very often we could hear the sharp rat-a-tat-tat of machine-guns in the trenches, which were only 3,000 yards away.

I woke up about 5 am and proceeded to fill the machine with the mechanic's assistance, and having run the engine up, I left the ground and flew to Abeele, with the night's mist running off my planes like water. The morning was very misty and I only found my aerodrome with difficulty, by taking some trees on the north end as a guide. I landed safely in a thick ground mist, and very nearly ran into some cows on the aerodrome, which I did not see until I was on the ground.

The same morning an insolent-looking German machine flew over us at a great height, but we could not get off to persue it, as the most was still thick on the aerodrome, although we could see through it vertically. Anyhow, I don't suppose the German got much information that morning unless the mist that was covering us was purely local.

I continued doing offensive patrols and escorts daily until 5 October, when I went to England on a week's leave. Just before this I had been awarded the Military Medal – on 1 October. I enjoyed a most interesting week's leave, which of course went all too soon.

★　　★　　★　　★

The morning of 9 November 1916 dawned bright, with good visibility, and as I dressed I remarked to Noakes that the Hun pilots were just about dressing too, saying among themselves how they were that morning going to strafe the *verfluchter Englander*.

Six of us left the ground about 7.30 am and got our height going towards Albert, intending to go round to Bapaume and then fly north to Arras with the intention of cutting off a good slice of Hunland and strafing any Hun that we found west of us.

By the time we got to Bapaume our patrol had dwindled down to three machines, Lieutenant Ball, Noakes and myself. So from Bapaume we flew bravely north, for up to the present we had not encountered any of the numerous Hun scouts that were reported to be always obnoxious in that sector.

We had just flown over Achiet-le-Grand at about 11,000 feet when I saw about six specks east of us. I drew Noakes' attention, and so we made off west a little as we were a long way east of the lines. Long before we got to Adinfer Wood the Hun machines overtook us, and directly they got within range we turned to fight.

One Hun came down at me nose on but then turned away, and in doing so I got a good view of the Hun which I had never seen before. It had a fuselage like the belly of a fish. Its wings were cut fairly square at the tips, and had no dihedral angle. The tail plane was of the shape of a spade. We learned later that these machines were the new German 'Albatros D1' chasers.

By now we were in the middle of six of them and were getting a bad time of it, for we were a long way east of the line, so we all knew that we had to fight hard or go down. At one time I saw a fat Hun about ten yards behind Ball absolutely filling him with lead, as Ball was flying straight, apparently changing a drum of ammunition, and had not seen the Hun.

I could not at the time go to Ball's assistance as I had two Huns after me fairly screaming for my blood. However, Ball did not go down. Noakes was having a good time too, and was putting up a wonderful show.

The Huns were co-operating very well. Their main tactic seemed to be for one of them to dive at one of us from the front and then turn away, inviting us to follow. I followed three times, but the third time I heard a terrific clack, bang, crash, rip behind me, and found a Hun was firing from about ten yards in the rear, and his guns seemed to be firing in my very ears. I at once did a half roll, and as the Hun passed over me I saw the black and white streams on his interplane struts. This fellow was the Hun leader, and I had previously noticed that he had manoeuvred very well.

By now, however, we had fought our way back to our lines, and all three of us had kept together, which was undoubtedly our salvation, but I had used all my ammunition and had to chase round after Huns without firing at them. However, the Huns had apparently had enough too, and as soon as we got back to our lines they withdrew east.

I now had time to look over my machine on my way back to the aerodrome and saw that it was in a bad way. My tail plane was a mass of torn fabric, and various wires were hanging, having been cut by bullets. We all landed, and in getting out of our machines were congratulated by our OC, who had been informed of the progress of the fight by telephone from our Archy section, who had seen the latter part of the fight and had said that it was the best they had seen for a long time.

I really think that fight was one of the best I have ever had, although we were outnumbered and the Huns had better machines than we.

I had a good look round my machine and found that the Huns had scored twenty-four hits. This was the greatest number I have ever had. I do not believe in being shot about. It is bad or careless flying to allow one's self to be shot about when one ought usually to be able to prevent it by properly timed manoeuvres.

The same afternoon I went out on another machine to do an offensive patrol and, having encountered a two-seater over Gommécourt, fired all my ammunition at him to no avail, so I landed at the nearest aerodrome for some more, after which I left the ground again to look for the Hun.

Whilst getting my height at about 4,000 feet, and feeling rather bucked with life, I thought I would try a loop; so I pushed the machine down till the speed got up to 90 mph, took a deep breath and pulled the stick back.

Half way up the loop I changed my mind and pushed the stick forward, with the result that I transferred my load from my flying to my landing wires. The resultant upward pressure was so great that all my ammunition drums shot out of my machine over my top plane and into the revolving propeller which, being a 'pusher', of course was behind me.

There was a mighty scrunch and terrific vibration as three out of my four propeller-blades disappeared in a cloud of splinters. I at once switched off and removed my gun from my knees, where it had fallen after having been wrenched from its mountings and thrown into the air owing to the terrific vibration caused by my engine doing 1,600 revs per minute with only one propeller-blade.

I now found that I wanted full right rudder to keep the machine straight and discovered, on looking round, that the lower right-hand tail boom had been cut clean in two by one of the flying propeller-blades, and all that was holding my tail on was a diagonal 10-cwt tail-boom bracing wire.

The machine was wobbling badly as the engine was still turning round slowly, and I had just about wits enough left to pick out a field and make a landing successfully.

As soon as I stopped running along the ground the machine tilted over on one wing, as the centre section bracing wires were broken, and there was nothing, now that the machine was at rest, to keep the wings in their correct position with the nacelle. I got out of the machine and thanked God for my salvation.

A few minutes later an officer from No 3 Squadron, on horseback, rode up to pick up my pieces, for as he had seen various portions of an aeroplane flying about the locality, he had come to inspect the biggest piece. I remained by the machine until the tender from No 3 Squadron arrived with a guard for the machine, and I then went to No 3 Squadron and telephoned to my Squadron what had happened, so they promised to send a car for me at once, and a breakdown party in the morning.

On Christmas Eve we were out on patrol east of Arras and saw a Hun miles east of us, so we went over to sing him carols with several Lewises as accompaniment, but the Hun objected, and discreetly withdrew further east.

We returned to our aerodrome soon after we had been out an hour, as the weather was very bad, and we also wanted to settle down to Christmas Eve. We had a quite successful concert that night and, one good thing, there was no flying on Christmas Day, so that we enjoyed a day's rest and recreation.

James McCudden was killed in April 1918. Taking off from a French aerodrome, his engine stalled, and in trying to get back on the runway his plane side-slipped into the ground.

Acknowledgements

Grateful acknowledgement is made to authors, publishers and proprietors for permission to include the works listed below.

ESCAPE FROM WAR FORT 9 from *The Escaping Club* by A. J. Evans reprinted by kind permission of The Bodley Head.

A FIGHT FOR LIFE from The *Scarlet Imposter* by Denis Wheatley by kind permission of the estate of Denis Wheatley.

ON THE FRINGE by George Hall by kind permission of William Blackwood and Sons Ltd.

THE MIRACLE OF UMANARSUK by Ralph Baker by kind permission of William Kimber & Co. and Ralph Baker.

NORTH FACE by Walter Unsworth by kind permission of The Hutchinson Publishing Group Limited.

IN THE SHADOW OF THE BLACK STONE from *The 39 Steps* by John Buchan by kind permission of Lord Tweedsmuir and A. P. Watt Ltd.

ROWING ACROSS THE ATLANTIC from *I Had to Dare* by Tom Maclean by kind permission of The Hutchinson Publishing Group Ltd.

THE WILD WASTE-PAPER from The *Incredible Adventures of Professor Branestawm* by Norman Hunter by kind permission of The Bodley Head.

THE OLD MAN OF THE SEA from *The Kontiki Expedition* by Thor Heyerdahl copyright © 1950 Thor Heyerdahl; published in the United States by Rand McNally & Co and in the British Commonwealth by George Allen and Unwin Publishers Ltd.

THE DESERT ROAD from *The Forgotten Path* by David Newman (originally published by Robert Hale) by kind permission of Curtis Brown and David Newman.

RAID ON ENTEBBE from *Counter Strike Entebbe* by Tony Williamson by kind permission of William Collins, Sons & Co. Ltd.

BLACK NIGHT ON THE THAMES from *My Escape From Donnington Hall* by Gunter Pluschow reprinted by kind permission of The Bodley Head.

The publishers have made every possible effort to clear all copyright, and trust that their apologies will be accepted for any omissions.